Murder by the Glass

Murder by the Glass

A Vintage Selection of Crime and
Mystery Stories

Edited by
Peter Haining

SOUVENIR PRESS

First published 1994 by
Souvenir Press Ltd,
43 Great Russell Street, London WC1B 3PA
and simultaneously in Canada

ISBN 0 285 63205 1

Phototypeset by Intype, London
Printed in Great Britain by
Mackays of Chatham

For
Hugh and Fiona Phillips
in memory of many a happy beaker,
and a lot more to come!

Contents

Introduction

Sherlock Holmes enjoys whisky and water, wine (preferably white) and the occasional glass of port. Lord Peter Wimsey is never happier than when drinking claret, and *Commissaire* Maigret, Inspector Morse and Detective Chief Inspector Wexford are all at peace when sipping a good pint of beer. Philip Marlowe, Mike Hammer, and Shell Scott, on the other hand (and on the other side of the Atlantic), are bourbon men, while Sam Spade, Matt Helm and the Boston private eye and *bon vivant* Spenser have slightly more esoteric tastes – Bacardi, Martini and Murphy's Irish Whiskey, respectively. And no one, of course, needs any reminding of what James Bond preferred, 'shaken, not stirred.'

Drink – usually *strong* drink – has been a part of crime and mystery fiction since the inception of the genre in a handful of stories by Edgar Allan Poe in the early years of the nineteenth century. Then from the days of the Bow Street Runners in the middle of the century, by way of the emergence of the Police Force and the arrival of a plethora of amateur and professional detectives in the wake of the opening of that celebrated 'consulting agency' in Baker Street, drink of one kind or another has played a major part as both the cause of crime and the stimulation of lawmen and criminals alike. Indeed, it has been rightly observed, I think, that without it, crime fiction would literally have dried up.

Consider for a moment all the mystery stories in which the wife or husband has put paid to her or his other half with a glass that has been doctored with poison, or the multitude of butlers who 'did it' with the night-cap of scotch, port or brandy. Think of the innumerable villains who have busily spiked the drinks of their enemies and unsuspecting victims, not to mention the officers of the law who have found a vital clue to a disappearance or a murder in the dregs of a glass or the lipstick marks around the rim. All these elements have been the meat and, if you'll excuse the pun, drink of the crime and mystery writer.

The indulgence of those who operate on either side of the law has swung the whole gamut from the restrained discernment of fine vintages displayed by the English gentlemen sleuths, to the unashamed boozing of their American private eye counterparts, who think nothing of consuming a bottle of the 'hard stuff' before contemplating their next course of action. While the first are evidently concerned with the preservation of their palates, the others seem hell bent on ruining their livers. In this context, I am reminded that Hercule Poirot considered that a small glass of sherry could 'enliven the little grey cells', while Dashiell Hammett's Continental Op had rather stronger opinions about the powers of stimulation in alcohol, as he revealed during the case of the *Red Harvest*.

'I would rather have been cold sober,' he reflected, 'but I wasn't. If the night held more work for me, I didn't want to go to it with alcohol dying in me. The snifter revived me a lot. I poured more of the King George into a flask, pocketed it, and went down to the taxi.'

Although over the years there have been countless anthologies of crime and detective fiction, as far as I have been able to ascertain there has never been one solely devoted to murder by the glass. As I have already indicated, wines, spirits and all the other varieties of strong drink have certainly featured in a great many novels and short stories, but this seems to be the first collection of short stories in which drink plays the central role.

During my research for this book I have read a large number of stories which, like alcohol itself, have been good and bad, with some really outstanding. The only headache my indulgence has left me has been the problem of picking those for my final choice. I hope the selection is to your liking, and if any personal favourite happens to be missing, then I can only suggest you write to my publisher with the title and urge him to order up another round.

Just one word of warning. There is a pretty heady brew in the following pages. The stories have all been written by some of the most accomplished practitioners of crime and mystery fiction, each of whom is equally knowledgeable about his or her tipple. The evils of drink, you might say, will be found here in plenty. I only hope that the combination of alcohol and murder does not give potential criminals ideas or help the abolitionist's cause by putting you off drink for life!

In the end, as that brilliant storyteller and wine-lover, Roald Dahl, infers in the opening story, it is all a matter of taste. I have done my best to ensure that each drop is of vintage quality. Cheers!

Peter Haining
Boxford, Suffolk.
December 1993

1

NAME YOUR POISON

Stories of the Connoisseurs

A CONNOISSEUR'S REVENGE

Roald Dahl

There were always two surprises in store for visitors to Roald Dahl's home in Great Missenden in Buckinghamshire—apart from the tall, commanding and combative author himself. One was the strange, yellowing, rather grisly object that floated in a jar on a small table in his living room (it was actually his own prolapsed intervertebral disc, the souvenir of an operation); and the second was his cellar in which he kept an enviable collection of over 3,000 bottles of vintage wine. Dahl (1916–1990) was not only one of this century's most ingenious writers of macabre stories, but probably the world's most popular writer of children's books. He was also very proud of his knowledge of wine, which he listed among his hobbies alongside rose-growing and picture-restoring. His stories were the inspiration for an American TV series Way Out, *in the early Sixties, which he also hosted; and the British-made* Tales of the Unexpected, *which ran for five years from 1979 to 1984. A highlight of this Anglia TV series was the following story which was screened in 1980 under the title 'Taste', starring Ron Moody. It is a fiendishly clever little chiller about a wine lover's challenge to a pompous expert to identify an obscure claret, and the story not only reveals Roald Dahl's own knowledge of vintage wine but makes a perfect beginning to this collection . . .*

There were six of us to dinner that night at Mike Schofield's house in London: Mike and his wife and daughter, my wife and I, and a man called Richard Pratt.

Richard Pratt was a famous gourmet. He was president of a small society known as the Epicures, and each month he circulated privately to its members a pamphlet on food and wines. He organized dinners where sumptuous dishes and rare wines were served. He refused to smoke for fear of harming his palate, and when discussing a wine, he had a curious, rather droll habit of referring to it as though it were a living being. 'A prudent wine,' he would say, 'rather diffident and evasive, but quite prudent.' Or, 'a good-humoured wine, benevolent and cheerful—slightly obscene, perhaps, but nonetheless good-humoured.'

I had been to dinner at Mike's twice before when Richard Pratt was there, and on each occasion Mike and his wife had gone out of their way to produce a special meal for the famous gourmet. And this one, clearly, was to be no exception. The moment we entered the dining room, I could see that the table was laid for a feast. The tall candles, the yellow roses, the quantity of shining silver, the three wineglasses to each person, and above all, the faint scent of roasting meat from the kitchen brought the first warm oozings of saliva to my mouth.

As we sat down, I remembered that on both Richard Pratt's previous visits Mike had played a little betting game with him over the claret, challenging him to name its breed and its vintage. Pratt had replied that that should not be too difficult provided it was one of the great years. Mike had then bet him a case of the wine in question that he could not do it. Pratt had accepted, and had won both times. Tonight I felt sure that the little game would be played over again, for Mike was quite willing to lose the bet in order to prove that his wine was good enough to be recognized, and Pratt, for his part, seemed to take a grave, restrained pleasure in displaying his knowledge.

The meal began with a plate of whitebait, fried very crisp in butter, and to go with it there was a Moselle. Mike got up and poured the wine himself, and when he sat down again, I could see that he was watching Richard Pratt. He had set the bottle in front of me so that I could read the label. It said, 'Geierslay Ohligsberg, 1945.' He leaned over and whispered to me that Geierslay was a tiny village in the Moselle, almost unknown outside Germany. He said that this wine we were drinking was something unusual, that the output of the vineyard was so small that it was almost impossible for a stranger to get any of it. He had visited Geierslay personally the previous summer in order to obtain the few dozen bottles that they had finally allowed him to have.

'I doubt anyone else in the country has any of it at the moment,' he said. I saw him glance again at Richard Pratt. 'Great thing about Moselle,' he continued, raising his voice, 'it's the perfect wine to serve before a claret. A lot of people serve a Rhine wine instead, but that's because they don't know any better. A Rhine wine will kill a delicate claret, you know that? It's barbaric to serve a Rhine before a claret. But a Moselle—ah!—a Moselle is exactly right.'

Mike Schofield was an amiable, middle-aged man. But he was a stock-broker. To be precise, he was a jobber in the stock market, and like a number of his kind, he seemed to be somewhat embarrassed, almost ashamed to find that he had made so much money with so slight a talent. In his heart he knew that he was not really much more than a bookmaker—an unctuous, infinitely respectable, secretly unscrupulous bookmaker—and he knew that his friends knew it, too. So he was seeking now to become a man of culture, to cultivate a literary and aesthetic taste, to collect paintings, music, books, and all the rest of it. His little sermon about Rhine wine and Moselle was a part of this thing, this culture that he sought.

'A charming little wine, don't you think?' he said. He was still watching Richard Pratt. I could see him give a rapid furtive glance down the table each time he dropped his head to take a mouthful of whitebait. I could almost *feel* him waiting for the moment when Pratt would take his first sip, and look up from his glass with a smile of pleasure, of astonishment, perhaps even of wonder, and then there would be a discussion and Mike would tell him about the village of Geierslay.

But Richard Pratt did not taste his wine. He was completely engrossed in conversation with Mike's eighteen-year-old daughter, Louise. He was half turned towards her, smiling at her, telling her, so far as I could gather, some story about a chef in a Paris restaurant. As he spoke, he leaned closer and closer to her, seeming in his eagerness almost to impinge upon her, and the poor girl leaned as far as she could away from him, nodding politely, rather desperately, and looking not at his face but at the topmost button of his dinner jacket.

We finished our fish, and the maid came round removing the plates. When she came to Pratt, she saw that he had not yet touched his food, so she hesitated, and Pratt noticed her. He waved her away, broke off his conversation, and quickly began to eat, popping the little crisp brown fish quickly into his mouth with rapid jabbing movements of his fork. Then, when he had finished, he reached for his glass, and in two short swallows he tipped the wine down his throat and turned immediately to resume his conversation with Louise Schofield.

Mike saw it all. I was conscious of him sitting there, very still, containing himself, looking at his guest. His round jovial face seemed to loosen slightly and to sag, but he contained himself and was still and said nothing.

Soon the maid came forward with the second course. This was a large roast of beef. She placed it on the table in front of Mike who stood up and carved it, cutting the slices very thin, laying them gently on the plates for the maid to take round. When he had served everyone, including himself, he put down the carving knife and leaned forward with both hands on the edge of the table.

'Now,' he said, speaking to all of us but looking at Richard Pratt. 'Now for the claret. I must go and fetch the claret, if you'll excuse me.'

'You go and fetch it, Mike?' I said. 'Where is it?'

'In my study, with the cork out—breathing.'

'Why the study?'

'Acquiring room temperature, of course. It's been there twenty-four hours.'

'But why the study?'

'It's the best place in the house. Richard helped me choose it last time he was here.'

At the sound of his name, Pratt looked round.

'That's right, isn't it?'Mike said.

'Yes,' Pratt answered, nodding gravely. 'That's right.'

'On top of the green filing cabinet in my study,' Mike said. 'That's the place we chose. A good draught-free spot in a room with an even temperature. Excuse me now, will you, while I fetch it.'

The thought of another wine to play with had restored his humour, and he hurried out of the door, to return a minute later more slowly, walking softly, holding in both hands a wine basket in which a dark bottle lay. The label was out of sight, facing downward. 'Now!' he cried as he came towards the table. 'What about this one, Richard? You'll never name this one!'

Richard Pratt turned slowly and looked up at Mike; then his eyes travelled down to the bottle nestling in its small wicker basket, and he raised his eyebrows, a slight, supercilious arching of the brows, and with it a pushing outward of the wet lower lip, suddenly imperious and ugly.

'You'll never get it,' Mike said. 'Not in a hundred years.'

'A claret?' Richard Pratt asked, condescending.

'Of course.'

'I assume, then, that it's from one of the smaller vineyards?'

'Maybe it is, Richard. And then again, maybe it isn't.'

'But it's a good year? One of the great years?'

'Yes, I guarantee that.'

'Then it shouldn't be too difficult,' Richard Pratt said, drawling his words, looking exceedingly bored. Except that, to me, there was something strange about his drawling and his boredom: between the eyes a shadow of something evil, and in his bearing an intentness that gave me a faint sense of uneasiness as I watched him.

'This one is really rather difficult,' Mike said, 'I won't force you to bet on this one.'

'Indeed. And why not?' Again the slow arching of the brows, the cool, intent look.

'Because it's difficult.'

'That's not very complimentary to me, you know.'

'My dear man,' Mike said, 'I'll bet you with pleasure, if that's what you wish.'

'It shouldn't be too hard to name it.'

'You mean you want to bet?'

'I'm perfectly willing to bet,' Richard Pratt said.

'All right, then, we'll have the usual. A case of the wine itself.'

'You don't think I'll be able to name it, do you?'

'As a matter of fact, and with all due respect, I don't,' Mike said. He was making some effort to remain polite, but Pratt was not bothering overmuch to conceal his contempt for the whole proceeding. And yet, curiously, his next question seemed to betray a certain interest.

'You like to increase the bet?'

'No, Richard. A case is plenty.'

'Would you like to bet fifty cases?'

'That would be silly.'

Mike stood very still behind his chair at the head of the table, carefully holding the bottle in its ridiculous wicker basket. There was a trace of whiteness around his nostrils now, and his mouth was shut very tight.

Pratt was lolling back in his chair, looking up at him, the eyebrows raised, the eyes half closed, a little smile touching the corners of his lips. And again I saw, or thought I saw, something distinctly disturbing about the man's face, that shadow of intentness between the eyes, and in the eyes themselves, right in their centres where it was black, a small slow spark of shrewdness, hiding.

'So you don't want to increase the bet?'

'As far as I'm concerned, old man, I don't give a damn,' Mike said. 'I'll bet you anything you like.'

The three women and I sat quietly, watching the two men. Mike's wife was becoming annoyed; her mouth had gone sour and I felt that at any moment she was going to interrupt. Our roast beef lay before us on our plates, slowly steaming.

'So you'll bet me anything I like?'

'That's what I told you. I'll bet you anything you damn well please, if you want to make an issue out of it.'

'Even ten thousand pounds?'

'Certainly I will, if that's the way you want it.' Mike was more confident now. He knew quite well that he could call any sum Pratt cared to mention.

'So you say I can name the bet?' Pratt asked again.

'That's what I said.'

There was a pause while Pratt looked slowly round the table, first at me, then at the three women, each in turn. He appeared to be reminding us that we were witness to the offer.

'Mike!' Mrs Schofield said. 'Mike, why don't we stop this nonsense and eat our food. It's getting cold.'

'But it isn't nonsense,' Pratt told her evenly. 'We're making a little bet.'

I noticed the maid standing in the background holding a dish of vegetables, wondering whether to come forward with them or not.

'All right, then,' Pratt said. 'I'll tell you what I want you to bet.'

'Come on, then,' Mike said, rather reckless. 'I don't give a damn what it is—you're on.'

Pratt nodded, and again the little smile moved the corners of his lips, and then, quite slowly, looking at Mike all the time, he said, 'I want you to bet me the hand of your daughter in marriage.'

Louise Schofield gave a jump. 'Hey!' she cried. 'No! That's not funny! Look here, Daddy, that's not funny at all.'

'No, dear,' her mother said. 'They're only joking.'

'I'm not joking,' Richard Pratt said.

'It's ridiculous,' Mike said. He was off balance again now.

'You said you'd bet anything I liked.'

'I meant money.'

'You didn't *say* money.'

'That's what I meant.'

'Then it's a pity you didn't say it. But anyway, if you wish to go back on your offer, that's quite all right with me.'

'It's not a question of going back on my offer, old man. It's a no-bet anyway, because you can't match the stake. You yourself don't happen to have a daughter to put up against mine in case you lose. And if you had, I wouldn't want to marry her.'

'I'm glad of that, dear,' his wife said.

'I'll put up anything you like,' Pratt announced. 'My house, for example. How about my house?'

'Which one?' Mike asked, joking now.

'The country one.'

'Why not the other one as well?'

'All right then, if you wish it. Both my houses.'

At that point I saw Mike pause. He took a step forward and placed the bottle in its basket gently down on the table. He moved the saltcellar to one side, then the pepper, and then he picked up

his knife, studied the blade thoughtfully for a moment, and put it
down again. His daughter, too, had seen him pause.

'Now, Daddy!' she cried. 'Don't be *absurd*! It's *too* silly for words.
I refuse to be betted on like this.'

'Quite right, dear,' her mother said. 'Stop it at once, Mike, and
sit down and eat your food.'

Mike ignored her. He looked over at his daughter and he smiled,
a slow, fatherly, protective smile. But in his eyes, suddenly, there
glimmered a little triumph. 'You know,' he said, smiling as he
spoke. 'You know, Louise, we ought to think about this a bit.'

'Now, stop it, Daddy! I refuse even to listen to you! Why, I've
never heard anything so ridiculous in my life!'

'No, seriously, my dear. Just wait a moment and hear what I
have to say.'

'But I don't *want* to hear it.'

'Louise! Please! It's like this. Richard here, has offered us a
serious bet. He is the one who wants to make it, not me. And if
he loses, he will have to hand over a considerable amount of
property. Now, wait a minute, my dear, don't interrupt. The point
is this. *He cannot possibly win.*'

'He seems to think he can.'

'Now listen to me, because I know what I'm talking about. The
expert, when tasting a claret—so long as it is not one of the famous
great wines like Lafite or Latour—can only get a certain way
towards naming the vineyard. He can, of course, tell you the
Bordeaux district from which the wine comes, whether it is from
St Emilion, Pomerol, Graves, or Médoc. But then each district has
several communes, little counties, and each county has many,
many small vineyards. It is impossible for a man to differentiate
between them all by taste and smell alone. I don't mind telling
you that this one I've got here is a wine from a small vineyard
that is surrounded by many other small vineyards, and he'll never
get it. It's impossible.'

'You can't be sure of that,' his daughter said.

'I'm telling you I can. Though I say it myself, I understand quite
a bit about this wine business, you know. And anyway, heavens
alive, girl, I'm your father and you don't think I'd let you in for—
for something you didn't want, do you? I'm trying to make you
some money.'

'Mike!' his wife said sharply. 'Stop it now, Mike, please!'

Again he ignored her. 'If you will take this bet,' he said to his
daughter, 'in ten minutes you will be the owner of two large
houses.'

'But I don't want two large houses, Daddy.'

'Then sell them. Sell them back to him on the spot. I'll arrange all that for you. And then, just think of it, my dear, you'll be rich! You'll be independent for the rest of your life!'

'Oh, Daddy, I don't like it. I think it's silly.'

'So do I,' the mother said. She jerked her head briskly up and down as she spoke, like a hen. 'You ought to be ashamed of yourself, Michael, ever suggesting such a thing! Your own daughter, too!'

Mike didn't even look at her. 'Take it!' he said eagerly, staring hard at the girl. 'Take it, quick! I'll guarantee you won't lose.'

'But I don't like it, Daddy.'

'Come on, girl. Take it!'

Mike was pushing her hard. He was leaning towards her fixing her with two hard bright eyes, and it was not easy for the daughter to resist him.

'But what if I lose?'

'I keep telling you, you can't lose. I'll guarantee it.'

'Oh, Daddy, must I?'

'I'm making you a fortune. So come on now. What do you say, Louise? All right?'

For the last time, she hesitated. Then she gave a helpless little shrug of the shoulders and said, 'Oh, all right, then. Just so long as you swear there's no danger of losing.'

'Good!' Mike cried. 'That's fine! Then it's a bet!'

'Yes,' Richard Pratt said, looking at the girl. 'It's a bet.'

Immediately, Mike picked up the wine, tipped the first thimble-ful into his own glass, then skipped excitedly round the table filling up the others. Now everyone was watching Richard Pratt, watching his face as he reached slowly for his glass with his right hand and lifted it to his nose. The man was about fifty years old and he did not have a pleasant face. Somehow, it was all mouth—mouth and lips—the full, wet lips of the professional gourmet, the lower lip hanging downward in the centre, a pendulous, permanently open taster's lip, shaped open to receive the rim of a glass or a morsel of food. Like a keyhole, I thought, watching it; his mouth is like a large wet keyhole.

Slowly he lifted the glass to his nose. The point of the nose entered the glass and moved over the surface of the wine, delicately sniffing. He swirled the wine gently around in the glass to receive the bouquet. His concentration was intense. He had closed his eyes, and now the whole top half of his body, the head and neck and chest, seemed to become a kind of huge sensitive smelling-machine, receiving, filtering, analysing the message from the sniffing nose.

Mike, I noticed, was lounging in his chair, apparently unconcerned, but he was watching every move. Mrs Schofield, the wife, sat prim and upright at the other end of the table, looking straight ahead, her face tight with disapproval. The daughter, Louise, had shifted her chair away a little, and sidewise, facing the gourmet, and she, like her father, was watching closely.

For at least a minute, the smelling process continued; then, without opening his eyes or moving his head, Pratt lowered the glass to his mouth and tipped in almost half the contents. He paused, his mouth full of wine, getting the first taste; then he permitted some of it to trickle down his throat and I saw his Adam's apple move as it passed by. But most of it he retained in his mouth. And now, without swallowing again, he drew in through his lips a thin breath of air which mingled with the fumes of the wine in the mouth and passed on down into his lungs. He held the breath, blew it out through his nose, and finally began to roll the wine around under the tongue, and chewed it, actually chewed it with his teeth as though it were bread.

It was a solemn, impressive performance, and I must say he did it well.

'Um,' he said, putting down the glass, running a pink tongue over his lips. 'Um—yes. A very interesting little wine—gentle and gracious, almost feminine in the aftertaste.'

There was an excess of saliva in his mouth, and as he spoke he spat an occasional bright speck of it onto the table.

'Now we can start to eliminate,' he said. 'You will pardon me for doing this carefully, but there is much at stake. Normally I would perhaps take a bit of a chance, leaping forward quickly and landing right in the middle of the vineyard of my choice. But this time—I must move cautiously this time, must I not?' He looked up at Mike and he smiled, a thick-lipped, wet-lipped smile. Mike did not smile back.

'First, then, which district in Bordeaux does this wine come from? That is not too difficult to guess. It is far too light in the body to be from either St Emilion or Graves. It is obviously a Médoc. There's no doubt about *that*.

'Now—from which commune in Médoc does it come? That also, by elimination, should not be too difficult to decide. Margaux? No. It cannot be Margaux. It has not the violent bouquet of a Margaux. Pauillac? It cannot be Pauillac, either. It is too tender, too gentle and wistful for a Pauillac. The wine of Pauillac has a character that is almost imperious in its taste. And also, to me, a Pauillac contains just a little pith, a curious, dusty, pithy flavour that the grape acquires from the soil of the district. No, no. This— this is a very gentle wine, demure and bashful in the first taste, emerging shyly but quite graciously in the second. A little arch, perhaps, in the second taste, and a little naughty also, teasing the tongue with a trace, just a trace, of tannin. Then, in the aftertaste, delightful—consoling and feminine, with a certain blithely generous quality that one associates only with the wines of the commune of St Julien. Unmistakably this is a St Julien.'

He leaned back in his chair, held his hands up level with his chest, and placed the fingertips carefully together. He was becoming ridiculously pompous, but I thought that some of it was deliberate, simply to mock his host. I found myself waiting rather tensely for him to go on. The girl Louise was lighting a cigarette. Pratt heard the match strike and he turned on her, flaring suddenly with real anger. 'Please!' he said. 'Please don't do that! It's a disgusting habit, to smoke at table!'

She looked up at him, still holding the burning match in one hand, the big slow eyes settling on his face, resting there a moment, moving away again, slow and contemptuous. She bent her head and blew out the match, but continued to hold the unlighted cigarette in her fingers.

'I'm sorry, my dear,' Pratt said, 'but I simply cannot have smoking at table.'

She didn't look at him again.

'Now, let me see—where were we?' he said. 'Ah, yes. This wine is from Bordeaux, from the commune of St Julien, in the district of Médoc. So far, so good. But now we come to the more difficult part—the name of the vineyard itself. For in St Julien there are many vineyards, and as our host so rightly remarked earlier on, there is often not much difference between the wine of one and the wine of another. But we shall see.'

He paused again, closing his eyes. 'I am trying to establish the "growth," ' he said. 'If I can do that, it will be half the battle. Now, let me see. This wine is obviously not from a first-growth vineyard—nor even a second. It is not a great wine. The quality, the—the—what do you call it?—the radiance, the power, is lacking. But a third growth—that it could be. And yet I doubt it. We know it is a good year—our host has said so—and this is probably flattering it a little bit. I must be careful. I must be very careful here.'

He picked up his glass and took another small sip.

'Yes,' he said, sucking his lips. 'I was right. It is a fourth growth. Now I am sure of it. A fourth growth from a very good year—from a great year, in fact. And that's what made it taste for a moment like a third—or even a second-growth wine. Good! That's better! Now we are closing in! What are the fourth-growth vineyards in the commune of St Julien?'

Again he paused, took up his glass, and held the rim against that sagging pendulous lower lip of his. Then I saw the tongue shoot out, pink and narrow, the tip of it dipping into the wine, withdrawing swiftly again—a repulsive sight. When he lowered the glass, his eyes remained closed, the face concentrated, only the lips moving, sliding over each other like two pieces of wet, spongy rubber.

'There it is again!' he cried. 'Tannin in the middle taste, and the quick astringent squeeze upon the tongue. Yes, yes, of course! Now I have it! This wine comes from one of those small vineyards around Beychevelle. I remember now. The Beychevelle district, and the river and the little harbour that has silted up so the wine ships can no longer use it. Beychevelle . . . could it actually be a Beychevelle itself? No, I don't think so. Not quite. But it is somewhere very close. Château Talbot? Could it be Talbot? Yes, it could. Wait one moment.'

He sipped the wine again, and out of the side of my eye I noticed Mike Schofield and how he was leaning farther and farther forward over the table, his mouth slightly open, his small eyes fixed upon Richard Pratt.

'No. I was wrong. It was not a Talbot. A Talbot comes forward to you just a little quicker than this one; the fruit is nearer to the surface. If it is a '34, which I believe it is, then it couldn't be Talbot. Well, well. Let me think. It is not a Beychevelle and it is not a Talbot, and yet—yet it is so close to both of them, so close, that the vineyard must be almost in between. Now, which could that be?'

He hesitated, and we waited, watching his face. Everyone, even Mike's wife, was watching him now. I heard the maid put down the dish of vegetables on the sideboard behind me, gently, so as not to disturb the silence.

'Ah!' he cried. 'I have it! Yes, I think I have it!'

For the last time, he sipped the wine. Then, still holding the glass up near his mouth, he turned to Mike and he smiled, a slow, silky smile, and he said, 'You know what this is? This is the little Château Branaire-Ducru.'

Mike sat tight, not moving.

'And the year, 1934.'

We all looked at Mike, waiting for him to turn the bottle round in its basket and show the label.

'Is that your final answer?' Mike said.

'Yes, I think so.'

'Well, is it or isn't it?'

'Yes, it is.'

'What was the name again?'

'Château Branaire-Ducru. Pretty little vineyard. Lovely old

château. Know it quite well. Can't think why I didn't recognize it at once.'

'Come on, Daddy,' the girl said. 'Turn it round and let's have a peek. I want my two houses.'

'Just a minute,' Mike said. 'Wait just a minute.' He was sitting very quiet, bewildered-looking, and his face was becoming puffy and pale, as though all the force was draining slowly out of him.

'Michael!' his wife called sharply from the other end of the table. 'What's the matter?'

'Keep out of this, Margaret, will you please.'

Richard Pratt was looking at Mike, smiling with his mouth, his eyes small and bright. Mike was not looking at anyone.

'Daddy!' the daughter cried, agonized. 'But, Daddy, you don't mean to say he's guessed it right!'

'Now, stop worrying, my dear,' Mike said. 'There's nothing to worry about.'

I think it was more to get away from his family than anything else that Mike then turned to Richard Pratt and said, 'I'll tell you what, Richard. I think you and I had better slip off into the next room and have a little chat?'

'I don't want a little chat,' Pratt said. 'All I want is to see the label on that bottle.' He knew he was a winner now; he had the bearing, the quiet arrogance of a winner, and I could see that he was prepared to become thoroughly nasty if there was any trouble. 'What are you waiting for?' he said to Mike. 'Go on and turn it round.'

Then this happened: The maid, the tiny, erect figure of the maid in her white-and-black uniform, was standing beside Richard Pratt, holding something out in her hand. 'I believe these are yours, sir,' she said.

Pratt glanced round, saw the pair of thin horn-rimmed spectacles that she held out to him, and for a moment he hesitated. 'Are they? Perhaps they are. I don't know.'

'Yes sir, they're yours.' The maid was an elderly woman—nearer seventy than sixty—a faithful family retainer of many years' standing. She put the spectacles down on the table beside him.

Without thanking her, Pratt took them up and slipped them into his top pocket, behind the white handkerchief.

But the maid didn't go away. She remained standing beside and slightly behind Richard Pratt, and there was something so unusual in her manner and in the way she stood there, small, motionless and erect, that I for one found myself watching her with a sudden apprehension. Her old grey face had a frosty, determined look, the lips were compressed, the little chin was out, and the hands were clasped together tight before her. The curious cap on her head and the flash of white down the front of her uniform made her seem like some tiny, ruffled, white-breasted bird.

'You left them in Mr Schofield's study,' she said. Her voice was unnaturally, deliberately polite. 'On top of the green filing cabinet in his study, sir, when you happened to go in there by yourself before dinner.'

It took a few moments for the full meaning of her words to penetrate, and in the silence that followed I became aware of Mike and how he was slowly drawing himself up in his chair, and the colour coming to his face, and the eyes opening wide, and the curl of the mouth, and the dangerous little patch of whiteness beginning to spread around the area of the nostrils.

'Now, Michael!' his wife said. 'Keep calm now, Michael, dear! Keep calm!'

THE CASK OF AMONTILLADO

Edgar Allan Poe

The first, and arguably still among the very best of the short stories that combine murder and drink is 'The Cask of Amontillado' by Edgar Allan Poe (1809–1849). Like Roald Dahl's tale, it concerns an overbearing connoisseur who has tormented another wine-lover beyond the point of endurance, although in this instance the setting is carnival time in nineteenth-century Italy. The expert is Fortunato, an unbearable boaster about his wine knowledge, while Montresor is the injured party who seeks revenge by tempting the vanity and palate of his adversary as they search his cellars for an unsurpassed amontillado. Poe, whose stories are famous for their mounting terror, wrote few better tales than this one which also mirrors his own love of drink that was ultimately to bring him to an early death. The reader will not easily forget the terrible events that occur in Montresor's subterranean crypt—which is just as well, for we shall be returning to this feud between two wine-loving Italians in a modern sequel that appears later in the book.

The thousand injuries of Fortunato I had borne as I best could; but when he ventured upon insult, I vowed revenge. You, who so well know the nature of my soul, will not suppose, however that I gave utterance to a threat. *At length* I would be avenged; this was a point definitely settled—but the very definiteness with which it was resolved precluded the idea of risk. I must not only punish, but punish with impunity. A wrong is unredressed when retribution overtakes its redresser. It is equally unredressed when the avenger fails to make himself felt as such to him who has done the wrong.

It must be understood that neither by word nor deed had I given Fortunato cause to doubt my good-will. I continued, as was my wont, to smile in his face, and he did not perceive that my smile *now* was at the thought of his immolation.

He had a weak point—this Fortunato—although in other

regards he was a man to be respected and even feared. He prided himself on his connoisseurship in wine. Few Italians have the true virtuoso spirit. For the most part their enthusiasm is adopted to suit the time and opportunity—to practise imposture upon the British and Austrian *millionnaires*. In painting and gemmary, Fortunato, like his countrymen, was a quack—but in the matter of old wines he was sincere. In this respect I did not differ from him materially: I was skilful in the Italian vintages myself, and bought largely whenever I could.

It was about dusk, one evening during the supreme madness of the carnival season, that I encountered my friend. He accosted me with excessive warmth, for he had been drinking much. The man wore motley. He had on a tight-fitting parti-striped dress, and his head was surmounted by the conical cap and bells. I was so pleased to see him that I thought I should never have done wringing his hand.

I said to him, 'My dear Fortunato, you are luckily met. How remarkably well you are looking today! But I have received a pipe of what passes for Amontillado, and I have my doubts.'

'How?' said he. 'Amontillado? A pipe? Impossible! And in the middle of the carnival!'

'I have my doubts,' I replied; 'and I was silly enough to pay the full Amontillado price without consulting you in the matter. You were not to be found, and I was fearful of losing a bargain.'

'Amontillado!'

'I have my doubts.'

'Amontillado!'

'And I must satisfy them.'

'Amontillado!'

'As you are engaged, I am on my way to Luchesi. If any one has a critical turn, it is he. He will tell me—'

'Luchesi cannot tell Amontillado from Sherry.'

'And yet some fools will have it that his taste is a match for your own.'

'Come, let us go.'

'Whither?'

'To your vaults.'

'My friend, no; I will not impose upon your good nature. I perceive you have an engagement, Luchesi—'

'I have no engagement—come.'

'My friend, no. It is not the engagement, but the severe cold with which I perceive you are afflicted. The vaults are insufferably damp. They are encrusted with nitre.'

'Let us go, nevertheless. The cold is merely nothing. Amontillado! You have been imposed upon. And as for Luchesi, he cannot distinguish Sherry from Amontillado.''

Thus speaking, Fortunato possessed himself of my arm. Putting on a mask of black silk, and drawing a *roquelaire* closely about my person, I suffered him to hurry me to my palazzo.

There were no attendants at home; they had absconded to make merry in honour of the time. I had told them that I should not return until the morning, and had given them explicit orders not to stir from the house. These orders were sufficient, I well knew, to insure their immediate disappearance, one and all, as soon as my back was turned.

I took from their sconces two flambeaux, and giving one to Fortunato, bowed him through several suites of rooms to the archway that led into the vaults. I passed down a long and winding staircase, requesting him to be cautious as he followed. We came at length to the foot of the descent, and stood together on the damp ground of the catacombs of the Montresors.

The gait of my friend was unsteady, and the bells upon his cap jingled as he strode.

'The pipe?' said he.

'It is farther on,' said I; 'but observe the white web-work which gleams from these cavern walls.'

He turned towards me, and looked into my eyes with two filmy orbs that distilled the rheum of intoxication.

'Nitre?' he asked, at length.

'Nitre,' I replied. 'How long have you had that cough?'

'Ugh! ugh! ugh!—ugh! ugh! ugh!—ugh! ugh! ugh!—ugh! ugh! ugh!—ugh! ugh! ugh!'

My poor friend found it impossible to reply for many minutes.

'It is nothing,' he said, at last.

'Come,' I said with decision, 'we will go back; your health is precious. You are rich, respected, admired, beloved; you are happy, as once I was. You are a man to be missed. For me it is no matter. We will go back; you will be ill, and I cannot be responsible. Besides, there is Luchesi—'

'Enough,' he said; 'the cough is a mere nothing; it will not kill me. I shall not die of a cough.'

'True—true,' I replied; 'and, indeed, I had no intention of alarming you unnecessarily; but you should use all proper caution. A draught of this Medoc will defend us from the damps.'

Here I knocked off the neck of a bottle which I drew from a long row of its fellows that lay upon the mould.

'Drink,' I said, presenting him the wine.

He raised it to his lips with a leer. He paused and nodded to me familiarly, while his bells jingled.

'I drink,' he said, 'to the buried that repose around us.'

'And I to your long life.'

He again took my arm, and we proceeded.

'These vaults,' he said, 'are extensive.'

'The Montresors,' I replied, 'were a great and numerous family.'

'I forget your arms.'

'A huge human foot d'or, in a field azure; the foot crushes a serpent rampant whose fangs are imbedded in the heel.'

'And the motto?'

'*Nemo me impune lacessit.*'

'Good!' he said.

The wine sparkled in his eyes and the bells jingled. My own fancy grew warm with the Medoc. We had passed through walls of piled bones, with casks and puncheons intermingling, into the inmost recesses of the catacombs. I paused again, and this time I made bold to seize Fortunato by an arm above the elbow.

'The nitre!' I said; 'see, it increases. It hangs like moss upon the vaults. We are below the river's bed. The drops of moisture trickle among the bones. Come, we will go back ere it is too late. Your cough—'

'It is nothing,' he said; 'let us go on. But first, another draught of the Medoc.'

I broke and reached him a flagon of De Gràve. He emptied it at a breath. His eyes flashed with a fierce light. He laughed and threw the bottle upward with a gesticulation I did not understand.

I looked at him in surprise. He repeated the movement—a grotesque one.

'You do not comprehend?' he said.

'Not I,' I replied.

'Then you are not of the brotherhood.'

'How?'

'You are not of the masons.'

'Yes, yes,' I said; 'yes, yes.'

'You? Impossible! A mason?'

'A mason,' I replied.

'A sign,' he said.

'It is this,' I answered, producing a trowel from beneath the folds of my *roquelaire*.

'You jest,' he exclaimed, recoiling a few paces. 'But let us proceed to the Amontillado.'

'Be it so,' I said, replacing the tool beneath the cloak, and again offering him my arm. He leaned upon it heavily. We continued our route in search of the Amontillado. We passed through a range of low arches, descended, passed on, and descending again, arrived at a deep crypt, in which the foulness of the air caused our flambeaux rather to glow than flame.

At the most remote end of the crypt there appeared another less spacious. Its walls had been lined with human remains, piled to the vault overhead, in the fashion of the great catacombs of Paris. Three sides of this interior crypt were still ornamented in this manner. From the fourth the bones had been thrown down, and lay promiscuously upon the earth, forming at one point a mound of some size. Within the wall thus exposed by the displacing of the bones, we perceived a still interior recess, in depth about four feet, in width three, in height six or seven. It seemed to have been constructed for no especial use within itself, but formed merely the interval between two of the colossal supports of the roof of the catacombs, and was backed by one of their circumscribing walls of solid granite.

It was in vain that Fortunato, uplifting his dull torch, endeavoured to pry into the depths of the recess. Its termination the feeble light did not enable us to see.

'Proceed,' I said; 'herein is the Amontillado. As for Luchesi—'

'He is an ignoramus,' interrupted my friend, as he stepped unsteadily forward, while I followed immediately at his heels. In an instant he had reached the extremity of the niche, and finding his progress arrested by the rock, stood stupidly bewildered. A moment more and I had fettered him to the granite. In its surface were two iron staples, distant from each other about two feet, horizontally. From one of these depended a short chain, from the other a padlock. Throwing the links about his waist, it was but the work of a few seconds to secure it. He was too much astounded to resist. Withdrawing the key, I stepped back from the recess.

'Pass your hand,' I said, 'over the wall; you cannot help feeling the nitre. Indeed it is *very* damp. Once more let me *implore* you to return. No? Then I must positively leave you. But I must first render you all the little attentions in my power.'

'The Amontillado!' ejaculated my friend, not yet recovered from his astonishment.

'True,' I replied; 'the Amontillado.'

As I said these words I busied myself among the pile of bones of which I have before spoken. Throwing them aside, I soon uncovered a quantity of building stone and mortar. With these materials and with the aid of my trowel, I began vigorously to wall up the entrance of the niche.

I had scarcely laid the first tier of the masonry when I discovered that the intoxication of Fortunato had in a great measure worn off. The earliest indication I had of this was a low moaning cry from the depth of the recess. It was *not* the cry of a drunken man.

There was then a long and obstinate silence. I laid the second tier, and the third and the fourth; and then I heard the furious vibrations of the chain. The noise lasted for several minutes, during which, that I might harken to it with the more satisfaction, I ceased my labours and sat down upon the bones. When at last the clanking subsided, I resumed the trowel, and finished without interruption the fifth, the sixth, and the seventh tier. The wall was now nearly upon a level with my breast. I again paused, and holding the flambeaux over the mason-work, threw a few feeble rays upon the figure within.

A succession of loud and shrill screams, bursting suddenly from the throat of the chained form, seemed to thrust me violently back. For a brief moment I hesitated—I trembled. Unsheathing my rapier, I began to grope with it about the recess; but the thought of an instant reassured me. I placed my hand upon the solid fabric of the catacombs and felt satisfied. I reapproached the wall. I replied to the yells of him who clamoured. I re-echoed—I aided—I surpassed them in volume and in strength. I did this, and the clamourer grew still.

It was now midnight, and my task was drawing to a close. I had completed the eighth, the ninth, and the tenth tier. I had finished a portion of the last and the eleventh; there remained but a single stone to be fitted and plastered in. I struggled with its weight; I placed it partially in its destined position. But now there came from out the niche a low laugh that erected the hairs upon my head. It was succeeded by a sad voice, which I had difficulty in recognizing as that of the noble Fortunato. The voice said,—

'Ha! ha! ha!—he! he!—a very good joke indeed—an excellent jest. We will have many a rich laugh about it at the palazzo—he! he! he!—over our wine—he! he! he!'

'The Amontillado!' I said.

'He! he! he!—he! he! he!—yes, the Amontillado. But is it not getting late? Will they not be awaiting us at the palazzo, the Lady Fortunato and the rest? Let us be gone.'

'Yes,' I said, 'let us be gone.'

'*For the love of God, Montresor!*'

'Yes,' I said, 'for the love of God!'

But to these words I harkened in vain for a reply. I grew impatient. I called aloud.

'Fortunato!'

No answer. I called again:

'Fortunato!'

No answer still. I thrust a torch through the remaining aperture and let it fall within. There came forth in return only a jingling of the bells. My heart grew sick—on account of the dampness of the

catacombs. I hastened to make an end of my labour. I forced
the last stone into its position; I plastered it up. Against the new
masonry I re-erected the old rampart of bones. For the half of a
century no mortal has disturbed them. *In pace requiescat!*

ALE CELESTIAL?

A. E. Coppard

This next story, which is also set in the not too distant past, happens to feature a very contemporary interest: the pursuit of better beer. What with the Campaign for Real Ale and the ever-increasing number of small breweries producing outstanding beers, connoisseurs of a good pint now have a bigger variety of choices open to them than ever before. Alfred Edgar Coppard (1878–1957) was, according to his own admission, 'rather fond of good ale' and, apart from brewing his own beer at his home in the village of Dunmow, Essex, often travelled far and wide in search of 'a better pint'. Coppard is now regarded as one of the most stylish short story writers of his time, with a special interest in rural life and folklore, and combines both in a highly individual way in 'Ale Celestial?' which he wrote in 1952. It is the story of a landlord who believes he has found an ale that gives his customers 'pure rapture', a drink 'fit for kings, for angels, for justices, for all good men and true'. But the manner of his discovering this secret and the outcome for himself and his business are not at all what he expects, as the reader will discover . . .

On a time, in the olden days, one Barnaby Barnes kept a crabby and rat-riddled tavern that stank of mildew and creaked when the wind came roughly. The man was a simpleton, and yet he was sly too, and had a curmudgeonly nature that could not be trusted; but sweet charity becomes us all, so let it be known that throughout his years of life he was unlucky, unfriended, and with no great spiel of happiness. About fifty he was, fifty years of hardship had been his measure. And devilishness too, for whenever the wheel of fortune's cart was turning towards his threshold Barnaby was not nigh, he was far afield, he was otherwise engaged; drunk say, getting married say; burying his first wife Kitsey, or chasing after Menanda Mears his second who had run away because he was not so very loving and said lustful things to her. All the same he was still hoping for happy days to come at him by a lucky twist, such as to find a bag of jewels dropped by a robber or a recipe for making gold out of the unwrought clay; any this or that notion of obtaining a fortune would attract him and he would try any fool way of getting it.

Not far from the tavern was a church, half in ruins and half not, that was thought to be haunted by reason of its constant loss of candles. It was a place where you could procure a candle to set alight for some holy purpose, but either the wicks were too thick or the wax was too thin for they were always consumed in remarkably quick time leaving not a trace of wax or smudge or soot. The folk of course were suspicious of false doing—a candle's a candle—but nothing was discovered and nothing more known so it was laid to the account of Hocus, king of the low world, or Pocus, queen of the high, because one of these persons—nobody was certain which one—was thought to perform some queer antics there on certain midsummer nights. And to be sure, the church was standing on a knoll that was known to have belonged to fairies in the days that are gone.

Now Barnaby Barnes was after asking about these antics of Hocus—or, as it might be, Pocus.

A man of courage—he was told—would receive a gift from them.

'What sort of a gift? What is the way of it?'

He would see something and get something, that was the way of it. It might look nothing—they said—but it would mean a lot. It might be very small but it would be very valuable; it would be worth—they told him—a king's ransom.

'I'll go,' said Barnaby Barnes.

Others around warned him that it was madness and not worth the danger. 'You'll be tempting the eye of heaven.'

'I'll tempt it,' said Barnaby Barnes.

And off he went one midnight, a crazy night when he was giddy with drink, to climb up the little hill. There was no more than half darkness anywhere, yet he blundered into a flock of ewes and lambs lying about for the night and the air for a while became dismal with the cries of the sheep. He came to the church. He took a glance around it. He peeped through the keyhole of the door but all was black as the inside of a hat. He took a stroll along by the church, past the ruins, and looked over the wall at the sheep strown about like rocks; they must have been sleeping again, they were so quiet. He strolled back and took another squint through the keyhole. Nothing seen, nothing at all, so he turned his back and stood easy with his hands sunk in his breeches pockets. A fine tender night it was too, dripping with stars, a piece of moon shining low through a shroud of trees, the air whiffling quietly among the weeds and bushes on the graves, and there was Barnaby Barnes waiting, as a man of courage should wait, for what might happen to him. And it came, abruptly and silently, a rough poke in his hinder parts that shocked him to the soul. He leapt round gasping. He saw a man with whiskers.

But he was such a teeny tiny figure of a man! And he must have been very old for his beard was long and white, reaching his knees. And he was not much bigger than a skittle. And he wore a queer conical hat. On each of his shoes a large buckle gleamed like silver. He was carrying a fat white candle, five or six feet long, carrying it on his shoulder like a navvy with a pole, and he puffed as though it was almost too heavy for him. It was the candle that had dug so rudely into Barnaby Barnes. And there was more to it than that: the church door had not been opened at all, it was locked, bolted, and barred; he must have come dashing clean through it, candle and all!

'Pardon me,' cried the dwarf. Barnaby Barnes at once recovered his composure; there was nothing to fear from such a mite, he could heave him over the graves and the wall as easy as a cheese.

'Sure,' said Barnaby in a cunning way. 'But who's been a-stealing candles!'

The other was quickly ruffled and piped up: 'Begone, don't pester me, silly bad man!'

'Be blowed!' growled Barnaby Barnes. 'You come a-dashing through that door like a comet, right through it you come, and do me an injury so I shan't be able to sit down for a fortnight.'

'Don't pester me, blockhead!' repeated the little one.

Barnaby said no more, but snatched the candle from him and held it aloft: 'Where'd ya get this candle, eh?'

Jumping with rage around him, the little man tried to wrench it back, although he could not manage any such thing with a big fellow like Barnaby Barnes, who only laughed at him. But pretty soon Barnaby did not laugh. A sheep leapt over the churchyard wall and came towards him, followed by another and another, the whole flock, marshalling warily in a ring around Barnaby and the little one. They did not do anything more, they did not bleat and baa, they stood stock still and stared and waited. Barnaby lifted his foot as though to take a kick at the nearest but it didn't stir hoof nor head. Unmoving and fearless, they were all ranked solidly together and the man felt it was no harmless flock now, it was more like a pack, uncommonly like a pack of wolves. Barnaby's courage was spirited away and he was quite subdued.

The dwarf marched up to him. 'The candle!' he commanded.

Barnaby humbly lowered it back on the imp's shoulder.

'Now remember, Barnaby Barnes, not a word of this matter to any human ear or it will be the worse for you!'

'No, sir; no, no,' Barnaby, all of a tremble, replied.

'Right then! Remember. Stick to that and I'll reward you, Barnaby Barnes, yes I will, I'll reward you and make your fortune as sure as larks are singers. I'm not boasting.'

With that, and the candle balanced on his shoulder, the troll disappeared and Barnaby never saw the going of him; one moment he was there before his eyes and the next instant he was not. What is more, the sheep turned and sauntered away and jumped back over the wall. It did not take Barnaby long to forget all about Hocus and Pocus—he put a smart piece of distance between the church and himself.

True to his promise he said naught to anybody about the events of that night, not so much as a whisper about the stolen candle or anything else, nothing, nothing at all, he was true to his promise. Well, not so very long after, he had a dream in which he seemed to encounter the little old man again and receive from him a recipe for making magic ale.

'What's the good of this?'

''Twill make your fortune,' was the reply, 'as sure as larks are singers.'

It was not at all easy to make, and Barnaby told him so.

'Thrifty thrives,' said the little old man.

It was not at all cheap to brew, either, and Barnaby told him so.

The old one answered: 'Greed grudges. Don't haggle in the path of fortune. Easy come, easy go; easy friend, easy foe.'

Barnaby woke up and remembered it all. He made some tubs of the stuff. It took time and a lot of time, gathering of the herbs almost broke his back. It took money and a lot of money, the cost of the sirups and malt nearly ruined him. But when he took a taste of the magic ale he knew it for a liquor that lined a belly with pure rapture; it was fit for kings, for angels, for justices, for all good men and true. And it was a moral ale as well as a magical, it would make one drunk as a lord or leave him sober as a judge— according to the goodness of the person. A few sips of it would plant a lordly villain on his back or, in a manner of speaking, tilt a worthy man up to the level of magistrates.

The fame of his wonderful ale soon spread and in a short while things began to go gaily with Barnaby Barnes. Tipplers and maltworms for miles around, and as far again and farther, rushed to his tavern to try this liquor, and having once tried it were seized by an everlasting loyalty. Songs were sung about it, anthems of tippling praise, and a mock tale was set going that it would cure death itself and endow a man with life for ever. 'It is the elixir,

the nurture of the phoenix! Quaffed of gods, it is the ale celestial!'
Profit keeps pace with good repute and Barnaby Barnes was in a
fair way to make an easy comfortable fortune. Even the Widow
Osmaston, a rich and beautiful person, began to take particular
notice of him.

And yet, there was a maddening drawback to his triumph. The
ale's virtue, the tone and competence of it all, was got, and was
only to be got, from the nectar of a certain herb used in the
commixion. It was no common herb and Barnaby Barnes would
not entrust the knowledge of it to any other man. Fresh gathered
the herb must be, and he would gather it himself alone. Silly
wretch! For as his custom spread and the fame of the ale increased
he was soon at his wits end, worn out search-and gathering and
wrecked with pangs of distemper and weariness. Covetise! Covetise! To have shared his secret with others would still have served
him well, but greed grudges even a scruple and grabs at every
dolt. He sent children of the village to gather for him, not the true
simple that was hard to find but a false weed that was close to it
in likeness and flourished like a pest. And he prepared the malt,
a great store of it from the kiln, with sirups of a meaner kind, and
set all in the vat and brewed it. And when he had brewed it he
was filled with joy for to his palate it was quite the same as before.

'Now I am a made man!' And rubbing his hands together he
gleefully cried: 'Fame is my portion and fortune is in my pouch.
Mother of mercy, though, here's Mrs. Osmaston to see me—and I
not shaved yet!'

But the very first drinker who came to taste the tipple at once
spat it out of his mouth. It was like water, he said. He swore it
was but filthy water and he refused to pay for it and went away
in dudgeon. Barnaby tasted it himself again, and to his palate it
was quite the same as before, but this was a figment—for it was
not so.

'Crazy hound!' he muttered, 'It is ale celestial!'

Another came and another. Each man vented his disgust and
cast the drink away. Others followed, crowding into the tavern at
the close of day, but on tasting the new brew all spat it from them
and upbraided Barnaby Barnes for an adulterater and purveyor
of dishonest ale. What could he do but deny it and manifest his
faith in the ale's virtue? Taking a cupful he gulped it down with
gusto, but before he could set back the empty cup upon the table
he swayed and dropped in a swoon to the ground. The onlookers
were contemptuous of his plight and left him to nose the dust of
the floor.

How pitiful is man's triumph! One hour he is perched on high
like a steeple cock and the next he is but a dry leaf flickering in a

ditch. Thus it was with Barney Barnes. Thenceforward his ale became a scoff, the tavern a derision. No one came there, no one drank there, only in mockery did its fame persist. And yet, to Barnaby the ale still had the same fragrant delicacy, authentic, genuine, pure, the primed elixir, ale celestial. With nothing else to be done with it he drank all up himself, drank it and drank it day after day until it was all consumed and he was but a walking shade, uncouth as a moulting hen squatting at death's door. Then one day he took heart again and set to work himself gathering the true herb once more. And when he had gathered a bushel of it he prepared the malt and bought the true sirups with the last of his silver. He brewed a tub or two of the ale, and he tasted it. And when his mouth savoured it it tasted rank, fell and foul, like filthy water indeed. But this was all a figment for it was not so— the ale was good, it was ale celestial again. Thus deceived, and in despair, his spirit left him and he fell with a crash down in his own dim cellar and died among the barrels.

He was dead for a day and a half before they found him, an ugly stiff corpse. And near his heels stood a fat white candle, as high as a well-wrought man, burning with strange luminosity. It burned, but did not consume a morsel of wax, and though there was no flicker of draught in the air the flame danced like a troll, leaping so merrily.

BITTER ALMONDS

Dorothy L. Sayers

Dorothy L. Sayers (1893–1957), who is today widely regarded as one of the 'Queens of Crime Fiction', was considered by her friends during her lifetime to have a particularly discerning palate where good sherry was concerned. The popularity of her fiction has tended to obscure the fact that in the years immediately after the First World War she was a brilliant copywriter in one of the largest London advertising agencies, S. H. Benson, and while working there coined the famous phrase, 'Guiness is Good for You' which is still in use today. Dorothy Sayers abandoned this profession, she said later, 'merely to make money'. Two of her characters share her appreciation of fine drink: the amateur detective Lord Peter Wimsey (who appears in the third part of this book) and the wine salesman, Montague Egg, who also doubles as a sleuth when the need arises. Dorothy Sayers wrote a dozen short tales about this knowledgeable little wine salesman, which, curiously, have never been collected in a single volume. 'Bitter Almonds', which is about the mysterious death of one of Egg's customers after drinking an after-dinner glass of crème de menthe *and which he solves in a particularly ingenious fashion, happens to be my favourite ...*

'Dash it!' exclaimed Mr Montague Egg, 'there's another perfectly good customer gone west.'

He frowned at his morning paper, which informed him that an inquest would be held that day on the body of Mr Bernard Whipley, a wealthy and rather eccentric old gentleman, to whom the firm of Plummett & Rose had from time to time sold a considerable quantity of their choice vintage wines, fine old matured spirits and liqueurs.

Monty had more than once been invited by Mr Whipley to sample his own goods, sitting in the pleasant study at Cedar Lawn—a bottle of ancient port, carried up carefully from the cellar by Mr Whipley himself or a liqueur brandy, brought out from the tall mahogany cabinet that stood in the alcove.

Mr Whipley never allowed anybody but himself to handle any-thing alcoholic. You never, he said, could trust servants, and he had no fancy for being robbed, or finding the cook with her head under the kitchen dresser.

So Mr Egg frowned and sighed, and then frowned still more, on seeing that Mr Whipley had been discovered dead, apparently from prussic acid poisoning, after drinking an after-dinner glass of crème de menthe.

It is not agreeable when customers suddenly died poisoned after partaking of the drinks one has supplied to them, and it is not good for business.

Mr Egg glanced at his watch. The town where he was at that moment reading the paper was only fifteen miles distant from the late Mr Whipley's place of residence. Monty decided that it might be just as well to run over and attend the inquest. He was, at any rate, in a position to offer testimony as to the harmless nature of crème de menthe as supplied by Messrs Plummett & Rose.

Accordingly he drove over there as soon as he had finished his breakfast, and by sending in his card to the coroner, secured for himself a convenient seat in the crowded little schoolroom where the inquest was being held.

The first witness was the housekeeper, Mrs Minchin, a stout, elderly person of almost exaggerated respectability. She said she had been over twenty years in Mr Whipley's service. He was nearly eighty years old, but very active and healthy, except that he had to be careful of his heart, as was only to be expected.

She had always found him an excellent employer. He had been, perhaps, a little close about financial matters and had kept a very sharp eye on the housekeeping, but personally she was not afraid of such, being as careful of his interests as she would be of her own. She had kept house for him ever since his wife's death.

'He was quite in his usual health on Monday evening,' Mrs Minchin went on. 'Mr Raymond Whipley had telephoned in the afternoon to say he would be down for dinner—'

'That is Mr Whipley's son?'

'Yes—his only child.' Here Mrs Minchin glanced across at a thin, sallow, young-old man, seated near Mr Egg on the bench reserved for witnesses, and sniffed rather meaningly. 'Mr and Mrs Cedric were staying in the house. Mr Cedric Whipley is Mr Whipley's nephew. He had no other relations.'

Mr Egg identified Mr and Mrs Cedric Whipley as the fashion-ably dressed young man and woman in black, who sat on the other side of Mr Raymond. The witness proceeded.

'Mr Raymond arrived in his car at half-past six, and went in at once to see his father in the study. He came out again when the dressing-gong rang for dinner, at a quarter-past seven. He passed me in the hall, and I thought he looked rather upset. As Mr Whipley didn't come out, I went in to him. He was sitting at his writing-table, reading something that looked to me like a legal paper.

'I said, "Excuse me, Mr Whipley, sir, but did you hear the gong?" He was sometimes a little hard of hearing, though wonderfully keen in all his faculties, considering his age. He looked up, and said, "All right, Mrs Minchin," and went back to what he was doing. I said to myself, "Mr Raymond's been putting him out again." At half-past—'

'One moment. What had you in your mind about Mr Raymond?'

'Well, nothing much, only Mr Whipley didn't always approve of Mr Raymond's goings-on, and they sometimes had words about it. Mr Whipley disliked Mr Raymond's business.

'At half-past seven,' continued the witness, 'Mr Whipley went upstairs to dress, and he seemed all right then, only his step was tired and heavy. I was waiting in the hall, in case he needed any assistance, and as he passed me he asked me to telephone to Mr Whitehead to ask him to come over the next morning—Mr Whitehead the lawyer. He did not say what it was for. I did as he asked me, and when Mr Whipley came down again, about ten minutes to eight, I told him Mr Whitehead had had the message, and would be with him at ten the next day.'

'Did anybody else hear you say that?'

'Yes. Mr Raymond and Mr and Mrs Cedric were in the hall, having their cocktails. They must all have heard me. Dinner was served at eight—'

'Were you present at dinner?'

'No. I have my meals in my own room. Dinner was over about a quarter to nine, and the parlourmaid took coffee into the drawing-room for Mr and Mrs Cedric, and into the study for Mr Whipley and Mr Raymond. I was alone in my room till nine o'clock, when Mr and Mrs Cedric came in to have a little chat. We were all together till just before half-past nine, when we heard the study door slam violently, and a few minutes later Mr Raymond came in, looking very queer. He had his hat and coat on.

'Mr Cedric said: "Hallo, Ray?" He took no notice, and said to me, "I shan't be staying the night, after all, Mrs Minchin. I'm going back to town at once." I said, "Very good, Mr Raymond. Does Mr Whipley know of your change of plans?" He laughed in a funny way, and said: "Oh, yes. He knows all about it." He went out again and Mr Cedric followed him and, I think, said something like, "Don't lose your hair, old man." Mrs Cedric said to me, she was afraid Mr Raymond might have had a quarrel with the old gentleman.

'About ten minutes later, I heard the two young gentlemen coming downstairs, and went out to see that Mr Raymond had left nothing behind him, as he was apt to be forgetful. He was just going out of the front door with Mr Cedric. I ran after him with his scarf, which he had left on the hallstand. He drove away in his car very quickly and I came back into the house with Mr Cedric.

'As we passed the study door, Mr Cedric said, "I wonder whether my uncle—" And then he stopped and said, "No, better let him alone till tomorrow." We went back to my room, where Mrs Cedric was waiting for us. She said, "What's the matter, Cedric?" and he answered, "Uncle Henry's found out about Ella. I told Ray he'd better be careful." She said, "Oh, dear!" and after that we changed the conversation.

'Mr and Mrs Cedric sat with me till about eleven-thirty, when they left me to go up to bed. I put my room in order and then came out to make my usual round of the house. When I put out the light in the hall, I noticed that the light was still on in Mr Whipley's study. It was unusual for him to be up so late, so I went to see if he had fallen asleep over a book.

'I got no answer when I knocked, so I went in, and there he was, lying back in his chair, dead. There were two empty coffee-cups and two empty liqueur glasses on the table and a half-empty flask of crème de menthe. I called Mr Cedric at once, and he told me to leave everything exactly as it was, and to telephone to Dr Baker.'

The next witness was the parlourmaid, who had waited at table. She said that nothing unusual had happened during dinner, except that Mr Whipley and his son both seemed rather silent and pre-occupied.

At the end of the meal, Mr Raymond had said, 'Look here, father, we can't leave it like this.' Mr Whipley had said, 'If you have changed your mind you had better tell me at once,' and had ordered coffee to be sent into the study. Mr Raymond said, 'I can't change my mind, but if you would only listen—' Mr Whipley did not reply.

On going into the study with the coffee and the liqueur glasses, the parlourmaid saw Mr Raymond seated at the table. Mr Whipley was standing at the cabinet, with his back turned to his son, apparently getting out the liqueurs.

He said to Mr Raymond, 'What will you have?' Mr Raymond replied, 'Crème de menthe.' Mr Whipley said, 'You would—that's

a woman's drink.' The parlourmaid then went out and did not
see either gentleman again.

Mr Egg smiled to himself as he listened. He could hear old Mr
Whipley saying it.

Then he composed his chubby face to a more serious expression,
as the coroner proceeded to call Mr Cedric Whipley.

Mr Cedric corroborated the housekeeper's story. He said he was
aged thirty-six, and was a junior partner in the publishing firm of
Freeman & Toplady. He was acquainted with the circumstance
of Mr Whipley's quarrel with his son. Mr Whipley had, in fact,
asked him and his wife to the house in order that he might discuss
the situation with them. The trouble had to do with Raymond's
engagement to a certain lady.

Mr Whipley had talked rather impulsively about altering his
will, but he (Cedric) had urged him to think the matter over
calmly. He had accompanied Raymond upstairs on the night of
the tragedy and had understood from him that Mr Whipley had
threatened to cut his son off with the proverbial shilling. He
had told Raymond to take things easy and the old man would
'simmer down'. Raymond had taken his interference in bad part.

After Raymond's departure he had thought it better to leave
the old man to himself. On leaving Mrs Minchin's room with his
wife, he had gone straight upstairs without entering the study. He
thought it would be about a quarter of an hour after that, that he
had come down in answer to Mrs Minchin's call, to find his uncle
dead.

He had bent over the body to examine it, and had then thought
he detected a faint smell of almonds about the lips. He had smelt
the liqueur glasses, but without touching them and, fancying that
one of them also smelt of almonds, had instructed Mrs Minchin
to leave everything exactly as it was. He had then formed the
impression that his uncle might have committed suicide.

There was a rustle in the little court when Mr Raymond Whipley
took his place at the coroner's table. He was a lean, effeminate
and rather unwholesome-looking person of anything between
thirty and forty years of age.

He said that he was 'a photographic artist' by profession. He
had a studio in Bond Street. His 'expressionist studies' of well-
known men and women had gained considerable notice in the
West End. His father had not approved of his activities. He had
old-fashioned prejudices.

'I understand,' said the coroner, 'that prussic acid is frequently
used in photography.'

Mr Raymond Whipley smiled winningly at this ominous
question.

'Cyanide of potassium,' he said. 'Oh, dear, yes. Quite frequently.'

'You are acquainted with its use for photography?'

'Oh, yes. I don't use it often. But I have some by me, if that's what you want to know.'

'Thank you. Now can you tell me about this alleged difference of opinion with your father?'

'Yes. He found out that I was engaged to marry a lady connected with the stage. I don't know who told him. Probably my cousin, Cedric. He'll deny it, of course, but I expect it was jolly old Cedric. My father sent for me and really cut up quite rough about it. Full of diehard prejudices, you know. We had quite a little rumpus before dinner. After dinner, I asked to see him again—thought I could talk him round. But he was really very offensive. I couldn't stand it. It upset me. So I barged off back to town.'

'Did he say anything about sending for Mr Whitehead?'

'Oh, yes. Said if I married Ella, he'd cut me out of his will. Quite the stern parent and all that. I said, cut away, then.'

'Did he say in whose favour he thought of making his new will?'

'No, he didn't say. I expect Cedric would have come in for something. He's the only other relation, of course.'

'Will you describe very carefully what happened in the study after dinner?'

'We went in, and I sat down at the table near the fire. My father went to the cabinet where he keeps his spirits and liqueurs and asked me what I would have. I said I would have a crème de menthe, and he sneered at me in his usual pleasant way. He fetched out the flask and told me to help myself, when the girl brought in the glasses. I did so. I had coffee and crème de menthe. He did not drink anything while I was there. He was rather excited and walked up and down, threatening me with this and that.

'After a bit I said, "Your coffee's getting cold, father." Then he told me to go to hell, and I said, "Right you are." He added a very disagreeable remark about my financée. I am afraid I then lost my temper and used some—shall we say, unfilial expressions. I went out and banged the door. When I left him, he was standing up behind the table, facing me.

'I went to tell Mrs Minchin that I was going back to town. Cedric started to butt in, but I told him I knew who it was I had to thank for all this trouble, and if he wanted the old man's money he was welcome to it. That's all I know about it.'

'If your father drank nothing while you were with him, how do you explain the fact that both the liqueur glasses and both the coffee-cups had been used?'

'I suppose he used his after I had gone. He certainly did not drink anything before I went.'

'And he was alive when you left the study?'

'Very much so.'

Mr Whitehead, the lawyer, explained the terms of the deceased man's will. It left an income of two thousand a year to Cedric Whipley, with reversion to Raymond, who was the residuary legatee.

'Did deceased ever express any intention of altering this will?'

'He did. On the day before his death he said that he was very much dissatisfied with his son's conduct, and that unless he could get him to see reason, he would cut him off with an annuity of a thousand a year, and leave the rest of the estate to Mr Cedric Whipley. He disliked Mr Raymond's financée and said he would not have that woman's children coming in for his money. I tried to dissuade him, but I think he supposed that when the lady heard of his intentions she would break off the engagement. When Mrs Minchin rang me up on the night in question I was convinced in my own mind that he intended to execute a new will.'

'But since he had no time to do so, the will in favour of Mr Raymond Whipley will now stand?'

'That is so.'

Inspector Brown of the County Police then gave evidence about finger-prints. He said that one coffee-cup and one liqueur glass bore the finger-prints of Mr Raymond Whipley, and the other cup and the glass which held the poison, those of Mr Whipley senior. There were no other prints, except, of course, those of the parlour-maid, on the cups or glasses, while the flask of crème de menthe bore those of both father and son.

Bearing in mind the possibility of suicide, the police had made a careful search of the room for any bottle or phial which might have contained the poison. They had found nothing either in the cabinet or elsewhere. They had, indeed, collected from the back of the fireplace the half-burnt fragment of a lead-foil capsule, which bore the letters '. . . AU . . . tier & Cie,' stamped round the edge.

From its size, however, it was clear that this capsule had covered the stopper of a half-litre bottle, and it seemed highly improbable that an intending suicide would purchase prussic acid by the half-litre, nor was there any newly opened bottle to which the capsule appeared to belong.

At this point a horrible thought began to emerge from Mr Egg's inner consciousness—a dim recollection of something he had once read in a book. He lost the remainder of Inspector Brown's evidence, which was purely formal, and only began to take notice

again when, after the cook and housemaid had proved that they
had been together the whole evening, the doctor was called to
give the medical evidence.

He said that deceased had undoubtedly died of prussic acid
poisoning. Only a very small amount of the cyanide had been
found in the stomach, but even a small dose would be fatal to a
man of his age and natural frailty. Prussic acid was one of the most
rapidly fatal of all known poisons, producing unconsciousness and
death within a very few minutes after being swallowed.

'When did you first see the body, doctor?'

'I arrived at the house at five minutes to twelve. Mr Whipley
had then been dead at least two hours, and probably a little more.'

'He could not possibly have died within, say, half an hour of
your arrival?'

'Not possibly. I place the death round about half-past nine,
certainly not later than ten-thirty.'

The analyst's report was next produced. The contents of the
flask of crème de menthe and the coffee dregs in both cups had
been examined and found to be perfectly harmless. Both liqueur
glasses contained a few drops of crème de menthe, and in one—
that which bore the finger-prints of old Mr Whipley—there was a
distinct trace of hydrocyanic acid.

Even before the coroner began his summing up it was plain that
things looked very black for Raymond Whipley. There was the
motive, the fact that he alone had easy access to the deadly cyanide, and the time of death, coinciding almost exactly with that of
his hasty and agitated flight from the house.

Suicide seemed to be excluded; the other members of the
household could prove each other's alibis; there was no suggestion
that any stranger had entered the house from outside. The jury
brought in the inevitable verdict of murder against Raymond
Whipley.

Mr Egg rapidly made his way out of court. Two things were
troubling him—Mrs Minchin's evidence and that half-remembered
warning that he had read in a book. He went down to the village
post-office and sent a telegram to his employers. Then he turned
to his steps to the local inn, ordered a high tea, and ate it slowly,
with his thoughts elsewhere. He had an idea that this case was
going to be bad for business.

In about an hour's time, the reply to his telegram was handed
to him. It ran: 'June 14, 1893. Freeman and Toplady, 1931,' and
was signed by the senior partner of Plummett and Rose.

Mr Egg's round and cheerful face became overcast by a cloud
of perplexity and distress. He shut himself into the landlord's
private room alone and put through an expensive trunk-call to

town. Emerging, less perplexed but still gloomy, he got into his car and set off in search of the coroner.

That official welcomed him cheerfully. He was a hearty and rubicund medical man with a shrewd eye and a brisk manner. Inspector Brown and the Chief Constable were with him when Monty was shown in.

'Well, Mr Egg,' said the coroner, 'I'm sure you're happy to be assured that this unfortunate case conveys no imputation against the purity of the goods supplied by your firm.'

'That's just what I've taken the liberty of coming to you about,' said Monty. 'Business is business, but, on the other hand, facts are facts, and our people are ready to face them. I've been on the 'phone to Mr Plummett, and he authorised me to put the thing before you.

'If I didn't,' added Mr Egg candidly, 'somebody else might, and that would make matters worse. Don't wait for unpleasant disclosures to burst. If the truth must be told, see that *you* tell it first. Monty's maxim—from "The Salesman's Handbook". Remarkable book, full of common sense. Talking of common sense, a spot of that commodity wouldn't have hurt our young friend, would it?'

'Meaning Raymond Whipley?' said the coroner. 'That young man is a pathological case, if you ask me.'

'You're right there, sir," agreed the inspector. 'I've seen a sight of foolish crooks, but he licks the lot. Barmy, I'd call him. Quarrelling with his dad, doing him in and running away in that suspicious manner—why didn't he put up an electric sign to say "I done it?" But as you say, I don't think he's quite all there.'

'Well, that may be,' said Monty, 'but over and above that, there's old Mr Whipley. You see, gentlemen, I know all my customers. It's my job, as you may say, to have their fancies by heart. No good offering an 1847 Oloroso to a gentleman that likes his sherry light and dry, or tantalising a customer that's under orders to stick to hock with bargains in vintage port.

'Now, what I'd like you to tell me is, how did the late Mr Whipley come to be drinking crème de menthe at all? He only kept it by him for ladies; it was a flavour he couldn't do with in any shape or form. You heard what he said about it to Mr Raymond.'

'That's a point,' said the Chief Constable. 'I may say it had already occurred to us. But he must have taken the poison in something.'

'Well, I only say, bear that in mind—that, and the foolishness of the murder, if it was done the way the jury brought it in. But now about this lead-foil capsule. I can tell you something about that. I didn't intrude myself at the inquest, because I hadn't got the facts, but I've got them now and here they are. You know, gentlemen, it stands to reason, if a capsule was taken off a bottle that day in the study, there must have been a bottle belonging to it. And where is it? It's got to be somewhere. A bottle's a bottle, when all's said and done.

'Now, gentlemen, Mr Whipley dealt with my employers, Plummett & Rose, for over fifty years. It's an old-established firm. And that capsule was put out by a firm of French shippers who went into liquidation in 1900—Prelatier & Cie was their name, and we were their agents in this country. Now, that capsule came off a bottle of Noyeau sent out by them—you can see the last two letters of the word on the stamp—and we delivered a bottle of Prelaitier's Noyeau to Mr Whipley, with some other samples of liqueur, on June 14, 1893.'

'Noyeau?' said the coroner, with interest.

'I see that means something to you, doctor,' said Mr Egg.

'It does, indeed,' said the coroner. 'Noyeau is a liqueur flavoured with oil of bitter almonds, or peach-stones—correct me if I'm wrong, Mr Egg—and contains, therefore, a small proportion of hydrocyanic acid.'

'That's it,' said Monty. 'Of course, in the ordinary way, there isn't enough of it to hurt anybody in a single glassful, or even two. But if you let a bottle stand long enough, the oil will rise to the top, and the first glass out of an old bottle of Noyeau has been known to cause death. I know that, because I read it in a book called *Foods and Poisons* published a few years ago by Freeman & Toplady.'

'Cedric Whipley's firm,' said the inspector.

'Exactly so,' said Monty.

'What precisely, are you suggesting, Mr Egg?' inquired the Chief Constable.

'Not murder, sir,' said Monty. 'No, not that—that I suppose it might have come to that, in a way. I'm suggesting that after Mr Raymond had left the study, the old gentleman got fidgety and restless, the way one does when one's been through a bit of an upset. I think he started to drink up his cold coffee, and then wanted a spot of liqueur to take with it.

'He goes to the cabinet—doesn't seem to fancy anything—roots about, and comes upon this old bottle of Noyeau that's been standing unopened for the last forty years. He takes it out, removes the capsule and throws it into the fire and draws the cork with his corkscrew, as I've seen him do many a time. Then he pours off the first glass, not thinking about the danger, drinks it

off as he's sitting in his chair and dies without hardly having time
to call out.'

'That's very ingenious,' said the Chief Constable. 'But what
became of the bottle and the corkscrew? And how do you account
for the crème de menthe in the glass?'

'Ah!' said Monty, 'there you are. Somebody saw to that, and it
wasn't Mr Raymond, because it would have been all to his advantage to leave things as they were. But suppose, round about half-
past eleven, when Mrs Minchin was tidying her room and the
other servants were in bed, another party had gone into the study
and seen Mr Whipley lying dead, with the bottle of Noyeau beside
him, and had guessed what had happened.

'Supposing this party had then put the corkscrew back in the
cupboard, tipped a few drops of crème de menthe from Mr Raymond's glass into the dead gentleman's, and carried the Noyeau
bottle away to be disposed of at leisure. What would it look like
then?'

'But how could the party do that, without leaving prints on Mr
Raymond's glass?'

'That's easy,' said Monty. 'He'd only to lift the glass by taking
the stem between the roots of his fingers. So. All you'd find would
be a faint smudge at the base of the bowl.'

'And the motive?' demanded the Chief Constable.

'Well, gentlemen, that's not for me to say. But if Mr Raymond
was to be hanged for murdering his father, I fancy his father's
money would go to the next of kin—to that gentleman who published the book that tells you all about Noyeau.

'It's very unfortunate,' added Mr Egg, 'that my firm should
have supplied the goods in question, but there you are. If accidents
happen and you are to blame, take steps to avoid repetition of
same. Not that we should admit any responsibility, far from it, the
nature of the commodity being what it is. But we might perhaps
insert a warning in our forthcoming catalogue.

'And à propos, gentlemen, let me make a note to send you our
New Centenary History of the House of Plummett & Rose. It will
be a very refined production, got up regardless, and worthy of a
position on any library shelf.'

THE INCOME TAX MYSTERY

Michael Gilbert

Mr Portway is, according to the narrator of this story, a solicitor who occasionally makes 'small earnings for articles on wine, on which he is an acknowledged expert'. Yet how does this man, who appears to have only a handful of clients, manage to dress well, drive a good car and also regularly spend 'hundreds of pounds at the wine merchant'? according to one of his disgruntled ex-employees. This is the mystery that Michael Gilbert (1912-), himself a noted London lawyer, sets out to resolve. Gilbert, who has been referred to by several experts as one of the finest of the post-World War Two detective story writers, has found the time away from his legal practice to write hundreds of short stories, many of them featuring the indomitable Detective Sergeant Patrick Petrella. There is more than a little of Gilbert's knowledge of both the law and wine in 'The Income Tax Mystery' in which the Pickwickian figure of Mr Portway is revealed to have a connoisseur's nose and palate matched to a scoundrel's ingenuity.

I qualified as a solicitor before the war and in 1937 I bought a share in a small partnership in the City. Then the War came along and I joined the Infantry. I was already thirty-five and it didn't look as if I was going to see much active service, so I cashed in on my knowledge of German and joined the Intelligence Corps.

When the War was finished, I got back to London and found our old office bombed and the other partner dead. As far as a legal practice can do so, it had vanished. I got a job without any difficulty in a firm in Bedford Row, but I didn't enjoy it. The work was easy enough but there was no real future in it. So I quit and joined the Legal Branch of Inland Revenue.

This may seem even duller than private practice, but in fact it wasn't. As soon as I had finished the subsidiary training in accountancy that all Revenue Officials have to take, I was invited to join a very select outfit known as IBA or Investigation Branch, Active.

If you ask a Revenue official about IBA, he'll tell you it doesn't exist. This may simply mean that he hasn't heard of it. Most ordinary Revenue investigation is done by accountants who examine balance sheets, profit and loss accounts, vouchers and receipts, then ask questions and go on asking questions until the truth emerges.

Some cases can't be treated like that. They need active investigation. Someone has got to go out and find the facts. That's where IBA comes in.

It isn't all big cases involving millions of pounds. The Revenue reckons to achieve the best results by making a few shrewd examples in the right places. One of our most spectacular coups was achieved when a member of the department once opened a greengrocers shop and—but that's another story.

When the name of Mr Portway cropped up in IBA records, it was natural that the dossier should get pushed across to me. For Mr Portway was a solicitor. I can't remember exactly how he first came to our notice—you'd be surprised what casual items can set IBA in motion: a conversation in a railway carriage, a hint from an insurance assessor, a bit of loud-voiced boasting in a pub. We don't go in for phone-tapping: it's inefficient and, from our point of view, quite unnecessary.

The thing about Mr Portway was simply this: he seemed to make a very substantial amount of money without working for it.

The first real confirmation came from a disgruntled girl who had been hired to look after his books and fired for inefficiency. Mr Portway ran a good car, she said; he dressed well, spent hundreds of pounds at the wine merchant (she'd seen one of his bills), and conducted an old-fashioned one-man practice which, by every law of economics, should have left him broke at the end of each year.

Some days he had no clients at all, she said, and spent the morning in his room reading a book (detective stories, chiefly); then he would take two hours off for lunch, snooze a little on his return, have a cup of tea, and go home. On other days a client or two would trickle in. The business was almost entirely the buying and selling of houses and the preparation of leases, mortgages, and sale agreements. Mr Portway did it all himself. He had one girl to do the typing and look after the outer office, and another (our informant) to keep the books.

I don't suppose you know anything about solicitors' accounting, and I'm not proposing to give you a dissertation on it; but the fact is that solicitors are bound by very strict rules—rules imposed by Act of Parliament and jealously enforced by the Law Society. And quite right, too. Solicitors handle a lot of other people's money.

When we'd made a quiet check to see if Mr Portway had any private means of his own and learned that he didn't, we decided that this was just the sort of case we ought to have a look at. It wasn't difficult. Mr Portway knew nothing about figures. However small his staff, he had to have someone with the rudiments of accountancy, or he couldn't have got through his annual audit. We simply watched the periodicals until we saw his advertisement, and I applied for the job.

I don't know if there were any other applicants, but I'm sure I was the only one who professed to know both law and book-keeping and who was prepared to accept the mouse-like salary he was offering.

Mr Portway proved to be a small, round, pink-cheeked, white-haired man. One would have said Pickwickian, except that he didn't wear glasses, nor was there anything in the least owl-like about his face. So far as any comparison suggested itself, he looked more like a tortoise. He had a sardonic, leathery, indestructible face, with the long upper lip of a philosopher.

He greeted me warmly and showed me to my room. The office occupied the ground floor and basement of the house. On the right as you came in, and overlooking the paved courtyard and fountain which is all that remains of the old 'Inn', was Mr Portway's sanctum, a very nice room, on the small side, and made smaller by the rows of bookcases full of bound reports. My own room was on the left of the entrance, and even smaller and more austere. Downstairs were storerooms of old files and records and a strong-room which ran back under the pavement.

I have given you some idea of the small scale of things so that you can gather how easy I thought my job was going to be. My guess was that a week would be more than enough to detect any funny business that was going on.

I was quite wrong.

A week was enough to confirm that something *was* wrong. But by the end of a month I hadn't got a step nearer to discovering what it was.

I reported my meagre findings to my superiors.

'Mr Portway,' I said, 'has a business which appears to produce, in fees, just about enough to pay the salaries of his two employees, the rent, lighting, and other outgoings, and to leave him no personal income at all. Indeed, in some instances, he has had to make up, from his own pocket, small deficiences in the office account. Nor does his money come from private means. It is part of my duty as accountant to prepare Mr Portway's personal tax returns'—(this, it is fair to him to say, was at his own suggestion)— 'and apart from a very small holding in War Stock and occasional

small earnings for articles on wine, on which he is an acknowledged expert, he has—or at least declares—no outside resources
at all. Nevertheless, enjoying as he does a minus income, he lives
very well, appears to deny himself little in the way of comfort.
He is not extravagant, but I would not hesitate to estimate his
personal expenditures at no less than three thousand pounds per
annum.'

My masters found this report so unsatisfactory that I was summoned to an interview. The head of the department at that time,
Dai Evans, was a tubby and mercurial Welshman, like Lloyd
George without the moustache. He was on Christian-name terms
with all his staff; but he wasn't a good man to cross.

'Are you asking me to believe in miracles, Michael?' he said.
'How can a man have an inexhaustible wallet of notes if he doesn't
earn them from somewhere?'

'Perhaps he makes them,' I suggested.

Dai elected to take this seriously. 'A forger you mean. I wouldn't
have thought it likely.'

'No,' I said. 'I didn't quite mean that.' (I knew as well as anyone
that the skill and organisation, to say nothing of the supplies of
special paper, necessary for banknote forgery were far beyond the
resources of an ordinary citizen.) 'I thought he might have a hoard.
Some people do, you know. There's nothing intrinsically illegal in
it. Suppose he made his money before the war and stowed it away
somewhere. In his strongroom downstairs, perhaps. He keeps the
keys himself and that's one room no one's allowed inside. Each
week he gets out a couple of dozen pound notes and spends
them.'

Dai grunted. 'Why should he trouble to keep up an office? You
say it actually costs him money. Why wouldn't he shift his hoard
to a safe deposit? That way he'd save himself money and work. I
don't like it, Michael. We're onto something here, boy. Don't let it
go.'

So I returned to Lombards Inn and kept my eyes and ears open.
And as the weeks passed the mystery grew more irritating and
seemingly more insoluble.

During the month which ensued I made a very careful calculation. In the course of that single month Mr Portway acted in the
purchase of one house for £5,000, and the sale of another at about
the same price. He drafted the lease of an office in the City and
fixed up a mortgage for an old lady with a Building Society. The
income he received for these transactions totalled exactly £171.50.
And that was just about five pounds *less* than he paid out—to
keep his office going for the same period . . .

One day, about three o'clock in the afternoon, I had occasion to take some papers in to him. I found him sitting in the chair beside the fireplace, the *Times* (which he read every day from first to last page) in one hand, and in the other a glass.

He said, 'You find me indulging in my secret vice. I'm one of the old school who thinks that claret should be drunk after lunch and burgundy after dinner.'

I am fond of French wines myself and he must have seen the quick glance I gave the bottle.

'It's a Pontet Canet,' he said, 'of 1943. Certainly the best of the war years, and almost the best Château of that year. You'll find a glass in the filing cabinet, Mr Gilbert.'

You can't drink wine standing up. Before I knew what I was doing, we were seated in front of the fireplace with the bottle between us. After a second glass Mr Portway fell into a mood of reminiscence. I kept my ears open, of course, for any useful information, but only half of me, at that moment, was playing the detective. The other half was enjoying an excellent claret, and the company of a philosopher.

It appeared that Mr Portway had come to the law late. He had studied art under Bertolozzi, the great Florentine engraver, and had then spent a couple of years in the workshops of Herr Groener, who specialised in intaglios and metal relief work. He took down from the mantelshelf a beautiful little reproduction in copper of the Papal Colophon which he had made himself. Then the first Word War, most of which he had spent in Egypt, had disorientated him.

'I felt the need,' he said, 'of something a little more tangible in my life than the art of metal relievo.' He had tried, and failed, to become an architect, and had then chosen the law, mostly to oblige an uncle who had no son.

'There have been Portways,' he said, 'in Lombards Inn for two centuries. I fear I shall be the last.'

The telephone broke up our talk and I went back to my room.

As I thought about things that night, I came to the conclusion that Mr Portway had presented me with the answer to one problem, in the act of setting me another.

'There have been Portways in Lombards Inn for two centuries.' The tie of sentiment? Was that perhaps why he was willing to finance, from his own pocket, a practice which no longer paid him? But where did the money come from? The more you looked at it, the more impossible the whole problem became.

As cashier, remember, I received and paid out every penny the firm earned and spent. And I knew—positively and actually knew—that no money went into Mr Portway's pocket. On the contrary, almost every month he had to draw a cheque on his own bank account to keep the office going. Nor did he draw, according to his bank statements, any money from that or any other account.

So from what source did the substantial wad of notes in his wallet come? As you see, I was being driven, step by step, to the only logical conclusion: that he had found some method, some perfectly safe and private method, of manufacturing money.

But not forgery, as the word is usually understood. Despite his bland admissions of an engraver's training, the difficulties were too great. Where would he get the special paper? And such notes as I had seen did not look in the least like forgeries.

I had come to one other conclusion. The heart of the secret lay in the strongroom. This was the one room that no one but Mr Portway ever visited, the room of which he alone had the key. Try as I would, I had never even glanced inside the door. If he wanted a deed out of it, Mr Portway would wait until I was at lunch before he went in to fetch it. And he was always the last one to leave the office.

The door of the strongroom was a heavy, old-fashioned affair, and if you have time to study it, and are patient enough, in the end you can get the measure of any lock. I had twice glimpsed the actual key, too, and that is a great help. It wasn't long before I had equipped myself with keys which I was pretty sure would open the door. The next thing was to find an opportunity to use them.

Eventually I hit on quite a simple plan.

At about three o'clock one afternoon I announced that I had an appointment with the local Inspector of Taxes. I thought it would take an hour or ninety minutes. Would it be all right if I went straight home? Mr Portway agreed. He was in the middle of drafting a complicated conveyance, and looked safely anchored in his chair.

I went back to my room, picked up my hat, raincoat and brief case, and tiptoed down to the basement. Quietly I opened the door of one of the storage rooms; I had used my last few lunch breaks, when I was alone in the office, in moving a rampart of deed boxes a couple of feet out from the wall and building up the top with bundles of old papers. Now I shut the door behind me and squeezed carefully into my lair. Apart from the fact that the fresh dust I had disturbed made me want to sneeze, it wasn't too bad. Soon the dust particles resettled themselves, and I fell into a state of somnolence.

It was five o'clock before I heard Mr Portway moving. His footsteps came down the passage outside, and stopped. I heard him open the door of the strongroom, opposite. A pause. The door shut again. The next moment my door opened and the lights sprung on.

I held my breath. The lights went out and the door closed. I heard the click of the key in the lock. Then the footsteps moved away.

He was certainly thorough. I even heard him look into the lavatory. (My first plan had been to lock myself in it. I was glad now that I had not.) At last the steps moved away upstairs; more pottering about, the big outer door slammed shut, and silence came down like a blanket.

I waited for nearly two hours. The trouble was the cleaning woman, an erratic old lady called Gertie. She had a key of her own and sometimes she came in the evening, and sometimes early in the morning. I had studied her movements for several weeks. The latest she had ever left the premises was a quarter to eight at night.

By half-past eight I felt it was safe for me to start investigating.

The storage room door presented no difficulties. The lock was on my side and I simply unscrewed it. The strongroom door was a different matter. I had got what is known in the trade as a set of 'approximates'—blank keys of the type and, roughly, the shape to open most old locks. My job was to find the one that worked best, and then file it down and fiddle it until it would open the lock. (You can't do this with a modern lock, which is tooled to a hundredth of an inch, but old locks, which rely on complicated convolutions and strong springs, though they look formidable, are actually much easier.)

By half-past ten I heard the sweet click which meant success, and I swung the steel door open, turned on the light switch, and stepped in.

It was a small vault with walls of whitewashed brick, with a run of wooden shelves round two of the sides, carrying a line of black deed boxes. I didn't waste much time on them; I guessed the sort of things they would contain.

On the left, behind the door, was a table and on the table stood a heavy, brass-bound teak box—the sort of thing that might have been built to contain a microscope, only larger. It was locked—with a small, Bramah-type lock which none of my implements was designed to cope with.

I worked for some time at it, but without much hope. The only solution seemed to be to lug the box away with me—it was very heavy, but just portable—and get someone outside to work on it. I reflected that I should look pretty silly if it did turn out to contain a valuable microscope that one of old Portway's clients had left with him for safekeeping.

Then I had an idea. On the shelf inside the door was a small black tin box with *E. Portway, Personal* painted on the front. It was the sort of thing in which a careful man might keep his War Savings Certificates and Passport. It too was locked, but with an ordinary deed-box lock, which one of the keys on my ring fitted. I opened it, and sure enough, lying on top of the stacked papers inside, the first thing that caught my eye was a worn leather key-holder containing a single, brass Bramah key.

I suddenly felt a little breathless. Perhaps the ventilation in that underground room was not all it should have been. Moving with deliberation, I fitted the brass key into the tiny keyhole, pressed home, and twisted. Then I lifted the top of the box—and came face to face with Mr Portway's secret.

At first sight it was disappointing. It looked like nothing more than a small handpress—the sort of thing you use for impressing a company seal, only a little larger. I lifted it out, picked up a piece of clean white paper off the shelf, slid the paper in, and pressed down the handle. Then I released it and extracted the paper.

Imprinted on the paper was a neat, orange, Revenue Stamp for £20. I went back to the box. Inside was a tray, and arranged in it were dies of various denominations—10s., £1, £2, £5, and upward. The largest was for £100.

I picked one of the dies out and held it up to the light. It was beautifully made. Mr Portway had not wasted his time at Bertolozzi's Florentine atelier. There was even an arrangement of cogs behind the die by which the three figures of the date could be set—tiny, delicate wheels, each a masterpiece of the watch-maker's art.

I heard the footsteps crossing the courtyard, and Mr Portway was through the door before I even had time to put the die down.

'What are you doing here?' I said stupidly.

'When anyone turns on the strongroom light,' he said, 'it also turns on the light in my office. I've got a private arrangement with the caretaker of the big block at the end who keeps an eye open for me. If he sees my light on, he telephones me at once.'

'I see,' I said. Once I had got over the actual shock of seeing him there, I wasn't alarmed. I was half his age and twice his size. 'I've just been admiring your private work. Every man his own revenue stamp office. A lovely piece of work, Mr Portway.'

'Is it not?' agreed my employer, blinking up at me under the strong light. I could read in his chelonian face neither fear nor anger, rather a sardonic amusement at the turn of affairs. 'Are you a private detective, by any chance?'

'IBA—Investigation Branch of the Inland Revenue.'

'And you have been admiring my little machine?'

'My only real surprise is that no one has thought of it before.'

'Yes,' he said. 'It's very useful. To a practising solicitor, of course. I used to find it a permanent source of irritation that my clients should pay more to the Government—who, after all, hadn't raised a finger to earn it—than they did to me. Do you realise that if I act for the purchaser of a London house for £5,000, I get about £43, whilst the Government's share is £100?'

'Scandalous,' I agreed. 'And so you devised this little machine to adjust the balance. Such a simple and foolproof form of forgery, when you come to think of it.' The more I thought of it the more I liked it. 'Just think of the effort you would have to expend—to say nothing of obtaining special stocks of paper—if you set out to forge one-hundred-pound notes. Whereas with this machine— a small die, a little pressure—'

'Oh, there's more to it than that,' said Mr Portway airily. 'A man would be a fool to forge treasury notes. They have to be passed into circulation, and each one is a potential danger to its maker. Here, when I have stamped a document, it goes directly into a deed box—and it may not be looked at again for twenty years. Possibly, never.'

'As a professional accountant,' I said, 'that is the angle which appeals to me most. Now, let me see. Take that purchase you were talking about. Your client would give you two cheques, one for your fee, which goes through the books in the ordinary way, and a separate one for the stamp duty.'

'Made out to cash.'

'Made out to cash, of course. Which you would yourself cash at the bank, then come back here—'

'I always took the trouble to walk through the Stamp Office in case anyone should be watching me.'

'Very sound precaution,' I agreed. 'Then you came back here, stamped the document yourself, and put the money in your pocket. It never appeared in your books at all.'

'That's precisely right,' said Mr Portway. He seemed gratified at the speed with which I had perceived the finer points of his arrangements.

'There's only one thing I can't quite see,' I went on. 'You're a bachelor, a man with simple tastes. Could you not—I don't want to sound pompous—but by working a little harder could you not have made sufficient money legitimately for your reasonable needs?'

Mr Portway looked at me for a moment, his smile broadening.

'I see,' he said, 'that you have not had time to examine the rest of this strongroom. My tastes are far from simple, Mr Gilbert, and owing to the scandalous and confiscatory nature of modern taxation—oh, I beg your pardon, I was forgetting for the moment—'

'Don't apologise,' I said. 'I have often thought the same thing myself. You were speaking of your expensive tastes—'

Mr Portway stepped over to a large, drop-fronted deed box, labelled *Lord Lampeter's Settled Estate*, and unlocked it with a key from his chain. Inside was a rack and in the rack I counted the dusty ends of a dozen bottles.

'Château Margaux. The 1934 vintage. I shouldn't say that even now it has reached its peak. Now here—' he unlocked *The Dean of Melchester, Family Affairs*—'I have a real treasure. A Mouton Rothschild of 1924.'

'1924!'

'In Magnums. I know that you appreciate a good wine and since this may perhaps be our last opportunity—'

'Well—'

Mr Portway took a corkscrew, a decanter, and two glasses from a small cupboard labelled *Estate Duty Forms, Miscellaneous*, drew the cork of the Mouton Rothschild with care and skill, and decanted it with a steady hand. Then he poured two glasses. We both held it up to the single unshaded light to note the dark, rich, almost black colour, and took our first, ecstatic, mouthful. It went down like oiled silk.

'What did you say you had in the other boxes?' I inquired reverently.

'My preference has been for the great clarets,' said Mr Portway. 'Of course, as I only really started buying in 1945, I have nothing that you could call a museum piece. But I picked up a small lot of 1927 Château Talbot which has to be tasted to be believed. And if a good burgundy was offered, I didn't say no to it.' He gestured towards the *Marchioness of Gravesend* box in one corner. 'There's a 1937 Romanée Conti—but your glass is empty—'

As we finished the Mouton Rothschild in companionable silence I looked at my watch. It was two o'clock in the morning.

'You will scarcely find any transport to get you home now,' said Mr Portway. 'Might I suggest that the only thing to follow a fine claret is a noble burgundy?'

'Well—' I said.

I was fully aware that I was compromising my official position. Actually, I think my mind had long since been made up. As dawn was breaking, and the Romanée Conti was sinking in the bottle, we agreed on provisional articles of partnership.

The name of the firm is Portway & Gilbert, of 7 Lombards Inn. If you are thinking, by any chance, of buying a house—

IN VINO VERITAS

Lawrence G. Blochman

Dr Frank Belling, the central character in this next story, is an American viniculturist who doubles as a private detective when murder intrudes into the normally placid world of wine-making. Dr Belling has appeared in a number of short stories by Lawrence G. Blochman (1900–1975) who is perhaps best known for the books he wrote about Dr Daniel Webster Coffee, the chief pathologist at Pasteur Hospital, and his imperturbable Hindu assistant, Dr Motilal Mookerji. Both Coffee and Dr Belling reflect their author's early training in forensic pathology, which he abandoned for a career in journalism that took him all over the world including France, India and the Far East. During his time in Paris, Blochman developed his interest in wine and cooking and contributed a regular column, 'Le Gourmet', to the now defunct Paris Times. But his hard-won knowledge—not to mention his particular interest in American wines which he pursued when he finally settled in Southern California— was put to good use in his fiction, and rarely better than in the case of murder which Dr Belling investigates in the following pages . . .

The fat Sheriff took his feet off the desk and gazed curiously at the precise, bespectacled little man opposite him.

'You sure don't look like a peace officer, Dr Belling,' he said. 'Not even any of the Eastern peace officers I ever saw.'

Dr Frank Belling smiled. 'As a matter of fact,' he explained, 'I've been deputised by the State Police for this one case only. I'm really professor of viticulture at Northeastern Agricultural College, and the police thought my special knowledge would be useful in this Tolman matter. Tell me what you know of Henry Tolman.'

'Well . . .' The Sheriff hesitated. 'Everyone around here knew Old Man Tolman, of course,' he said, 'and we knew his son Henry when he was just a kid. But when Henry started growing up, he was away at school most of the time. Then when he was twenty-one, he went to Europe to learn about the wine business in France and Italy. Three years later the old man died and left Henry his vineyards here. Henry got back to California six months after we cabled. He was wearing a reddish beard—seems like all American youngsters raise beards when they get to France—so naturally he would look different, even if it hadn't been more than three years since we'd seen him. What makes you think he might be an imposter, Dr Belling?'

'If he's not an imposter, he may be a murderer,' Dr Belling replied. 'A few weeks ago the New York State Police found a skeleton in the woods about twenty miles from New York City. The skeleton had obviously been lying there for a number of years, and the few fragments of rotted clothing that remained were no help in establishing an identity. There was no other identification, but there was a bullet rattling around inside the skull.

'The Missing Persons Bureau, after measuring the bones, reported that the skeleton might have been that of a petty racketeer and ex-bootlegger called Rusty Hull, who disappeared six years ago. Hull didn't have a police record, so the police had nothing to go on except his size and build, and the colour of his hair—all of which tally pretty closely with Henry Tolman's, I've discovered since. The police went back to the woods where the skeleton was found and about a hundred yards away they picked up a gold watch engraved *To Henry Tolman on his Twenty-First Birthday.*

'Checking further, the police discovered that Tolman and Rusty Hull had been seen together in New York shortly before Hull disappeared. This was natural enough, since Hull had numerous winery connections dating back to Prohibition days. It is possible that Tolman killed Hull and dropped his watch while hiding the body in the woods. It is much more likely, however, that Hull killed Tolman in order to pose as the heir to a profitable winery, and that the watch was dropped while he was carrying Tolman's body from a car into the woods. I'm working on the second supposition. That's why I want to see Tolman.'

The Sheriff reached for his Stetson. 'I'll drive you to the vineyards,' he said. 'But Henry Tolman seems OK to me. Of course, he's had six years to build up his alibis, but he does know all about the wines that the old man used to make.'

'That's exactly what I'm counting on,' Dr Belling said. 'I may not be much of a cop, but I do know my wines. That's why I phoned Tolman this morning. I told him I represented an Eastern syndicate interested in buying the winery.'

'And you think, if he's an imposter, he'll swallow that story?'

'I hope not, I'd rather he were suspicious. Shall we go?'

The Sheriff drove Dr Belling five miles through the sunny afternoon. The Northern California valley, with its stone houses nestling against the vine-covered slopes, might well have been somewhere in Europe, Belling reflected as the car swung off the main highway and took a road winding up the cultivated hillside.

'This is the Tolman vineyard,' the Sheriff announced.

'Stop here a moment, please,' Dr Belling said. He left the car to walk briefly among the vines. He examined the stocks, the leaves, the ripening clusters of grapes.

'Sylvaner grapes,' he said, as he climbed back into the car. 'They make a nice, sound, white wine.'

'Around here they call it California Riesling,' the Sheriff said.

'There are very few true Riesling grapes in California,' Dr Belling countered, 'and these are not among them. However, the Sylvaner grape does make a wine that resembles the Rhine wines in general type.'

The car groaned in second gear as it climbed to the stone winery buildings on the hilltop, where the bearded Henry Tolman met them. He ushered the two men into a cool sitting-room, full of old-fashioned furniture, faded family photographs, and lace curtains. A half-written letter lay on the table.

After they had talked about wines in general and the Tolman vineyard in particular, Henry Tolman said: 'You can tell your East-coast principals, Dr Belling, that this is not one of those upstart wineries. My father was not caught in the early Volstead panic of California wine-growers who pulled up their grapes to plant walnuts. He made wine right through Prohibition—good wine. So he didn't have to start out all over again after Repeal. I remember just before I went to Europe, my father laid down a wine that he said was the best Riesling vintage this state has ever seen. I'll see if I can't find a bottle. I know there are a few left, and I'd like you to taste it. I remember writing the labels.'

When Tolman left the room, the Sheriff winked at Belling. 'What did I tell you? He's going to prove he was here ten years ago.'

Tolman came back to place a dusty, cobwebbed bottle on the table beside the half-finished letter. Then he went in search of glasses and a corkscrew, giving Belling and the Sheriff ample opportunity to compare the handwriting in the letter with that of the dusty label. The writing was identical.

'See?' the Sheriff declared.

Tolman returned to pour the wine. Dr Belling held his glass up to the light. He breathed its fragrance. He admired its pale gold colour, its flowery bouquet, before he sipped it. Then he took a full swallow, rolled it around his tongue. The wine was excellent, with a robust, fruity tang.

'Great wine, isn't it, Dr Belling?' Tolman asked.

Belling took another swallow, closed his eyes appreciatively.

'Perfect,' he said at last. 'Much too perfect to fit your story. Arrest this man, Sheriff.'

'Say, what—?'

'You're going back to New York, Rusty Hull, to stand trial for the murder of Henry Tolman.'

'But I am Henry Tolman!'

'You are Rusty Hull,' Belling insisted, 'and this superb wine was made, bottled, and labelled within the last three or four years. If you were Henry Tolman, you would know better than to try to pass this wine off as ten years old. You would know that white wine made from Sylvaner grapes reaches its peak at the age of three; that unlike most wines which mellow and achieve greatness in the bottle for decades, its best qualities fade after its early youth. This wine is brilliant. After ten years in the bottle, it would have been ordinary, dull, and insipid.'

The Sheriff put down his glass and dangled a pair of handcuffs.

'Just a moment, Sheriff,' Dr Belling said. 'Before we get down to business, let's finish this bottle.'

THE LAST BOTTLE IN THE WORLD

Stanley Ellin

The quest for an elusive wine and the nightmare situation into which it thrusts the wine merchant narrator, Monsieur Drummond, is the theme of this 'vintage tale about wine' as Ellery Queen described it when first publishing it in his magazine in February 1968. It is a situation brought about by Max de Marechal, the opinionated editor of La Cave, a wine magazine for connoisseurs, who enlists Drummond's aid to help him write a series of articles about legendary vintages. The story displays all the knowledge of wine mixed with clever twists of plot for which Stanley Ellin (1916–1986) remains famous almost a decade after his death. Ellin, whose name has been linked in the field of mystery writers with those of Sir Arthur Conan Doyle and Dashiell Hammett, is the author of several novels which have been filmed (including The Big Night, *1951;* Nothing But The Best, *1964; and* House of Cards, *1968) and a number of outstanding short stories including* 'The House Party' *which won the Mystery Writers of America 'Edgar' Award in 1954. He is in similarly brilliant form in 'The Last Bottle in the World', a story with body and bouquet and a little something else even more disturbing . . .*

It was a bad moment. This cafe on the rue de Rivoli near the Meurice had looked tempting, I had taken a chair at one of its sidewalk tables, and then, glancing casually across at the next table, had found myself staring into the eyes of a young woman who was looking at me with startled recognition. It was Madame Sophia Kassoulas. Suddenly, the past towered over me like a monstrous genie released from a bottle. The shock was so great that I could actually feel the blood draining from my face.

Madame Kassoulas was instantly at my side.

'Monsieur Drummond, what is it? You look so ill. Is there anything I can do?'

'No, no. A drink, that's all. Cognac, please.'

She ordered me one, then sat down to solicitously undo the

buttons of my jacket. 'Oh, you men. The way you dress in this summer heat.'

This might have been pleasant under other conditions, but I realised with embarrassment that the picture we offered the other patrons of the café must certainly be that of a pitiful, white-haired old grandpa being attended to by his soft-hearted granddaughter.

'Madame, I assure you—'

She pressed a finger firmly against my lips. 'Please. Not another word until you've had your cognac and feel like yourself again. Not one little word.'

I yielded the point. Besides, turnabout was fair play. During that nightmarish scene six months before when we were last in each other's company she had been the one to show weakness and I had been the one to apply the restoratives. Meeting me now, the woman must have been as hard hit by cruel memory as I was. I had to admire her for bearing up so well under the blow.

My cognac was brought to me, and even *in extremis*, so to speak, I automatically held it up to the sunlight to see its colour. Madame Kassoulas' lips quirked in a faint smile.

'Dear Monsieur Drummond,' she murmured. 'Always the connoisseur.'

Which, indeed, I was. And which, I saw on grim reflection, was how the whole thing had started on a sunny Parisian day like this the year before . . .

That was the day a man named Max de Marechal sought me out in the offices of my company, Broulet and Drummond, wine merchants, on the rue de Berri. I vaguely knew of de Marechal as the editor of a glossy little magazine, *La Cave*, published solely for the enlightenment of wine connoisseurs. Not a trade publication, but a sort of house organ for *La Société de la Cave*, a select little circle of amateur wine fanciers. Since I generally approved the magazine's judgements, I was pleased to meet its editor.

Face to face with him, however, I found myself disliking him intensely. In his middle forties, he was one of those dapper, florid types who resemble superannuated leading men. And there was a feverish volatility about him which put me on edge. I tend to be low-geared and phlegmatic myself. People who are always bouncing about on top of their emotions like a ping pong ball on a jet of water make me acutely uncomfortable.

The purpose of his visit, he said, was to obtain an interview from me. In preparation for a series of articles to be run in his magazine, he was asking various authorities on wine to express their opinions about the greatest vintage they had ever sampled.

This way, perhaps, a consensus could be made and placed on record. If—

'If,' I cut in, 'you ever get agreement on the greatest vintage. Ask a dozen experts about it and you'll get a dozen different opinions.'

'It did look like that at the start. By now, however, I have found some small agreement on the supremacy of two vintages.'

'Which two?'

'Both are Burgundies. One is the Richebourg 1923. The other is the Romanée-Conti 1934. And both, of course, indisputably rank among the noblest wines.'

'Indisputably.'

'Would one of these be your own choice as the vintage without peer?'

'I refuse to make any choice, Monsieur de Marechal. When it comes to wines like these, comparisons are not merely odious, they are impossible.'

'Then you do not believe any one vintage stands by itself beyond comparison?'

'No, it's possible there is one. I've never tasted it, but the descriptions written of it praise it without restraint. A Burgundy, of course, from an estate which never again produced anything like it. A very small estate. Have you any idea which vintage I'm referring to?'

'I believe I do.' De Marechal's eyes gleamed with fervour. 'The glorious Nuits Saint-Oen 1929. Am I right?'

'You are.'

He shrugged helplessly. 'But what good is knowing about it when I've never yet met anyone who has actually tasted it? I want my series of articles to be backed by living authorities. Those I've questioned all know about this legendary Saint-Oen, but not one has even seen a bottle of it. What a disaster when all that remains of such a vintage—possibly the greatest of all—should only be a legend. If there were only one wretched bottle left on the face of the earth—'

'Why are you so sure there isn't?' I said.

'Why?' De Marechal gave me a pitying smile. 'Because, my dear Drummond, there can't be. I was at the Saint-Oen estate myself not long ago. The *vigneron's* records there attest that only forty dozen cases of the 1929 were produced altogether. Consider. A scant forty dozen cases spread over all the years from then to now, and with thousands of connoisseurs thirsting for them. I assure you, the last bottle was emptied a generation ago.'

I had not intended to come out with it, but that superior smile of his got under my skin.

'I'm afraid your calculations are a bit off, my dear de Marechal.'
It was going to be a pleasure setting him back on his heels. 'You
see, a bottle of Nuits Saint-Oen 1929 is, at this very moment,
resting in my company's cellars.'

The revelation jarred him as hard as I thought it would. His jaw
fell. He gaped at me in speechless wonderment. Then his face
darkened with suspicion.

'You're joking,' he said. 'You must be. You just told me you've
never tasted the vintage. Now you tell me—'

'Only the truth. After my partner's death last year I found the
bottle among his private stock.'

'And you haven't been tempted to open it?'

'I resist the temptation. The wine is dangerously old. It would
be extremely painful to open it and find it has already died.'

'Ah, no!' De Marechal clapped a hand to his brow. 'You're an
American, monsieur, that's your trouble. Only an American could
talk this way, someone who's inherited the obscene Puritan
pleasure in self-denial. And for the last existing bottle of Nuits
Saint-Oen 1929 to have such an owner! It won't do. It absolutely
will not do. Monsieur Drummond, we must come to terms. What
price do you ask for this Saint-Oen?'

'None. It is not for sale.'

'It must be for sale!' de Marechal said explosively. With an effort
he got himself under control. 'Look, I'll be frank with you. I am
not a rich man. You could get at least a thousand francs—possibly
as much as two thousand—for that bottle of wine, and I'm in no
position to lay out that kind of money. But I am close to someone
who can meet any terms you set. Monsieur Kyros Kassoulas.
Perhaps you know of him?'

Since Kyros Kassoulas was one of the richest men on the Conti-
nent, someone other magnates approached with their hats off, it
would be hard not to know of him despite his well-publicised
efforts to live in close seclusion.

'Of course,' I said.

'And do you know of the one great interest in his life?'

'I can't say I do. According to the newspapers, he seems to be
quite the man of mystery.'

'A phrase concocted by journalists to describe anyone of such
wealth who chooses to be reticent about his private affairs. Not
that there is anything scandalous about them. You see, Monsieur
Kassoulas is a fanatic connoisseur of wines.' De Marechal gave
me a meaningful wink. 'That's how I interested him in founding
our Société de la Cave and in establishing its magazine.'

'And in making you its editor.'

'So he did,' said de Marechal calmly. 'Naturally, I'm grateful to him for that. He, in turn, is grateful to me for giving him sound instruction on the great vintages. Strictly between us, he was a sad case when I first met him. A man without any appetite for vice, without any capacity to enjoy literature or music or art, he was being driven to distraction by the emptiness of his life. I filled that emptiness the day I pointed out to him that he must cultivate his extraordinarily true palate for fine wine. The exploration of the worthier vintages since then has been for him a journey through a wonderland. By now, as I have said, he is a fanatic connoisseur. He would know without being told that your bottle of Nuits Saint-Oen 1929 is to other wines what the Mona Lisa is to other paintings. Do you see what that means to you in a business way? He's a tough man to bargain with, but in the end he'll pay two thousand francs for that bottle. You have my word on it.'

I shook my head. 'I can only repeat, Monsieur de Marechal, the wine is not for sale. There is no price on it.'

'And I insist you set a price on it!'

That was too much.

'All right,' I said, 'then the price is one hundred thousand francs. And without any guarantee the wine isn't dead. One hundred thousand francs exactly.'

'Ah,' de Marechal said furiously, 'so you really don't intend to sell it! But to play dog in the manger—!'

Suddenly he went rigid. His features contorted, his hands clutched convulsively at his chest. As crimson with passion as his face had been the moment before, it was now ghastly pale and bloodless. He lowered himself heavily into a chair.

'My heart,' he gasped in agonised explanation. 'It's all right. I have pills—'

The pill he slipped under his tongue was nitroglycerine, I was sure. I had once seen my late partner Broulet undergo a seizure like this.

'I'll call a doctor,' I said, but when I went to the phone de Marechal made a violent gesture of protest.

'No, don't bother. I'm used to this. It's an old story with me.'

He was, in fact, looking better now.

'If it's an old story you should know better,' I told him. 'For a man with a heart condition you allow yourself to become much too emotional.'

'Do I? And how would you feel, my friend, if you saw a legendary vintage suddenly appear before you and then found it remained just out of reach? No, forgive me for that. It's your privilege not to sell your goods if you don't choose to.'

'It is.'

'But one small favour. Would you, at least, allow me to see the bottle of Saint-Oen? I'm not questioning its existence. It's only that the pleasure of viewing it, of holding it in my hands—'

It was a small enough favour to grant him. The cellars of Broulet and Drummond were near the Halles au Vin, a short trip by car from the office. There I conducted him through the cool, stony labyrinth bordering the Seine, led him to the Nuits Saint-Oen racks where, apart from all the lesser vintages of later years, the one remaining bottle of 1929 rested in solitary grandeur. I carefully took it down and handed it to de Marechal, who received it with reverence.

He examined the label with an expert eye, delicately ran a fingertip over the cork. 'The cork is in good condition.'

'What of it? That can't save the wine if its time has already come.'

'Naturally. But it's an encouraging sign.' He held the bottle up to peer through it. 'And there seems to be only a normal sediment. Bear in mind, Monsieur Drummond, that some great Burgundies have lived for fifty years. Some even longer.'

He surrendered the bottle to me with reluctance. His eyes remained fixed on it so intensely as I replaced it in the rack that he looked like a man under hypnosis. I had to nudge him out of the spell before I could lead him upstairs to the sunlit outer world.

We parted there.

'I'll keep in touch with you,' he said as we shook hands. 'Perhaps we can get together for lunch later this week.'

'I'm sorry,' I said without regret, 'but later this week I'm leaving for New York to look in on my office there.'

'Too bad. But of course you'll let me know as soon as you return to Paris.'

'Of course,' I lied.

However, there was no putting off Max de Marechal now that he had that vision of the Nuits Saint-Oen 1929 before his eyes. He must have bribed one of the help in my Paris office to tell him when I was back from the States, because no sooner was I again at my desk on the rue de Berri than he was on the phone. He greeted me with fervour. What luck he had timed his call so perfectly! My luck, as well as his. Why? Because *La Société de la Cave* was to have a dinner the coming weekend, a positive orgy of wine sampling, and its presiding officer, Kyros Kassoulas himself, had requested my presence at it!

My first impulse was to refuse the invitation. For one thing, I knew its motive. Kassoulas had been told about the Nuits Saint-Oen 1929 and wanted to get me where he could personally bargain for it without losing face. For another thing, these wine-tasting sessions held by various societies of connoisseurs were not for me. Sampling a rare and excellent vintage is certainly among life's most rewarding experiences, but, for some reason I could never fathom, doing it in the company of one's fellow *aficionados* seems to bring out all the fakery hidden away in the soul of even the most honest citizen. And to sit there, watching ordinarily sensible men vie with each other in their portrayals of ecstasy over a glass of wine, rolling their eyes, flaring their nostrils, straining to find the most incongruous adjectives with which to describe it, has always been a trial to me.

Weighed against all this was simple curiosity. Kyros Kassoulas was a remote and awesome figure, and here I was being handed the chance to actually meet him. In the end, curiosity won. I attended the dinner, I met Kassoulas there, and quickly realised, with gratification, that we were striking it off perfectly.

It was easy to understand why. As de Marechal had put it, Kyros Kassoulas was a fanatic on wines, a man with a single-minded interest in their qualities, their history, and their lore; and I could offer him more information on the subject than anyone else he knew. More, he pointed out to me, than even the knowledgeable Max de Marechal.

As the dinner progressed, it intrigued me to observe that where everyone else in the room deferred to Kassoulas—especially de Marechal, a shameless sycophant—Kassoulas himself deferred to me. I enjoyed that. Before long I found myself really liking the man instead of merely being impressed by him.

He was impressive, of course. About fifty, short and barrel-chested, with a swarthy, deeply lined face and almost simian ears, he was ugly in a way that some clever women would find fascinating. Somehow, he suggested an ancient idol roughhewn out of a block of mahogany. His habitual expression was a granite impassivity, relieved at times by a light of interest in those veiled, ever-watchful eyes. That light became intense when he finally touched on the matter of my bottle of Saint-Oen.

He had been told its price, he remarked with wry humour, and felt that a hundred thousand francs—twenty thousand hard American dollars—was, perhaps, a little excessive. Now if I would settle for two thousand francs—

I smilingly shook my head.

'It's a handsome offer,' Kassoulas said. 'It happens to be more than I've paid for any half dozen bottles of wine in my cellar.'

'I won't dispute that, Monsieur Kassoulas.'

'But you won't sell, either. What are the chances of the wine's being fit to drink?'

'Who can tell? The 1929 vintage at Saint-Oen was late to mature, so it may live longer than most. Or it may already be dead. That's why I won't open the bottle myself or sell anyone else the privilege of opening it. This way, it's a unique and magnificent treasure. Once its secret is out, it may simply be another bottle of wine gone bad.'

To his credit, he understood that. And, when he invited me to be a guest at his estate near Saint-Cloud the next weekend, it was with the blunt assurance that it was only my company he sought, not the opportunity to further dicker for the bottle of Saint-Oen. In fact, said he, he would never again broach the matter. All he wanted was my word that if I ever decided to sell the bottle, he would be given first chance to make an offer for it. And to that I cheerfully agreed.

The weekend at his estate was a pleasant time for me, the first of many I spent there. It was an enormous place, but smoothly run by a host of efficient help under the authority of a burly, grizzled majordomo named Joseph. Joseph was evidently Kassoulas' devoted slave. It came as no surprise to learn he had been a sergeant in the Foreign Legion. He responded to orders as if his master was the colonel of his regiment.

What did come as a surprise was the lady of the house, Sophia Kassoulas. I don't know exactly what I expected Kassoulas' wife to be like, but certainly not a girl young enough to be his daughter, a gentle, timid creature whose voice was hardly more than a whisper. By today's standards which require a young woman to be a lank-haired rack of bones she was, perhaps, a little too voluptuous, a little too ripely curved, but I am an old-fashioned sort of man who believes women should be ripely curved. And if, like Sophia Kassoulas, they are pale, dark-eyed, blushing beauties, so much the better.

As time passed and I became more and more a friend of the family, I was able to draw from her the story of her marriage, now approaching its fifth anniversary. Sophia Kassoulas was a distant cousin of her husband. Born to poor parents in a mountain village of Greece, convent bred, she had met Kassoulas for the first time at a gathering of the family in Athens, and, hardly out of her girlhood, had married him soon afterwards. She was, she assured me in that soft little voice, the most fortunate of women. Yes, to have been chosen by a man like Kyros to be his wife, surely the most fortunate of women—

But she said it as if she were desperately trying to convince herself of it. In fact, she seemed frightened to death of Kassoulas. When he addressed the most commonplace remark to her she shrank away from him. It became a familiar scene, watching this happen, and watching him respond to it by then treating her with an icily polite disregard that only intimidated her the more.

It made an unhealthy situation in that household because, as I saw from the corner of my eye, the engaging Max de Marechal was always right there to soothe Madame's fears away. It struck me after a while how very often an evening at Saint-Cloud wound up with Kassoulas and myself holding a discussion over our brandy at one end of the room while Madame Kassoulas and Max de Marechal were head to head in conversation at the other end. There was nothing indecorous about those *tête-á-têtes*, but still I didn't like the look of them. The girl appeared to be as wide-eyed and ingenuous as a doe, and de Marechal bore all the earmarks of the trained predator.

Kassoulas himself was either unaware of this or remarkably indifferent to it. Certainly, his regard for de Marechal was genuine. He mentioned it to me several times and once, when de Marechal got himself dangerously heated up in an argument with me over the merits of some vintage or other, Kassoulas said to him with real concern, 'Gently, Max, gently. Remember your heart. How many times has the doctor warned you against becoming over-excited?'—which, for Kassoulas, was an unusual show of feeling. Generally, like so many men of his type, he seemed wholly incapable of expressing any depth of emotion.

Indeed, the only time he ever let slip any show of his feelings about his troublesome marriage was once when I was inspecting his wine cellar with him and pointed out that a dozen Volnay-Caillerets 1955 he had just laid in were likely to prove extremely uneven. It had been a mistake to buy it. One never knew, in uncorking a bottle, whether or not he would find it sound.

Kassoulas shook his head.

'It was a calculated risk, Monsieur Drummond, not a mistake. I don't make mistakes.' Then he gave an almost imperceptible little shrug. 'Well, one perhaps. When a man marries a mere child—'

He cut it short at that. It was the first and last time he ever touched on the subject. What he wanted to talk about was wine, although sometimes under my prodding and because I was a good listener, he would recount stories about his past. My own life has been humdrum. It fascinated me to learn, in bits and pieces, about the life of Kyros Kassoulas, a Piraeus wharf rat who was a thief in his childhood, a smuggler in his youth, and a multimillionaire before he was thirty. It gave me the same sense of drama Kassoulas appeared to feel when I would recount to him stories about some of the great vintages which, like the Nuits Saint-Oen 1929, had been cranky and uncertain in the barrel until, by some miracle of nature, they had suddenly blossomed into their full greatness.

It was at such times that Max de Marechal himself was at his best. Watching him grow emotional in such discussions, I had to smile inwardly at the way he had once condescendingly described Kassoulas as a fanatic about wines. It was a description which fitted him even better. Whatever else might be false about Max de Marechal, his feelings about any great vintage were genuine.

During the months that passed, Kassoulas proved to be as good as his word. He had said he wouldn't again bargain with me for the precious bottle of Saint-Oen, and he didn't. We discussed the Saint-Oen often enough—it was an obsession with de Marechal—but no matter how much Kassoulas was tempted to renew the effort to buy it, he kept his word.

Then, one dismally cold and rainy day in early December, my secretary opened my office door to announce in awestruck tones that Monsieur Kyros Kassoulas was outside waiting to see me. This was a surprise. Although Sophia Kassoulas, who seemed to have no friends in the world apart from de Marechal and myself, had several times been persuaded to have lunch with me when she was in town to do shopping, her husband had never before deigned to visit me in my domain, and I was not expecting him now.

He came in accompanied by the ever dapper de Marechal who, I saw with increased mystification, was in a state of feverish excitement.

We had barely exchanged greetings when de Marechal leaped directly to the point.

'The bottle of Nuits Saint-Oen 1929, Monsieur Drummond,' he said. 'You'll remember you once set a price on it. One hundred thousand francs.'

'Only because it won't be bought at any such price.'

'Would you sell it for less?'

'I've already made clear I wouldn't.'

'You drive a hard bargain, Monsieur Drummond. But you'll be pleased to know that Monsieur Kassoulas is now prepared to pay your price.'

I turned incredulously to Kassoulas. Before I could recover my voice, he drew a cheque from his pocket and, impassive as ever, handed it to me. Involuntarily, I glanced at it. It was for one hundred thousand francs. It was worth, by the going rate of exchange, twenty thousand dollars.

'This is ridiculous,' I finally managed to say. 'I can't take it.'

'But you must!' de Marechal said in alarm.

'I'm sorry. No wine is worth a fraction of this. Especially a wine that may be dead in the bottle.'

'Ah,' said Kassoulas lightly, 'then perhaps that's what I'm paying for—the chance to see whether it is or not.'

'If that's your reason—' I protested, and Kassoulas shook his head.

'It isn't. The truth is, my friend, this wine solves a difficult problem for me. A great occasion is coming soon, the fifth anniversary of my marriage, and I've been wondering how Madame and I could properly celebrate it. Then inspiration struck me. What better way of celebrating it than to open the Saint-Oen and discover it is still in the flush of perfect health, still in its flawless maturity? What could be more deeply moving and significant on such an occasion?'

'That makes it all the worse if the wine is dead,' I pointed out. The cheque was growing warm in my hand. I wanted to tear it up but couldn't bring myself to do it.'

'No matter. The risk is all mine,' said Kassoulas. 'Of course, you'll be there to judge the wine for yourself. I insist on that. It will be a memorable experience, no matter how it goes. A small dinner with just the four of us at the table, and the Saint–Oen as climax to the occasion.'

'The *pièce de résistance* must be an *entrecôte*,' breathed de Marechal. 'Beef, of course. It will suit the wine perfectly.'

I had somehow been pushed past the point of no return. Slowly I folded the cheque for the hundred thousand francs and placed it in my wallet. After all, I was in the business of selling wine for a profit.

'When is this dinner to be held?' I asked. 'Remember that the wine must stand a few days before it's decanted.'

'Naturally, I'm allowing for that,' said Kassoulas. 'Today is Monday; the dinner will be held Saturday. That means more than enough time to prepare every detail perfectly. On Wednesday I'll see that the temperature of the dining room is properly adjusted, the table set, and the bottle of Saint-Oen placed upright on it for the sediment to clear properly. The room will then be locked to avoid any mishap. By Saturday the last of the sediment should have settled completely. But I don't plan to decant the wine. I intend to serve it directly from the bottle.'

'Risky,' I said.

'Not if it's poured with a steady hand. One like this.' Kassoulas held out a stubby-fingered, powerful-looking hand which showed not a sign of tremor. 'Yes, this supreme vintage deserves the honour of being poured from its own bottle, risky as that may be.

Surely you now have evidence, Monsieur Drummond, that I'm a man to take any risk if it's worthwhile to me.'

I had good cause to remember those concluding words at a meeting I had with Sophia Kassoulas later in the week. That day she phoned early in the morning to ask if I could meet her for lunch at an hour when we might have privacy in the restaurant, and, thinking this had something to do with her own plans for the anniversary dinner, I cheerfully accepted the invitation. All the cheerfulness was washed out of me as soon as I joined her at our table in a far corner of the dimly lit, almost deserted room. She was obviously terrified.

'Something is very wrong,' I said to her. 'What is it?'

'Everything,' she said piteously. 'And you're the only one I can turn to for help, Monsieur Drummond. You've always been so kind to me. Will you help me now?'

'Gladly. If you tell me what's wrong and what I can do about it.'

'Yes, there's no way around that. You must be told everything.' Madame Kassoulas drew a shuddering breath. 'It can be told very simply. I had an affair with Max de Marechal. Now Kyros has found out about it.'

My heart sank. The last thing in the world I wanted was to get involved in anything like this.

'Madame,' I said unhappily, 'this is a matter to be settled between you and your husband. You must see that it's not my business at all.'

'Oh, please! If you only understood—'

'I don't see what there is to understand.'

'A great deal. About Kyros, about me, about my marriage. I didn't want to marry Kyros, I didn't want to marry anybody. But my family arranged it, so what could I do? And it's been dreadful from the start. All I am to Kyros is a pretty little decoration for his house. He has no feeling for me. He cares more about that bottle of wine he bought from you than he does for me. Where I'm concerned, he's like stone. But Max—'

'I know,' I said wearily. 'You found that Max was different. Max cared very much for you. Or, at least, he told you he did.'

'Yes, he told me he did,' Madame Kassoulas said with defiance. 'And whether he meant it or not, I needed that. A woman must have some man to tell her he cares for her or she has nothing. But it was wicked of me to put Max in danger. And now that Kyros knows about us Max is in terrible danger.'

'What makes you think so? Has your husband made any threats?'

'No, he hasn't even said he knows about the affair. But he does. I can swear he does. It's in the way he's been behaving toward me these past few days, in the remarks he makes to me, as if he were enjoying a joke that only he understood. And it all seems to have something to do with that bottle of Saint-Oen locked up in the dining room. That's why I came to you for help. You know about these things.'

'Madame, all I know is that the Saint-Oen is being made ready for your dinner party on Saturday.'

'Yes, that's what Kyros said. But the way he said it—' Madame Kassoulas leaned toward me intently. 'Tell me one thing. Is it possible for a bottle of wine to be poisoned without its cork being drawn? Is there any way of doing that?'

'Oh, come now. Do you seriously believe for a moment that your husband intends to poison Max?'

'You don't know Kyros the way I do. You don't know what he's capable of.'

'Even murder?'

'Even murder, if he was sure he could get away with it. They tell a story in my family about how, when he was very young, he killed a man who had cheated him out of a little money. Only it was done so cleverly that the police never found out who the murderer was.'

That was when I suddenly recalled Kassoulas' words about taking any risk if it were worthwhile to him and felt a chill go through me. All too vividly, I had a mental picture of a hypodermic needle sliding through the cork in that bottle of Saint-Oen, of drops of deadly poison trickling into the wine. Then it struck me how wildly preposterous the picture was.

'Madame,' I said, 'I'll answer your question this way. Your husband does not intend to poison anyone at your dinner party unless he intends to poison us all, which I am sure he does not. Remember that I've also been invited to enjoy my share of the Saint-Oen.'

'What if something were put into Max's glass alone?'

'It won't be. Your husband has too much respect for Max's palate for any such clumsy trick. If the wine is dead, Max will know it at once and won't drink it. If it's still good, he'd detect anything foreign in it with the first sip and not touch the rest. Anyhow, why not discuss it with Max? He's the one most concerned.'

'I did try to talk to him about it, but he only laughed at me. He said it was all in my imagination. I know why. He's so insanely eager to try that wine that he won't let anything stop him from doing it.'

'I can appreciate his feelings about that.' Even with my equanimity restored I was anxious to get away from this unpleasant topic. 'And he's right about your imagination. If you really want my advice, the best thing you can do is to behave with your husband as if nothing has happened and to steer clear of Monsieur de Marechal after this.'

It was the only advice I could give her under the circumstances. I only hoped she wasn't too panic-stricken to follow it. Or too infatuated with Max de Marechal.

Knowing too much for my own comfort, I was ill at ease the evening of the party, so when I joined the company it was a relief to see that Madame Kassoulas had herself well in hand. As for Kassoulas, I could detect no change at all in his manner toward her or de Marechal. It was convincing evidence that Madame's guilty conscience had indeed been working overtime on her imagination, and that Kassoulas knew nothing at all about her *affaire*. He was hardly the man to take being cuckolded with composure, and he was wholly composed. As we sat down to dinner, it was plain that his only concern was about its menu, and, above all, about the bottle of Nuits Saint-Oen 1929 standing before him.

The bottle had been standing there three days, and everything that could be done to insure the condition of its contents had been done. The temperature of the room was moderate; it had not been allowed to vary once the bottle was brought into the room, and, as Max de Marechal assured me, he had checked this at regular intervals every day. And, I was sure, had taken time to stare rapturously at the bottle, marking off the hours until it would be opened.

Furthermore, since the table at which our little company sat down was of a size to seat eighteen or twenty, it meant long distances between our places, but it provided room for the bottle to stand in lonely splendour clear of any careless hand that might upset it. It was noticeable that the servants waiting on us all gave it a wide berth. Joseph, the burly, hardbitten majordomo who was supervising them with a dangerous look in his eye, must have put them in fear of death if they laid a hand near it.

Now Kassoulas had to undertake two dangerous procedures as preludes to the wine-tasting ritual. Ordinarily, a great vintage like the Nuits Saint-Oen 1929 stands until all its sediment has collected in the base of the bottle, and is then decanted. This business of transferring it from bottle to decanter not only insures that sediment and cork crumbs are left behind, but it also means that the wine is being properly aired. The older a wine, the more it needs to breathe the open air to rid itself of mustiness accumulated in the bottle.

But Kassoulas, in his determination to honour the Saint-Oen by serving it directly from its original bottle, had imposed on himself the delicate task of uncorking it at the table so skilfully that no bits of cork would filter into the liquid. Then, after the wine had stood open until the entrée was served, he would have to pour it with such control that none of the sediment in its base would roil up. It had taken three days for that sediment to settle. The least slip in uncorking the bottle or pouring from it, and it would be another three days before it was again fit to drink.

As soon as we were at the table, Kassoulas set to work on the first task. We all watched with baited breath as he grasped the neck of the bottle firmly and centred the point of the corkscrew in the cork. Then, with the concentration of a demolitions expert defusing a live bomb, he slowly, very slowly, turned the corkscrew, bearing down so lightly that the corkscrew almost had to take hold by itself. His object was to penetrate deep enough to get a grip on the cork so that it could be drawn, yet not to pierce the cork through; it was the one sure way of keeping specks of cork from filtering into the wine.

It takes enormous strength to draw a cork which has not been pierced through from a bottle of wine which it has sealed for decades. The bottle must be kept upright and immobile, the pull must be straight up and steady without any of the twisting and turning that will tear a cork apart. The old-fashioned corkscrew which exerts no artificial leverage is the instrument for this because it allows one to feel the exact working of the cork in the bottleneck.

The hand Kassoulas had around the bottle clamped it so hard that his knuckles gleamed white. His shoulders hunched, the muscles of his neck grew taut. Strong as he appeared to be, it seemed impossible for him to start the cork. But he would not give way, and in the end it was the cork that gave way. Slowly and smoothly it was pulled clear of the bottle-mouth, and for the first time since the wine had been drawn from its barrel long years before, it was now free to breathe the open air.

Kassoulas waved the cork back and forth under his nose, sampling its bouquet. He shrugged as he handed it to me.

'Impossible to tell anything this way,' he said, and of course he was right. The fumes of fine Burgundy emanating from the cork meant nothing, since even dead wine may have a good bouquet.

De Marechal would not even bother to look at the cork.

'It's only the wine that matters,' he said fervently. 'Only the wine. And in an hour we'll know its secret for better or worse. It will seem like a long hour, I'm afraid.'

I didn't agree with that at first. The dinner we were served was more than sufficient distraction for me. Its menu, in tribute to the Nuits Saint-Oen 1929, had been arranged the way a symphony conductor might arrange a short programme of lighter composers in preparation for the playing of a Beethoven masterwork. Artichoke hearts in a butter sauce, *langouste* in mushrooms, and, to clear the palate, a lemon ice unusually tart. Simple dishes flawlessly prepared.

And the wines Kassoulas had selected to go with them were, I was intrigued to note, obviously chosen as settings for his diamond. A sound Chablis, a respectable Muscadet. Both were good, neither was calculated to do more than draw a small nod of approval from the connoisseur. It was Kassoulas' way of telling us that nothing would be allowed to dim the glorious promise of that open bottle of Nuits Saint-Oen standing before us.

Then my nerves began to get the better of me. Old as I was at the game, I found myself more and more filled with tension and as the dinner progressed I found the bottle of Saint-Oen a magnet for my eyes. It soon became an agony, waiting until the entrée would be served and the Saint-Oen poured.

Who, I wondered, would be given the honour of testing the first few drops? Kassoulas, the host, was entitled to that honour, but as a mark of respect he could assign it to anyone he chose. I wasn't sure whether or not I wanted to be chosen. I was braced for the worst, but I knew that being the first at the table to discover the wine was dead would be like stepping from an aeroplane above the clouds without a parachute. Yet, to be the first to discover that this greatest of vintages had survived the years—! Watching Max de Marechal, crimson with mounting excitement, sweating so that he had to constantly mop his brow, I suspected he was sharing my every thought.

The entrée was brought in at last, the *entrecôte* of beef that de Marechal had suggested. Only a salver of *petits pois* accompanied it. The *entrecôte* and peas were served. Then Kassoulas gestured at Joseph, and the majordomo cleared the room of the help. There must be no chance of disturbance while the wine was being poured, no possible distraction.

When the servants were gone and the massive doors of the dining room were closed behind them, Joseph returned to the table and took up his position near Kassoulas, ready for anything that might be required of him.

The time had come.

Kassoulas took hold of the bottle of Nuits Saint-Oen 1929. He lifted it slowly, with infinite care, making sure not to disturb the treacherous sediment. A ruby light flickered from it as he held it at arm's length, staring at it with brooding eyes.

'Monsieur Drummond, you were right,' he said abruptly.

'I was?' I said, taken aback. 'About what?'

'About your refusal to unlock the secret of this bottle. You once said that as long as the bottle kept its secret it was an extraordinary treasure, but that once it was opened it might prove to be nothing but another bottle of bad wine. A disaster. Worse than a disaster, a joke. That was the truth. And in the face of it I now find I haven't the courage to learn whether or not what I am holding here is a treasure or a joke.'

De Marechal almost writhed with impatience.

'It's too late for that!' he protested violently. 'The bottle is already open!'

'But there's a solution to my dilemma,' Kassoulas said to him. 'Now watch it. Watch it very closely.'

His arm moved carrying the bottle clear of the table. The bottle slowly tilted. Stupefied, I saw wine spurt from it, pour over the polished boards of the floor. Drops of wine spattered Kassoulas' shoes, stained the cuffs of his trousers. The puddle on the floor grew larger. Trickles of it crept out in thin red strings between the boards.

It was an unearthly choking sound from de Marechal which tore me free of the spell I was in. A wild cry of anguish from Sophia Kassoulas.

'Max!' she screamed. 'Kyros, stop! For God's sake, stop! Don't you see what you're doing to him?'

She had reason to be terrified. I was terrified myself when I saw de Marechal's condition. His face was ashen, his mouth gaped wide open, his eyes, fixed on the stream of wine relentlessly gushing out of the bottle in Kassoulas' unwavering hand, were starting out of his head with horror.

Sophia Kassoulas ran to his side but he feebly thrust her away and tried to struggle to his feet. His hands reached out in supplication to the fast emptying bottle of Nuits Saint-Oen 1929.

'Joseph,' Kassoulas said dispassionately, 'see to Monsieur de Marechal. The doctor warned that he must not move during these attacks.'

The iron grasp Joseph clamped on de Marechal's shoulder prevented him from moving, but I saw his pallid hand fumbling into a pocket, and at last regained my wits.

'In his pocket!' I pleaded. 'He has pills!'

It was too late. De Marechal suddenly clutched at his chest in that familiar gesture of unbearable pain, then his entire body went

limp, his head lolling back against the chair, his eyes turning up
in his head to glare sightlessly at the ceiling. The last thing they
must have seen was the stream of Nuits Saint-Oen 1929 become
a trickle, the trickle become an ooze of sediment clotting on the
floor in the middle of the vast puddle there.

Too late to do anything for de Marechal, but Sophia Kassoulas
stood swaying on her feet ready to faint. Weak-kneed myself, I
helped her to her chair, saw to it that she downed the remains of
the Chablis in her glass.

The wine penetrated her stupor. She sat there breathing hard,
staring at her husband until she found the strength to utter words.

'You knew it would kill him,' she whispered. 'That's why you
bought the wine. That's why you wasted it all.'

'Enough, madame,' Kassoulas said frigidly. 'You don't know
what you're saying. And you're embarrassing our guest with this
emotionalism.' He turned to me. 'It's sad that our little party had
to end this way, monsieur, but these things do happen. Poor Max.
He invited disaster with his temperament. Now I think you had
better go. The doctor must be called in to make an examination
and fill out the necessary papers, and these medical matters can
be distressing to witness. There's no need for you to be put out
by them. I'll see you to the door.'

I got away from there without knowing how. All I knew was
that I had seen a murder committed and there was nothing I could
do about it. Absolutely nothing. Merely to say aloud that what I
had seen take place was murder would be enough to convict me
of slander in any court. Kyros Kassoulas had planned and
executed his revenge flawlessly, and all it would cost him, by my
bitter calculations, were one hundred thousand francs and the loss
of a faithless wife. It was unlikely that Sophia Kassoulas would
spend another night in his house even if she had to leave it with
only the clothes on her back.

I never heard from Kassoulas again after that night. For that
much, at least, I was grateful . . .

Now, six months later, here I was at a café table on the rue de
Rivoli with Sophia Kassoulas, a second witness to the murder and
as helplessly bound to silence about it as I was. Considering the
shock given me by our meeting, I had to admire her own composure as she hovered over me solicitously, saw to it that I took
down a cognac and then another, chattered brightly about incon-
sequential things as if that could blot the recollection of the past
from our minds.

She had changed since I had last seen her. Changed all for the
better. The timid girl had become a lovely woman who glowed

with self-assurance. The signs were easy to read. Somewhere, I was sure, she had found the right man for her and this time not a brute like Kassoulas or a shoddy Casanova like Max de Marechal.

The second cognac made me feel almost myself again, and when I saw my Samaritan glance at the small, brilliantly jewelled watch on her wrist I apologised for keeping her and thanked her for her kindness.

'Small kindness for such a friend,' she said reproachfully. She rose and gathered up her gloves and purse. 'But I did tell Kyros I would meet him at—'

'Kyros!'

'But of course. Kyros. My husband.' Madame Kassoulas looked at me with puzzlement.

'Then you're still living with him?'

'Very happily.' Then her face cleared. 'You must forgive me for being so slow-witted. It took a moment to realise why you should ask such a question.'

'Madame, I'm the one who should apologise. After all—'

'No, no, you had every right to ask it.' Madame Kassoulas smiled at me. 'But it's sometimes hard to remember I was ever unhappy with Kyros, the way everything changed so completely for me that night—

'But you were there, Monsieur Drummond. You saw for yourself how Kyros emptied the bottle of Saint-Oen on the floor, all because of me. What a revelation that was! What an awakening! And when it dawned on me that I really did mean more to him than even the last bottle of Nuits Saint-Oen 1929 in the whole world, when I found the courage to go to his room that night and tell him how this made me feel—oh, my dear Monsieur Drummond, it's been heaven for us ever since!'

CELLAR COOL

Geoffrey Household

Like Stanley Ellin, Geoffrey Household (1900-) has won international acclaim for his novels and short stories, in particular the thriller Rogue Male *(1939) in which a young sportsman goes hunting for an unnamed European dictator which readers everywhere assumed to be Hitler. Household led an adventurous life himself, working in Spain, America (during the Depression where he kept himself from starvation by writing children's plays for the radio) and Latin America, before finally settling in England. He has an expert knowledge of wine and a cellar boasting many exotic vintages—and doubtless drew part of his inspiration from this collection in writing the following story of intrigue. I say only part of his inspiration for reasons which will become obvious as you read on . . .*

You might as well listen, darling . . . All right, then, I won't call you darling. Just a matter of habit. One can't drop it at once . . . No, of course it wasn't just a habit.

How the devil do I know if you can use the same evidence? I've never been cited as a co-respondent before. It certainly was *not* the merest luck. I've always been faithful to you. I was this time, too. I can't help it if the lawyers say the bastard is bound to win his case. So what? Because the blasted Law says I am guilty, it doesn't mean I am.

Yes, I know it doesn't do any good, swearing. But if I want to, I shall. After all, you aren't on speaking terms with me. I'm a lonely man with every right to talk to himself in strong language. And there'll be plenty of it before I get used to being a co-respondent. Damn it, I admit we looked like co, but there was no responding whatever!

You won't understand . . . Yes, I know you can understand anything I can . . . But this is difficult. You see, we start with the fact that you like swilling cocktails before dinner, and I like wine with

it . . . No, please don't walk off! I agree. I agree entirely that one
cocktail before dinner cannot be described as swilling.

All I mean is that people who are devoted to one way of living
can't ever quite believe in enthusiasts for another. That rich, incompetent
slob, that white-nosed twerp, that hypocritical, dirty-minded
financier, is much worse than—I mean, he drinks water.
He's a rabid teetotaller. He should have married a Welsh preacher,
not a charming Belgian who was the daughter of a hotelier and
had the wine list in her nursery along with Peter Rabbit.

I used the word *charming*, darling . . . Yes, of course I'll cut that
out . . . I used it in the sense of cultivated, civilised. Her—er—
personal charms I have never considered at all. She has a face like
a very amiable horse, even if she does have a pretty figure.

No, I am *not* in a position to judge. And if I was, which I deny,
it's not my fault.

I'd never seen the woman before. It was her husband who asked
me to dine and stay the night. He could hardly do anything else
when I had just missed the last train because he'd sacked his
chauffeur for keeping turpentine in a gin bottle. And a dream of
a dinner it was. Naturally one would expect a woman like that . . .
No, I wasn't implying any criticism at all! What I meant was that
she had the training to see that he used his money properly. French
chef. Butler. Gardeners. All that.

But only water to go with the meal! His blasted principles! You
wouldn't think that he'd compel his poor wife to be teetotal as
well. He wouldn't have a drop under his roof.

Yes, I know! I'm coming to the cellar. He had bought the house
from executors as it stood—pictures, cellar, and all. And he was
too damn mean to sell off the wines when he thought they were
bound to improve in value over the years. The bloody fool was
quite wrong. Some of those clarets and white Burgundies were
long past their best and growing more worthless every day.

No, I am not giving a lecture on wine. I am just trying to make
the position clear.

When we had finished the coffee, he pushed off upstairs to
annoy his Dictaphone. All the noble thoughts inspired by water
had to go down on the tape ready for his secretaries next day. He
said that no doubt Gabrielle would entertain me. Hardly polite. I
could see her raise an eyebrow. That sort of remark does suggest
to a sensitive woman that she is safely unattractive.

She was very easy to talk to. I could see we had a good deal in
common. We both enjoyed simple pleasures—of the palate, and
so forth. We were getting on fine, except that in the absence of
anything to drink there were occasional silences which we would
each try to break at the same time. She must have felt that it was

a pity our social intercourse—That was quite unworthy of you, my dear. And anyway I think the courts call it Intimacy like the Sunday papers—She felt, as I was saying, that it was a pity the going should be so hard.

At last she asked me, very confidentially, if I would like a brandy after my coffee. And when I said I would, she got up and told me to take one of her husband's overcoats out of the hall.

Now, that should be a good point in Court. After all a man doesn't borrow an overcoat to ... Well, the Judge will understand it even if you don't!

M'Lud, I shall say, if these allegations were correct, we should not have chosen the cold and discomfort of a cellar. There was a large garden where impropriety could have taken place in idyllic surroundings. And it was a warm evening. The lady did not need her second-best mink nor I an overcoat. An overcoat implies, as I need hardly tell Your Lordship ...

No, I am not blathering. I maintain that the overcoat is evidence that there was no *mens rea*, if we may so describe the intention to commit adultery.

Entry to the cellar was strictly forbidden. It was a shameful secret, like Bluebeard's. But Gabrielle had had a private key cut for herself. And I assure you that the cellar wasn't furnished as a love nest. There was just a bench.

She told me that she had never been down there before with anyone who really cared—for wine, that is. She took me on a conducted tour of the bins. I don't know who laid down those wines, but he knew what he was about.

A family cellar, we decided. Father training son. It was so traditional that I was surprised to find comparatively little port. She said that the butler had been selling it off. Of course the crook— a teetotaller like his boss—had had his own key made. The chance was too good to miss. By careful marketing he could put anything from five to ten thousand pounds in his own pocket.

Her situation was difficult. She couldn't report that the butler visited the cellar without giving herself away. Nor could he drop a hint that she did. Armed neutrality. I gathered there was an unspoken agreement that he could make away with the port— which didn't interest her—so long as there were no sudden gaps in the table wines.

Slipping down for a quick nip—well, she had been doing that ever since they bought the house. But it was no way to treat such a cellar, and she knew it. My heart bleeds for her. She might as well have kept a bottle of hooch wrapped up in her nightdresses at the back of the bedroom wardrobe ...

That is most unkind! It would *not* have been a more convenient place!

Everything we could possibly want was on the spot... Yes, I know I said the cellar wasn't furnished at all. It was not. When I say *everything*, I mean corkscrews of suitable sizes, a wonderful range of the right glasses, and a box of dry biscuits.

It's seldom one finds the perfect partner for any really delicate hobby. What I didn't know, she did. Occasionally I knew something she didn't. And with all those wines simply asking to be opened and tasted, we were able to illustrate our theories on the spot. I think we had quite forgotten each other's sex.

Don't snort in that way! It was very natural. There's a proper time for everything. If you found yourself in Aladdin's Cave with diamonds and rubies all over the floor, all you'd think about would be spreading out your skirt and filling it.

No, I am not accusing you of being mercenary! When I said *you* I meant *one*. Me! Anybody!

Orgy, indeed! There was no question of an orgy. I was opening bottles in order to add a little to the world's store of knowledge. The stuff was so good that it didn't affect me in the least. I was feeling extremely sane and active, except perhaps for the slightest touch of indigestion as a result of eating so many biscuits. Naturally I took a biscuit to clear my palate between one glass and another, and they added up.

Gabrielle was just taking sips of our choices, whereas I may have swallowed half a glass of each. I thought she was holding her own very well, allowing for normal feminine discretion.

I was about to say when you interrupted me that I have never believed in the superstition that you must always let a claret breathe. Many of them are at their best if drunk as soon as the cork is pulled. I was just developing this point—with examples from some of the '52s—when I was surprised to notice that she was fast asleep with her back against an old beer barrel.

She looked very uncomfortable. I could hardly leave such a perfect hostess in that position... No, her mouth was not open... I did exactly what any old family friend of hers would have done. I put a half bottle of 1947 Pauillac within easy reach of my left hand. I sat down beside her on her husband's overcoat and drew her poor, tired head down on my shoulder.

Yes, I know the depositions state that she was in a state of undress. She must have caught the zip on something, or perhaps tried to loosen herself up under the impression that she was fainting. With the dam' fool evening frocks you women wear, it's amazing you aren't always in a state of undress. I didn't feel that I ought to start tinkering with the mechanics of whale-bone and such when she was fast asleep. Suppose she had woken up and entirely misunderstood my intentions?

I did at one point—when I wanted to get up and try a Margaux against the Pauillac—give her a shake, and all she did was to snuggle up and say No.

I don't know what you mean by *what else could she say*? It was a quite unmistakeable shake. Her reply simply indicated that she wished to go on sleeping and that I was not to disentangle myself . . . No, I am not asking you to believe she was three years old. She must be about thirty.

What I ought to have done—I admit that—was to pick her up, deposit her in the drawing-room and go to bed. But it wasn't so easy. I was not at all sure of the right direction to turn on reaching the top of the cellar steps. I was trying to draw a kind of mental map of the passages when I fell asleep, too. I must have unconsciously pulled her mink over the pair of us.

No, we were not lying on the floor. Sitting! I don't care what the depositions say. We may have slipped down a bit. But our position would properly be described as sitting.

I suppose that damned thief of a butler had been keeping an eye on her movements. He wasn't going to miss a chance like that. With Gabrielle out of the way, nobody would be any the wiser if he sold off the whole cellar. He could fill the racks up with empty bottles, and take the first plane to Australia.

I woke up to see him measuring us with his eyes as if he had been the managing director of a funeral parlour. And his blasted boss was dancing around and throwing bottles on the floor without any of his usual reverence for his own property.

Yet I give you my word that what the butler saw was nothing. And what that obscene teetotaller saw was not enough to disturb any reasonably broadminded husband.

I didn't know what attitude to take. There ought to be a school for co-respondents. I see now that it's only too easy for an innocent person to find himself in that distasteful position. A week's quick course should be enough to teach the etiquette and a few manly phrases which would lower the painful tone of excitement—no harder than learning to write a good business letter.

Gabrielle rebuked him, I thought, with dignity. But she met with no response. It is most unjust that the poor woman should have to suffer for irreproachable hospitality. What really made the intolerable fellow boil when he stirred up the coats was not the slight disorder in her dress, as Herrick calls it, but the signs of what he called alcoholism.

Alcoholism! I ask you! As if anyone would willingly drink

himself into a beastly stupor when such joys for the palate still remained to be explored!

I understand that the settlement will be amicable. Gabrielle stood out for the contents of the cellar and got them. I may find myself compelled to help her with the inventory and the moving. It's the least I can do, though for the sake of the wines she would be wiser to choose a professional. That's most important. I think I can find her an experienced man.

You believe me, darling? You really see that there is nothing to forgive? Bless you! I felt sure that if you would only listen you would understand.

THE FRIENDS OF PLONK

Kingsley Amis

Readers familiar with the work of Kingsley Amis (1922-) will be only too aware of his expert knowledge of wine and spirits—revealed in books such as On Drink *and* How's Your Glass?—*as well as his frequent use of alcohol in short stories like 'Who or What Was It?' about a haunted pub, and 'A Twitch on the Thread' describing the plight of a long reformed alcoholic who falls back into addiction. Recently,* The Independent *described him as the 'laureate of the comic hangover, a committed non-abstainer'. Amis is also the inventor of a sub-genre called 'SF-drink', a series of time travel stories in which investigators journey into the future to find out what has happened to English drinking habits. In one of these tales, 'The 2003 Claret', for example, the traveller discovers that the working class have become connoisseurs of fine wines, while the fashionable upper classes prefer to frequent dreary pubs where they drink pints of bitter and eat three-day-old cheese rolls. 'The Friends of Plonk' is also about a return to London, but forty years later, where the connoisseurs are now known as 'conozers' and their favourite drink is—well, read on and find out for yourself in Amis' inimitable style!*

The (technical) success of Simpson's trip to the year 2010 encouraged the authorities to have similar experiments conducted for a variety of time-objectives. Some curious and occasionally alarming pieces of information about the future came to our knowledge in this way; I'm thinking less of politics than of developments in the domain of drink.

For instance, let me take this opportunity of warning every youngster who likes any kind of draught beer and has a high life-expectancy to drink as much of the stuff as he can while he can, because they're going to stop making it in 2016. Again, just six months ago Simpson found that, in the world of 2045, alcoholic diseases as a whole accounted for almost exactly a third of all deaths, or nearly as many as transport accidents and suicide com-

bined. This was universally put down to the marketing, from 2039
onwards, of wines and spirits free of all the congeneric elements
that cause hangovers, and yet at the same time indistinguishable
from the untreated liquors even under the most searching tests—
a triumph of biochemitechnology man had been teasingly on the
brink of since about the time I was downing my first pints of beer.

Anyway, by a lucky accident, the authorities suddenly became
anxious to know the result of the 2048 Presidential election in
America, and so Simpson was able to travel to that year and
bring back news, not only of the successful Rosicrucian candidate's
impending installation at the Black House, but also of the rigorous
outlawing of the new drink process and everything connected
with it. After one veiled reference to the matter in conversation,
Simpson had considered himself lucky to escape undamaged from
the bar of the Travellers' Club.

For a time, our section's exploration of the rather more distant
future was blocked by a persistent fault in the TIOPEPE, whereby
the projection circuits cut off at approximately 83.63 years in
advance of time-present. Then, one day in 1974, an inspired guess
of Rabaiotti's put things right, and within a week Simpson was
off to 2145. We were all there in the lab as usual to see him back
safely. After Schneider had given him the usual relaxing shots,
Simpson came out with some grave news. A quarrel about spy-
flights over the moons of Saturn had set Wales and Mars—the
two major powers in the Inner Planets at that period—at each
other's throats and precipitated a system-wide nuclear war in
2101. Half of Venus, and areas on Earth the size of Europe, had
been virtually obliterated.

Rabaiotti was the first to speak when Simpson had stopped.
'Far enough off not to bother most of our great-grandchildren,
anyway,' he said.

'That's true. But what a prospect.'

'I know,' I said.

'Well, no use glooming, Baker,' the Director said. 'Nothing we
can do about it. We've got a full half-hour before the official
conference—tell us what's happened to drink.'

Simpson rubbed his bald head and sighed. I noticed that his
eyes were bloodshot, but then they nearly always were after one
of these trips. A very conscientious alcohologist, old Simpson.
'You're not going to like it.'

We didn't.

Simpson's landing in 2145 had been a fair enough success, but
there had been an unaccountable error in the ground-level esti-
mates, conducted a week earlier by means of our latest brain-

child, the TIAMARIA (Temporal Inspection Apparatus and Meteorological - Astronomical - Regional - Interrelation Assessor). This had allowed him to materialize twelve feet up in the air and given him a nasty fall—on to a flower-bed, by an unearned piece of luck, but shaking him severely. What followed shook him still further.

The nuclear war had set everything back so much that the reconstructed world he found himself in was little more unfamiliar than the ones he had found on earlier, shorter-range time-trips. His official report, disturbing as it was, proved easy enough to compile, and he had a couple of hours to spare before the TIOPE-PE's field should snatch him back to the present. He selected a restaurant within easy range of his purse—the TIAMARIA's cameras, plus our counterfeiters in the Temporal Treasury, had taken care of the currency problem all right—found a vacant table, and asked for a drink before dinner.

'Certainly, sir,' the waiter said. 'The Martian manatee-milk is specially good today. Or there's a new delivery of Iapetan carnivorous-lemon juice, if you've a liking for the unusual. Very, uh, full-blooded sir.'

Simpson swallowed. 'I'm sure,' he said, 'but I was thinking of something—you know—a little stronger?'

The waiter's manner suffered an abrupt change. 'Oh, you mean booze, do you?' he said coldly. 'Sometimes I wonder what this town's coming to, honest. All right, I'll see what I can do.'

The 'booze' arrived on a tin tray in three chunky cans arranged like equal slices of a round cake. The nearest one had the word BEAR crudely stamped on it. Simpson poured some muddy brown liquid from it into a glass. It tasted like last week's swipes topped up with a little industrial alcohol. Then he tried the can stamped BOOJLY. (We all agreed later that this must be a corruption of 'Beaujolais'.) That was like red ink topped up with a good deal of industrial alcohol. Lastly there was BANDY. Industrial alcohol topped up with a little cold tea.

Wondering dimly if some trick of the TIOPEPE had managed to move him back into some unfrequented corner of the 1960s, Simpson became aware that a man at the next table had been watching him closely. When their eyes met, the stranger came over and, with a word of apology, sat down opposite him. (It was extraordinary, Simpson was fond of remarking, how often people did just this sort of thing when he visited the future.)

'Do excuse me,' the man said politely, 'but from your expression just now I'd guess you're a conozer—am I right? Oh, my name's Piotr Davies, by the way, on leave from Greenland Fruiteries. You're not Earth-based, I take it?'

'Oh . . . no, I'm just in from Mercury. My first trip since I was a lad, in fact,' Simpson noticed that Piotr Davies's face was covered by a thick network of burst veins, and his nose carried the richest growth of grog-blossom Simpson had ever seen. (He avoided looking at the Director when he told us this.) 'Yes,' he struggled on after giving his name, 'I am a bit of a connoiss—conozer, I suppose. I do try to discriminate a little in my—'

'You've hit it,' Piotr Davies said excitedly. 'Discrimination. That's it, the very word. I knew I was right about you. Discrimination. And tradition. Well, you won't find much of either on Earth these days, I'm afraid. Nor on Mercury, from what I hear.'

'No—no, you certainly won't.'

'We conozers are having a hard time. The Planetary War, of course. And the Aftermath.' Davies paused, and seemed to be sizing up Simpson afresh. Then: 'Tell me, are you doing anything tonight? More or less right away?'

'Well, I have got an appointment I must keep in just under two hours, but until then I—'

'Perfect. Let's go.'

'But what about my dinner?'

'You won't want any after you've been where I'm going to take you.'

'But where are you—?'

'Somewhere absolutely made for a conozer like you. What a bit of luck you happened to run into me. I'll explain on the way.'

Outside, they boarded a sort of wheelless taxicab and headed into what seemed to be a prosperous quarter. Davies's explanations were copious and complete; Simpson made full use of his supposed status as one long absent from the centre of things. It appeared that the Planetary War had destroyed every one of the vast, centralised, fully automated distilleries of strong liquors; that bacteriological warfare had put paid to many crops, including vines, barley, hops and even sugar; that the fanatical religious movements of the Aftermath, many of them with government backing, had outlawed all drink for nearly twenty years. Simpson shuddered at that news.

'And when people came to their senses,' Davies said glumly, 'it was too late. The knowledge had died. Oh, you can't kill a process like distillation. Too fundamental. Or fermentation, either. But the special processes, the extra ingredients, the skills, the *tradition*— gone for ever. Whisky—what a rich, evocative word. What can the stuff have tasted like? What little there is about it in the surviving literature gives a very poor idea. Muzzle—that was a white wine, we're pretty sure, from Germany, about where the

Great Crater is. Gin—a spirit flavoured with juniper, we know that much. There isn't any juniper now, of course.

'So, what with one thing and another, drinking went out. Real, civilised drinking, that is—I'm not talking about that stuff they tried to give you back there. I and a few like-minded friends tried to get some of the basic information together, but to no avail. And then, quite by chance, one of us, an archaeologist, turned up a primitive two-dimensional television film that dated back almost two hundred years, giving a full description of some ancient drinks and a portrayal of the habits that went with them—all the details. The film was called "The Down-and-Outs", which is an archaic expression referring to people of limited prosperity, but which we immediately understood as being satirically or ironically intended in this instance. That period, you know, was very strong on satire. Anyway, the eventual result of our friend's discovery was . . . this.'

With something of a flourish, Davies drew a pasteboard card from his pocket and passed it to Simpson. It read:

THE FRIENDS OF PLONK
Established 2139 for the drinking of
traditional liquors in traditional
dress and in traditional surroundings

Before Simpson could puzzle this out, his companion halted the taxi and a moment later was shepherding him through the portals of a large and magnificent mansion. At the far end of a thickly carpeted foyer was a steep, narrow staircase, which they descended. When they came to its foot, Davies reached into a cupboard and brought out what Simpson recognised as a trilby hat of the sort his father had used to wear, a cloth cap, a large piece of sacking and a tattered brown blanket. All four articles appeared to be covered with stains and dirt. At the same time Simpson became aware of a curious and unpleasant mixture of smells and a subdued grumbling of voices.

In silence, Davies handed him the cap and the blanket and himself donned the sacking, stole-fashion, and the trilby. Simpson followed his lead. Then Davies ushered him through a low doorway.

The room they entered was dimly lit by candles stuck into bottles, and it was a moment before Simpson could take in the scene. At first he felt pure astonishment. There was no trace here of the luxury he had glimpsed upstairs: the walls, of undressed stone, were grimy and damp, the floor was covered at random with sacks and decaying lumps of matting. A coke stove made the cellar stiflingly hot; the air swam with cigarette smoke; the

atmosphere was thick and malodorous. Against one wall stood a
trestle table piled with bottles and what looked like teacups.
Among other items Simpson uncomprehendingly saw there were
several loaves of bread, some bottles of milk, a pile of small
circular tins and, off in a corner, an old-fashioned and rusty gas-
cooker or its replica.

But his surprise and bewilderment turned to mild alarm when
he surveyed the dozen or so men sitting about on packing-cases
or broken chairs and squatting or sprawling on the floor, each
wearing some sort of battered headgear and with a blanket or
sack thrown round his shoulders. All of them were muttering
unintelligibly, in some instances to a companion, more often just
to themselves. Davies took Simpson's arm and led him to a splin-
tery bench near the wall.

'These blankets and so on must have been a means of asserting
the essential democracy of drink,' Davies whispered. 'Anyway,
we're near the end of the purely ritualistic part now. Our film
didn't make its full significance clear, but it was obviously a kind
of self-preparation, perhaps even prayer. The rest of the proceedings will be much less formal. Ah . . .'

Two of the men had been muttering more loudly at each other
and now closed physically, but their blows and struggles were
symbolic, a mime, as in ballet or the Japanese theatre. Soon one
of them had his adversary pinned to the floor and was raining
token punches upon him. ('We're rather in the dark about this
bit,' Davies murmured. 'Perhaps an enacted reference to the
ancient role of drink as a sequel to physical exertion.') When
the prostrate combatant had begun to feign unconsciousness, a
loud and authoritative voice spoke.

'End of Part One.'

At once all was animation: everybody sprang up and threw off
his borrowed garments, revealing himself as smartly clad in the
formal dress of the era. Davies led Simpson up to the man who
had made the announcement, probably a member of one of the
professions and clearly the host of the occasion. His face was
sprayed with broken veins to a degree that outdid Davies's.

'Delighted you can join us,' the host said when Simpson's presence had been explained. 'A privilege to have an Outworlder at
one of our little gatherings. Now for our Part Two. Has Piotr
explained to you about the ancient film that taught us so much?
Well, its second and third sections were so badly damaged as to
be almost useless to us. So what's to follow is no more than an
imaginative reconstruction, I fear, but I think it can be said that
we've interpreted the tradition with taste and reverence. Let's
begin, shall we?'

He signed to an attendant standing at the table; the man began filling the teacups with a mixture of two liquids. One came out of something like a wine-bottle and was red, the other came out of something like a medicine bottle and was almost transparent, with a faint purplish tinge. Courteously passing Simpson the first of the cups, the host said: 'Please do us the honour of initiating the proceedings.'

Simpson drank. He felt as if someone had exploded a tear-gas shell in his throat and then sprayed his gullet with curry-powder. As his own coughings and weepings subsided he was surprised to find his companions similarly afflicted in turn as they drank.

'Interesting, isn't it?' the host asked, wheezing and staggering. 'A fine shock to the palate. One might perhaps say that it goes beyond the merely gustatory and olfactory to the purely tactile. Hardly a sensuous experience at all—ascetic, almost abstract. An invention of genius, don't you think?'

'What—what's the . . .?'

'Red Biddy, my dear fellow,' Piotr Davies put in proudly. There was reverence in his voice when he added: 'Red wine and methylated spirits. Of course, we can't hope to reproduce the legendary Empire Burgundy-characters that used to go into it, but our own humble Boojly isn't a bad substitute. Its role is purely ancillary, after all.'

'We like to use a straw after the first shock.' The host passed one to Simpson. 'I hope you approve of the teacups. A nice traditional touch, I think. And now, do make yourself comfortable. I must see to the plonk in person—one can't afford to take risks.'

Simpson sat down near Davies on a packing-case. He realized after a few moments that it was actually carved out of a single block of wood. Then he noticed that the dampness of the walls was maintained by tiny water-jets at intervals near the ceiling. Probably the sacks on the floor had been specially woven and then artificially aged. Pretending to suck at his straw, he said nervously to Davies: 'What exactly do you mean by plonk? In my time, people usually . . .' He broke off, fearful of having betrayed himself, but the man of the future had noticed nothing.

'Ah, you're in for a great experience, my dear friend, something unknown outside this room for countless decades. To our ancestors in the later twentieth century it may have been the stuff of daily life, but to us it's a pearl beyond price, a precious fragment salvaged from the wreck of history. Watch carefully—every bit of this is authentic.'

With smarting eyes, Simpson saw his host pull the crumb from a loaf and stuff it into the mouth of an enamel jug. Then, taking a candle from a nearby bottle, he put the flame to a disc-shaped cake of brownish substance that the attendant was holding between tongs. A flame arose; liquid dropped on to the bread and began to soak through into the jug; the assembled guests clapped and cheered. Another brownish cake was treated in the same way, then another. 'Shoe-polish,' Simpson said in a cracked voice.

'Exactly. We're on the dark tans this evening, with just a touch of ox-blood to give body. Makes a very big, round, pugnacious drink. By the way, that's processed bread he's using. Wholemeal's too permeable, we've found.'

Beaming, the host came over to Simpson with a half-filled cup, a breakfast cup this time. 'Down in one, my dear chap,' he said.

They were all watching; there was nothing for it. Simpson shut his eyes and drank. This time a hundred blunt dental drills seemed to be working at once on his nose and throat and mouth. Fluid sprang from all the mucous membranes in those areas. It was like having one's face pushed into a bath of acid. Simpson's shoulders sagged and his eyes filmed over.

'I'd say the light tans have got more bite,' a voice said near him. 'Especially on the gums.'

'Less of a follow-through, on the other hand.' There was the sound of swallowing and then a muffled scream. 'Were you here for the plain-tan tasting last month? Wonderful fire and vehemence. I was blind for the next four days.'

'I still say you can't beat a straight brown for all-round excoriation. Amazing results on the uvula and tonsils.'

'What's wrong with black?' This was a younger voice.

An embarrassed silence, tempered by a fit of coughing and a heart-felt moan from different parts of the circle, was ended by someone saying urbanely: 'Each to his taste, of course, and there is impact there, but I think experience shows that that sooty, oilsmoke quality is rather meretricious. Most of us find ourselves moving tanwards as we grow older.'

'Ah, good, he's . . . yes, he's using a tin of transparent in the next jug. Watch for the effect on the septum.'

Simpson lurched to his feet. 'I must be going,' he muttered. 'Important engagement.'

'What, you're not staying for the coal-gas in milk? Turns the brain to absolute jelly, you know.'

'Sorry . . . friend waiting for me.'

'Goodbye, then. Give our love to Mercury. Perhaps you'll be able to start a circle of the Friends of Plonk on your home planet. That would be a magnificent thought.'

'Magnificent,' the Director echoed bitterly. 'Just think of it. The idea of an atomic war's too much to take in, but those poor devils ... Baker, we must prepare some information for Simpson to take on his next long-range trip, something that'll show them how to make a decent vodka or gin even if the vines have all gone.'

I was hardly listening. 'Aren't there some queer things about that world, sir? Shoe-polish in just the same variants that we know? Wholemeal bread when the crops are supposed to have—'

I was interrupted by a shout from the far end of the lab, where Rabaiotti had gone to check the TIAMARIA. He turned and came racing towards us, babbling at the top of his voice.

'Phase distortion, sir! Anomalous tracking on the output side! Completely new effect!'

'And the TIOPEPE's meshed with it, isn't it?' Schneider said.

'Of course!' I yelled. 'Simpson was on a different time-path, sir! An alternative probability, a parallel world. No wonder the ground-level estimate was off. This is amazing!'

'No nuclear war in our time-path—no certainty, anyway,' the Director sang, waving his arms.

'No destruction of the vines.'

'No Friends of Plonk.'

'All the same,' Simpson murmured to me as we strolled towards the Conference Room, 'in some ways they're better off than we are. At least the stuff they use is genuine. Nobody's going to doctor bloody shoe-polish to make it taste smoother or to preserve it or so that you'll mistake it for a more expensive brand. And it can only improve, what they drink.'

'Whereas we ...'

'Yes. That draught beer you go on about isn't draught at all: it comes out of a giant steel bottle these days, because it's easier that way. And do you think the Germans are the greatest chemists in the world for nothing? Ask Schneider about the 1972 Moselles. And what do you imagine all those scientists are doing in Bordeaux?'

'There's Italy and Spain and Greece. They'll—'

'Not Italy any more. Ask Rabaiotti, or rather don't. Spain and Greece'll last longest, probably, but by 1980 you'll have to go to Albania if you want real wine. Provided the Chinese won't have started helping them to get the place modernized.'

'What are you going to do about it?'

'Switch to whisky. That's still real. In fact I'm going to take a bottle home tonight. Can you lend me twenty-five quid?'

2

DYING FOR A DRINK

Cocktails of Mystery and Death

THE OPENER OF THE CRYPT

John Jakes

The impact of Edgar Allan Poe's story 'The Cask of Amontillado' has continued to influence readers and writers to the present day, and there are those who say that they are never able to take a glass of this lightly-coloured, medium dry sherry without thinking of that terrifying story. Among such authors is John Jakes (1932-) who began his writing career with stories of SF and fantasy, but during the past decade has become an international best seller with his novels dramatising American history, such as North and South *(1988) and* Homeland *(1993). For years, he says, he was haunted by Poe's tale of Montresor and Fortunato—'the classic horror story of all time'—and was determined to write a sequel. He has finally achieved this ambition with 'The Opener of the Way', a compelling tale that, with the passage of time, will surely earn its own acclaim.*

I first read the story when I was very young. Even then it seemed real in a way none of the other stories I read were real. As I grew up I tried to tell myself that it was nothing but a boy's imagination which gave me that sense of reality. But then I would read the story again and it wouldn't be a story any longer. It would become a real and vital truth, distorted somehow, but still real. A voice at the back of my mind always spoke to me then, whispering with a hollow solemn softness.

This is truth, the voice would say. *This is fact. This is not imagination or legend.* And I believed it. It filled every part of me, and as a grown man I was more aware of the truth than I had been as a child. And so I worked at my job on the *Gazette* and led my life along the streets of Paris. But I read the story again and again, until it was a part of me, until I knew that somewhere, sometime, it had existed.

Of course, I wanted to prove it to myself, to justify that quiet voice in my mind, but for years I never had the chance. And then one summer evening when the sky over the city was filled with a pale twilight, I had dinner with Dr Armand, a good friend of mine and a historian of high standing. I remember how it was as we sat smoking our cigars and sipping our brandy. How I came one step closer to the realisation of the truth that lived in my mind.

Dr Armand reached over to a small table beside his chair and picked up a letter. He nodded his white head at me. 'This ought to interest you, Paul.'

'What's that you have?' I asked.

He glanced at the finely written script. 'A letter from a friend of mine in Rome. It seems he was touring the seacoast last month and he ran across a highly interesting house in a small village.'

I took a puff on the cigar. I tried to be calm, but something stirred inside of me. 'What's so interesting about this house?'

'Well,' said Dr Armand, his gaze going out the window to the peaceful evening sky, 'it's quite an old house, and almost fallen to the ground, but one of the innkeepers said it once belonged to a family named Montresor.'

I sat there stupefied.

Dr Armand waved the letter again. 'Coincidence, of course, but I thought you might be interested.' He chuckled quietly and continued his talk on various topics. But I didn't hear. The voice was in my mind again, speaking softly to me. *He does not believe. But you know the truth.*

'Yes!' my voice was intense.

'What did you say?' Dr. Armand looked at me, puzzled.

I made up a hasty excuse and left him, after I had pressed him for all the details. When I got back to my flat, I couldn't go to sleep. There it was! Something to prove what I believed. This bit of news made me want more proof. When morning came I went to the editor of the *Gazette* and quit my job. I took my savings out of the bank, bought a small motor car and started south.

I drove rapidly. A desire filled me and pulled me toward Italy, toward that small village, toward the proof of the legend that was for me a living truth. It was more than a desire, because I felt vaguely that a force outside myself was pulling me there. I slept at the roadside slumped over in the seat of the car, and ate only when the growling in my stomach became painful. The countryside raced by and I was in Italy, roaring across the plains, through the river valleys, across the rivers, disturbing the sleepy plazas and throwing up dust behind me. But I had to know!

I got tired, of course. Very tired. By the time I had gotten lost once or twice, found my way again and at last reached the coast,

I was sore all over. My face felt dirty and I knew my beard had grown out quite a bit. But it was worth it. With each kilometre I drove, I knew I was getting closer to the truth.

It was early evening when I finally reached the town. I had been driving along the coast for two hours with the sea spread out to my left in a glistening sheet, when at last I pulled over the top of a small hill. I stopped the car. The town lay before me at the foot of the hill. Music and shouting drifted up from below. The streets were brightly lit. My hands gripped the steering wheel. A skyrocket shot up into the air over the town and exploded in a shower of red stars, and I knew it was carnival season!

I drove down the hill. The streets were jammed with people dressed in costume, singing and dancing and running in every direction. I pushed my way through those streets on foot, paying hardly any attention to the people, watching the houses for the name of the inn mentioned in the letter. At last I found it. I think I was a little crazy then, feeling so close to my goal, because I shoved my way roughly through the crowd and a couple of young men turned to look at me, their eyes glaring darkly through slits in their masks. I went through the door of the inn, ignoring them.

The landlord's name was Giacomo. He looked me up and down, his ancient tanned forehead wrinkling into a frown. I was a foreigner and I was not in costume. He must have felt that something was certainly wrong. And from the way I must have looked, bearded and dirty, my clothes rumpled, I suppose I couldn't blame him.

'What does the signor wish?' the old man asked me. He poured himself a glass of wine and downed it quickly.

I could hardly say the words. Excitement had made me tense, nervous. 'I . . . I am looking for an old house.'

He laughed loudly. I could tell he thought I was mad, and it made me angry. I wanted to lean across the table and choke the words out of him. 'We have many old houses, signor. This town is full of old houses.'

'This is a particular house. It belonged to a particular family. The family's name was Montresor.'

He thought a minute, staring into the wine dregs. Then he nodded. 'Yes, the Montresor house is in this town. It is a ruin, signor, tumbling to the ground. No one goes there at all any more. Why do you wish to find that particular house?'

'Never mind. Where is it?'

He gave me directions. The southern edge of the village. I tossed some coins on the table and hurried out. This time I shoved people brutally out of my way, pushing against the sticky tide of humanity roistering through the streets. The rockets blazed above me, the noise dinned in my ears, but I pushed on, driven by my desire. People hurled angry curses at me but I did not heed them. At last I broke free of the crowd and found myself in a deserted street, quite dark, with immense patches of purple shadow hiding the walls of the houses in inky impenetrability.

I hurried along the street, which suddenly became a dead end. My heart fell. I stopped at what seemed to be an iron gate and took out a match. I lit it and held it up, the reddish light flickering in an eerie manner. And my heart pounded within my chest.

For there, blazoned on the stone, was a coat of arms that I knew only too well. The large human foot grinding down upon a snake as the snake sank its fangs into the heel of that same foot. Above the symbol was the motto, and I had only to glance at the first word. *Nemo* . . . My match was suddenly extinguished by a gust of stale wind. With trembling hands I lit another. *Nemo me impune lacessit.* And below the coat—I felt a force seize me and transform me into a wildly quivering creature of fear and anguish. The name, carved in capitals that were heavy and ponderous; *Montresor!*

The second match flickered out into darkness. My heart thudding wildly, I pushed at the gate. There was a horrendous screeching noise, and I stepped quickly backward as the gate came free of its hinges and fell with a mighty clang onto the stone of the courtyard. This was the very house, and I was close to the heart of my secret! I raced across the courtyard, conscious within myself that soon I would know the reason for which I had been drawn over the years to this dark and malignantly brooding place. I would know what strange and demonically real impulse made me believe the legend as truth and made me seek proof.

The oppressive air of obsolescence and decay filled my nostrils as I stepped through the front portal into the first of the dark rooms. I knew the way . . . oh, God! I knew the way and could not turn aside! For here was the place to which I had been destined to come. Why I had been so destined, only the spirits that brooded here could explain.

I reached up to the wall and found a torch resting in its socket. With violently trembling hands I applied a match and soon had a flickering reddish light to guide me. My feet clattered hollowly on the cold and hoary stone. I paced quickly through the various suites of ancient rooms, each with its own particular odour of decay and desolation. The entrance to the staircase loomed before me and I hurried on, plunging downward at a rapid rate, watching as the shadows unfolded in the guttering torch glare, watching as I saw the reality of my brain becoming the reality of matter itself. Then the air became suddenly colder and I stood on damp ground.

Around me stretched endless rows of wine racks, long empty of their casques, deserted and left to the scurrying rodents and the webs of dust and age that spread like grotesque mantles over the empty tiers.

The voice called to me now, surging through my brain, whirling me on and on and I could not resist its mighty power. *Come, come, make haste, make haste, the task must be performed.* What task I knew not, but I raced on nonetheless. I was will-less now, a creature drugged by the commands of an unknown preternatural force. The nitre depended from the vaulted ceiling in strangely deformed shapes, and the torchlight danced and whirled on the primeval stone of the walls. I felt the chill of the air pierce to the very marrow of my bones.

Again the vaults descended and my light fell upon the hollow black sockets of ancient skulls, scattered askew on mounds of human remains, and new terror thrilled through me as my mind signalled that I was descending beneath the river. Droplets of moisture trickled over the yellowed skulls, and rodents scratched and chittered among the piled bones. The voice spoke again, its volume increased now, its tone imperious and sonorous. *Come; make haste to perform the task!*

I passed through the low arches, descended once more, pursued my way through another lengthy passage, stepping over piles of those grisly remains, and once again hurled myself down an incline, until at last I realised with a start of overwhelming terror that I was in the deepest crypt, far in the bowels of the dark earth. My torch was seized with a gust of fetid air that made it dim and lose its intensity, so that an unearthly light of a bluish colour pervaded the crypt. Here the bleached relics of human life had been mounded up to the very roof. And directly before me was a wall of masonry, and lying before it upon the ground was an ancient tool with which the masons plied their trade.

I stood in wonder and awe, realising that here at last I had found the utter actuality of that which I had once only sensed vaguely. The speaker thundered his monstrous tones into the remotest crevices of my brain, and I realised that he was lodged behind the wall of masonry, imprisoned, yet powerful in all of his fiendish strength.

Break the masonry!

The command echoed and reechoed in my confused brain. I reeled dizzily and nearly dropped my light. I staggered forward, no longer a mortal, but an agent of some weird and terrible force from the great dark gulfs of supernatural power that lie far beyond the ken of mere human knowledge. I knelt and placed my torch in a heap of grisly bones, propping it up as best I could. And then I took the mason's tool into my hand and gazed at it wonderingly, my brow hot and feverish. I leaped forward, and with a fury that approached madness I attacked the masonry.

I have no conception of how long I laboured. The torch dwindled slowly and I battered at the ancient stonework, chipping it away fragment by fragment, until the blood streamed off my injured hands and stained the stone with its red colour. I worked feverishly, emitting whimpering sounds, howling insane curses to unknown gods, exciting myself to a pitch of brutal mindless automatism. At the end of this period of madness, I had created an opening in the masonry scarcely a foot square. I took my torch with faltering hand and thrust it before me into the aperture. And my demented eyes saw the speaker who had sought me.

There in the flickering illumination I beheld the figure floating, as in a mist, above the floor of the smaller crypt. I grew cognisant of the garb of motley, of the delicate tinkle of bells on the peaked cap, of the almost overpowering reek of wine. From out of that spectral face two orbs burned, intense as the innermost fires of the underworld. The voice that spoke to me issued from that unearthly apparition.

'You have fulfilled the obligation placed upon your family by your ignoble ancestor. You have released me from my prison and set my spirit free to roam the outer spheres. The debt is paid.'

'Who is speaking?' I shrieked in a frenzy. 'Who addresses me thus?'

'Fortunato,' was the reply. 'My tormented spirit has survived my flesh.'

'Fortunato!' I cried. 'But why have I been chosen? Why has it been my task and mine alone to free you? Who am I to be called here thus? In God's name, speak!'

'You are Montresor,' came the shade's reply.

'*Montresor!*' This I shrieked in a voice completely and utterly saturated with a wild madness.

'The last of the Montresor line. I have kept alive within you the spirit of that first Montresor, that infamous spirit which fed upon its own guilt and transformed itself into the spirit of a man inflamed with guilt. I have placed a compulsion upon you to free me, and you have answered.'

And then I was aware of what I had only sensed before, that the immaterial substance of that first hateful Montresor who walled up the insufferable Fortunato had been transferred to me, until I was in spirit and in actuality two separate and individual beings united into a single creature!

My torch wavered once more. I reeled unsteadily on my feet, my eyes filming with the mists of madness. I swooned, but in the instant before complete unconsciousness threw its healing cloak over me, I felt a prescience whisper past me from out that small crypt, rushing by as with a great wind, flinging the tiny musical tinkle of bells behind it in supreme triumph as it ascended upward toward the earth and the starred heavens, liberated and unfettered after age upon age in the depths of the planet. I swooned completely.

And only at this moment have I awakened. My torch is extinguished. I am faint from my labour at the masonry, and am lying upon the chill earth of the crypt with its stillness penetrating into me, and I have not the will or the strength to stir. In the darkness there are the remotest of scurrying sounds. The rodents are awaiting my demise. I shall rest until the infernal shade descends, for my debt has been fully rendered.

BEFORE THE PARTY

Somerset Maugham

Widely acclaimed as one of the greatest storytellers of this century, William Somerset Maugham (1874–1965) drew on his years of travel around the world, his experiences as a secret agent in both World Wars, and his insight into human nature to become one of the modern masters of the short story. Drink plays a substantial part in a number of his best novels and plays, and is at the heart of this story of life in the Far East, where he was, of course, a resident for some years. Maugham was a great admirer of the detective and mystery story, and in this whisky-soaked tale describes a doomed relationship in which a violent death seems to be the only possible outcome . . .

Mrs Skinner liked to be in good time. She was already dressed, in black silk as befitted her age and the mourning she wore for her son-in-law, and now she put on her toque. She was a little uncertain about it, since the egrets' feathers which adorned it might very well arouse in some of the friends she would certainly meet at the party acid expostulations; and of course it was shocking to kill those beautiful white birds, in the mating season too, for the sake of their feathers; but there they were, so pretty and stylish, and it would have been silly to refuse them, and it would have hurt her son-in-law's feelings. He had brought them all the way from Borneo and he expected her to be so pleased with them. Kathleen had made herself rather unpleasant about them, she must wish she hadn't now, after what had happened, but Kathleen had never really liked Harold. Mrs Skinner, standing at her dressing table, placed the toque on her head, it was after all the only nice hat she had, and put in a pin with a large jet knob. If anybody spoke to her about the ospreys she had her answer.

'I know it's dreadful,' she would say, 'and I wouldn't dream of buying them, but my poor son-in-law brought them back the last time he was home on leave.'

That would explain her possession of them and excuse their use. Everyone had been very kind. Mrs Skinner took a clean handkerchief from a drawer and sprinkled a little Eau de Cologne on it. She never used scent, and she had always thought it rather fast, but Eau de Cologne was so refreshing. She was very nearly ready now and her eyes wandered out of the window behind her looking glass. Canon Heywood had a beautiful day for his garden party. It was warm and the sky was blue; the trees had not yet lost the fresh green of the spring. She smiled as she saw her little granddaughter in the strip of garden behind the house busily raking her very own flowerbed. Mrs Skinner wished Joan were not quite so pale, it was a mistake to have kept her so long in the tropics; and she was so grave for her age, you never saw her run about; she played quiet games of her own invention and watered her garden. Mrs Skinner gave the front of her dress a little pat, took up her gloves, and went downstairs.

Kathleen was at the writing table in the window busy with lists she was making, for she was honorary secretary of the Ladies' Golf Club and when there were competitions had a good deal to do. But she too was ready for the party.

'I see you've put on your jumper after all,' said Mrs Skinner.

They had discussed at luncheon whether Kathleen should wear her jumper or her black chiffon. The jumper was black and white, and Kathleen thought it rather smart, but it was hardly mourning. Millicent, however, was in favour of it.

'There's no reason why we should all look as if we'd just come from a funeral,' she said. 'Harold's been dead eight months.'

To Mrs Skinner it seemed rather unfeeling to talk like that. Millicent was strange since her return from Borneo.

'You're not going to leave off your weeds yet, darling?' she asked.

Millicent did not give a direct answer.

'People don't wear mourning in the way they used,' she said. She paused a little and when she went on there was a tone in her voice which Mrs Skinner thought quite peculiar. It was plain that Kathleen noticed it too, for she gave her sister a curious look. 'I'm sure Harold wouldn't wish me to wear mourning for him indefinitely.'

'I dressed early because I wanted to say something to Millicent,' said Kathleen in reply to her mother's observation.

'Oh?'

Kathleen did not explain. But she put her lists aside and with knitted brows read for the second time a letter from a lady who complained that the committee had most unfairly marked down her handicap from twenty-four to eighteen. It requires a good deal of tact to be Honorary Secretary to a ladies' golf club. Mrs Skinner began to put on her new gloves. The sun blinds kept the room cool and dark. She looked at the great wooden hornbill, gaily painted, which Harold had left in her safekeeping; and it seemed a little odd and barbaric to her, but he had set much store on it. It had some religious significance and Canon Heywood had been greatly struck by it. On the wall, over the sofa, were Malay weapons, she forgot what they were called, and here and there on occasional tables pieces of silver and brass which Harold at various times had sent to them. She had liked Harold and involuntarily her eyes sought his photograph which stood on the piano with photographs of her two daughters, her grandchild, her sister and her sister's son.

'Why, Kathleen, where's Harold's photograph?' she asked.

Kathleen looked round. It no longer stood in its place.

'Someone's taken it away,' said Kathleen.

Surprised and puzzled, she got up and went over to the piano. The photographs had been rearranged so that no gap should show.

'Perhaps Millicent wanted to have it in her bedroom,' said Mrs Skinner.

'I should have noticed it. Besides, Millicent has several photographs of Harold. She keeps them locked up.'

Mrs Skinner had thought it very peculiar that her daughter should have no photographs of Harold in her room. Indeed she had spoken of it once, but Millicent had made no reply. Millicent had been strangely silent since she came back from Borneo, and had not encouraged the sympathy Mrs Skinner would have been so willing to show her. She seemed unwilling to speak of her great loss. Sorrow took people in different ways. Her husband had said the best thing was to leave her alone. The thought of him turned her ideas to the party they were going to.

'Father asked if I thought he ought to wear a top hat,' she said. 'I said I thought it was just as well to be on the safe side.'

It was going to be quite a grand affair. They were having ices, strawberry and vanilla, from Boddy, the confectioner, but the Heywoods were making the iced coffee at home. Everyone would be there. They had been asked to meet the Bishop of Hong Kong, who was staying with the Canon, an old college friend of his, and he was going to speak on the Chinese missions. Mrs Skinner, whose daughter had lived in the East for eight years and whose son-in-law had been Resident of a district in Borneo, was in a flutter of interest. Naturally it meant more to her than to people who had never had anything to do with the Colonies and that sort of thing.

' "What can they know of England who only England know?" ' as Mr Skinner said.

He came into the room at that moment. He was a lawyer, as his father had been before him, and he had offices in Lincoln's Inn Fields. He went up to London every morning and came down every evening. He was only able to accompany his wife and daughters to the Canon's garden party because the Canon had very wisely chosen a Saturday to have it on. Mr Skinner looked very well in his tailcoat and pepper-and-salt trousers. He was not exactly dressy, but he was neat. He looked like a respectable family solicitor, which indeed he was; his firm never touched work that was not perfectly above-board, and if a client went to him with some trouble that was not quite nice, Mr Skinner would look grave.

'I don't think this is the sort of case that we very much care to undertake,' he said. 'I think you'd do better to go elsewhere.'

He drew towards him his writing block and scribbled a name and address on it. He tore off a sheet of paper and handed it to his client.

'If I were you I think I would go and see these people. If you mention my name I believe they'll do anything they can for you.'

Mr Skinner was clean-shaven and very bald. His pale lips were tight and thin, but his blue eyes were shy. He had no colour in his cheeks and his face was much lined.

'I see you've put on your new trousers,' said Mrs Skinner.

'I thought it would be a good opportunity,' he answered. 'I was wondering if I should wear a buttonhole.'

'I wouldn't, Father,' said Kathleen. 'I don't think it's awfully good form.'

'A lot of people will be wearing them,' said Mrs Skinner.

'Only clerks and people like that,' said Kathleen. 'The Heywoods have had to ask everybody, you know. And besides, we are in mourning.'

'I wonder if there'll be a collection after the Bishop's address,' said Mr Skinner.

'I should hardly think so,' said Mrs Skinner.

'I think it would be rather bad form,' agreed Kathleen.

'It's as well to be on the safe side,' said Mr Skinner. 'I'll give for all of us. I was wondering if ten shillings would be enough or if I must give a pound.'

'If you give anything I think you ought to give a pound, Father,' said Kathleen.

'I'll see when the time comes. I don't want to give less than anyone else, but on the other hand I see no reason to give more than I need.'

Kathleen put away her papers in the drawer of the writing table and stood up. She looked at her wrist watch.

'Is Millicent ready?' asked Mrs Skinner.

'There's plenty of time. We're only asked at four and I don't think we ought to arrive much before half-past. I told Davis to bring the car round at four-fifteen.'

Generally Kathleen drove the car, but on grand occasions like this Davis, who was the gardener, put on his uniform and acted as chauffeur. It looked better when you drove up and naturally Kathleen didn't much want to drive herself when she was wearing her new jumper. The sight of her mother forcing her fingers one by one into her new gloves reminded her that she must put on her own. She smelt them to see if any odour of the cleaning still clung to them. It was very slight. She didn't believe anyone would notice.

At last the door opened and Millicent came in. She wore her widow's weeds. Mrs Skinner never could get used to them, but of course she knew that Millicent must wear them for a year. It was a pity they didn't suit her; they suited some people. She had tried on Millicent's bonnet once, with its white band and long veil, and thought she looked very well in it. Of course she hoped dear Alfred would survive her, but if he didn't she would never go out of weeds. Queen Victoria never had. It was different for Millicent; Millicent was a much younger woman; she was only thirty-six; it was very sad to be a widow at thirty-six. And there wasn't much chance of her marrying again. Kathleen wasn't very likely to marry now, she was thirty-five; last time Millicent and Harold had come home she had suggested that they should have Kathleen to stay with them; Harold had seemed willing enough, but Millicent said it wouldn't do. Mrs Skinner didn't know why not. It would give her a chance. Of course they didn't want to get rid of her, but a girl ought to marry, and somehow all the men they knew at home were married already. Millicent said the climate was trying. It was true she was a bad colour. No one would think now that Millicent had been the prettier of the two. Kathleen had fined down as she grew older (of course some people said she was too thin) but now that she had cut her hair, with her cheeks red from playing golf in all weathers, Mrs Skinner thought her quite pretty. No one could say that of poor Millicent; she had lost her figure completely; she had never been tall and now that she had filled out she looked stocky. She was a good deal too fat; Mrs Skinner supposed it was due to the tropical heat that prevented her from taking exercise. Her skin was sallow and muddy; and her blue eyes, which had been her best feature, had gone quite pale.

'She ought to do something about her neck,' Mrs Skinner reflected. 'She's becoming dreadfully jowly.'

She had spoken of it once or twice to her husband. He remarked that Millicent wasn't as young as she was: that might be, but she needn't let herself go altogether. Mrs Skinner made up her mind to talk to her daughter seriously, but of course she must respect her grief and she would wait till the year was up. She was just as glad to have this reason to put off a conversation the thought of which made her slightly nervous. For Millicent was certainly changed. There was something sullen in her face which made her mother not quite at home with her. Mrs Skinner liked to say aloud all the thoughts that passed through her head, but Millicent when you made a remark (just to say something, you know), had an awkward habit of not answering so that you wondered whether she had heard. Sometimes Mrs Skinner found it so irritating, that not to be quite sharp with Millicent she had to remind herself that poor Harold had only been dead eight months.

The light from the window fell on the widow's heavy face as she advanced silently, but Kathleen stood with her back to it. She watched her sister for a moment.

'Millicent, there's something I want to say to you,' she said. 'I was playing golf with Gladys Heywood this morning.'

'Did you beat her?' asked Millicent.

Gladys Heywood was the Canon's only unmarried daughter.

'She told me something about you which I think you ought to know.'

Millicent's eyes passed beyond her sister to the little girl watering flowers in the garden.

'Have you told Annie to give Joan her tea in the kitchen, Mother?' she said.

'Yes, she'll have it when the servants have theirs.'

Kathleen looked at her sister coolly.

'The Bishop spent two or three days at Singapore on his way home,' she went on. 'He's very fond of travelling. He's been to Borneo and he knows a good many of the people that you know.'

'He'll be interested to see you, dear,' said Mrs Skinner. 'Did he know poor Harold?'

'Yes, he met him at Kuala Solor. He remembers him very well. He says he was shocked to hear of his death.'

Millicent sat down and began to put on her black gloves. It seemed strange to Mrs Skinner that she received these remarks with complete silence.

'Oh, Millicent,' she said, 'Harold's photo has disappeared. Have you taken it?'

'Yes, I put it away.'

'I should have thought you'd like to have it out.'

Once more Millicent said nothing. It really was an exasperating habit.

Kathleen turned slightly in order to face her sister.

'Millicent, why did you tell us that Harold died of fever?'

The widow made no gesture, she looked at Kathleen with steady eyes, but her sallow skin darkened with a flush. She did not reply.

'What do you mean, Kathleen?' asked Mr Skinner, with surprise.

'The Bishop says that Harold committed suicide.'

Mrs Skinner gave a startled cry, but her husband put out a deprecating hand.

'Is it true, Millicent?'

'It is.'

'But why didn't you tell us?'

Millicent paused for an instant. She fingered idly a piece of Brunei brass which stood on the table by her side. That too had been a present from Harold.

'I thought it better for Joan that her father should be thought to have died of fever. I didn't want her to know anything about it.'

'You've put us in an awfully awkward position,' said Kathleen, frowning a little. 'Gladys Heywood said she thought it rather nasty of me not to have told her the truth. I had the greatest difficulty in getting her to believe that I knew absolutely nothing about it. She said her father was rather put out. He says, after all the years we've known one another, and considering that he married you, and the terms we've been on, and all that, he does think we might have had confidence in him. And at all events if we didn't want to tell him the truth we needn't have told him a lie.'

'I must say I sympathise with him there,' said Mrs Skinner acidly.

'Of course I told Gladys that we weren't to blame. We only told them what you told us.'

'I hope it didn't put you off your game,' said Millicent.

'Really, my dear, I think that is a most improper observation,' exclaimed her father.

He rose from his chair, walked over to the empty fireplace, and from force of habit stood in front of it with parted coat-tails.

'It was my business,' said Millicent, 'and if I chose to keep it to myself I didn't see why I shouldn't.'

'It doesn't look as if you had any affection for your mother if you didn't even tell her,' said Mrs Skinner.

Millicent shrugged her shoulders.

'You might have known it was bound to come out,' said Kathleen.

'Why? I didn't expect that two gossiping old parsons would have nothing else to talk about than me.'

'When the Bishop said he'd been to Borneo it's only natural that the Heywoods should ask him if he knew you and Harold.'

'All that's neither here nor there,' said Mr Skinner. 'I think you should certainly have told us the truth and we could have decided what was the best thing to do. As a solicitor I can tell you that in the long run it only makes things worse if you attempt to hide them.'

'Poor Harold,' said Mrs Skinner, and the tears began to trickle down her raddled cheeks. 'It seems dreadful. He was always a good son-in-law to me. Whatever induced him to do such a dreadful thing?'

'The climate.'

'I think you'd better give us all the facts, Millicent,' said her father.

'Kathleen will tell you.'

Kathleen hesitated. What she had to say really was rather dreadful. It seemed terrible that such things should happen to a family like theirs.

'The Bishop says he cut his throat.'

Mrs Skinner gasped and she went impulsively up to her bereaved daughter. She wanted to fold her in her arms.

'My poor child,' she sobbed.

But Millicent withdrew herself.

'Please don't fuss me, Mother. I really can't stand being mauled about.'

'Really, Millicent,' said Mr Skinner, with a frown.

He did not think she was behaving very nicely.

Mrs Skinner dabbed her eyes carefully with her handkerchief and with a sigh and a little shake of the head returned to her chair. Kathleen fidgeted with the long chain she wore round her neck.

'It does seem rather absurd that I should have to be told the details of my brother-in-law's death by a friend. It makes us all look such fools. The Bishop wants very much to see you, Millicent; he wants to tell you how much he feels for you.' She paused, but Millicent did not speak. 'He says that Millicent had been away with Joan and when she came back she found poor Harold lying dead on his bed.'

'It must have been a great shock,' said Mr Skinner.

Mrs Skinner began to cry again, but Kathleen put her hand gently on her shoulder.

'Don't cry, Mother,' she said. 'It'll make your eyes red and people will think it so funny.'

They were all silent while Mrs Skinner, drying her eyes, made a successful effort to control herself. It seemed very strange to her that at this very moment she should be wearing in her toque the ospreys that poor Harold had given her.

'There's something else I ought to tell you,' said Kathleen.

Millicent looked at her sister again, without haste, and her eyes were steady, but watchful. She had the look of a person who is waiting for a sound which he is afraid of missing.

'I don't want to say anything to wound you, dear,' Kathleen went on, 'but there's something else and I think you ought to know it. The Bishop says that Harold drank.'

'Oh, my dear, how dreadful!' cried Mrs Skinner. 'What a shocking thing to say. Did Gladys Heywood tell you? What did you say?'

'I said it was entirely untrue.'

'This is what comes of making secrets of things,' said Mr Skinner irritably. 'It's always the same. If you try and hush a thing up all sorts of rumours get about which are ten times worse than the truth.'

'They told the Bishop in Singapore that Harold had killed himself while he was suffering from delirium tremens. I think for all our sakes you ought to deny that, Millicent.'

'It's such a dreadful thing to have said about anyone who's dead,' said Mrs Skinner. 'And it'll be so bad for Joan when she grows up.'

'But what is the foundation of this story, Millicent?' asked her father. 'Harold was always very abstemious.'

'Here,' said the widow.

'Did he drink?'

'Like a fish.'

The answer was so unexpected, and the tone so sardonic, that all three of them were startled.

'Millicent, how can you talk like that of your husband when he's dead?' cried her mother, clasping her neatly gloved hands. 'I can't understand you. You've been so strange since you came back. I could never have believed that a girl of mine could take her husband's death like that.'

'Never mind about that, Mother,' said Mr Skinner. 'We can go into all that later.'

He walked to the window and looked out at the sunny little garden, and then walked back into the room. He took his pince-nez out of his pocket and, though he had no intention of putting them on, wiped them with his handkerchief. Millicent looked at him and in her eyes, unmistakably, was a look of irony which was quite cynical. Mr Skinner was vexed. He had finished his week's work and he was a free man till Monday morning. Though he had told his wife that his garden party was a great nuisance and he would much sooner have tea quietly in his own garden, he had been looking forward to it. He did not care very much about Chinese missions, but it would be interesting to meet the Bishop. And now this! It was not the kind of thing he cared to be mixed up in; it was most unpleasant to be told on a sudden that his son-in-law was a drunkard and a suicide. Millicent was thoughtfully smoothing her white cuffs. Her coolness irritated him; but instead of addressing her he spoke to his younger daughter.

'Why don't you sit down, Kathleen? Surely there are plenty of chairs in the room.'

Kathleen drew forward a chair and without a word seated herself. Mr Skinner stopped in front of Millicent and faced her.

'Of course I see why you told us Harold had died of fever. I think it was a mistake, because that sort of thing is bound to come out sooner or later. I don't know how far what the Bishop has told the Heywoods coincides with the facts, but if you will take my advice you will tell us everything as circumstantially as you can, then we can see. We can't hope that it will go no further now that Canon Heywood and Gladys know. In a place like this people are bound to talk. It will make it easier for all of us if we at all events know the exact truth.'

Mrs Skinner and Kathleen thought he put the matter very well. They waited for Millicent's reply. She had listened with an impassive face; that sudden flush had disappeared and it was once more, as usual, pasty and sallow.

'I don't think you'll much like the truth if I tell it you,' she said.

'You must know that you can count on our sympathy and understanding,' said Kathleen gravely.

Millicent gave her a glance and the shadow of a smile flickered across her set mouth. She looked slowly at the three of them. Mrs Skinner had an uneasy impression that she looked at them as though they were mannequins at a dressmaker's. She seemed to live in a different world from theirs and to have no connection with them.

'You know, I wasn't in love with Harold when I married him,' she said reflectively.

Mrs Skinner was on the point of making an exclamation when a rapid gesture of her husband, barely indicated, but after so many years of married life perfectly significant, stopped her. Millicent went on. She spoke with a level voice, slowly, and there was little change of expression in her tone.

'I was twenty-seven, and no one else seemed to want to marry me. It's true he was forty-four, and it seemed rather old, but he had a very good position, hadn't he? I wasn't likely to get a better chance.'

Mrs Skinner felt inclined to cry again, but she remembered the party.

'Of course I see now why you took his photograph away,' she said dolefully.

'Don't, Mother,' exclaimed Kathleen.

It had been taken when he was engaged to Millicent and was a very good photograph of Harold. Mrs Skinner had always thought him quite a fine man. He was heavily built, tall and perhaps a little too fat, but he held himself well, and his presence was imposing. He was inclined to be bald, even then, but men did go bald very early nowadays, and he said that topees, sun-helmets, you know, were very bad for the hair. He had a small dark moustache and his face was deeply burned by the sun. Of course his best feature was his eyes; they were brown and large, like Joan's. His conversation was interesting. Kathleen said he was pompous, but Mrs Skinner didn't think him so, she didn't mind it if a man laid down the law; and when she saw, as she very soon did, that he was attracted by Millicent she began to like him very much. He was always very attentive to Mrs Skinner and she listened as though she were really interested when he spoke of his district and told her of the big game he had killed. Kathleen said he had a pretty good opinion of himself, but Mrs Skinner came of a generation which accepted without question the good opinion that men had of themselves. Millicent saw very soon which way the wind blew and, though she said nothing to her mother, her mother knew that if Harold asked her she was going to accept him.

Harold was staying with some people who had been thirty years in Borneo and they spoke well of the country. There was no reason why a woman shouldn't live there comfortably; of course the children had to come home when they were seven; but Mrs Skinner thought it unnecessary to trouble about that yet. She asked Harold to dine and she told him they were always in to tea. He seemed to be at a loose end and when his visit to his old friends was drawing to a close she told him they would be very much pleased if he would come and spend a fortnight with them. It was towards the end of this that Harold and Millicent became engaged. They had a very pretty wedding, they went to Venice for their honeymoon, and then they started for the East. Millicent wrote from the various ports at which the ship touched. She seemed happy.

'People were very nice to me at Kuala Solor,' she said. Kuala

Solor was the chief town of the state of Sembulu. 'We stayed with
the Resident and everyone asked us to dinner. Once or twice I
heard men ask Harold to have a drink but he refused; he said he
had turned over a new leaf now he was a married man. I didn't
know why they laughed. Mrs Gray, the Resident's wife, told me
they were all so glad Harold was married. She said it was dreadfully lonely for a bachelor on one of the outstations. When we left
Kuala Solor Mrs Gray said good-bye to me so funnily that I was
quite surprised. It was as if she was solemnly putting Harold in
my charge.'

They listened to her in silence. Kathleen never took her eyes off
her sister's impassive face, but Mr Skinner stared straight in front
of him at the Malay arms, krises and parangs, which hung on the
wall above the sofa on which his wife sat.

'It wasn't till I went back to Kuala Solor a year and a half later
that I found out why their manner had seemed so odd.' Millicent
gave a queer little sound like the echo of a scornful laugh. 'I knew
then a good deal that I hadn't known before. Harold came to
England that time in order to marry. He didn't much mind who
it was. Do you remember how we spread ourselves out to catch
him, Mother? We needn't have taken so much trouble.'

'I don't know what you mean, Millicent,' said Mrs Skinner, not
without acerbity, for the insinuation of scheming did not please
her. 'I saw he was attracted by you.'

Millicent shrugged her heavy shoulders.

'He was a confirmed drunkard. He used to go to bed every
night with a bottle of whisky and empty it before morning. The
Chief Secretary told him he'd have to resign unless he stopped
drinking. He said he'd give him one more chance. He could take
his leave then and go to England. He advised him to marry so
that when he got back he'd have someone to look after him.
Harold married me because he wanted a keeper. They took bets
in Kuala Solor on how long I'd make him stay sober.'

'But he was in love with you,' Mrs Skinner interrupted. 'You
don't know how he used to speak to me about you, and at that
time you're speaking of, when you went to Kuala Solor to have
Joan, he wrote me such a charming letter about you.'

Millicent looked at her mother again and a deep colour dyed
her sallow skin. Her hands, lying on her lap, began to tremble a
little. She thought of those first months of her married life. The
Government launch took them to the mouth of the river and they
spent the night at the bungalow which Harold said jokingly was
their seaside residence. Next day they went upstream in a prahu.
From the novels she had read she expected the rivers of Borneo
to be dark and strangely sinister, but the sky was blue, dappled

with little white clouds, and the green of the mangroves and the nipas, washed by the flowing water, glistened in the sun. On each side stretched the pathless jungle, and in the distance, silhouetted against the sky, was the rugged outline of a mountain. The air in the early morning was fresh and buoyant. She seemed to enter upon a friendly, fertile land, and she had a sense of spacious freedom. They watched the banks for monkeys sitting on the branches of the tangled trees and once Harold pointed out something that looked like a log and said it was a crocodile. The Assistant Resident, in ducks and a topee, was at the landing stage to meet them, and a dozen trim little soldiers were lined up to do them honour. The Assistant Resident was introduced to her. His name was Simpson.

'By Jove, sir,' he said to Harold, 'I'm glad to see you back. It's been deuced lonely without you.'

The Resident's bungalow, surrounded by a garden in which grew wildly all manner of gay flowers, stood on the top of a low hill. It was a trifle shabby and the furniture was sparse, but the rooms were cool and of generous size.

'The kampong is down there,' said Harold, pointing.

Her eyes followed his gesture, and from among the coconut trees rose the beating of a gong. It gave her a queer little sensation in the heart.

Though she had nothing much to do the days passed easily enough. At dawn a boy brought them their tea and they lounged about the veranda, enjoying the fragrance of the morning (Harold in a singlet and a sarong, she in a dressing gown), till it was time to dress for breakfast. Then Harold went to his office and she spent an hour or two learning Malay. After tiffin he went back to his office while she slept. A cup of tea revived them both and they went for a walk or played golf on the nine-hole links which Harold had made on a level piece of cleared jungle below the bungalow. Night fell at six and Mr Simpson came along to have a drink. They chatted till their late dinner hour, and sometimes Harold and Mr Simpson played chess. The balmy evenings were enchanting. The fireflies turned the bushes just below the veranda into coldly sparkling, tremulous beacons, and flowering trees scented the air with sweet odours. After dinner they read the papers which had left London six weeks before and presently went to bed. Millicent enjoyed being a married woman, with a house of her own, and she was pleased with the native servants, in their gay sarongs, who went about the bungalow, with bare feet, silent but friendly. It gave her a pleasant sense of importance to be the wife of the Resident. Harold impressed her by the fluency with which he spoke the language, by his air of command, and by his dignity.

She went into the courthouse now and then to hear him try cases. The multifariousness of his duties and the competent way in which he performed them aroused her respect. Mr Simpson told her that Harold understood the natives as well as any man in the country. He had the combination of firmness, tact, and good humour which was essential in dealing with that timid, revengeful, and suspicious race. Millicent began to feel a certain admiration for her husband.

They had been married nearly a year when two English naturalists came to stay with them for a few days on their way to the interior. They brought a pressing recommendation from the Governor and Harold said he wanted to do them proud. Their arrival was an agreeable change. Millicent asked Mr Simpson to dinner (he lived at the Fort and only dined with them on Sunday nights) and after dinner the men sat down to play bridge. Millicent left them presently and went to bed, but they were so noisy that for some time she could not get to sleep. She did not know at what hour she was awakened by Harold staggering into the room. She kept silent. He made up his mind to have a bath before getting into bed; the bath-house was just below their room and he went down the steps that led to it. Apparently he slipped, for there was a great clatter, and he began to swear. Then he was violently sick. She heard him sluice the buckets of water over himself and in a little while, walking very cautiously this time, he crawled up the stairs and slipped into bed. Millicent pretended to be asleep. She was disgusted. Harold was drunk. She made up her mind to speak about it in the morning. What would the naturalists think of him? But in the morning Harold was so dignified that she hadn't quite the determination to refer to the matter. At eight Harold and she, with their two guests, sat down to breakfast. Harold looked round the table.

'Porridge,' he said. 'Millicent, your guests might manage a little Worcester Sauce for breakfast, but I don't think they'll much fancy anything else. Personally I shall content myself with a whisky and soda.'

The naturalists laughed, but shamefacedly.

'Your husband's a terror,' said one of them.

'I should not think I had properly performed the duties of hospitality if I sent you sober to bed on the first night of your visit,' said Harold, with his round, stately way of putting things.

Millicent, smiling acidly, was relieved to think that her guests had been as drunk as her husband. The next evening she sat up with them and the party broke up at a reasonable hour. But she was glad when the strangers went on with their journey. Their life resumed its placid course. Some months later Harold went on a tour of inspection of his district and came back with a bad attack of malaria. This was the first time she had seen the disease of which she had heard so much, and when he recovered it did not seem strange to her that Harold was very shaky. She found his manner peculiar. He would come back from the office and stare at her with glazed eyes; he would stand on the veranda, swaying slightly, but still dignified, and make long harangues about the political situation in England; losing the thread of his discourse, he would look at her with an archness which his natural stateliness made somewhat disconcerting and say:

'Pulls you down dreadfully, this confounded malaria. Ah, little woman, you little know the strain it puts upon a man to be an empire builder.'

She thought that Mr Simpson began to look worried, and once or twice, when they were alone, he seemed on the point of saying something to her which his shyness at the last moment prevented. The feeling grew so strong that it made her nervous and one evening when Harold, she knew not why, had remained later than usual at the office she tackled him.

'What have you got to say to me, Mr Simpson?' she broke out suddenly.

He blushed and hesitated.

'Nothing. What makes you think I have anything in particular to say to you?'

Mr Simpson was a thin, weedy youth of four and twenty, with a fine head of waving hair which he took great pains to plaster down very flat. His wrists were swollen and scarred with mosquito bites. Millicent looked at him steadily.

'If it's something to do with Harold, don't you think it would be kinder to tell me frankly?'

He grew scarlet now. He shuffled uneasily on his rattan chair. She insisted.

'I'm afraid you'll think it awful cheek,' he said at last. 'It's rotten of me to say anything about my chief behind his back. Malaria's a rotten thing and after one's had a bout of it one feels awfully down and out.'

He hesitated again. The corners of his mouth sagged as if he were going to cry. To Millicent he seemed like a little boy.

'I'll be as silent as the grave,' she said with a smile, trying to conceal her apprehension. 'Do tell me.'

'I think it's a pity your husband keeps a bottle of whisky at the office. He's apt to take a nip more often than he otherwise would.'

Mr Simpson's voice was hoarse with agitation. Millicent felt a sudden coldness shiver through her. She controlled herself, for she knew that she must not frighten the boy if she were to get out of him all there was to tell. He was unwilling to speak. She pressed him, wheedling, appealing to his sense of duty, and at last she began to cry. Then he told her that Harold had been drunk more or less for the last fortnight, the natives were talking about it, and they said that soon he would be as bad as he had been before his marriage. He had been in the habit of drinking a good deal too much then, but details of that time, notwithstanding all her attempts, Mr Simpson resolutely declined to give her.

'Do you think he's drinking now?' she asked.

'I don't know.'

Millicent felt herself on a sudden hot with shame and anger. The Fort, as it was called because the rifles and ammunition were kept there, was also the courthouse. It stood opposite the Resident's bungalow in a garden of its own. The sun was just about to set and she did not need a hat. She got up and walked across. She found Harold sitting in the office behind the large hall in which he administered justice. There was a bottle of whisky in front of him. He was smoking cigarettes and talking to three or four Malays who stood in front of him listening with obsequious and at the same time scornful smiles. His face was red.

The natives vanished.

'I came to see what you were doing,' she said.

He rose, for he always treated her with elaborate politeness, and lurched. Feeling himself unsteady he assumed an elaborate stateliness of demeanour.

'Take a seat, my dear, take a seat. I was detained by press of work.'

She looked at him with angry eyes.

'You're drunk,' she said.

He stared at her, his eyes bulging a little, and a haughty look gradually traversed his large and fleshy face.

'I haven't the remotest idea what you mean,' he said.

She had been ready with a flow of wrathful expostulation, but suddenly she burst into tears. She sank into a chair and hid her face. Harold looked at her for an instant, then the tears began to trickle down his cheeks; he came towards her with outstretched arms and fell heavily on his knees. Sobbing, he clasped her to him.

'Forgive me, forgive me,' he said. 'I promise you it shall not happen again. It was that damned malaria.'

'It's so humiliating,' she moaned.

He wept like a child. There was something very touching in the self-abasement of that big dignified man. Presently Millicent looked up. His eyes, appealing and contrite, sought hers.

'Will you give me your word of honour that you'll never touch liquor again?'

'Yes, yes. I hate it.'

It was then she told him that she was with child. He was overjoyed.

'That is the one thing I wanted. That'll keep me straight.'

They went back to the bungalow. Harold bathed himself and had a nap. After dinner they talked long and quietly. He admitted that before he married her he had occasionally drunk more than was good for him: in outstations it was easy to fall into bad habits. He agreed to everything that Millicent asked. And during the months before it was necessary for her to go to Kuala Solor for her confinement Harold was an excellent husband, tender, thoughtful, proud and affectionate: he was irreproachable. A launch came to fetch her, she was to leave him for six weeks, and he promised faithfully to drink nothing during her absence. He put his hands on her shoulders.

'I never break a promise,' he said in his dignified way. 'But even without it, can you imagine that while you are going through so much, I should do anything to increase your troubles?'

Joan was born. Millicent stayed at the Resident's and Mrs Gray, his wife, a kindly creature of middle age, was very good to her. The two women had little to do during the long hours they were alone but to talk, and in course of time Millicent learnt everything there was to know of her husband's alcoholic past. The fact which she found most difficult to reconcile herself to was that Harold had been told that the only condition upon which he would be allowed to keep his post was that he should bring back a wife. It caused in her a dull feeling of resentment. And when she discovered what a persistent drunkard he had been she felt vaguely uneasy. She had a horrid fear that during her absence he would not have been able to resist the craving. She went home with her baby and a nurse. She spent a night at the mouth of the river and sent a messenger in a canoe to announce her arrival. She scanned the landing stage anxiously as the launch approached it. Harold and Mr Simpson were standing there. The trim little soldiers were lined up. Her heart sank, for Harold was swaying slightly, like a man who seeks to keep his balance on a rolling ship, and she knew he was drunk.

It wasn't a very pleasant home-coming. She had almost forgotten her mother and father and her sister who sat there silently listening to her. Now she roused herself and became once more aware of their presence. All that she spoke of seemed very far away.

'I knew that I hated him then,' she said. 'I could have killed him.'

'Oh, Millicent, don't say that,' cried her mother. 'Don't forget that he's dead, poor man.'

Millicent looked at her mother, and for a moment a scowl darkened her impassive face. Mr Skinner moved uneasily.

'Go on,' said Kathleen.

'When he found out that I knew all about him he didn't bother very much more. In three months he had another attack of d.t.'s.'

'Why didn't you leave him?' said Kathleen.

'What would have been the good of that? He would have been dismissed from the service in a fortnight. Who was to keep me and Joan? I had to stay. And when he was sober I had nothing to complain of. He wasn't in the least in love with me, but he was fond of me: I hadn't married him because I was in love with him but because I wanted to be married. I did everything I could to keep liquor from him; I managed to get Mr Gray to prevent whisky being sent from Kuala Solor, but he got it from the Chinese. I watched him as a cat watches a mouse. He was too cunning for me. In a little while he had another outbreak. He neglected his duties. I was afraid complaints would be made. We were two days from Kuala Solor and that was our safeguard, but I suppose something was said, for Mr Gray wrote a private letter of warning to me. I showed it to Harold. He stormed and blustered, but I saw he was frightened, and for two or three months he was quite sober. Then he began again. And so it went on till our leave became due.

'Before we came to stay here I begged and prayed him to be careful. I didn't want any of you to know what sort of man I had married. All the time he was in England he was all right and before we sailed I warned him. He'd grown to be very fond of Joan, and very proud of her, and she was devoted to him. She always liked him better than she liked me. I asked him if he wanted to have his child grow up knowing that he was a drunkard, and I found out that at last I'd got a hold on him. The thought terrified him. I told him that I wouldn't allow it, and if he ever let Joan see him drunk I'd take her away from him at once. Do you know, he grew quite pale when I said it. I fell on my knees that night and thanked God because I'd found a way of saving my husband.

'He told me that if I would stand by him he would have another try. We made up our minds to fight the thing together. And he tried so hard. When he felt as though he *must* drink he came to me. You know he was inclined to be rather pompous: with me he was humble, he was like a child; he depended on me. Perhaps he didn't love me when he married me, but he loved me then, me and Joan. I'd hated him, because of the humiliation, because when he was drunk and tried to be dignified and impressive he was loathsome; but now I got a strange feeling in my heart. It wasn't love, but it was a queer, shy tenderness. He was something more than my husband, he was like a child that I'd carried under my heart for long and weary months. He was so proud of me and you know, I was proud too. His long speeches didn't irritate me any more and I only thought his stately ways rather funny and charming. At last we won. For two years he never touched a drop. He lost his craving entirely. He was even able to joke about it.

'Mr Simpson had left us then and we had another young man called Francis.

' "I'm a reformed drunkard you know, Francis", Harold said to him once. "If it hadn't been for my wife I'd have been sacked long ago. I've got the best wife in the world, Francis."

'You don't know what it meant to me to hear him say that. I felt that all I'd gone through was worth while. I was so happy.'

She was silent. She thought of the broad, yellow and turbid river on whose banks she had lived so long. The egrets, white and gleaming in the tremulous sunset, flew down the stream in a flock, flew low and swift, and scattered. They were like a ripple of snowy notes, sweet and pure and springlike, which an unseen hand drew forth, a divine arpeggio, from an unseen harp. They fluttered along between the green banks, wrapped in the shadows of evening, like the happy thoughts of a contented mind.

'Then Joan fell ill. For three weeks we were very anxious. There was no doctor nearer than Kuala Solor and we had to put up with the treatment of a native dispenser. When she grew well again I took her down to the mouth of the river in order to give her a breath of sea air. We stayed there a week. It was the first time I had been separated from Harold since I went away to have Joan. There was a fishing village, on piles, not far from us, but really we were quite alone. I thought a great deal about Harold, so tenderly, and all at once I knew that I loved him. I was so glad when the prahu came to fetch us back, because I wanted to tell him. I thought it would mean a good deal to him. I can't tell you how happy I was. As we rowed upstream the headman told me that Mr Francis had had to go up country to arrest a woman who had murdered her husband. He had been gone a couple of days.

'I was surprised that Harold was not on the landing stage to meet me; he was always very punctilious about that sort of thing; he used to say that husband and wife should treat one another as politely as they treated acquaintances; and I could not imagine what business had prevented him. I walked up the little hill on which the bungalow stood. The ayah brought Joan behind me. The bungalow was strangely silent. There seemed to be no servants about and I could not make it out; I wondered if Harold hadn't expected me so soon and was out. I went up the steps. Joan was thirsty and the ayah took her to the servants' quarters to give her something to drink. Harold was not in the sitting room. I called him, but there was no answer. I was disappointed, because I should have liked him to be there. I went into our bedroom. Harold wasn't out after all: he was lying on the bed asleep. I was really very much amused because he always pretended he never slept in the afternoon. He said it was an unnecessary habit that we white people got into. I went up to the bed softly. I thought I would have a joke with him. I opened the mosquito curtains. He was lying on his back, with nothing on but a sarong, and there was an empty whisky bottle by his side. He was drunk.

'It had begun again. All my struggles for so many years were wasted. My dream was shattered. It was all hopeless. I was seized with rage.'

Millicent's face grew once again darkly red and she clenched the arms of the chair she sat in.

'I took him by the shoulders and shook him with all my might. "You beast," I cried, "you beast." I was so angry I don't know what I did, I don't know what I said. I kept on shaking him. You don't know how loathsome he looked, that large fat man, half naked; he hadn't shaved for days, and his face was bloated and purple. He was breathing heavily. I shouted at him, but he took no notice. I tried to drag him out of bed, but he was too heavy. He lay there like a log. "Open your eyes," I screamed. I shook him again. I hated him. I hated him all the more because for a week I'd loved him with all my heart. He'd let me down. He'd let me down. I wanted to tell him what a filthy beast he was. I could make no impression on him. "You shall open your eyes," I cried. I was determined to make him look at me.'

The widow licked her dry lips. Her breath seemed hurried. She was silent.

'If he was in that state I should have thought it best to have let him go on sleeping,' said Kathleen.

'There was a parang on the wall by the side of the bed. You know how fond Harold was of curios.'

'What's a parang?' said Mrs Skinner.

'Don't be silly, Mother,' her husband replied irritably. 'There's one on the wall immediately behind you.'

He pointed to the Malay sword on which for some reason his eyes had been unconsciously resting. Mrs Skinner drew quickly

into the corner of the sofa, with a little frightened gesture, as
though she had been told that a snake lay curled up beside her.

'Suddenly the blood spurted out from Harold's throat. There
was a great red gash across it.

'Millicent,' cried Kathleen, springing up and almost leaping
towards her, 'what in God's name do you mean?'

Mrs Skinner stood staring at her with wide startled eyes, her
mouth open.

'The parang wasn't on the wall any more. It was on the bed.
Then Harold opened his eyes. They were just like Joan's.'

'I don't understand,' said Mr Skinner. 'How could he have
committed suicide if he was in the state you describe?'

Kathleen took her sister's arm and shook her angrily.

'Millicent, for God's sake, explain.'

Millicent released herself.

'The parang was on the wall, I told you. I don't know what
happened. There was all the blood and Harold opened his eyes.
He died almost at once. He never spoke, but he gave a sort of
gasp.'

At last Mr Skinner found his voice.

'But, you wretched woman, it was murder.'

Millicent, her face mottled with red, gave him such a look of
scornful hatred that he shrank back. Mrs Skinner cried out.

'Millicent, you didn't do it, did you?'

Then Millicent did something that made them all feel as though
their blood were turned to ice in their veins. She chuckled.

'I don't know who else did,' she said.

'My God,' muttered Mr Skinner.

Kathleen had been standing bolt upright, with her hands to her
heart, as though its beating were intolerable.

'And what happened then?' she said.

'I screamed. I went to the window and flung it open. I called
for the ayah. She came across the compound with Joan. "Not
Joan," I cried. "Don't let her come." She called the cook and told
him to take the child. I cried to her to hurry. And when she came
I showed her Harold. "The Tuan's killed himself!" I cried. She
gave a scream and ran out of the house.

'No one would come near. They were all frightened out of their
wits. I wrote a letter to Mr Francis, telling him what had happened,
and asking him to come at once.'

'How do you mean you told him what had happened?'

'I said, on my return from the mouth of the river, I'd found
Harold with his throat cut. You know, in the tropics you have to
bury people quickly. I got a Chinese coffin, and the soldiers dug
a grave behind the Fort. When Mr Francis came Harold had been

buried for nearly two days. He was only a boy. I could do anything I wanted with him. I told him I'd found the parang in Harold's hand and there was no doubt he'd killed himself in an attack of delirium tremens. I showed him the empty bottle. The servants said he'd been drinking hard ever since I left to go to the sea. I told the same story at Kuala Solor. Everyone was very kind to me, and the Government granted me a pension.'

For a little while nobody spoke. At last Mr Skinner gathered himself together.

'I am a member of the legal profession. I'm a solicitor. I have certain duties. We've always had a most respectable practice. You've put me in a monstrous position.'

He fumbled, searching for the phrases that played at hide and seek in his scattered wits. Millicent looked at him with scorn.

'What are you going to do about it?'

'It was murder, that's what it was; do you think I can possibly connive at it?'

'Don't talk nonsense, Father,' said Kathleen sharply. 'You can't give your own daughter up.'

'You've put me in a monstrous position,' he repeated.

Millicent shrugged her shoulders again.

'You made me tell you. And I've borne it long enough by myself. It was time that all of you bore it too.'

At that moment the door was opened by the maid.

'Davis has brought the car round, sir,' she said.

Kathleen had the presence of mind to say something, and the maid withdrew.

'We'd better be starting,' said Millicent.

'I can't go to the party now,' cried Mrs Skinner, with horror. 'I'm far too upset. How can we face the Heywoods? And the Bishop will want to be introduced to you.'

Millicent made a gesture of indifference. Her eyes held their ironical expression.

'We must go, Mother,' said Kathleen. 'It would look so funny if we stayed away.' She turned on Millicent furiously. 'Oh, I think the whole thing is such frightfully bad form.'

Mrs Skinner looked helplessly at her husband. He went to her and gave her his hand to help her from the sofa.

'I'm afraid we must go, Mother,' he said.

'And me with the ospreys in my toque that Harold gave me with his own hands,' she moaned.

He led her out of the room, Kathleen followed close on their heels, and a step or two behind came Millicent.

'You'll get used to it, you know,' she said quietly. 'At first I thought of it all the time, but now I forget it for two or three days together. It's not as if there was any danger.'

They did not answer. They walked through the hall and out of the front door. The three ladies got into the back of the car and Mr Skinner seated himself beside the driver. They had no self-starter; it was an old car, and Davis went to the bonnet to crank it up. Mr Skinner turned round and looked petulantly at Millicent.

'I ought never to have been told,' he said. 'I think it was most selfish of you.'

Davis took his seat and they drove off to the Canon's garden party.

A BOTTLE OF GIN

Robert Bloch

Robert Bloch (1917-) is famous as the author of Psycho *(1959), the novel which Alfred Hitchcock adapted into probably the most popular horror film ever made. He is also one of the most highly regarded writers of short stories in the same genre, ranging from outright terror to graveyard humour. A most convivial man by nature, he can endow even the most ordinary objects with frightening possibilities—as he demonstrates in 'A Bottle of Gin'. It is a mystery story tinged with Bloch's knowledge of the supernatural and his clever use of black humour to illustrate yet another of the dangers of drink.*

Mr Collins scampered up the steps. His twitching chin, long, wobbly ears, and pinkly bloodshot eyes gave him the appearance of a frightened rabbit. Rabbit-fashion, he glanced fearfully over his shoulder, then scurried into the burrow of the building.

Little Mr Collins bounded down a long hall on short legs. The museum corridor was deserted, but his pink eyes revolved fearfully. With a sigh of relief, he made for a door marked *Curator's Office* and hurried inside.

The young lady in the outer waiting room rose from her desk with a look of vague solicitude.

'Tom,' she exclaimed. 'Tom—where have you been? You worried me sick these past three days. Why didn't you call me?'

Mr Collins gave her a fleeting glance.

'Sorry, Edith. I can't explain now. Is the Doctor in?'

The young lady marched around the desk. Her lips curled, not in solicitude, but in sudden scorn.

'Tom—you've been drinking again! Out on another bender, I suppose. Just look at you! A fine wreck you are. Haven't been to bed for three days, I suppose.'

Little Mr Collins groaned. 'That's right. I haven't. But it's not what you think, Edith, honest it's not. I haven't touched a drop—'

'Huh!' Edith snorted scornfully. It was a most unpleasant sound, and Mr Collins winced. Then he straightened.

'I've got to see Doctor Sweet at once,' he insisted.

'He's busy. Can't be disturbed. Now, Tom, look at me! I want you to explain right this instant just what you've been up to and—'

Mr Collins suddenly darted past her and whirled through an inner door. His sweaty palm locked it behind him.

He stood, gasping for breath, in Doctor Sweet's private office. The Curator's sanctum was large, and necessarily so. For the room was literally and incredibly stuffed with objects. Rows of books. Shelves of books. Piles of books. Statuary. Idols. Figurines. Tables filled with jars. Tables filled with vases. Tables filled with bottles. The floor was carpeted with papers and manuscripts. The desk in the centre of the room was completely submerged beneath a miscellany of paraphernalia.

It took a full minute before Mr Collins was able to detect the figure of Doctor Sweet, buried behind the debris on his desk. Then the Doctor rose, as if to fully establish his presence.

'Well?' said the old man. His hands raked upward over a dome-like forehead and into a tangle of bushy white hair. They finally encountered a pair of spectacles, which Doctor Sweet now drew down to eye level.

'By Bel and Astarte!' he exclaimed. 'Collins!'

Little Mr Collins took a step forward and gulped. 'I'm back,' he announced.

'So I see. Burn me in Moloch's mouth if you aren't! Have you got it, man? Have you got it?'

'Here.'

Mr Collins fumbled inside his coat, drew out an object wrapped in tissue-paper.

Doctor Sweet grabbed for it with careful haste. He undid the wrappings, then cupped the object in his hands.

'Perfect!' he muttered. 'Early Korean. This vase completes the collection. By the Cabala, it's a gem. I congratulate you.'

Mr Collins turned pale. 'You'd better offer me condolences,' he whispered.

'What's the matter?'

'What's the matter? Don't you *know*?'

'I've been very busy, son. Very busy. Going through my collection. Three days now.'

'Well, while you've been going through your collection, I've been going through hell.'

'Very interesting.' Doctor Sweet turned, his hands caressing the tear-vase. 'You must tell me about it some time. Right now I'm very busy. Excuse me.'

'Listen, Doctor.' Collins was tense. 'If you don't hear me now, there may not be another time.'

'Quit talking nonsense, son. I asked you to go up to Mr Sung's house to buy this vase. You've done so. What you've been doing in the past three days does not concern me. Out on a rip-snorter, I'll bet.' The old man cackled suddenly.

Collins lost his temper.

'You make me sick!' he shouted. 'You and your secretary both! Out on a tear, was I? I'll have you know that for the past three days I've been riding the subway in fear of my life.'

'Very dangerous things, subways,' Doctor Sweet observed. 'Never ride them myself.'

Mr Collins uttered a low moan.

'Get this through your head,' he screeched. 'When I went up to Sung's place to buy the vase, his downstairs shop was robbed. Some thugs held up the antique place and we heard them. Sung went down the stairs after them and they shot him. They saw me with the vase in my hand and started after me—three of them. Gorillas.'

'My goodness!' clucked the Doctor, as though humouring a child. 'Must have been after that fine antique collection of his.'

'Of course they were,' Collins wailed. 'But that's not important. They were after me, too.'

'This vase is worth twenty thousand,' the Doctor gloated. 'I don't blame them. By Eblis, I don't at that.'

Collins muttered something under his breath, then recovered. 'So I ran out the back entrance and made for the subway. They followed me. And for the last three days I've been dodging them from train to train. They're after me in shifts. I recognise all three of them now. Naturally I couldn't go to the police because there's no record that Sung sold the vase to me before he was murdered. So I've had to ride the damned trains until I could get away, without sleep or rest or food or—'

'How distressing.' Doctor Sweet placed the vase carefully on a shelf. 'Well, the vase is safe now. Why don't you go home and shave? You look awful.'

Mr Collins danced a cadenza of fright about the room.

'I'll look quite awful if they catch up with me,' he answered. 'I'm afraid to leave for fear they're waiting outside.'

'By the Four Books!' exclaimed the Doctor. 'That's very exciting, isn't it? If I were in your place then, I wouldn't go outside.'

Mr Collins suddenly slumped into a chair.

'What's the matter?'

'I'm dying,' he groaned. 'Dying from hunger. For mercy's sake, get me something to eat.'

'I have a sandwich left from lunch in the other office,' said Doctor Sweet, dubiously. 'Do you care for minced ham?'

'I'll swallow anything,' Collins gasped.

Abruptly, the little man's eyes swivelled to the row of bottles and beakers on the desk. There were tall bottles and small bottles, some stoppered and some open. Green ones and brown ones.

'That's what I need,' he mumbled to himself. 'A drink.'

'What's that?' Doctor Sweet paused at the door.

'I merely asked you what was in that bottle.'

Collins levelled a finger at random, selecting a tall brown bottle which stood apart from the rest at the back of the table.

'That bottle?' Doctor Sweet eyed him curiously.

'Yes.'

The Doctor told Collins in a single word. He left the room.

Two seconds later Collins was at the table. His frantic fingers scrabbled at the bottle, tore at the tight cork. He wrenched it free, held the brown bottle to his lips, and gulped. Then he sank back and tottered over to his chair.

When Doctor Sweet re-entered the room he found Mr Collins sitting slumped in his seat with a most peculiar expression on his face.

Suddenly he gave a little hiccup.

The Doctor ignored it and extended a sandwich.

'Here's the minced ham,' he said.

Collins peered at the offering with pale distaste.

'I don't want it,' he said.

'What's that?'

Collins hiccuped again.

'Something wrong?'

'Hic.'

'Collins—what's the matter?'

'Hic.'

Doctor Sweet shook the little man's shoulders.

'What did you do?' he demanded.

'I—hic—took a swig out of that bottle of—hic—gin you have.'

'Gin?' said Doctor Sweet. 'By Allah's beard, I haven't any gin here.'

'You said so before you left,' Collins accused. 'You told—hic—me that there was gin in that brown bottle.'

'Great jumping dervishes!'

'What's—hic—wrong?'

'I didn't say there was gin in that bottle.'

'No?'

'I said there was a *djinn* in there.'

Doctor Sweet goggled. 'A *djinn*,' he repeated. 'A genie. An elemental spirit imprisoned in a bottle. And you've *swallowed* him!'

Collins nodded weakly.

'I just took a gulp,' he whispered. 'Something went down into my stomach, hard. Hic.'

'Dear me,' the Doctor wailed. 'One of my most priceless treasures, too. That bottle was hundreds of years old. Found off the Persian Gulf. I've always been careful to keep it sealed, too. These *djinn* are terribly dangerous if let free. That's why Solomon imprisoned them. And now you've got to go and swallow one.'

Collins tottered to his feet.

'You mean I have a guy in my stomach?' he croaked. 'Well, get him out of there.' Excitement stifled his hiccups.

Doctor Sweet ran his hand into cottony hair. 'I'm afraid I can't,' he whispered. 'You don't understand. If the *djinn* is released, he'll run wild. You'll just have to keep him there.'

'Not on your life,' Collins announced. 'I want a meal on my stomach, not a midget.'

'That's just it,' the Doctor answered. 'The *djinn* is a small creature when he is imprisoned. But once released, his substance grows like a cloud of smoke. He becomes a huge pillar in human shape. Perhaps fifty feet tall. He wants to destroy, wreak havoc.'

Collins wasn't listening. He was busily engaged in thrusting a finger down his throat.

Doctor Sweet jumped for his hand.

'No, don't!' he gasped. 'He'll escape.'

'I want him to. You think I'm going to walk around with this— monster—inside of me? Get him back in his bottle.'

'I wish I could,' sighed the Doctor. 'But he wouldn't go back. From now on, *you're* his bottle.'

'*Me?*' Collins stared at his paunch. 'I'm a human bottle for some oriental demon?'

'I'm afraid so. We'll just have to find a way out, somehow.'

Collins glanced despairingly at the ham sandwich.

'I'm so hungry,' he wailed. He reached for the bread.

'You can't eat.' Doctor Sweet snatched his hand back. 'Don't you understand? Food will *displace* the *djinn*.'

'What'll we do, then?' Stomach pump?'

'And let him out? Certainly not!'

'You've got to think of something, quick!'

'I know, I know.' The Doctor moved towards the window, head bowed. He wheeled, suddenly. 'Do you snore?'

'Snore? What's that matter?'

'Do you snore?' the Doctor demanded.

'Suppose so.'

'Then,' decided the old man, 'I must forbid you to sleep. Once you fall asleep and let your mouth hang open, the *djinn* comes out.'

'Oh!' groaned Collins. 'Fine help you are!'

'Of course,' the Doctor mused, 'you can have three wishes.'

'Wishes?'

'Yes. It is a custom of *djinns* to offer their captors three wishes before being released. You might make a deal with the *djinn*.'

'How?'

'Maybe you can talk to him,' suggested Doctor Sweet.

'Talk to my own stomach?'

'Ventriloquists do.'

Mr Collins drew a long breath. 'All right,' he muttered. 'All right, then.' He paused. His voice receded peculiarly in his throat.

'Hey! Hey you down there.'

A sound came from Collins' mouth. It wasn't his voice, but a voice spoke. A hollow voice. An entombed voice.

'Yes, Master.'

The actual sound of the reply disconcerted both men. Collins shuddered. When he attempted to go on, he discovered that there was really nothing his trembling voice could say. What would one say to a *djinn* under such circumstances?

'How's—how's things down there?' was the only inanity he could bring forth.

'Very distressing, Master. Please permit me to leave.'

'He wants out,' Collins whispered.

The Doctor nodded. 'Naturally.'

'What about my three wishes?' Collins asked.

The voice from his stomach grew soft. 'But certainly, Master! Three wishes—whatever your esteemed presence desires.'

Collins turned to Doctor Sweet. 'You heard him? Suppose I wish he was back in his bottle?'

Sweet shook his head. 'Wouldn't work, I'm afraid. That's destroying part of the agreement, you see.'

'Yes, I suppose so.'

The Doctor took Collins by the shoulder. 'On second thought, I don't believe it's safe for you to wish at all. Because on the third wish he comes out.'

'But I could make two—'

A voice interrupted them. It was the *djinn*.

'Will you release me then, oh Master?'

'I've got to think about it for a while,' Collins temporised. He

turned to the window with a sigh of despair. His eyes suddenly
revolved in their sockets.

'There!' he breathed. 'Look down there!'

'What's the matter?'

'You see those three men?'

'Yes?'

'They're the gorillas who've been following me. They're coming
in—I've got to get out of here.'

'But the *djinn*—'

'Never mind him.' Collins bolted for the door.

The Doctor wheezed after him.

'Here,' he urged. 'Take this with you. And good luck.' He held
out the brown bottle and its cork. Collins grabbed for them hastily.

'Remember,' warned Doctor Sweet. 'Don't let them shoot you,
or anything. The *djinn* would escape through the holes.'

With a sob, Collins rushed through the door.

The girl in the outer office confronted him with an icy stare. Her
eyes wandered to the bottle he was clutching in his hand.

'So!' she accused.

'But Edith—it's empty. Look?' Collins held it upside down.

'I know it is. Drank it all, did you?'

'I haven't touched a drop,' Collins began.

But another voice broke in.

'Who is this houri, Master?'

Edith whirled.

'What did you say, Tom?'

'Is it your wish that I destroy her?' the *djinn* continued, blandly.

'No, no—nothing.' Collins answered both voices at once. The
effort was too much. He hiccuped softly.

'Tom, you're sick.'

Collins nodded. 'Stomach trouble,' he said.

'Let me get you some bicarbonate,' Edith suggested, softening.

'No, don't. He wouldn't like it.'

'Who wouldn't like it?'

'Why the thing down there—inside me,' Collins began, then
checked himself.

'Are you raving, Tom?'

'I don't know!' The little man's eyes blinked rapidly. 'Let me
out of here,' he commanded. 'Quick! They'll be after me in a
minute.'

'What's after you? Tom Collins—you have d.t.s., that's what's
the matter.'

'Hold your lying tongue, wench.' The voice came from the
stomach.

Edith gasped. As her mouth opened, Collins made a break for the door.

Dodging along the hall, he neared the entrance. Then he halted, sick with sudden dread.

Standing squarely on the steps below were the figures of three men—the stocky little fellow in the blue overcoat, the tall, thin man wearing a derby, and the ugly fat gentleman with his hand significantly inside his coat pocket.

Collins stared into the three blue-jowled faces. He saw tight lips and little eyes; a kaleidoscope of hairy knuckles, protruding jaws, and jutting brows.

They were waiting for him to come out.

Collins slipped the glass bottle into his coat. He crouched back in the doorway and mopped his forehead.

Let them wait, he decided. He was willing. Just as long as he was inside and they were outside—

But they weren't going to stay outside.

Collins saw the three huddle together. The man with the derby whispered, gesturing significantly towards the building. Then the three wheeled. They began to march slowly up the steps.

'Oh, oh!' breathed Collins.

'Master?' inquired the voice from within his stomach.

But 'Master' didn't have the time to reply. With a courage born of desperation alone, Collins decided to dash for it. If he could run through them as they were caught coming up the steps now—

He burst from the building and clattered down the stairs. They saw him coming, attempted to dodge. He cannoned into the trio, hurling his body forward at the fat man in the centre.

With a grunt of surprise, the fat man staggered back. His two companions tripped over his legs, sprawled down the steps.

Mr Collins hurdled their tangled bodies and continued down. Then he turned. They were on their feet again, and this time the fat man waved a gun. He didn't wave it long. He began to point it. He pointed it directly where it would do Mr Collins the least possible good.

Collins looked around wildly for a hole in the pavement. There was none. No place to hide, no place to run to for shelter. He was in the open; a visible target.

'This is it!' he groaned.

'What, Master?'

The voice came through a fog. Then Collins remembered.

'*Djinn*,' he croaked. 'Now's the chance to show your stuff. I wish you'd take care of these babies, quick.'

'Your wish,' echoed the *djinn*, 'is my command.'

Almost without volition, Collins felt himself running towards the man with the gun.

The three hoodlums faced him in astonishment. The fat man steadied his aim, ready to fire. And then—

Collins *felt* it happen. The feeling of growth, stealing along his throat. The trio before him *saw* it happen.

They were gaping at his mouth. It was a small mouth, but from it protruded the largest tongue in the world. Or something.

Something—something long and black. Something muscled and menacing. Something that writhed forth like a snake of smoke, swelling to unbelievable proportions from Collins' opened mouth. Something that waved in the air, extending claws and a fist.

'Look out!' shrilled the thin man, suddenly. 'He's on fire— smoke's coming out of his mouth!'

But it was not smoke that darted forward a dozen feet in advance of the charging Mr Collins.

The fat man realised this when he felt the black column against his chin. He didn't have a chance to realise anything else before he sagged to the pavement.

The gun fell from his hand. His stocky little companion snatched it up and cursed.

'You will, will ya?' he snarled. A shot pumped into the black pillar rising from Collins' throat. It thudded home, but the huge inky paw of smoke merely swirked about his head and descended.

There was the sound of a walnut cracking, magnified ten times.

'Hey!' yelled the third party, as Collins turned, and the horrid limb reared once more. 'Holy Moses!'

But Moses, sanctified or not, did nothing to help him. The black triphammer descended and sent the last man to join his fellows on the ground in a soggy heap.

Slowly, the emanation disappeared from before Mr Collins's face.

He stood there for a moment and rubbed his aching jaws.

'Whew!' he panted. 'How did you do that?'

'It is simple, Master. Any wish of yours—to hear is to obey.'

'Was that really your arm?' Collins asked, weakly.

'Indeed. Am I not many cubits tall?'

'Don't talk about it,' begged the rescued man. 'It upsets my stomach just to think about it.'

'Your other two wishes?' pursued the voice of the *djinn*. 'Perhaps you would like some stomach tablets?' it went on, craftily.

'No, not that,' said Collins. 'Give me a little more time to think.'

'But I desire my freedom from this prison,' the *djinn* complained. 'I am no Jonah.'

'I'm no whale, either,' Collins snapped. 'Believe me, this hurts me more than it does you.'

It was true. Collins had a terrific stomach ache. The *djinn* was moving around down there. Let's see—if it fitted into the brown bottle, it could reduce its size to about four inches. Still, that was quite a bellyful at that.

Too much for Collins. But at the moment, he had other matters to consider.

He took one more glance at the three forms on the pavement. He trembled, thinking of what might have happened if any passersby had chanced to wander down the street while the battle was in progress.

'Must get away before somebody comes along,' he muttered. He started up the block and rounded a corner rapidly. He moved briskly along for ten minutes before slackening his panic-driven pace.

During this time he was becoming more and more aware of the load he carried under his belt. The *djinn*, unused to his queer surroundings, was evidently pacing back and forth.

'Will you kindly cut out walking around inside of me?' Collins begged, hoping no one else was listening.

'Is that a wish?' asked the *djinn*.

'No. Oh, let it go.'

Collins shrugged. An old woman walking ahead of him glanced back. Collins closed his lips and tried to look sedate.

But not in time. A hiccup escaped from his mouth.

'Excuse me,' mumbled Collins.

'Me also,' said the voice from his stomach.

The woman quickly glanced away again.

'Drunken sot,' she muttered.

Collins blushed.

'I wish they wouldn't—' he began then stopped.

No. That wouldn't do. He had to be careful about wishes. He mustn't say he wished he could get some sleep, or some food, or a moment's peace. The price to pay was too great.

Yet he must do something. And quickly. Collins realised the impossibility of his situation. The *djinn* must be disposed of.

'Could I wish he wasn't here?' Collins wondered. 'Or was Doctor Sweet right when he said I couldn't get rid of him that way?'

He glanced down at the brown bottle he still carried under one arm. The *djinn's* bottle. How to get him back in? That was the problem. That's what he must wish for.

Ouch! The *djinn* was evidently doing a tap dance now. Collins patted his stomach gingerly.

'Who's there?' came the voice.

'Oh, shut up!' Collins barked.

A man beside him suddenly shied away. He cast a leering glance at the bottle under Collins' arm.

Collins ducked into an alley.

'Now see what you're doing,' he complained. 'Everybody keeps thinking I'm drunk. This simply can't go on'

'Make a wish,' the *djinn* coaxed.

Collins brandished his brown bottle in futile rage.

Suddenly he smiled, as inspiration came. He stared at the bottle curiously. Here was his solution, after all!

'All right,' he whispered. I'll make a wish. Get this one, *djinn*. And get it right, because this wish is important.'

'To hear is to obey.'

Collins took a deep breath in anticipation. He gloated over the words.

'*I wish this bottle you came in had never even existed!*'

For a moment there was a stunning silence. And then—

Collins felt it in his fingers. A lessening of weight. He glanced down at the bottle he was holding in his hand. But there was no bottle! There was nothing at all between his fingers.

With a curious shock, Collins realised that there never *had* been anything there. He had never carried a bottle, never seen one. He couldn't exactly *remember* what it looked like.

The little man sighed deeply. 'That's that,' he breathed.

'You spoke, Master?'

The incredible voice, again. And still from his stomach.

'What the—thought you were gone!'

'Not *I*,' the *djinn* corrected. 'Merely the bottle. But I'm not in the bottle, remember. I'm in you.'

Collins clasped both hands to his head. 'All right,' he groaned. 'I can't get rid of you. I give up.'

'And let me out?' persisted the *djinn* eagerly.

'I don't know.'

Collins lurched out of the alley. He walked along in a daze.

'That does it,' he told himself. 'Now the bottle's gone. I can never get him back into what doesn't exist.'

'Master!'

That hateful voice again.

'What is it?'

'Your third wish, Master?'

Collins couldn't answer. His third wish? He had so many of them. He wished the damned genie wouldn't keep calling him 'Master' for one thing. Because in reality, the *djinn* was *his* master. The *djinn* kept him from eating, from sleeping, from associating with human beings. And how Collins wished he could eat and sleep and meet his fellow men again!

But he dare not wish aloud. He dare not release this creature and he couldn't keep on going this way. He couldn't.

Automatically his feet led him up the stairs to his own apartment. On the way the *djinn* joggled up and down inside him with every step. It complained bitterly about the climb, too. Collins was glad the hall was empty.

Oh well, it wouldn't be for long.

Once inside, Collins went straight to his pantry. There was a fifth of gin there. Gin, by all that was ironic! He opened it and took a swig. A healthy swig. It gave him the courage he needed for what he was about to do.

Collins sat down at the phone and dialled the museum. He had to. He owed it to the girl to tell her. In a moment she answered.

'Edith?'

'Yes—oh, Tom, it's you.'

'Edith, I want to say good-bye.'

'But Tom, where are you going?'

Collins didn't hesitate before he answered.

'Down to the pier.'

'Tom, you're not going to—'

Collins hung up quickly. He'd made a damned fool of himself again. But it was no use. He couldn't tell Edith what he meant to tell her. About the *djinn*. About the way he loved her.

It was loving her that drove him to drink in the first place. That feeling of inferiority. She was always so calm, so cool. So unapproachable. And he was just a little museum clerk.

That's why he had clung to the vase the last three days, even with those men on his trail. Because Doctor Sweet had promised him an assistant curatorship if he managed to get it. Then he and Edith could be married. But now the *djinn* had come and there was no way out.

These were the things he meant to tell her. But he couldn't. And what was the use? He'd go down to the pier now and take the plunge. He and the *djinn* together. It was the only way out.

Collins pocketed his fifth and left. Before going out the hall door, he took another drink. It consoled. And it enabled Collins to walk the five blocks down to the beach.

The *djinn* was mercifully silent. It threshed around from time to time, but Collins didn't care. In a few moments it would all be over.

Collins scanned the deserted autumn vista of the beach. With plodding steps he moved out along the short white stretch of the pier. The water churned icily around the stones.

His head was clearing. That would never do.

Collins took out his gin and drank. Deeply. Then he sat down at the end of the pier. He stared at the greenish-black depths of the water. Water—how he hated it! Gin was better.

He took another swig. The fifth was going down. It would go down and then he would. He drank again. It warmed him.

'Master.'

The damned voice again! Collins forced himself to reply.

'What is it?'

'Where are we? I'm warm.'

'Never mind.'

'But I feel very strange, Master.'

Good! The gin was displeasing to the demon. Collins took another drink, a long one. With malicious satisfaction, he tilted the fifth back.

'Ooooh, Master—that burns!'

'It feels fine.'

And it did feel fine. Collins was aware of tipsiness. A pleasant sensation.

'I'm getting all wet,' the *djinn* pleaded.

'You'll be wetter in a minute,' Collins chuckled.

He would be, too. Because when Collins jumped off the pier—
But that could wait. Another drink now.

Collins began to feel good. He anticipated the moment of release. The water looked inviting now.

'Master—what is this?'

'A little stomach medicine. Just what you advised me.'

'But it smells strange.'

'You'll get used to it.'

'Strong. It's like fire.'

Collins began to laugh. 'Best stuff I ever drank,' he chortled.

'You drink this?' The *djinn* was incredulous.

'Of course.'

'Oh.'

Then there was silence. Collins drank recklessly.

'This is good.' The *djinn*'s voice rose on a note of discovery.

'Glad you like it.'

'Let's have some more.'

'Why not?' Collins took another sip.

'You are right, Master. It is excellent. Warming.'

This was the last straw. The *djinn* was actually getting drunk on the gin Collins absorbed!

'Let's have a lot more of it,' the voice suggested. It was loud, yet oddly blurred.

Collins obliged with enthusiasm.

'Say, Master.'

'Yeah?'

'How 'bout that other wish of yours?'

'Forget it.'

'Very kind of you. Very. Have a drink on that.'

They drank.

'Hot down here. Makes me thirsty.' The *djinn* was slurring his words now. 'Can't stand up right.'

'Lie down, then.'

'Can't lie down. Want another drink.'

Again the fifth was lifted. Collins drained the last drop.

'Good. You're th' mos' exalted of all Mas'ters.'

Collins could feel the *djinn* swaying around. He stood up. Now the gin was gone, and it was time to act. The party had been swell while it lasted, but it was over. The thought of entertaining two hangovers at once was impossible. Collins looked down at the water again and took a deep breath.

'Mas'ter!'

'What is it?'

'Wanna 'nother drink.'

'No,' replied Collins brusquely. 'No more drinks.'

'Please. Got to have one.'

Collins exulted. The *djinn* was frankly begging now. Let him— it served him right for the misery he caused.

'Just one. Please.'

'No! Why should I give you a drink? What have you ever done for me? You wreck my life, you plot against me, you take possession of my nice warm stomach and jump around. You think I like to walk around feeling as though I were going to have a baby or something?'

'Jus' one little drink!' the *djinn* begged.

'Absolutely none,' Collins retorted.

'But I wanna—enchanting stuff—do anything.'

Collins felt the *djinn*'s drunken frame quiver with eagerness. He glanced down at the empty fifth beside him, then looked at the water again.

Suddenly Collins sat down.

'Listen,' he whispered, softly.

'Lis'ning,' the *djinn* mumbled.

'You really want that drink?'

'I swear it, Mas'er.'

'Then,' said Collins, 'you can come and get it.'

'Wha'ssat?'

'I said you'll have to come after it—I'm tired of pouring the stuff down to you.'

'You'll let me out?'

'Why not? If you want a drink, come and get it.'

'To hear,' mumbled the *djinn*, 'is to 'bey.'

Collins opened his mouth to reply.

The reply never came. His throat was choked—choked with smoke. A cloud welled from his parted lips, an ebony pillar poured forth in the air above him. Not an arm this time, but a gigantic billow that swirled inchoately in mid-air.

Collins caught a glimpse of a coalescing pattern—an unbelievably huge torso, towering coal-black limbs, and a pair of blood-shot rolling eyes like striated billiard balls.

'Wait!' he whispered. 'It's down in there.' His trembling finger indicated the fifth of gin.

The inky column wavered drunkenly. Materialisation halted.

'You'll never get it that way,' Collins repeated. 'You're too big.'

The smoke spiralled in woozy indecision. Suddenly it began to contract.

Swiftly it was shrinking to human size, then to child's height. A little black smoke doll danced over to the standing fifth.

'Smaller still,' Collins whispered.

Obediently, the *djinn* contracted. A tiny ebony wisp hovered about the neck of the fifth.

'In there,' Collins directed.

The wisp hesitated. A shrill little piping voice rose.

'But it's inside the bottle,' it protested maudlinly.

Collins gasped.

'Yes,' he breathed. 'And so are you!'

His darting hand pushed the smoky wraith down the neck of the empty fifth bottle. His fingers rammed the cap over the top. He twisted it tightly.

Inside the gin bottle, the *djinn* danced up and down in drunken rage. Its wrinkled little black face was contorted, and Collins saw its mouth shaping curses he could not hear.

Nor did he hear the shrill honking of the horn from the beach behind him.

It was not until Edith had jumped from the car and ran clattering out onto the pier to where he stood that Collins turned his head.

Then she was in his arms, sobbing just a little as she poured out her words in a torrent of tenderness.

'Oh, Tom, thank goodness I'm in time . . . poor dear . . . suicide over me . . . Doctor Sweet explained about everything, how you got his vase for him . . . promotion . . . and when I looked out the window and saw those three awful men lying there . . . what you did to them . . . never knew you were so strong and wonderful . . . get married.'

It went something like that, between sobs and hugs and quite undignified kisses.

Collins liked it a lot.

Edith retrieved her dignity just once, and only for a moment. She saw the gin bottle standing there on the pier edge and turned away.

'But Tom . . . you'll have to promise me you'll stop drinking.'

'Certainly, dear,' whispered the little man. 'From now on I'm off the bottled goods forever.'

Edith smiled happily. Stooping, she picked up the fifth bottle with an impulsive gesture. She flung it into the water.

Collins watched appreciatively. It was a good throw. The bottle bobbed far out on the waves.

'That's a load off my mind,' the girl murmured, happily.

'That's a load off my—'

But Collins didn't say it. He merely held Edith very closely to him, so that he couldn't see the *djinn* bottle as it floated away toward the open sea.

MARMALADE WINE

Joan Aiken

Joan Aiken (1924-) is another writer with a reputation for outstanding short stories of psychological horror and macabre humour, following in the footsteps of her distinguished father, Conrad Aiken. She was inspired to write 'Marmalade Wine' by her chemist brother who, she says, brews bottles of this unique wine 'of unusual potency'. The story was adapted for Rod Serling's very popular TV series, 'Night Gallery' in 1971, with Robert Morse as Roger Blacker, the writer who ill-advisedly samples a few glasses of the very special brew made by Dr Francis Deeking (played by the veteran singer-actor, Rudee Vallee) and thereafter finds himself plunged into a far worse nightmare than any hangover might induce . . .

'Paradise,' Blacker said to himself, moving forward into the wood. 'Paradise. Fairyland.'

He was a man given to exaggeration; poetic licence he called it, and his friends called it 'Blacker's little flights of fancy', or something less polite, but on this occasion he spoke nothing but the truth. The wood stood silent about him, tall, golden, with afternoon sunlight slanting through the half-unfurled leaves of early summer. Underfoot, anemones palely carpeted the ground. A cuckoo called.

'Paradise,' Blacker repeated, closed the gate behind him, and strode down the overgrown path, looking for a spot in which to eat his ham sandwich. Hazel bushes thickened at either side until the circular blue eye of the gateway by which he had come in dwindled to a pinpoint and vanished. The taller trees overtopping the hazels were not yet in full leaf and gave little cover; it was very hot in the wood and very still.

Suddenly Blacker stopped short with an exclamation of surprise and regret: lying among the dog's-mercury by the path was the body of a cock-pheasant in the full splendour of its spring plumage. Blacker turned the bird over with the townsman's pity and curiosity at such evidence of nature's unkindness; the feathers, purple-bronze, green, and gold, were smooth under his hand as a girl's hair.

'Poor thing,' he said aloud, 'what can have happened to it?'

He walked on, wondering if he could turn the incident to account. 'Threnody for a Pheasant in May.' Too precious? Too sentimental? Perhaps a weekly would take it. He began choosing rhymes, staring at his feet as he walked, abandoning his conscious rapture at the beauty around him.

> *Stricken to death ... and something ... leafy ride,*
> *Before his ... something ... fully flaunt his pride.*

Or would a shorter line be better, something utterly simple and heartfelt, limpid tears of grief like spring rain dripping off the petals of a flower?

It was odd, Blacker thought, increasing his pace, how difficult he found writing nature poetry; nature was beautiful, maybe, but it was not stimulating. And it was nature poetry that *Field and Garden* wanted. Still, that pheasant ought to be worth five guineas. *Tread lightly past, Where he lies still, And something last ...*

Damn! In his absorption he had nearly trodden on *another* pheasant. What was happening to the birds? Blacker, who objected to occurrences with no visible explanation, walked on frowning. The path bore downhill to the right, and leaving the hazel coppice, crossed a tiny valley. Below him Blacker was surprised to see a small, secretive flint cottage, surrounded on three sides by trees. In front of it was a patch of turf. A deckchair stood there, and a man was peacefully stretched out in it, enjoying the afternoon sun.

Blacker's first impulse was to turn back; he felt as if he had walked into somebody's garden, and was filled with mild irritation at the unexpectedness of the encounter; there ought to have been some warning signs, dash it all. The wood had seemed as deserted as Eden itself. But his turning round would have an appearance of guilt and furtiveness; on second thoughts he decided to go boldly past the cottage. After all there was no fence, and the path was not marked private in any way; he had a perfect right to be there.

'Good afternoon,' said the man pleasantly as Blacker approached. 'Remarkably fine weather, is it not?'

'I do hope I'm not trespassing.'

Studying the man, Blacker revised his first guess. This was no gamekeeper; there was distinction in every line of the thin, sculptured face. What most attracted Blacker's attention were the hands, holding a small gilt coffee-cup; they were as white, frail, and attenuated as the pale roots of water-plants.

'Not at all,' the man said cordially. 'In fact you arrive at a most opportune moment; you are very welcome. I was just wishing for a little company. Delightful as I find this sylvan retreat, it becomes, all of a sudden, a little *dull*, a little *banal*. I do trust that you have time to sit down and share my afternoon coffee and liqueur.'

As he spoke he reached behind him and brought out a second deck-chair from the cottage porch.

'Why, thank you; I should be delighted,' said Blacker, wondering if he had the strength of character to take out the ham sandwich and eat it in front of this patrician hermit.

Before he made up his mind the man had gone into the house and returned with another gilt cup full of black, fragrant coffee, hot as Tartarus, which he handed to Blacker. He carried also a tiny glass, and into this, from a blackcurrant-cordial bottle, he carefully poured a clear, colourless liquor. Blacker sniffed his glassful with caution, mistrusting the bottle and its evidence of home brewing, but the scent, aromatic and powerful, was similar to that of curaçao, and the liquid moved in its glass with an oily smoothness. It certainly was not cowslip wine.

'Well,' said his host, reseating himself and gesturing slightly with his glass, 'how do you do?' He sipped delicately.

'Cheers,' said Blacker, and added, 'My name's Roger Blacker.' It sounded a little lame. The liqueur was not curaçao, but akin to it, and quite remarkably potent; Blacker, who was very hungry, felt the fumes rise up inside his head as if an orange tree had taken root there and was putting out leaves and golden glowing fruit.

'Sir Francis Deeking,' the other man said, and then Blacker understood why his hands had seemed so spectacular, so portentously out of the common.

'The surgeon? But surely you don't live down here?'

Deeking waved a hand deprecatingly. 'A weekend retreat. A hermitage, to which I can retire from the strain of my calling.'

'It certainly is very remote,' Blacker remarked. 'It must be five miles from the nearest road.'

'Six. And you, my dear Mr Blacker, what is your profession?'

'Oh, a writer,' said Blacker modestly. The drink was having its usual effect on him; he managed to convey not that he was a journalist on a twopenny daily with literary yearnings, but that he was a philosopher and essayist of rare quality, a sort of second Bacon. All the time he spoke, while drawn out most flatteringly by the questions of Sir Francis, he was recalling journalistic scraps of information about his host: the operation on the Indian Prince;

the Cabinet Minister's appendix; the amputation performed on that unfortunate ballerina who had both feet crushed in a railway accident; the major operation which had proved so miraculously successful on the American heiress.

'You must feel like a god,' he said suddenly, noticing with surprise that his glass was empty. Sir Francis waved the remark aside.

'We all have our godlike attributes,' he said, leaning forward. 'Now you, Mr Blacker, a writer, a creative artist—do you not know a power akin to godhead when you transfer your thought to paper?'

'Well, not exactly then,' said Blacker, feeling the liqueur moving inside his head in golden and russet-coloured clouds. 'Not *so* much then, but I do have one unusual power, a power not shared by many people, of foretelling the future. For instance, as I was coming through the wood, I *knew* this house would be here. I knew I should find you sitting in front of it. I can look at the list of runners in a race, and the name of the winner fairly leaps out at me from the page, as if it was printed in golden ink. Forthcoming events—air disasters, train crashes—I always sense in advance. I begin to have a terrible feeling of impending doom, as if my brain was a volcano just on the point of eruption.'

What was that other item of news about Sir Francis Deeking, he wondered, a recent report, a tiny paragraph that had caught his eye in *The Times*? He could not recall it.

'*Really?*' Sir Francis was looking at him with the keenest interest; his eyes, hooded and fanatical under their heavy lids, held brilliant points of light. 'I have always longed to know somebody with such a power. It must be a terrifying responsibility.'

'Oh, it is,' Blacker said. He contrived to look bowed under the weight of supernatural cares; noticed that his glass was full again, and drained it. 'Of course I don't use the faculty for my own ends; something fundamental in me rises up to prevent that. It's as basic, you know, as the instinct forbidding cannibalism or incest—'

'Quite, quite,' Sir Francis agreed. 'But for another person you would be able to give warnings, advise profitable courses of action—? My dear fellow, your glass is empty. Allow me.'

'This is marvellous stuff,' Blacker said hazily. 'It's like a wreath of orange blossom.' He gestured with his finger.

'I distil it myself; from marmalade. But do go on with what you were saying. Could you, for instance, tell me the winner of this afternoon's Manchester Plate?'

'Bow Bells,' Blacker said unhesitatingly. It was the only name he could remember.

'You interest me enormously. And the result of today's Aldwych by-election? Do you know that?'

'Unwin, the Liberal, will get in by a majority of two hundred and eighty-two. He won't take his seat, though. He'll be killed at seven this evening in a lift accident at his hotel.' Blacker was well away by now.

'Will he, indeed?' Sir Francis appeared delighted. 'A pestilent fellow. I have sat on several boards with him. Do continue.'

Blacker required little encouragement. He told the story of the financier whom he had warned in time of the oil company crash; the dream about the famous violinist which had resulted in the man's cancelling his passage on the ill-fated *Orion*; and the tragic tale of the bullfighter who had ignored his warning.

'But I'm talking too much about myself,' he said at length, partly because he noticed an ominous clogging of his tongue, a refusal of his thoughts to marshal themselves. He cast about for an impersonal topic, something simple.

'The pheasants,' he said. 'What's happened to the pheasants? Cut down in their prime. It—it's terrible. I found four in the wood up there, four or five.'

'Really?' Sir Francis seemed callously uninterested in the fate of the pheasants. 'It's the chemical sprays they use on the crops, I understand. Bound to upset the ecology; they never work out the probable results beforehand. Now if *you* were in charge, my dear Mr Blacker—but forgive me, it is a hot afternoon and you must be tired and footsore if you have walked from Witherstow this morning—let me suggest that you have a short sleep . . .'

His voice seemed to come from farther and farther away; a network of sun-coloured leaves laced themselves in front of Blacker's eyes. Gratefully he leaned back and stretched out his aching feet.

Some time after this Blacker roused a little—or was it only a dream?—to see Sir Francis standing by him, rubbing his hands, with a face of jubilation.

'My dear fellow, my dear Mr Blacker, what a *lusus naturae* you are. I can never be sufficiently grateful that you came my way. Bow Bells walked home—positively *ambled*. I have been listening to the commentary. What a misfortune that I had no time to place money on the horse—but never mind, never mind, that can be remedied another time.

'It is unkind of me to disturb your well-earned rest, though; drink this last thimbleful and finish your nap while the sun is on the wood.'

As Blacker's head sank back against the deck-chair again, Sir Francis leaned forward and gently took the glass from his hand.

Sweet river of dreams, thought Blacker, fancy the horse actually winning. I wish I'd had a fiver on it myself; I could do with a new pair of shoes. I should have undone these before I dozed off, they're too tight or something. I must wake up soon, ought to be on my way in half an hour or so . . .

When Blacker finally woke he found that he was lying on a narrow bed, indoors, covered with a couple of blankets. His head ached and throbbed with a shattering intensity, and it took a few minutes for his vision to clear; then he saw that he was in a small white cell-like room which contained nothing but the bed he was on and a chair. It was very nearly dark.

He tried to struggle up but a strange numbness and heaviness had invaded the lower part of his body, and after hoisting himself on to his elbow he felt so sick that he abandoned the effort and lay down again.

That stuff must have the effect of a knockout drop, he thought ruefully; what a fool I was to drink it. I'll have to apologise to Sir Francis. What time can it be?

Brisk light footsteps approached the door and Sir Francis came in. He was carrying a portable radio which he placed on the window sill.

'Ah, my dear Blacker, I see you have come round. Allow me to offer you a drink.'

He raised Blacker skilfully, and gave him a drink of water from a cup with a rim and a spout.

'Now let me settle you down again. Excellent. We shall soon have you—well, not on your feet, but sitting up and taking nourishment.' He laughed a little. 'You can have some beef tea presently.'

'I am so sorry,' Blacker said. 'I really need not trespass on your hospitality any longer. I shall be quite all right in a minute.'

'No trespass, my dear friend. You are not at all in the way. I hope that you will be here for a long and pleasant stay. These surroundings, so restful, so conducive to a writer's inspiration— what could be more suitable for you? You need not think that I shall disturb you. I am in London all week, but shall keep you company at weekends—pray, pray don't think that you will be a nuisance or *de trop*. On the contrary, I am hoping that you can do me the kindness of giving me the Stock Exchange prices in advance, which will amply compensate for any small trouble I have taken. No, no, you must feel quite at home—please consider, indeed, that this *is* your home.'

Stock Exchange prices? It took Blacker a moment to remember, then he thought, Oh lord, my tongue has played me false as usual.

He tried to recall what stupidities he had been guilty of. 'Those stories,' he said lamely, 'they were all a bit exaggerated, you know. About my foretelling the future. I can't really. That horse's winning was a pure coincidence, I'm afraid.'

'Modesty, modesty.' Sir Francis was smiling, but he had gone rather pale, and Blacker noticed a beading of sweat along his cheekbones. 'I am sure you will be invaluable. Since my retirement I find it absolutely necessary to augment my income by judicious investment.'

All of a sudden Blacker remembered the gist of that small paragraph in *The Times*. Nervous breakdown. Complete rest. Retirement.

'I—I really must go now,' he said uneasily, trying to push himself upright. 'I meant to be back in town by seven.'

'Oh, but Mr Blacker, that is quite out of the question. Indeed, so as to preclude any such action, I have amputated your feet. But you need not worry; I know you will be very happy here. And I feel certain that you are wrong to doubt your own powers. Let us listen to the nine o'clock news in order to be quite satisfied that the detestable Unwin did fall down the hotel lift shaft.'

He walked over to the portable radio and switched it on.

THE WINE GLASS

A. A. Milne

Tokay, the sweetish, heavy wine with its distinctive aromatic flavour which originated from the town of that name in Hungary, was one of the favourite drinks of Alan Alexander Milne (1882–1956) whose fame was assured by his stories of Winnie-the-Pooh and Christopher Robin. He was also one of the leading humorists of his day (contributing to Punch *for many years) and a devotee of the crime and detective story. His landmark novel,* The Red House Mystery, *published in 1922, was hailed by Alexander Woollcott as 'one of the three best mystery stories of all time', and his play* The Perfect Alibi *(1928) was popular in both London and on Broadway. He also wrote several short stories, of which 'The Wine Glass' admirably fulfils the criteria for this collection. The bottle of the author's favourite Tokay which has been tampered with and thereby poisons a butler is only the beginning of a puzzling mystery with a most startling denouement.*

I am in a terrible predicament, as you will see directly. I don't know what to do . . .

'One of the maxims which I have found most helpful in my career at Scotland Yard,' the superintendent was saying, 'has been the simple one that appearances are not always deceptive. A crime may be committed exactly as it seems to have been committed and exactly as it was intended to be committed.' He helped himself and passed the bottle.

'I don't think I follow you,' I said, hoping thus to lead him on.

I am a writer of detective stories. If you have never heard of me, it can only be because you don't read detective stories. I wrote 'Murder on the Back Stairs' and 'The Mystery of the Twisted Eglantine,' to mention only two of my successes. It was this fact, I think, which first interested Superintendent Frederick Mortimer in me, and, of course, me in him. He is a big fellow with the face of a Roman Emperor; I am the small neat type. We gradually became friends and so got into the habit of dining together once a month. He liked talking about his cases, and naturally I liked listening. But this evening the wine seemed to be making itself felt.

'I don't think I follow you,' I said again.

'I mean that the simple way of committing a murder is often the best way. This doesn't mean that the murderer is a man of simple mind. On the contrary. He is subtle enough to know that the simple solution is too simple to be credible.'

This sounded anything but simple, so I said, 'Give me an example.'

'Well, take the case of the bottle of wine which was sent to the Marquis of Hedingham on his birthday. Have I never told you about it?'

'Never,' I said, and I helped myself and passed the bottle.

He filled his glass and considered. 'Give me a moment to get it clear,' he said. 'It was a long time ago.' While he closed his eyes and let the past drift before him, I ordered up another bottle of the same.

'Yes,' said Mortimer, opening his eyes. 'I've got it now.'

I leaned forward, listening eagerly. This is the story he told me.

The first we heard of it at the Yard (said Mortimer) was a brief announcement over the telephone that the Marquis of Hedingham's butler had died suddenly at His Lordship's town house in Brook Street, and that poison was suspected. This was at seven o'clock. We went round at once. Inspector Totman had been put in charge of the case; I was a young detective sergeant at the time, and I generally worked under Totman. He was a brisk, military sort of fellow, with a little prickly ginger moustache, good at his job in a showy, orthodox way, but he had no imagination, and he was thinking all the time of what Inspector Totman would get out of it. Quite frankly I didn't like him. Outwardly we kept friendly, for it doesn't do to quarrel with one's superiors; indeed, he was vain enough to think that I had a great admiration for him; but I knew that he was just using me for his own advantage, and I had a shrewd suspicion that I should have been promoted before this, if he hadn't wanted to keep me under him so that he could profit by my brains.

We found the butler in his pantry, stretched out on the floor. An open bottle of Tokay, a broken wine glass with the dregs of the liquid still in it, the medical evidence of poisoning, all helped to build up the story for us. The wine had arrived about an hour before, with the card of Sir William Kelso attached to it. On the card was a typewritten message, saying, 'Bless you, Tommy, and here's something to celebrate with.' I can't remember the exact words, of course, but that was the idea. Apparently it was His Lordship's birthday, and he was having a small family party of about six people for the occasion. Sir William Kelso, I should explain, was his oldest friend and a relation by marriage, Lord Hedingham having married his sister; in fact, Sir William was to have been one of the party present that evening. He was a bachelor, about fifty, and a devoted uncle to his nephew and nieces.

Well, the butler had brought up the bottle and the card to His Lordship—this was about six o'clock; and Lord Hedingham, as he told us, had taken the card, said something like, 'Good old Bill. We'll have that tonight, Perkins,' and Perkins had said, 'Very good, My Lord,' and gone out again with the bottle. The card had been left lying on the table. Afterwards, there could be little doubt what had happened. Perkins had opened the bottle with the intention of decanting it but had been unable to resist the temptation to sample it first. I suspect that in his time he had sampled most of His Lordship's wine but had never before come across a Tokay of such richness. So he had poured himself out a full glass, drunk it, and died almost immediately.

'Good heavens!' I interrupted. 'But how extremely providential—I mean, of course, for Lord Hedingham and the others.'

'Exactly,' said Mortimer, as he twirled his own wine glass.

The contents of the bottle were analysed (he went on) and found to contain a more-than-fatal dose of prussic acid. Of course we did all the routine things. With young Roberts, a nice young fellow who often worked with us, I went around to all the chemists' shops in the neighbourhood. Totman examined everybody from Sir William and Lord Hedingham downwards.

Roberts and I took the bottle round to all the wine merchants in the neighbourhood. At the end of a week all we could say was this:

One: The murderer had a motive for murdering Lord Hedingham; or, possibly, somebody at his party; or, possibly, the whole party. In accordance with the usual custom, His Lordship would be the first to taste the wine. A sip would not be fatal, and in a wine of such richness the taste might not be noticeable; so that the whole party would then presumably drink His Lordship's health. He would raise his glass to them, and in this way they would all take the poison, and be affected according to how deeply they drank. On the other hand, His Lordship might take a good deal more than a sip in the first place, and so be the only one to suffer. My deduction from this was that the motive was revenge rather than gain. The criminal would avenge himself on Lord Hedingham if His Lordship or *any* of his family were seriously poisoned; he could only profit if *definite* people were definitely *killed*. It took a little time to get Totman to see this, but he did eventually agree.

Two: The murderer had been able to obtain one of Sir William Kelso's cards, and knew that John Richard Mervyn Plantagenet Carlow, tenth Marquis of Hedingham, was called 'Tommy' by his intimates. Totman deduced from this that he was therefore one of the Hedingham-Kelso circle of relations and friends. I disputed this. I pointed out: (a) that it was to strangers rather than to intimate friends that cards were presented, except in the case of formal calls, when they were left in a bowl or tray in the hall, and anybody could steal one; (b) that the fact that Lord Hedingham was called Tommy must have appeared in society papers and be known to many people; and, most convincing of all, (c) that the murderer did *not* know that Sir William Kelso was to be in the party that night. For obviously some reference would have been made to the gift, either on his arrival or when the wine was served; whereupon he would have disclaimed any knowledge of it, and the bottle would immediately have been suspected. As it was, of course, Perkins had drunk from it before Sir William's arrival. Now both Sir William and Lord Hedingham assured us that they *always* dined together on each other's birthday, and they were convinced that any personal friend of theirs would have been aware of the fact. I made Totman question them about this, and he then came round to my opinion.

Three: There was nothing to prove that the wine in the bottle corresponded to the label; and wine experts were naturally reluctant to taste it for us. All they could say from the smell was that it was a Tokay of sorts. This, of course, made it more difficult for us. In fact I may say that neither from the purchase of wine nor the nature of the poison did we get any clue.

We had, then, the following picture of the murderer. He had a cause of grievance, legitimate or fancied, against Lord Hedingham, and did not scruple to take the most terrible revenge. He knew that Sir William Kelso was a friend of His Lordship and called him Tommy, and that he might reasonably give him a bottle of wine on his birthday. He did *not* know that Sir William would be dining there that night; that is to say, *even as late as six o'clock that evening, he did not know.* He was not likely, therefore, to be anyone at present employed or living in Lord Hedingham's house. Finally, he had had an opportunity to get hold of a card of Sir William's.

As it happened, there was somebody who fitted completely into this picture. It was a fellow called—wait a bit—Merrivale, Medley—oh, well, it doesn't matter. Merton, that was it. Merton. He had been His Lordship's valet for six months, had been suspected of stealing and had been dismissed without a character

reference. Just the man we wanted. So for a fortnight we searched
for Merton. And then, when at last we got on to him, we discovered that he had the most complete alibi imaginable. (*The
superintendent held up his hand, and it came into my mind that he must
have stopped the traffic as a young man with just that gesture.*) Yes, I
know what you're going to say, what you detective-story writers
always say—the better an alibi, the worse it is. Well, sometimes, I
admit; but not in this case. For Merton was in jail, under another
name, and he had been inside for the last two months. And what
do you think he was suspected of, and was waiting trial for? Oh,
well, of course you guess; I've as good as told you. He was on a
charge of murder—and murder, mark you, by poison.

'Good heavens!' I interjected. I seized the opportunity to refill
my friend's glass. He said, 'Exactly,' and took a long drink.

You can imagine (he went on) what a shock this was to us. You
see, a certain sort of murder had been committed; we had deduced
that it was done by a certain man, without knowing whether he
was in the least capable of such a crime; and now, having proved
to the hilt that he *was* capable of it, we had simultaneously
proved that he didn't do it.

I said to Totman, 'Let's take a couple of days off, and each of
us think it out, then pool our ideas and start afresh.'

Totman frisked up his little moustache and laughed in his con-
ceited way. 'You don't think I'm going to admit myself wrong, do
you, when I've just proved I'm right?' (Totman saying 'I,' when
he had got everything from me!) 'Merton's my man. He'd got the
bottle ready, and somebody else delivered it for him. That's all.
He had to wait for the birthday, you see, and when he found
himself in prison, his wife or somebody—'

'—took round the bottle, all nicely labelled, "Poison; not to be
delivered till Christmas Day." ' I had to say it, I was so annoyed
with him.

'Don't be more of a damned fool than you can help,' he shouted,
'and don't be insolent, or you'll get into trouble.'

I apologised humbly and told him how much I liked working
with him. He forgave me, and we were friends again. He patted
me on the shoulder.

'You take a day off,' he said kindly, 'you've been working too
hard. Take a bus into the country and make up a good story for
me; the story of that bottle, and how it came from Merton's lodging
to Brook Street, and who took it and why. I admit I don't see it at
present, but that's the bottle, you can bet your life. I'm going
down to Leatherhead. Report here on Friday morning, and we'll
see what we've got. My birthday as it happens, and I feel I'm
going to be lucky.' Leatherhead was where an old woman had

been poisoned. That was the third time in a week he'd told me when his wretched birthday was.

I took a bus to Hampstead Heath. I walked round the Leg of Mutton Pond twenty times. And each time that I went round, Totman's theory seemed sillier than the last time. And each time I felt more and more strongly that we were being *forced* into an entirely artificial interpretation of things. It sounds fantastic, I know, but I could almost feel the murderer behind us, pushing us along the way he wanted us to go.

I sat down on a seat and filled a pipe, and I said, 'Right! The murderer's a man who wanted me to believe all that I have believed. When I've told myself that the murderer intended to do so-and-so, he intended me to believe that, and therefore he didn't do so-and-so. When I've told myself that the murderer wanted to mislead me, he wanted me to think he wanted to mislead me, which meant the truth was exactly as it seemed to be. Now then, Fred, you'll begin all over again, and you'll take things as they are and won't be too clever about them. Because the murderer expects you to be clever, and wants you to be clever, and from now on you aren't going to take your orders from *him*.'

And of course, the first thing which leaped to my mind was that the murderer *meant* to murder the butler!

It seemed incredible now that we could ever have missed it. Didn't every butler sample his master's wines? Why, it was an absolute certainty that Perkins would be the first victim of a poisoned bottle of a very special vintage. What butler could resist pouring himself out a glass as he decanted it?

Wait, though. Mustn't be in a hurry. Two objections. One: Perkins might be the one butler in a thousand who wasn't a wine-sampler. Two: Even if he were like any other butler, he might be out of sorts on that particular evening and have put by a glass to drink later. Wouldn't it be much too risky for a murderer who only wanted to destroy Perkins, and had no grudge against Lord Hedingham's family, to depend so absolutely on the butler drinking first?

For a little while this held me up, but not for long. Suddenly I saw the complete solution.

It would *not* be risky if (a) the murderer had certain knowledge of the butler's habits; and (b) could, if necessary, at the last moment, prevent the family from drinking. In other words, if he were an intimate of the family, were himself present at the party, and, without bringing suspicion on himself, could bring the wine under suspicion.

In other words, only if he were Sir William Kelso! For Sir William was the only man in the world who could say, 'Don't drink this wine. I'm supposed to have sent it to you, and I didn't, so that proves it's a fake.' The *only* man.

Why hadn't we suspected him from the beginning? One reason, of course, was that we had supposed the intended victim to be one of the Hedingham family, and of Sir William's devotion to his sister, brother-in-law, nephew and nieces, there was never any doubt. But the chief reason was our assumption that the last thing a murderer would do would be to give himself away by sending his own card with the poisoned bottle. 'The *last* thing a murderer would do'—and therefore the *first* thing a really clever murderer would do.

To make my case complete to myself, for I had little hope as yet of converting Totman, I had to establish motive. Why should Sir William want to murder Perkins? I gave myself the pleasure of having tea that afternoon with Lord Hedingham's housekeeper. We had caught each other's eye on other occasions when I had been at the house, and—well, I suppose I can say it now—I had a way with the women in those days. When I left, I knew two things. Perkins had been generally unpopular, not only downstairs, but upstairs. 'It was a wonder how they put up with him.' And Her Ladyship had been 'a different woman lately'.

'How different?' I asked.

'So much younger, if you know what I mean, Sergeant Mortimer. Almost like a girl again, bless her heart.'

I did know. And that was that. Blackmail.

What was I to do? What did my evidence amount to? Nothing. It was all corroborative evidence. If Kelso had done one suspicious thing, or left one real clue, then the story I had made up would have convinced any jury. As it was, in the eyes of a jury he had done one completely unsuspicious thing and had left one real clue to his innocence—his visiting card. Totman would just laugh at me.

I disliked the thought of being laughed at by Totman. I wondered how I could get the laugh on him. I took a bus to Baker Street, and walked into Regent's Park, not minding where I was going, but just thinking. And then, as I got opposite Hanover Terrace, who should I see but young Roberts.

'Hallo, young fellow, what have *you* been up to?'

'Hallo, Sarge,' he grinned. 'Been calling on my old school chum, Sir William Kelso—or rather, his valet. Tottie thought he might have known Merton. Speaking as one valet to another, so to speak.'

'Is Inspector Totman back?' I asked.

Roberts stood to attention, and said, 'No, Sergeant Mortimer, Inspector Totman is not expected to return from Leatherhead, Surrey, until a late hour tonight.'

You couldn't be angry with the boy. At least I couldn't. He had no respect for anybody, but he was a good lad. And he had an eye like a hawk. Saw everything and forgot none of it.

I said, 'I didn't know Sir William lived up this way.'

Roberts pointed across the road. 'Observe the august mansion. Five minutes ago you'd have found me in the basement, talking to a housemaid who thought Merton was a town in Surrey. As it is, of course.'

I had a sudden crazy idea.

'Well, now you're going back there,' I said. 'I'm going to call on Sir William, and I want you handy. Would they let you in at the basement again, or are they sick of you?'

'Sarge, they just love me. When I went, they said, "Must you go?"'

We say at the Yard, 'Once a murderer, always a murderer.' Perhaps that was why I had an absurd feeling that I should like young Roberts within call. Because I was going to tell Sir William Kelso what I'd been thinking about by the Leg of Mutton Pond. I'd only seen him once, but he gave me the idea of being the sort of man who wouldn't mind killing, but didn't like lying. I thought he would give himself away . . . and then—well, there might be a roughhouse, and Roberts would be useful.

As we walked in at the gate together, I looked in my pocket-book for a card. Luckily I had one left, though it wasn't very clean. It was a bit ink-stained, in fact. Roberts, who never missed anything, said, 'Personally I always use blotting paper,' and went on whistling. If I hadn't known him, I shouldn't have known what he was talking about. I said, 'Oh, do you?' and rang the bell. I gave the maid my card and asked if Sir William could see me, and at the same time Roberts gave her a wink and indicated the back door. She nodded to him, and asked me to come in. Roberts went down and waited for her in the basement. I felt safer.

Sir William was a big man, as big as I was. But of course a lot older. He said, 'Well, Sergeant, what can I do for you?' twiddling my card in his fingers. He seemed quite friendly about it. 'Sit down, won't you?'

I said, 'I think I'll stand, Sir William. I want just to ask you one question, if I may?' Yes, I know I was crazy, but somehow I felt inspired.

'By all means,' he said, obviously not much interested.

'When did you first discover that Perkins was blackmailing Lady Hedingham?'

He was standing in front of his big desk, and I was opposite him. He stopped fiddling with my card and became absolutely still; and there was a silence so complete that I could feel it in every nerve of my body. I kept my eyes on his, you may be sure. We stood there, I don't know how long.

'Is that the only question?' he asked. The thing that frightened me was that his voice was just the same as before. Ordinary.

'Well, just one more. Have you a typewriter in your house?' Just corroborative evidence again, that's all. But it told him that I knew.

He gave a long sigh, tossed the card into the wastepaper basket and walked to the window. He stood there with his back to me, looking out but seeing nothing. Thinking. He must have stood there for a couple of minutes. Then he turned around, and to my amazement he had a friendly smile on his face. 'I think we'd both better sit down,' he said. We did.

'There is a typewriter in the house which I sometimes use,' he began. 'I daresay you use one too.'

'I do.'

'And so do thousands of other people—including, it may be, the murderer you are looking for.'

'Thousands of people, including the murderer,' I agreed.

He noticed the difference, and smiled. 'People' I had said, not 'other people.' And I didn't say I was looking for him. Because I had found him.

'And then,' I went on, 'there was the actual wording of the typed message.'

'Was there anything remarkable about it?'

'No. Except that it was exactly right.'

'Oh, my dear fellow, anyone could have got it right. A simple birthday greeting.'

'Anyone in your own class, Sir William, who knew you both. But that's all. It's Inspector Totman's birthday tomorrow.' I added to myself: As he keeps telling us, damn him! 'If I sent him a bottle of whisky, young Roberts—that's the constable who's in on this case; you may have seen him about, he's waiting for me now down below'—I thought this was rather a neat way of getting that in—'Roberts could make a guess at what I'd say, and so could anybody at the Yard who knows us both, and they wouldn't be far wrong. But *you* couldn't, Sir William.'

He looked at me. He couldn't take his eyes off me. I wondered what he was thinking. At last he said, 'You'd probably say, "A long life and all the best, with the admiring good wishes of—" How's that?'

It was devilish. First that he had really been thinking it out when he had so much else to think about, and then that he'd got it so right. That 'admiring' which meant that he'd studied Totman just as he was studying me, and knew how I'd play up to him.

'You see,' he smiled, 'it isn't really difficult. And the fact that my card was used is in itself convincing evidence of my innocence, don't you think?'

'To a jury perhaps,' I said, 'but not to me.'

'I wish I could convince *you*,' he murmured to himself. 'Well, what are you doing about it?'

'I shall, of course, put my reconstruction of the case in front of Inspector Totman tomorrow.'

'Ah! A nice birthday surprise for him. And, knowing your Totman, what do you think he will do?'

He had me there, and he knew it.

'I think *you* know him too, Sir,' I said.

'I do,' he smiled.

'And me, I daresay, and anybody else you meet. Quick as lightning. But even ordinary men like me have a sort of sudden understanding of people sometimes. As I've got of you, Sir. And I've a sort of feeling that, if ever we get you into a witness box, and you've taken the oath, you won't find perjury so much to your liking as murder. Or what the law calls murder.'

'But *you* don't?' he said quickly.

'I think,' I said, 'that there are a lot of people who *ought* to be killed. But I'm a policeman, and what I think isn't evidence. You killed Perkins, didn't you?'

He nodded; and then said, almost with a grin at me, 'A nervous affection of the head, if you put it in evidence. I could get a specialist to swear to it.'

My God, he was a good sort of man. I was really sorry when they found him next day, after he'd put a bullet through his head. And yet what else could he do? He knew I should get him.

I was furious with Fred Mortimer. That was no way to end a story. Suddenly, like that, as if he were tired of it. I told him so.

'My dear little friend,' he said, 'it isn't the end. We're just coming to the exciting part. This will make your hair curl.'

'Oh!' I said sarcastically. 'Then I suppose all that you've told me so far is just introduction?'

'That's right. Now you listen. On Friday morning, before we heard of Sir William's death, I went in to report to Inspector Totman. He wasn't there. Nobody knew where he was. They rang up his apartment house. Now hold tight to the leg of the table or something. When the porter got into his flat, he found Totman's body. Poisoned.'

'Good heavens!' I ejaculated.

'You may say so. There he was, and on the table was a newly opened bottle of whisky, and by the side of it a visiting card. And whose card do you think it was? *Mine!* And what do you think it said? 'A long life and all the best, with the admiring good wishes of—' *me!* Lucky for me I had had young Roberts with me. Lucky for me he had this genius for noticing and remembering. Lucky for me he could swear to the exact shape of the smudge of ink on that card. And I might add, lucky for me that they believed me when I told them word for word what had been said at my interview with Sir William, as I have just told you. I was reprimanded, of course, for exceeding my duty, as I most certainly had, but that was only official. Unofficially they were very pleased with me. We couldn't prove anything, naturally, and Sir William's suicide was left unexplained. But a month later I was promoted to Inspector.'

Mortimer fixed his glass and drank, while I revolved his extraordinary story in my mind.

'The theory,' I said, polishing my glasses thoughtfully, 'was, I suppose, that Sir William sent the poisoned whisky, not so much to get rid of Totman, from whom he had little to fear, as to discredit you by bringing you under suspicion, and to discredit entirely your own theory of the other murder.'

'Exactly.'

'And then, at the last moment he realised that he couldn't go on with it, or the weight of his crimes became suddenly too much for him, or—'

'Something of the sort. Nobody ever knew, of course.'

I looked across the table with sudden excitement; almost with awe.

'Do you remember what he said to you?' I asked, giving the words their full meaning as I slowly quoted them. ' "The fact that my card was used is in itself convincing evidence of my innocence...." And you said, "Not to me." And he said, "I wish I could convince *you.*" *And that was how he did it!* The fact that your card was used *was* convincing evidence of your innocence!'

'With the other things. The proof that he was in possession of the particular card of mine which was used, and the certainty that he had committed the other murder. Once a poisoner, always a poisoner.'

'True ... yes.... Well, thanks very much for the story, Fred. All the same, you know,' I said, shaking my head at him, 'it doesn't altogether prove what you set out to prove.'

'What was that?'

'That the simple explanation is generally the true one. In the case of Perkins, yes. But not in the case of Totman.'

'Sorry, I don't follow.'

'My dear fellow,' I said, putting up a finger to emphasise my point, for he seemed a little hazy with the wine suddenly; 'the *simple* explanation of Totman's death—surely?—would have been that *you* had sent him the poisoned whisky.'

Superintendent Mortimer looked a little surprised, 'But I did,' he said.

So now you see my terrible predicament. I could hardly listen as he went on dreamily: 'I never liked Totman, and he stood in my way; but I hadn't seriously thought of getting rid of him until I got that card into my hands again. As I told you, Sir William dropped it into the basket and turned to the window, and I thought: Damn it, *you* can afford to chuck about visiting cards, but I can't. It's the only one I've got left, and if you don't want it, I do. So I bent down very naturally to tie my shoelace and felt in the basket behind me, because, of course, it was rather an undignified thing to do, and I didn't want to be seen; and just as I was putting it into my pocket I saw that ink smudge again, and I remembered that Roberts had seen it. And in a flash the whole plan came to me; simple; foolproof. And from that moment everything I said to him was in preparation for it. Of course we were quite alone, but you never knew who might be listening, and besides'—he twiddled the stem of his wine glass—'p'raps I'm like Sir William, rather tell the truth than not. And it was true, all of it—how Sir William came to know about Totman's birthday, and knew that those were the very words I should have used.

'Don't think I wanted to put anything on to Sir William that wasn't his. I liked him. But he as good as told me he wasn't going to wait for what was coming to him, and he'd done one murder anyway. That was why I slipped down with the bottle that evening and left it outside Totman's flat. Didn't dare wait till the morning, in case Sir William closed his account that night.' He stood up and stretched himself. 'Ah, well, it was a long time ago. Goodbye, old man, I must be off. Thanks for a grand dinner. Don't forget, you're dining with *me* next Tuesday. I've got a new Burgundy for you. You'll like it.'

He drained his wine glass and swaggered out, leaving me to my thoughts.

THE LIQUEUR GLASS

Phyllis Bottome

The name Phyllis Bottome (1884–1963) may well be familiar as a novelist who came to wide public attention in 1926 through her novel Old Wine. *Rather less well-known is the fact that she was also one of the formative influences on Ian Fleming, creator of James Bond, the spy who likes his dry martinis 'shaken, not stirred'. The young Fleming met Phyllis Bottome in 1927 while he was preparing to enter the diplomatic service and, discovering his flair for language, she encouraged him to write his first short story. Her husband, Captain Ernan Forbes Dennis, was also a former Intelligence Officer, and on visits to their home regaled Fleming with tales of espionage which certainly fired his interest in the subject and probably made it his first choice when he decided to try writing novels. Phyllis Bottome herself also provided the writer with the model for his famous villain, Goldfinger, from accounts she gave him of a mysterious figure she had once met named Baron Hofflinger, who carried his entire wealth about with him in the form of bags of diamonds. Sadly, Phyllis Bottome did not live to see James Bond become a twentieth-century legend, and much of her own writing is now rather neglected. But among her short stories there are few better than 'The Liqueur Glass' in which a glass of the famous liqueur made from the berries of the blackthorn bush plays a crucial part. It is not a tale to recommend to any wife who is disenchanted with her husband . . .*

Mrs Henry Watkins loved going to church. She could not have told you why she loved it. It had perhaps less to do with religious motives than most people's reason for attending divine service; and she took no interest in other people's clothes.

She gazed long and fixedly at the stained glass window in which St Peter, in a loose magenta blouse, was ladling salmon-coloured sardines out of a grassgreen sea; but she did not really see St Peter or notice his sleight-of-hand, preoccupation with the fish. She was simply having a nice, quiet time.

She always sat where she could most easily escape seeing the back of Henry Watkins's head. She had never liked the back of his head and twenty years' married life had only deepened her distaste for it.

Hetty and Paul sat between her and their father, and once or twice it had occurred to Mrs Watkins as strange that she should owe the life of these two beloved beings to the man she hated.

It was no use pretending at this time of the day that she didn't hate Henry Watkins. She hated him with all the slow, quiet force of a slow quiet nature.

She had hated him for some time before she discovered that she no longer loved him.

Mrs Watkins arrived slowly at the recognition of a new truth; she would go on provisionally for years with a worn-out platitude, but when she once dropped it, she never returned to pick it up again; and she acted upon her discoveries.

The choir began to sing 'O God, Our Help in Ages Past'. Mrs Watkins disliked this hymn; and she had never found God much of a help. She thought the verse that compared men's lives to the flight of dreams was nonsense. Nobody could imagine Henry Watkins flying like a dream.

The first lesson was more attractive. Mrs Watkins enjoyed Jael's reception of Sisera. 'She brought him butter in a lordly dish,' boomed the curate. Henry Watkins ate a lot of butter, though he insisted, from motives of economy, upon its being Danish. Sisera, worn out with battle, slumbered. Jael took up the nail and carried on with efficiency and dispatch her inhospitable deed. Mrs Watkins thought the nails in those days must have been larger than they are now and probably sharper at the end.

The curate cleared his throat a little over the story; it seemed to him to savour of brutality.

'Why tarry the wheels of his chariot?' cried Sisera's mother.

Mrs Watkins leaned back in her seat and smiled. Sisera was done for, his mother would never hear the sound of those returning chariot wheels.

Jael had permanently recouped herself for the butter.

A little later on the vicar swept out of his stall and up to the pulpit covered by the prolonged 'Amen' of the accompanying hymn. Henry looked at his watch and shut it with a click. Then his hard blue eyes closed suddenly—he had no eyelashes. Mrs Watkins folded her hands in her lap and fixed her attention upon St Peter.

This was her nice, quiet time, and she spent it considering how she could most easily kill Henry Watkins.

She was not in the least touched by the sight of her wedding ring. Her marriage had been an accident, one of those accidents that happened frequently twenty years ago, and which happen, though more seldom, now. An unhappy blunder of ignorance and family pressure.

She had liked making Henry Watkins jump, and her mother had explained to her that the tendency to jump on Henry's part was ardent, manly love, and that her own amused contemplation of the performance was deep womanly inclination.

It was then that Mrs Watkins urged that she did not like the back of Henry's head. She had been told that it was immodest to notice it. His means were excellent and her own parents were poor. Twenty years ago Mrs Watkins had known very little about life, and what she did know she was tempted to enjoy. She knew a good deal about it now, and she had long ago outgrown the temptation to enjoy it.

Still, that in itself wouldn't have given her any idea of killing her husband. She was a just woman and she knew that her husband had not invented the universe; if he had, she thought it would have been more unpleasant still.

Henry's idea of marriage was very direct; he knew that he had done his wife an enormous favour. She was penniless and he had the money; she was to come to him for every penny and all she had was his as a matter of course. She could do him no favours, she had no rights, and her preferences were silly.

It had occurred to Mrs Watkins in one awful moment of early resentment that she would rather be bought by a great many men than by one. There would be more variety, and some of them, at least, wouldn't be like Henry.

Then her children came; she aged very rapidly. Nothing is so bad for the personal appearance as the complete abrogation of self-respect. Henry continually threw her birthdays in her teeth. 'A woman of your age,' he would say with deep contempt.

He was a man of favourite phrases. Mrs Watkins was not constitutionally averse to repetition, but the repetition of a phrase that means to hurt can be curiously unpleasant. Still, as her mother had pointed out to her long years ago, you can get used to the unpleasant.

She never complained, and her parents were gratefully conscious of how soon she had settled down.

But there was a strange fallacy that lingered deep in Mrs Watkins's heart.

She had given up her rights as a woman, since presumably her marriage necessitated the sacrifice. But she believed that she would be allowed the rights of a mother. This, of course, was where she made her mistake.

Henry Watkins meant to be master in his own house. The house was his own, so was his wife, so were his children. There is no division of property where there is one master. This was a great religious truth to Henry, so that when his son displeased him he thrashed him, and when his daughter got in his way he bullied her.

Mrs Watkins disputed this right not once but many times, till she found the results were worse for the children. Then she dropped her opposition. Henry Watkins saw that she had learnt her lesson. It taught the children a lesson, too; they saw that it made no difference what mother said to father.

Nothing happened to alter either her attitude or Henry's.

They went to the same church twice every Sunday, except when it rained; and ate roast beef afterwards.

In spite of Henry, Hetty had grown into a charming, slightly nervous young woman, and in spite of Henry, Paul had become a clever, highly strung, regrettably artistic young man.

But if Henry couldn't help their temperaments he could put his foot down about their future.

Paul should go into the bank and learn to be a man. (By learning to be a man, Henry meant learning to care more for money than for anything else); and Hetty should receive no assistance toward marrying an impecunious young architect to whom she had taken a fancy.

Hetty could do as she chose: she could marry Henry's old friend Badeley, who had a decent income; or she could stay at home and pretend to be ill; but she certainly shouldn't throw herself away on a young fool who hadn't the means (rather fortunately, as it happened) to support her.

Henry looked at his watch; the sermon had already lasted twenty minutes.

Mrs Watkins went over once more in her mind how she had better do it. 'And now to God the Father,' said the vicar. The sermon had lasted twenty-seven minutes, and Henry meant to point it out to the vicar in the vestry. 'Oh, what the joy and the glory must be!' sang the choir. 'And if I am hanged,' said Mrs Watkins to herself, 'they'll get the money just the same. I shall try not to be, because it would be so upsetting for them, poor young things; still it's wonderful what you can get over when you're young.'

At lunch Henry made Hetty cry and ordered her from the room.

Paul flashed out in his sister's defence. 'You're unbearable, sir—why can't you leave us alone?'

His mother strangely interposed.

'Never mind, Paul,' she said. 'Let father have his own way.'

Paul looked at her in astonishment, and Henry was extremely annoyed. He was perfectly capable of taking his own way without his wife's interference, and he told her so.

It was the cook's evening out, and the house parlour-maid—a flighty creature—was upstairs in her room, trimming a new hat. There was no one downstairs in the kitchen after supper.

Paul went out to smoke in the garden, and Hetty had gone to finish her tears in her own room. That was something Mrs Watkins hadn't got; but she needed no place for finishing her tears, because she had never yet begun them. She did not see the use of tears.

Mrs Watkins stood and looked at her husband as he sprawled at his ease in the most comfortable chair.

'Henry,' she said, 'would you like some of that sloe gin your brother sent you? You haven't tried it yet.'

'I don't mind trying a glass,' said Henry good-naturedly.

His wife paused at the door. She came back a step or two. 'You've not changed your mind,' she asked, 'about the children's futures?'

'No! Why should I change my mind?' said Henry. 'Do I ever change my mind? They can make as much fuss as they like, but the man who pays the piper calls the tune!'

'I've heard you say that before,' said his wife reflectively.

'I dare say you'll hear me say it again!' said Henry with a laugh.

Mrs Watkins's hand went toward the handle of the door; she did not think she would ever hear Henry say this favourite maxim again; but still she lingered.

'Hurry up with that liqueur!' said her husband.

Mrs Watkins went into the pantry and took out a liqueur-glass. She poured a little sloe gin into it, then she put down the bottle and left the pantry. She went into the children's dark-room—they were allowed that for their photography.

She still had the glass in her hand. There was a bottle on the highest shelf. She took it down and measured it carefully with her eye. The children's manual of photography and the medical dictionary in Henry's dressing-room had been a great help.

She poured out into the deep red of the sloe gin some of the contents of the bottle; it looked very white and harmless and hardly smelt at all. She wondered if it was enough, and she tipped up the bottle a little to make sure. She used a good deal more than the medical dictionary said was necessary, but the medical dictionary might have underestimated Henry's constitution. She put the bottle back where she found it, and returned to the pantry. There she filled up the liqueur-glass with more sloe gin.

She saw Paul on a garden seat through the window. 'I wish you'd come out, Mother,' he said.

'I will in a minute, dear,' she answered quietly. Then she went back to her husband. 'Here it is, Henry.'

'What a slow woman you are!' he grumbled. 'Still I must say you have a steady hand.'

She held the full glass toward him and watched him drink it in a gulp.

'It tastes damned odd,' said Henry thoughtfully. 'I don't think I shall take any more of it.'

Mrs Watkins did not answer; she took up the liqueur-glass and went back into the pantry.

She took out another glass, filled it with sloe gin, drank it, and put it on the pantry table.

The first glass she slipped up her long sleeve and went out into the garden.

'I thought you were never coming, Mother!' Paul exclaimed. 'Oh, I do feel sick about everything! If this kind of thing goes on, I shall do something desperate! I sometimes think I should like to kill father.'

Mrs Watkins drew a long breath of relief. Once or twice lately it had occurred to her while she was thinking things over in church that Paul might get desperate and attack his father. He couldn't now.

'Don't talk like that dear,' she said gently. 'I sometimes think your father can't help himself. Besides, it's very natural he should want you and Hetty to have money; he values money.'

'He doesn't want us to have it!' Paul exclaimed savagely. 'He only wants to keep us in his power because we haven't got it, and can't get away! What money has he ever given you—or let us have for our own freedom?'

Mrs Watkins looked up at the substantial house and around the well-stocked garden. Henry had gone in especially for cabbages. She looked as if she were listening for something.

'I don't like to hear you talk like that, Paul,' she said at last. 'I want you to go up to Hetty's room and bring her out into the garden. She ought to have some air. It'll be church time presently.'

'But if I bring her down, won't *he* come out and upset her?' Paul demanded.

'I don't think he is coming out again,' said Mrs Watkins. She watched her son disappear into the house, and then walked on into the thick shrubbery at the end of the garden. She slipped the liqueur-glass out of her sleeve and broke it into fragments against the garden wall, then she covered the pieces with loose earth.

She had hardly finished before she heard a cry from the house. 'Mother! Mother! Oh, Mother!'

'I've done the best I can,' she said suddenly, between the kitchen garden and the house.

There was an inquest the following week, and Mrs Watkins dressed in decent black, gave her evidence with methodical carefulness.

Her husband had been quite well before dinner, she explained. At dinner he had been a little disturbed with one of the children, but nothing out of the ordinary at all. He had merely said a few sharp words. After dinner he had gone to sit in the drawing room, and at his request she had brought him a glass of sloe gin sent him by his brother; when he had finished it she had carried the glass back into the pantry. She did not see him again. The maids were not downstairs at the time. The sloe gin was examined, the pantry was examined, the whole household was examined. The parlour-maid had hysterics, and the cook gave notice to the coroner for asking her if she kept her pans clean. The verdict was death through misadventure, though a medical officer declared that poison was evidently the cause.

It was considered possible that Henry had privately procured it and taken it himself.

It is true he had no motive for suicide, but there was still less motive for murder. Nobody wished ardently that Henry might live, but, on the other hand, nobody benefited by his interesting and mysterious death—that is to say, nobody but Henry's family; and it is not considered probable that well-dressed, respectable people benefit by a parent's death.

Mrs Watkins was never tempted to confession; and she continued to gaze just as fixedly at St Peter and the sardines every Sunday. She thought about quite different subjects now; but she still had a nice quiet time.

It was the day before Hetty's wedding to the young architect that Mrs Watkins made her final approach to the question of her husband's death. She never referred to it afterwards.

'Do you know, Mummy darling,' Hetty said, 'I was sure there were a dozen liqueur-glasses in the cupboard. I always looked after them myself. Father was so particular about them; and they put back the horrid inquest one, I know, and yet I can only find eleven.'

Mrs Watkins looked at her daughter with a curious expression, then she asked abruptly, 'Are you very happy, child?' Hetty assented radiantly. Her mother nodded. 'And Paul,' said Mrs Watkins thoughtfully, 'he seems very contented in his painting. He wants me to go with him to Paris.'

'Paul can't be as happy as I am,' Hetty triumphantly assured her, 'because he hasn't got Dick—but it does seem as if both our wildest dreams had come true in the most extraordinary way, doesn't it, Mummy?'

Mrs Watkins did not answer her daughter at once. She turned toward the cupboard. She seemed to be counting the broken set over again.

'Well, I don't think it matters about that liqueur-glass,' she said finally. 'I'm not as particular as your father.'

OVER AN ABSINTHE BOTTLE

W. C. Morrow

Absinthe, the curious liqueur containing extract of wormwood, has always had an exotic and slightly sinister reputation, and featured particularly in a number of stories by some of the decadent writers who belonged to the late nineteenth-century French school of symbolists and their like. There are, though, few tales which utilise the drink better than 'Over an Absinthe Bottle' by the American writer, William Chambers Morrow (1853–1923) whose fame rests solely on one collection of short stories, curiously entitled The Ape, the Idiot and Other People, *published in 1897. Morrow died mysteriously in San Francisco of drink-related problems, which adds an extra frisson to this grim tale of two strangers drinking and gambling away their lives in a bar . . .*

Arthur Kimberlin, a young man of very high spirit, found himself a total stranger in San Francisco one rainy evening, at a time when his heart was breaking; for his hunger was of that most poignant kind in which physical suffering is forced to the highest point without impairment of the mental functions. There remained in his possession not a thing he might have pawned for a morsel to eat; and even as it was, he had stripped his body of all articles of clothing except those which a remaining sense of decency compelled him to retain. Hence it was that cold assailed him and conspired with hunger to complete his misery. Having been brought into the world and reared a gentleman, he lacked the courage to beg and the skill to steal. Had not an extraordinary thing occurred to him, he either would have drowned himself in the bay within twenty-four hours or died of pneumonia in the street. He had been seventy hours without food, and his mental desperation had driven him far in its race with his physical needs to consume the strength within him; so that now, pale, weak, and tottering, he took what comfort he could find in the savoury odours which came steaming up from the basement kitchen of the restaurants in Market Street, caring more to gain them than to avoid the rain. His teeth chattered; he shambled, stooped, and gasped. He was too desperate to curse his fate—he could only long for food. He could not reason; he could not understand that ten thousand hands might gladly have fed him; he could think only of the hunger which consumed him, and of food that could give him warmth and happiness.

When he had arrived at Mason Street, he saw a restaurant a little way up that thoroughfare, and for that he headed, crossing the street diagonally. He stopped before the window and ogled the steaks, thick and lined with fat; big oysters lying on ice; slices of ham as large as his hat; whole roasted chickens, brown and juicy. He ground his teeth, groaned, and staggered on.

A few steps beyond was a drinking-saloon, which had a private door at once side, with the words 'Family Entrance' painted thereon. In the recess of the door (which was closed) stood a man. In spite of his agony, Kimberlin saw something in this man's face that appalled and fascinated him. Night was on, and the light in the vicinity was dim; but it was apparent that the stranger had an appearance of whose character he himself must have been ignorant. Perhaps it was the unspeakable anguish of it that struck through Kimberlin's sympathies. The young man came to an uncertain halt and stared at the stranger. At first he was unseen, for the stranger looked straight out into the street with singular fixity, and the death-like pallor of his face added a weirdness to the immobility of his gaze. Then he took notice of the young man.

'Ah,' he said, slowly and with peculiar distinctness, 'the rain has caught you, too, without overcoat or umbrella! Stand in this doorway—there is room for two.'

The voice was not unkind, though it had an alarming hardness. It was the first word that had been addressed to the sufferer since hunger had seized him, and to be spoken to at all, and have his comfort regarded in the slightest way, gave him cheer. He entered the embrasure and stood beside the stranger, who at once relapsed into his fixed gaze at nothing across the street. But presently the stranger stirred himself again.

'It may rain a long time,' said he; 'I am cold, and I observe that you tremble. Let us step inside and get a drink.'

He opened the door and Kimberlin followed, hope beginning to lay a warm hand upon his heart. The pale stranger led the way into one of the little private booths with which the place was furnished. Before sitting down he put his hand into his pocket and drew forth a roll of bank-bills.

'You are younger than I,' he said; 'won't you go to the bar and buy a bottle of absinthe, and bring a pitcher of water and some glasses? I don't like the waiters to come round. Here is a twenty-dollar bill.'

Kimberlin took the bill and started down through the corridor towards the bar. He clutched the money tightly in his palm; it felt warm and comfortable, and sent a delicious tingling through his arm. How many glorious hot meals did that bill represent? He clutched it tighter and hesitated. He thought he smelled a broiled steak, with fat little mushrooms and melted butter in the steaming dish. He stopped and looked back towards the door of the booth. He saw that the stranger had closed it. He could pass it, slip out of the door, and buy something to eat. He turned and started, but the coward in him (there are other names for this) tripped his resolution; so he went straight to the bar and made the purchase. This was so unusual that the man who served him looked sharply at him.

'Ain't goin' to drink all o' that, are you?' he asked.

'I have friends in the box,' replied Kimberlin, 'and we want to drink quietly and without interruption. We are in Number 7.'

'Oh, beg pardon. That's all right,' said the man.

Kimberlin's step was very much stronger and steadier as he returned with the liquor. He opened the door of the booth. The stranger sat at the side of the little table, staring at the opposite wall just as he had stared across the street. He wore a wide-brimmed, slouch hat, drawn well down. It was only after Kimberlin had set the bottle, pitcher, and glasses on the table, and seated himself opposite the stranger and within his range of vision, that the pale man noticed him.

'Oh! you have brought it? How kind of you! Now please lock the door.'

Kimberlin had slipped the change into his pocket, and was in the act of bringing it out when the stranger said—

'Keep the change. You will need it, for I am going to get it back in a way that may interest you. Let us first drink, and then I will explain.'

The pale man mixed two drinks of absinthe and water, and the two drank. Kimberlin, unsophisticated, had never tasted the liquor before, and he found it harsh and offensive; but no sooner had it reached his stomach than it began to warm him, and sent the most delicious thrill through his frame.

'It will do us good,' said the stranger; 'presently we shall have more. Meanwhile, do you know how to throw dice?'

Kimberlin weakly confessed that he did not.

'I thought not. Well, please go to the bar and bring a dice-box. I would ring for it, but I don't want the waiters to be coming in.'

Kimberlin fetched the box, again locked the door, and the game began. It was not one of the simple old games, but had complications, in which judgement, as well as chance, played a part. After a game or two without stakes, the stranger said—

'You now seem to understand it. Very well—I will show you that you do not. We will now throw for a dollar a game, and in that way I shall win the money that you received in change. Otherwise I should be robbing you, and I imagine you can not afford to lose. I mean no offence. I am a plain-spoken man, but I believe in honesty before politeness. I merely want a little diversion, and you are so kind-natured that I am sure you will not object.'

'On the contrary,' replied Kimberlin, 'I shall enjoy it.'

'Very well; but let us have another drink before we start. I believe I am growing colder.'

They drank again, and this time the starving man took his liquor with relish—at least, it was something in his stomach, and it warmed and delighted him.

The stake was a dollar a side. Kimberlin won. The pale stranger smiled grimly, and opened another game. Again Kimberlin won. Then the stranger pushed back his hat and fixed that still gaze upon his opponent, smiling yet. With this full view of the pale stranger's face, Kimberlin was more appalled than ever. He had begun to acquire a certain self-possession and ease, and his marvelling at the singular character of the adventure had begun to weaken, when this new incident threw him back into confusion. It was the extraordinary expression of the stranger's face that alarmed him. Never upon the face of a living being had he seen a pallor so death-like and chilling. The face was more than pale; it was white. Kimberlin's observing faculty had been sharpened by the absinthe, and, after having detected the stranger in an absent-minded effort two or three times to stroke a beard which had no existence, he reflected that some of the whiteness of the face might be due to the recent removal of a full beard. Besides the pallor, there were deep and sharp lines upon the face, which the electric light brought out very distinctly. With the exception of the steady glance of the eyes and an occasional hard smile, which seemed out place upon such a face, the expression was that of stone inartistically cut. The eyes were black, but of heavy expression; the lower lip was purple; the hands were fine, white, and thin, and dark veins bulged out upon them. The stranger pulled down his hat.

'You are lucky,' he said. 'Suppose we try another drink. There is nothing like absinthe to sharpen one's wits, and I see that you and I are going to have a delightful game.'

After the drink the game proceeded. Kimberlin won from the very first, rarely losing a game. He became greatly excited. His eyes shone; colour came to his cheeks. The stranger, having exhausted the roll of bills which he first produced, drew forth another, much larger and of higher denominations. There were several thousand dollars in the roll. At Kimberlin's right hand were his winnings—something like two hundred dollars. The stakes were raised, and the game went rapidly on. Another drink was taken. Then fortune turned the stranger's way, and he won easily. It went back to Kimberlin, for he was now playing with all the judgement and skill he could command. Once only did it occur to him to wonder what he should do with the money if he should quit winner; but a sense of honour decided him that it would belong to the stranger.

By this time the absinthe had so sharpened Kimberlin's faculties that, the temporary satisfaction which it had brought to his hunger having passed, his physical suffering returned with increased aggressiveness. Could he not order a supper with his earnings? No; that was out of the question, and the stranger said nothing about eating. Kimberlin continued to play, while the manifestations of hunger took the form of sharp pains, which darted through him viciously, causing him to writhe and grind his teeth. The stranger paid no attention, for he was now wholly absorbed in the game. He seemed puzzled and disconcerted. He played with great care, studying each throw minutely. No conversation passed between them now. They drank occasionally, the dice continued to rattle, the money kept piling up at Kimberlin's hand.

The pale man began to behave strangely. At times he would start and throw back his head, as though he were listening. For a moment his eyes would sharpen and flash, and then sink into heaviness again. More than once Kimberlin, who had now begun to suspect his antagonist was some kind of monster, saw a frightfully ghastly expression sweep over his face, and his features would become fixed for a very short time in a peculiar grimace. It was noticeable, however, that he was steadily sinking deeper and deeper into a condition of apathy. Occasionally he would raise his eyes to Kimberlin's face after the young man had made an astonishingly lucky throw, and keep them fixed there with a steadiness that made the young man quail.

The stranger produced another roll of bills when the second was gone, and this had a value many times as great as the others together. The stakes were raised to a thousand dollars a game, and still Kimberlin won. At last the time came when the stranger braced himself for a final effort. With speech somewhat thick, but very deliberate and quiet, he said,—

'You have won seventy-four thousand dollars, which is exactly the amount I have remaining. We have been playing for several hours. I am tired, and I suppose you are. Let us finish the game. Each will now stake his all and throw a final game for it.'

Without hesitation, Kimberlin agreed. The bills made a considerable pile on the table. Kimberlin threw, and the box held but one combination that could possibly beat him; this combination might be thrown once in ten thousand times. The starving man's heart beat violently as the stranger picked up the box with exasperating deliberation. It was a long time before he threw. He made his combination and ended by defeating his opponent. He sat looking at the dice a long time, and then he slowly leaned back in his chair, settled himself comfortably, raised his eyes to Kimberlin's, and fixed that unearthly stare upon him. He said not a word; his face contained not a trace of emotion or intelligence. He simply looked. One cannot keep one's eyes open very long without winking, but the stranger did. He sat so motionless that Kimberlin began to be tortured.

'I will go now,' he said to the stranger—said that when he had not a cent and was starving.

The stranger made no reply, but did not relax his gaze; and under that gaze the young man shrank back in his own chair, terrified. He became aware that two men were cautiously talking in an adjoining booth. As there was now a deathly silence in his own, he listened, and this is what he heard:

'Yes; he was seen to turn into this street about three hours ago.'

'And he had shaved?'

'He must have done so; and to remove a full beard would naturally make a great change in a man.'

'But it may not have been he.'

'True enough; but his extreme pallor attracted attention. You know that he has been troubled with heart-disease lately, and it has affected him seriously.'

'Yes, but his old skill remains. Why, this is the most daring bank-robbery we ever had here. A hundred and forty-eight thousand dollars—think of it! How long has it been since he was let out of Joliet?'

'Eight years. In that time he has grown a beard, and lived by dice-throwing with men who thought they could detect him if he should swindle them; but that is impossible. No human being can come winner out of a game with him. He is evidently not here; let us look farther.'

Then the two men clinked glasses and passed out.

The dice-players—the pale one and the starving one—sat gazing at each other, with a hundred and forty-eight thousand dollars piled up between them. The winner made no move to take in the money; he merely sat and stared at Kimberlin, wholly unmoved by the conversation in the adjoining room. His imperturbability was amazing, his absolute stillness terrifying.

Kimberlin began to shake with an ague. The cold, steady gaze of the stranger sent ice into his marrow. Unable to bear longer this unwavering look, Kimberlin moved to one side, and then he was amazed to discover that the eyes of the pale man, instead of following him, remained fixed upon the spot where he had sat, or, rather, upon the wall behind it. A great dread beset the young man. He feared to make the slightest sound. Voices of men in the bar-room were audible, and the sufferer imagined that he heard others whispering and tiptoeing in the passage outside his booth. He poured out some absinthe, watching his strange companion all the while, and drank alone and unnoticed. He took a heavy drink, and it had a peculiar effect upon him: he felt his heart bounding with alarming force and rapidity, and breathing was difficult. Still his hunger remained, and that and the absinthe gave him an idea that the gastric acids were destroying him by digesting his stomach. He leaned forward and whispered to the stranger, but was given no attention. One of the man's hands lay upon the table; Kimberlin placed his upon it, and then drew back in terror—the hand was as cold as a stone.

The money must not lie there exposed. Kimberlin arranged it into neat parcels, looking furtively every moment at his immovable companion, and *in mortal fear that he would stir!* Then he sat back and waited. A deadly fascination impelled him to move back into his former position, so as to bring his face directly before the gaze of the stranger. And so the two sat and stared at each other.

Kimberlin felt his breath coming heavier and his heart-beats growing weaker, but these conditions gave him comfort by reducing his anxiety and softening the pangs of hunger. He was growing more and more comfortable and yawned. If he had dared he might have gone to sleep.

Suddenly a fierce light flooded his vision and sent him with a bound to his feet. Had he been struck upon the head or stabbed to the heart? No; he was sound and alive. The pale stranger still sat there staring at nothing and immovable; but Kimberlin was no longer afraid of him. On the contrary, an extraordinary buoyancy of spirit and elasticity of body made him feel reckless and daring. His former timidity and scruples vanished, and he felt equal to any adventure. Without hesitation he gathered up the money and bestowed it in his several pockets.

'I am a fool to starve,' he said to himself, 'with all this money ready to my hand.'

As cautiously as a thief he unlocked the door, stepped out, reclosed it, and boldly and with head erect stalked out upon the street. Much to his astonishment, he found the city in the bustle of the early evening, yet the sky was clear. It was evident to him that he had not been in the saloon as long as he had supposed. He walked along the street with the utmost unconcern of the dangers that beset him, and laughed softly but gleefully. Would he not eat now—ah, would he not? Why, he could buy a dozen restaurants! Not only that, but he would hunt the city up and down for hungry men and feed them with the fattest steaks, the juiciest roasts, and the biggest oysters that the town could supply. As for himself, he must eat first; after that he would set up a great establishment for feeding other hungry mortals without charge. Yes, he would eat first; if he pleased, he would eat till he should burst. In what single place could he find sufficient to satisfy his hunger? Could he live sufficiently long to have an ox killed and roasted whole for his supper? Besides an ox he would order two dozen broiled chickens, fifty dozen oysters, a dozen crabs, ten dozen eggs, ten hams, eight young pigs, twenty wild ducks, fifteen fish of four different kinds, eight salads, four dozen bottles each of claret, burgundy, and champagne; for pastry, eight plum-puddings, and for dessert, bushels of nuts, ices, and confections. It would require time to prepare such a meal, and if he could only live until it could be made ready it would be infinitely better than to spoil his appetite with a dozen or two meals of ordinary size. He thought he could live that long, for he felt amazingly strong and bright. Never in his life before had he walked with so great ease and lightness; his feet hardly touched the ground—he ran and leaped. It did him good to tantalise his hunger, for that would make his relish of the feast all the keener. Oh, but how they would stare when he would give his order, and how comically they would hang back, and how amazed they would be when he would throw a few thousands of dollars on the counter and tell them to take their money out of it and keep the change! Really, it was worth while to be so hungry as that, for then eating became an unspeakable luxury. And one must not be in too great a hurry to eat when one is so hungry—that is beastly. How much of the joy of living do rich people miss from eating before they are hungry—before they have gone three days and nights without food! And how manly it is, and how great self-control it shows, to dally with starvation when one has a dazzling fortune in one's pocket and every restaurant has an open door! To be hungry without money— that is despair; to be starving with a bursting pocket—that is sublime! Surely the only true heaven is that in which one famishes in the presence of abundant food, which he might have for the taking, and then a gorged stomach and a long sleep.

The starving wretch, speculating thus, still kept from food. He felt himself growing in stature, and the people whom he met became pigmies. The streets widened, the stars became suns and dimmed the electric lights, and the most intoxicating odours and the sweetest music filled the air. Shouting, laughing, and singing, Kimberlin joined in a great chorus that swept over the city, and then—

* * *

The two detectives who had traced the famous bank-robber to the saloon in Mason Street, where Kimberlin had encountered the stranger of the pallid face, left the saloon; but, unable to pursue the trail farther, had finally returned. They found the door of booth No. 7 locked. After rapping and calling and receiving no answer, they burst open the door, and there they saw two men— one of middle age and the other very young—sitting perfectly still, and in the strangest manner imaginable staring at each other across the table. Between them was a great pile of money, arranged neatly in parcels. Near at hand were an empty absinthe bottle, a water-pitcher, glasses, and a dice-box, with the dice lying before the elder man as he had thrown them last. One of the detectives covered the elder man with a revolver and commanded—

'Throw up your hands!'

But the dice-thrower paid no attention. The detectives exchanged startled glances. They looked closer into the faces of the two men, and then they discovered that both were dead.

THE WIDOW

Margery Allingham

Margery Allingham (1904–1966) came from a literary family and first made her name as a serious historical novelist. It was after her marriage to Philip Youngman Carter, the artist and editor of The Tatler, *that she turned her attention to mystery stories and eventually created the detective, Albert Campion, for whom she is now best remembered. Margery and her husband (who also compiled* The Complete Imbiber, *a periodical miscellany sponsored by Gilbey's Gin) divided their time between a flat in London, in Great Russell Street, and a large house at Tolleshunt D'Arcy, an isolated little village on the edge of the Essex marshes. Here they threw legendary parties at which punch, made from one of Margery's own secret recipes, and vintage brandy were the favourite drinks for their guests. Drink also features in a number of the detective novels, including* Tiger in the Smoke *(1952) which was filmed in 1956 starring Donald Sinden and Muriel Pavlow, and in several short stories such as 'The Widow' which also happens to feature the perceptive and discerning sleuth, Mr Campion.*

The second prettiest girl in Mayfair was thanking Superintendent Stanislaus Oates for the recovery of her diamond bracelet and the ring with the square-cut emerald in it, and Mr Campion, who had accompanied her to the ceremony, was admiring her technique.

She was doing it very charmingly; so charmingly, in fact, that the Superintendent's depressing little office had taken on an air of garden-party gaiety which it certainly did not possess in the ordinary way, while the Superintendent himself had undergone an even more sensational change.

His long dyspeptic face was transformed by a blush of smug satisfaction and he quite forgot the short lecture he had prepared for his visitor on The Carelessness Which Tempts the Criminal, or its blunter version, Stupidity Which Earns Its Own Reward.

It was altogether a most gratifying scene, and Mr Campion

seated in the visitor's chair, his long thin legs crossed and his pale eyes amused behind his horn-rimmed spectacles, enjoyed it to the full.

Miss Leonie Peterhouse-Vaughn raised her remarkable eyes to the Superintendent's slightly sheepish face and spoke with deep earnestness.

'I honestly think you're wonderful,' she said.

Realising that too much butter can have a disastrous effect on any dish, and not being at all certain of his old friend's digestive capabilities, Mr Campion coughed.

'He has his failures too,' he ventured. 'He's not omnipotent, you know. Just an ordinary man.'

'Really?' said Miss Peterhouse-Vaughn with gratifying surprise.

'Oh, yes; well, we're only human, miss.' The Superintendent granted Mr Campion a reproachful look. 'Sometimes we have our little disappointments. Of course on those occasions we call in Mr Campion here,' he added with a flash of malice.

Leonie laughed prettily and Mr. Oates's ruffled fur subsided like a wave.

'Sometimes even he can't help us,' he went on, encouraged, and, inspired no doubt by the theory that the greater the enemy the greater the honour, launched into an explanation perhaps not altogether discreet. 'Sometimes we come up against a man who slips through our fingers every time. There's a man in London today who's been responsible for more trouble than I can mention. We know him, we know where he lives, we could put our hands on him any moment of the day or night, but have we any proof against him? Could we hold him for ten minutes without getting into serious trouble for molesting a respectable citizen? Could we? Well, we couldn't.'

Miss Peterhouse-Vaughn's expression of mystified interest was very flattering.

'This is incredibly exciting,' she said. 'Who is he?—or mustn't you tell?'

The Superintendent shook his head.

'Entirely against the regulations,' he said regretfully, and then, on seeing her disappointment and feeling, no doubt, that his portentous declaration had fallen a little flat, he relented and made a compromise between his conscience and a latent vanity which Mr Campion had never before suspected. 'Well, I'll show you this,' he conceded. 'It's a very curious thing.'

With Leonie's fascinated eyes upon him, he opened a drawer in his desk and took out a single sheet torn from a week-old London evening paper. A small advertisement in the Situations Vacant column was ringed with blue pencil. Miss Peterhouse-Vaughn took it eagerly and Mr Campion got up lazily to read it over her shoulder.

> WANTED: *Entertainer suitable for children's party. Good money offered to right man. Apply in person any evening. Widow, 13 Blakenham Gardens, W1.*

Leonie read the lines three times and looked up.

'But it seems quite ordinary,' she said.

The Superintendent nodded. 'That's what any member of the public would think,' he agreed, gracefully keeping all hint of condescension out of his tone. 'And it would have escaped our notice too except for one thing, and that's the name and address. You see, the man I was telling you about happens to live at 13 Blakenham Gardens.'

'Is his name Widow? How queer!'

'No, miss, it's not.' Oates looked uncomfortable, seeing the pitfall too late. 'I ought not to be telling you this,' he went on severely. 'This gentleman—and we've got nothing we can pin on him, remember—is known as "The Widow" to the criminal classes. That's why this paragraph interested us. As it stands it's an ad for a crook, and the fellow has the impudence to use his own address! Doesn't even hide it under a box number.'

Mr Campion eyed his old friend. He seemed mildly interested.

'Did you send someone along to answer it?' he enquired.

'We did.' The Superintendent spoke heavily. 'Poor young Billings was kept there singing comic songs for three-quarters of an hour while W—I mean this fellow—watched him without a smile. Then he told him he'd go down better at a police concert.'

Miss Peterhouse-Vaughn looked sympathetic.

'What a shame!' she said gravely, and Mr Campion never admired her more.

'We sent another man,' continued the Superintendent, 'but when he got there the servant told him the vacancy had been filled. We kept an eye on the place, too, but it wasn't easy. The whole crescent was a seething mass of would-be child entertainers.'

'So you haven't an idea what he's up to?' Mr Campion seemed amused.

'Not the faintest,' Oates admitted. 'We shall in the end, though; I'll lay my bottom dollar. He was the moving spirit in that cussed Featherstone case, you know, and we're pretty certain it was he who slipped through the police net in the Barking business.'

Mr Campion raised his eyebrows. 'Blackmail and smuggling?' he said. 'He seems to be a versatile soul, doesn't he?'

'He's up to anything,' Oates declared. 'Absolutely anything. I'd

give a packet to get my hands on him. But what he wants with a
kids' entertainer—if it is an entertainer he's after—I do not know.'

'Perhaps he just wants to give a children's party?' suggested
Miss Peterhouse-Vaughn and while the policeman was considering this possibility, evidently the one explanation which had not
crossed his mind, she took her leave.

'I must thank you once again, Mr Oates,' she said. 'I can't tell
you how terribly, terribly clever I think you are, and how awfully
grateful I am, and how frightfully careful I'll be in future not to
give you any more dreadful trouble.'

It was a charming little speech in spite of her catastrophic adjectives and the Superintendent beamed.

'It's been a pleasure, miss,' he said.

As Mr Campion handed her into her mother's Daimler he
regarded her coldly.

'A pretty performance,' he remarked. 'Tell me, what do you say
when a spark of genuine gratitude warms your nasty little heart?
My poor Oates!'

Miss Peterhouse-Vaughn grinned.

'I did do it well, didn't I?' she said complacently. 'He's rather a
dear old goat.'

Mr Campion was shocked and said so.

'The Superintendent is a distinguished officer. I always knew
that, of course, but this afternoon I discovered a broad streak of
chivalry in him. In his place I think I might have permitted myself
a few comments on the type of young woman who leaves a
diamond bracelet and an emerald ring in the soap-dish at a public
restaurant and then goes smiling to Scotland Yard to ask for it
back. The wretched man had performed a miracle for you and
you call him a dear old goat.'

Leonie was young enough to look abashed without losing her
charm.

'Oh, but I am grateful,' she said. 'I think he's wonderful. But
not so absolutely brilliant as somebody else.'

'That's very nice of you, my child.' Mr Campion prepared to
unbend.

'Oh, not you, darling.' Leonie squeezed his arm. 'I was talking
about the other man—The Widow. He's got real nerve, don't you
think?—using his own address and making the detective sing and
all that. . . . So amusing!'

Her companion looked down at her severely.

'Don't make a hero out of *him*,' he said.

'Why not?'

'Because, my dear little hideous, he's a crook. It's only while he
remains uncaught that he's faintly interesting. Sooner or later your

elderly admirer, the Superintendent, is going to clap him under lock and key and then he'll just be an ordinary convict, who is anything but romantic, believe me.'

Miss Peterhouse-Vaughn shook her head.

'He won't get caught,' she said. 'Or if he does—forgive me, darling—it'll be by someone much cleverer than you or Mr Oates.'

Mr Campion's professional pride rebelled.

'What'll you bet?'

'Anything you like,' said Leonie. 'Up to two pounds,' she added prudently.

Campion laughed. 'The girl's learning caution at last!' he said. 'I may hold you to that.'

The conversation changed to the charity matinée of the day before, wherein Miss Peterhouse-Vaughn had appeared as Wisdom, and continued its easy course, gravitating naturally to the most important pending event in the Peterhouse-Vaughn family, the christening of Master Brian Desmond Peterhouse-Vaughn, nephew to Leonie, son to her elder brother, Desmond Brian, and godson to Mr Albert Campion.

It was his new responsibility as a godfather which led Mr Campion to take part in yet another elegant little ceremony some few days after the christening and nearly three weeks after Leonie's sensational conquest of Superintendent Oates's susceptible heart.

Mr. Campion called to see Mr Thistledown in Cheese Street, EC, and they went reverently to the cellars together.

Mr. Thistledown was a small man, elderly and dignified. His white hair was inclined to flow a little and his figure was more suited, perhaps, to his vocation than to his name. As head of the small but distinguished firm of Thistledown, Friend and Son, Wine Importers since 1798, he very seldom permitted himself a personal interview with any client under the age of sixty-five, for at that year he openly believed the genus *homo sapiens*, considered solely as a connoisseur of vintage wine, alone attained full maturity.

Mr Campion, however, was an exception. Mr. Thistledown thought of him as a lad still, but a promising one. He took his client's errand with all the gravity he felt it to deserve.

'Twelve dozen of port to be laid down for Master Brian Desmond Peterhouse-Vaughn,' he said, rolling the words round his tongue as though they, too, had their flavour. 'Let me see, it is now the end of '36. It will have to be a '27 wine. Then by the time your godson is forty—he won't want to drink it before that age, surely?—there should be a very fine fifty-year-old vintage awaiting him.'

A long and somewhat heated discussion, or, rather, monologue, for Mr Campion was sufficiently experienced to offer no opinion, followed. The relative merits of Croft, Taylor, Da Silva, Noval and Fonseca were considered at length, and in the end Mr Campion followed his mentor through the sacred tunnels and personally affixed his seal upon a bin of Taylor, 1927.

Mr Thistledown was in favour of a stipulation to provide that Master Peterhouse-Vaughn should not attain full control over his vinous inheritance until he attained the age of thirty, whereas Mr Campion preferred the more conventional twenty-one. Finally a compromise of twenty-five was agreed upon and the two gentlemen retired to Mr Thistledown's consulting-room glowing with the conscious virtue of men who had conferred a benefit upon posterity.

The consulting-room was comfortable. It was really no more than an arbour of bottles constructed in the vault of the largest cellar and was furnished with a table and chairs of solid ship's timber. Mr Thistledown paused by the table and hesitated before speaking. There was clearly something on his mind and Campion, who had always considered him slightly inhuman, a sort of living port crust, was interested.

When at last the old gentleman unburdened himself it was to make a short speech.

'It takes an elderly man to judge a port or a claret,' he said, 'but spirits are definitely in another category. Some men may live to be a hundred without ever realising the subtle differences of the finest rums. To judge a spirit one must be born with a certain kind of palate. Mr Campion, would you taste a brandy for me?'

His visitor was startled. Always a modest soul, he made no pretensions to connoisseurship and now he said so firmly.

'I don't know.' Mr Thistledown regarded him seriously. 'I have watched your taste for some years now and I am inclined to put you down as one of the few really knowledgeable younger men. Wait for me a moment.'

He went out, and through the arbour's doorway Campion saw him conferring with the oldest and most cobwebby of the troglodyte persons who lurked about the vaults.

Considerably flattered in spite of himself, he sat back and awaited developments. Presently one of the younger myrmidons, a mere youth of fifty or so, appeared with a tray and a small selection of balloon glasses. He was followed by an elder with two bottles, and at the rear of the procession came Mr Thistledown himself with something covered by a large silk handkerchief. Not until they were alone did he remove the veil. Then, whipping the handkerchief aside, he produced a partly full half-bottle with a new cork and no label. He held it up to the light and Mr Campion saw that the liquid within was of the true dark amber.

Still with the ritualistic air, Mr Thistledown polished a glass and poured a tablespoonful of the spirit, afterwards handing it to his client.

Feeling like a man with his honour at stake, Campion warmed the glass in his hand, sniffed at it intelligently, and finally allowed a little of the stuff to touch his tongue.

Mr Thistledown watched him earnestly. Campion tasted again and inhaled once more. Finally he set down his glass and grinned.

'I may be wrong,' he said, 'but it tastes like the real McKay.'

Mr Thistledown frowned at the vulgarism. He seemed satisfied, however, and there was a curious mixture of pleasure and discomfort on his face.

'I put it down at a Champagne Fine, 1835,' he said. 'It has not, perhaps, quite the superb caress of the true Napoleon—but a brave, yes, a brave brandy! The third best I have ever tasted in my life. And that, let me tell you, Mr Campion, is a very extraordinary thing.'

He paused, looking like some old white cockatoo standing at the end of the table

'I wonder if I might take you into my confidence?' he ventured at last. 'Ah—a great many people do take you into their confidence, I believe? Forgive me for putting it that way.'

Campion smiled. 'I'm as secret as the grave,' he said, 'and if there's anything I can do I shall be delighted.'

Mr Thistledown sighed with relief and became almost human.

'This confounded bottle was sent to me some little time ago,' he said. 'With it was a letter from a man called Gervaise Papulous; I don't suppose you've ever heard of him, but he wrote a very fine monograph on brandies some years ago which was greatly appreciated by connoisseurs. I had an idea he lived a hermit's life somewhere in Scotland, but that's neither here nor there. The fact remains that when I had this note from an address in Half Moon Street I recognised the name immediately. It was a very civil letter, asking me if I'd mind, as an expert, giving my opinion of the age and quality of the sample.'

He paused and smiled faintly.

'I was a little flattered, perhaps,' he said. 'After all, the man is a well-known authority himself. Anyway, I made the usual tests, tasted it and compared it with the oldest and finest stuff we have in stock. We have a few bottles of 1848 and one or two of the 1835. I made the most careful comparisons and at last I decided that the sample was a '35 brandy, but not the same blend as our own. I wrote him; I said I did not care to commit myself, but I gave him my opinion for what it was worth and I appended my reasons for forming it.'

Mr Thistledown's precise voice ceased and his colour heightened.

'By return I received a letter thanking me for mine and asking me whether I would care to consider an arrangement whereby I could buy the identical spirit in any quantity I cared to name at a hundred and twenty shillings a dozen, excluding duty—or, in other words, ten shillings per bottle.'

Mr Campion sat up. 'Ten shillings?' he said.

'Ten shillings,' repeated Mr Thistledown. 'The price of a wireless licence,' he added with contempt. 'Well, as you can imagine, Mr Campion, I thought there must be some mistake. Our own '35 is listed at sixty shillings a bottle and you cannot get finer value anywhere in London. The stuff is rare. In a year or two it will be priceless. I considered this sample again and reaffirmed my own first opinion. Then I re-read the letter and noticed the peculiar phrase—"an arrangement whereby you will be able to purchase." I thought about it all day and finally I put on my hat and went down to see the man.'

He glanced at his visitor almost timidly. Campion was reassuring.

'If it was genuine it was not a chance to be missed,' he murmured.

'Exactly.' Mr Thistledown smiled. 'Well, I saw him, a younger man than I had imagined but well informed, and I received quite a pleasant impression. I asked him frankly where he got the brandy and he came out with an extraordinary suggestion. He asked me first if I was satisfied with the sample, and I said I was or I should hardly have come to see him. Then he said the whole matter was a secret at the moment, but that he was asking certain well-informed persons to a private conference and something he called a scientific experiment. Finally he offered me an invitation. It is to take place next Monday evening in a little hotel on the Norfolk coast where Mr Papulous says the ideal conditions for his experiment exist.'

Mr Campion's interest was thoroughly aroused.

'I should go,' he said.

Mr Thistledown spread out his hands.

'I had thought of it,' he admitted. 'As I came out of the flat at Half Moon Street I passed a man I knew on the stairs. I won't mention his name and I won't say his firm is exactly a rival of ours, but—well, you know how it is. Two or three old firms get the reputation for supplying certain rare vintages. Their names are equally good and naturally there is a certain competition between them. If this fellow has happened on a whole cellar full of this brandy I should like to have as good a chance of buying it as the next man, especially at the price. But in my opinion and in my experience that is too much to hope for, and that is why I have ventured to mention the matter to you.'

A light dawned upon his client.

'You want me to attend the conference and make certain everything's above-board?'

'I hardly dared to suggest it,' he said, 'but since you are such an excellent judge, and since your reputation as an investigator— if I may be forgiven the term—is so great, I admit the thought did go through my mind.'

Campion picked up his glass and sniffed its fragrance.

'My dear man, I'd jump at it,' he said. 'Do I pass myself off as a member of the firm?'

Mr Thistledown looked owlish.

'In the circumstances I think we might connive at that little inexactitude,' he murmured. 'Don't you?'

'I think we'll have to,' said Mr Campion.

When he saw the 'little hotel on the Norfolk coast' at half-past six on the following Monday afternoon the thought came to him that it was extremely fortunate for the proprietor that it should be so suitable for Mr Papulous's experiment, for it was certainly not designed to be of much interest to any ordinary winter visitor. It was a large country public-house, not old enough to be picturesque, standing by itself at the end of a lane some little distance from a cold and sleepy village. In the summer, no doubt, it provided a headquarters for a great many picnic parties, but in winter it was deserted.

Inside it was warm and comfortable enough, however, and Campion found a curious little company seated round the fire in the lounge. His host rose to greet him and he was aware at once of a considerable personality.

He saw a tall man with a shy ingratiating manner, whose clothes were elegant and whose face was remarkable. His deep-set eyes were dark and intelligent and his wide mouth could smile disarmingly, but the feature which was most distinctive was the way in which his iron-grey hair drew into a clean-cut peak in the centre of his high forehead, giving him an odd, Mephistophelean appearance.

'Mr Fellowes?' he said, using the alias Campion and Mr Thistledown had agreed upon. 'I heard from your firm this morning. Of course I'm very sorry not to have Mr Thistledown here. He says in his note that I am to regard you as his second self. You handle the French side, I understand?'

'Yes. It was only by chance that I was in England yesterday when Mr Thistledown asked me to come.'

'I see.' Mr Papulous seemed contented with the explanation. Campion looked a mild, inoffensive young man, even a little foolish.

He was introduced to the rest of the company round the fire and was interested to see that Mr Thistledown had been right in his guess. Half a dozen of the best-known smaller and older wine firms were represented, in most cases by their senior partners.

Conversation, however, was not as general as might have been expected among men of such similar interests. On the contrary, there was a distinct atmosphere of restraint, and it occurred to Mr Campion that they were all close rivals and each man had not expected to see the others.

Mr Papulous alone seemed happily unconscious of any discomfort. He stood behind his chair at the head of the group and glanced round him with satisfaction.

'It's really very kind of you all to have come,' he said in his deep musical voice. 'Very kind indeed. I felt we must have experts, the finest experts in the world, to test this thing, because it's revolutionary—absolutely revolutionary.'

A large old gentleman with a hint of superciliousness in his manner glanced up.

'When are we going to come to the horses, Mr Papulous?'

His host turned to him with a deprecatory smile.

'Not until after dinner, I'm afraid, Mr Jerome. I'm sorry to seem so secretive, but the whole nature of the discovery is so extraordinary that I want you to see the demonstration with your own eyes.'

Mr Jerome, whose name Campion recognised as belonging to the moving spirit of Bolitho Brothers, of St Mary Axe, seemed only partly mollified. He laughed.

'Is it the salubrious air of this particular hotel that you need for your experiment, may I ask?' he enquired.

'Oh no, my dear sir. It's the stillness.' Mr Papulous appeared to be completely oblivious of any suggestion of a sneer. 'It's the utter quiet. At night, round about ten o'clock, there is a lack of vibration here, so complete that you can almost feel it, if I may use such a contradiction in terms. Now, Mr Fellowes, dinner's at seven-thirty. Perhaps you'd care to see your room?'

Campion was puzzled. As he changed for the meal—a gesture which seemed to be expected of him—he surveyed the situation with growing curiosity. Papulous was no ordinary customer. He managed to convey an air of conspiracy and mystery while appearing himself as open and simple as the day. Whatever he was up to, he was certainly a good salesman.

The dinner was simple and well cooked and was served by

Papulous's own man. There was no alcohol and the dishes were not highly seasoned, out of deference, their host explained, to the test that was to be put to their palates later on.

When it was over and the mahogany had been cleared of dessert, a glass of clear water was set before each guest and from the head of the table Mr Papulous addressed his guests. He made a very distinguished figure, leaning forward across the polished wood, the candle-light flickering on his deeply lined face and high heart-shaped forehead.

'First of all let me recapitulate,' he said. 'You all know my name and you have all been kind enough to say that you have read my little book. I mention this because I want you to realise that by asking you down here to witness a most extraordinary demonstration I am taking my reputation in my hands. Having made that point, let me remind you that you have, each of you, with the single exception of Mr Fellowes, been kind enough to give me your considered views on a sample of brandy which I sent you. In every case, I need hardly mention, opinion was the same—a Champagne Fine of 1835.'

A murmur of satisfaction not untinged with relief ran round the table and Mr Papulous smiled.

'Well,' he said, 'frankly that would have been my own opinion had I not known—mark you, I say "known"—that the brandy I sent you was a raw cognac of nearly a hundred years later—to be exact, of 1932.'

There was a moment of bewilderment, followed by an explosion from Mr Jerome.

'I hope you're not trying to make fools of us, sir,' he said severely. 'I'm not going to sit here, and—'

'One moment, one moment.' Papulous spoke soothingly. 'You really must forgive me. I know you all too well by repute to dare to make such a statement without following it immediately by the explanation to which you are entitled. As you're all aware, the doctoring of brandy is an old game. Such dreadful additions as vanilla and burnt sugar have all been used in their time and will, no doubt, be used again, but such crude deceptions are instantly detected by the cultured palate. This is something different.'

Mr Jerome began to seethe.

'Are you trying to interest us in a fake, sir?' he demanded. 'Because, if so, let me tell you I, for one, am not interested.'

There was a chorus of hasty assent in which Mr Campion virtuously joined.

Gervaise Papulous smiled faintly.

'But of course not,' he said. 'We are all experts. The true expert knows that no fake can be successful, even should we so far forget ourselves as to countenance its existence. I am bringing you a discovery—not a trick, not a clever fraud, but a genuine discovery which may revolutionise the whole market. As you know, time is the principal factor in the maturing of spirits. Until now time has been the only factor which could not be artificially replaced. An old brandy, therefore, is quite a different thing from a new one.'

Mr Campion blinked. A light was beginning to dawn upon him.

Mr Papulous continued. There seemed to be no stopping him. At the risk of boring his audience he displayed a great knowledge of technical detail and went through the life history of an old liqueur brandy from the time it was an unripe grapeskin on a vine outside Cognac.

When he had finished he paused dramatically, adding softly:

'What I hope to introduce to you tonight, gentlemen, is the latest discovery of science, a method of speeding up this long and wearisome process so that the whole business of maturing the spirit takes place in a few minutes instead of a hundred years. You have all examined the first-fruits of this method already and have been interested enough to come down here. Shall we go on?'

The effect of his announcement was naturally considerable. Everybody began to talk at once save Mr Campion, who sat silent and thoughtful. It occurred to him that his temporary colleagues were not only interested in making a great deal of money but very much alarmed at the prospect of losing a considerable quantity also.

'If it's true it'll upset the whole damned trade,' murmured his next-door neighbour, a little thin man with wispy straw-coloured hair.

Papulous rose. 'In the next room the inventor, M. Philippe Jessant, is waiting to demonstrate,' he said. 'He began work on the idea during the period of prohibition in America and his researches were assisted there by one of the richest men in the world, but when the country was restored to sanity his patron lost interest in the work and he was left to perfect it unassisted. You will find him a simple, uneducated, unbusiness-like man, like many inventors. He came to me for help because he had read my little book and I am doing what I can for him by introducing him to you. Conditions are now ideal. The house if perfectly still. Will you come with me?'

The sceptical but excited little company filed into the large 'commercial' room on the other side of the passage. The place had been stripped of furniture save for a half-circle of chairs and a large deal table. On the table was a curious contraption, vaguely resembling two or three of those complicated coffee percolators which seemed to be designed solely for the wedding-present trade.

An excitable little man in a long brown overall was standing behind the table. If not an impressive figure, he was certainly an odd one, with his longish hair and gold-rimmed pince-nez.

'Quiet, please. I must beg of you quiet,' he commanded, holding up his hand as they appeared. 'We must have no vibration, no vibration at all, if I am to succeed.'

He had a harsh voice and a curious foreign accent, which Campion could not instantly trace, but his manner was authoritative and the experts tiptoed gently to their seats.

'Now,' said M. Jessant, his small eyes flashing, 'I leave all explanations to my friend here. For me, I am only interested in the demonstration. You understand?'

He glared at them and Papulous hastened to explain.

'M. Jessant does not mean the human voice, of course,' he murmured. 'It is vibration, sudden movement, of which he is afraid.'

'Quiet,' cut in the inventor impatiently. 'When a spirit matures in the ordinary way what does it have?—quiet, darkness, peace. These conditions are essential. Now we will begin, if you please.'

It was a simple business. A clear-glass decanter of brandy was produced and duly smelt and sampled by each guest. Papulous himself handed round the glasses and poured the liquid. By unanimous consent it was voted a raw spirit. The years 1932 and 1934 were both mentioned.

Then the same decanter was emptied into the contraption on the table and its progress watched through a system of glass tubes and a filter into a large retort-shaped vessel at the foot of the apparatus.

M. Jessant looked up.

'Now,' he said softly. 'You will come, one at a time, please, and examine my invention. Walk softly.'

The inspection was made and the man in the brown overall covered the retort with a hood composed of something that looked like black rubber. For a while he busied himself with thermometers and a little electric battery.

'It is going on now,' he explained, suppressed excitement in his voice. 'Every second roughly corresponds to a year—a long, dark, dismal year. Now—we shall see.'

The hood was removed, fresh glasses were brought, and the retort itself carefully detached from the rest of the apparatus.

Mr Jerome was the first to examine the liquid it contained and his expression was ludicrous in its astonishment.

'It's incredible!' he said at last. 'Incredible! I can't believe it. . . .

There are certain tests I should like to make, of course, but I could swear this is an 1835 brandy.'

The others were of the same opinion and even Mr Campion was impressed. The inventor was persuaded to do his experiment again. To do him justice he complied willingly.

'It is the only disadvantage,' he said. 'So little can be treated at the one time. I tell my friend I should like to make my invention foolproof and sell the machines and the instructions to the public, but he tells me no.'

'No indeed!' ejaculated Mr Campion's neighbour. 'Good heavens! it would knock the bottom out of half my trade....'

When at last the gathering broke up in excitement it was after midnight. Mr Papulous addressed his guests.

'It is late,' he said. 'Let us go to bed now and consider the whole matter in the morning when M. Jessant can explain the theory of his process. Meanwhile, I am sure you will agree with me that we all have something to think about.'

A somewhat subdued company trooped off upstairs. There was little conversation. A man does not discuss a revolutionary discovery with his nearest rival.

Campion came down in the morning to find Mr Jerome already up. He was pacing the lounge and turned on the young man almost angrily.

'I like to get up at six,' he said without preamble, 'but there were no servants in the place. A woman, her husband and a maid came along at seven. It seems Papulous made them sleep out. Afraid of vibration, I suppose. Well, it's an extraordinary discovery, isn't it? If I hadn't seen it with my own eyes I should never have believed it. I suppose one's got to be prepared for progress, but I can't say I like it. Never did.'

He lowered his voice and came closer.

'We shall have to get together and suppress it, you know,' he said. 'Only thing to do. We can't have a thing like this blurted out to the public and we can't have any single firm owning the secret. Anyway, that's my opinion.'

Campion murmured that he did not care to express his own without first consulting Mr Thistledown.

'Quite, quite. There'll be a good many conferences in the City this afternoon,' said Mr Jerome gloomily. 'And that's another thing. D'you know there isn't a telephone in this confounded pub?'

Campion's eyes narrowed.

'Is that so?' he said softly. 'That's very interesting.'

Mr Jerome shot him a suspicious glance.

'In my opinion . . . ,' he began heavily, but got no further. The door was thrust open and the small wispy-haired man, who had been Campion's neighbour at dinner, came bursting into the room.

'I say,' he said, 'a frightful thing! The little inventor chap has been attacked in the night. His machine is smashed and the plans and formula are stolen. Poor old Papulous is nearly off his head.'

Both Campion and Jerome started for the doorway and a moment later joined the startled group on the landing. Gervaise Papulous, an impressive figure in a long black dressing-gown, was standing with his back to the inventor's door.

'This is terrible, terrible!' he was saying. 'I beseech you all, go downstairs and wait until I see what is best to be done. My poor friend has only just regained consciousness.'

Jerome pushed his way through the group.

'But this is outrageous,' he began.

Papulous towered over him, his eyes dark and angry.

'It is just as you say, outrageous,' he said, and Mr Jerome quailed before the suppressed fury in his voice.

'Look here,' he began, 'you surely don't think . . . you're not insinuating. . . .'

'I am only thinking of my poor friend,' said Mr Papulous.

Campion went quietly downstairs.

'What on earth does this mean?' demanded the small wispy-haired gentleman, who had remained in the lounge.

Campion grinned. 'I rather fancy we shall all find that out pretty clearly in about an hour,' he said.

He was right. Mr Gervaise Papulous put the whole matter to them in the bluntest possible way as they sat dejectedly looking at the remains of what had proved a very unsatisfactory breakfast.

M. Jessant, his head in bandages and his face pale with exhaustion, had told a heart-breaking story. He had awakened to find a pad of chloroform across his mouth and nose. It was dark and he could not see his assailant, who also struck him repeatedly. His efforts to give the alarm were futile and in the end the anaesthetic had overpowered him.

When at last he had come to himself his apparatus had been smashed and his precious black pocket-book, which held his calculations and which he always kept under his pillow, had gone.

At this point he had broken down completely and had been led away by Papulous's man. Mr Gervaise Papulous then took the floor. He looked pale and nervous and there was an underlying suggestion of righteous anger and indignation in his manner which was very impressive.

'I won't waste time by telling you how appalled I am by this monstrous attack,' he began, his fine voice trembling. 'I can only tell you the facts. We were alone in this house last night. Even my own man slept out in the village. I arranged this to ensure ideal conditions for the experiment. The landlady reports that the doors were locked this morning and the house had not been entered from the outside. Now you see what this means? Until last night only the inventor and I knew of the existence of a secret which is of such great importance to all of you here. Last night we told you, we took you into our confidence, and now . . .' he shrugged his shoulders. 'Well, we have been robbed and my friend assaulted. Need I say more?'

An excited babble of protest arose and Mr Jerome seemed in danger of apoplexy. Papulous remained calm and a little contemptuous.

'There is only one thing to do,' he said, 'but I hesitated before calling in the police, because, of course, only one of you can be guilty and the secret must still be in the house, whereas I know the publicity which cannot be avoided will be detrimental to you all. And not only to yourselves personally, but to the firms you represent.'

He paused and frowned.

'The Press is so ignorant,' he said. 'I am so afraid you may all be represented as having come here to see some sort of faking process—new brandy into old. It doesn't sound convincing, does it?'

His announcement burst like a bomb in the quiet room. Mr Jerome sat very still, his mouth partly open. Somebody began to speak, but thought better of it. A long unhappy silence supervened.

Gervaise Papulous cleared his throat.

'I am sorry,' he said. 'I must either have my friend's note-book back and full compensation, or I must send for the police. What else can I do?'

Mr Jerome pulled himself together.

'Wait,' he said in a smothered voice. 'Before you do anything rash we must have a conference. I've been thinking over this discovery of yours, Mr Papulous, and in my opinion it raises very serious considerations for the whole trade.'

There was a murmur of agreement in the room and he went on.

'The one thing none of us can afford is publicity. In the first place, even if the thing becomes generally known it certainly won't become generally believed. The public doesn't rely on its palate; it relies on our labels, and that puts us in a very awkward position. This final development precipitates everything. We must clear up this mystery in private and then decide what is best to be done.'

There was a vigorous chorus of assent, but Mr Papulous shook his head.

'I'm afraid I can't agree,' he said coldly. 'In the ordinary way M. Jessant and I would have been glad to meet you in any way, but this outrage alters everything. I insist on a public examination unless, of course,' he added deliberately, 'unless you care to take the whole matter out of our hands.'

'What do you mean?' Mr Jerome's voice was faint.

The tall man with the deeply lined face regarded him steadily.

'Unless you care to club together and buy us out,' said Mr Papulous. 'Then you can settle the matter as you like. The sum M. Jessant had in mind was fifteen thousand pounds, a very reasonable price for such a secret.'

There was silence after he had spoken.

'Blackmail,' said Mr Campion under his breath and at the same moment his glance lighted on Mr Papulous's most outstanding feature. His eyebrows rose and an expression of incredulity, followed by amazement, passed over his face. Then he kicked himself gently under the breakfast table. He rose.

'I must send a wire to my principal,' he said. 'You'll understand I'm in an impossible position and must get in touch with Mr Thistledown at once.'

Papulous regarded him.

'If you will write your message my man will despatch it from the village,' he said politely and there was no mistaking the implied threat.

Campion understood he was not to be allowed to make any private communication with the outside world. He looked blank.

'Thank you,' he said and took out a pencil and a loose-leaf notebook.

'Unexpected development,' he wrote. 'Come down immediately. Inform Charlie and George cannot lunch Tuesday. A. C. Fellowes.'

Papulous took the message, read it and went out with it, leaving a horrified group behind him.

Mr Thistledown received Mr Campion's wire at eleven o'clock and read it carefully. The signature particularly interested him. Shutting himself in his private room, he rang up Scotland Yard and was fortunate in discovering Superintendent Oates at his desk. He dictated the wire carefully and added with a depreciatory cough:

'Mr Campion told me to send on to you any message from him signed with his own initials. I don't know if you can make much of this. It seems very ordinary to me.'

'Leave all that to us, sir.' Oates sounded cheerful. 'Where is he, by the way?'

Mr Thistledown gave the address and hung up the receiver. At the other end of the wire the superintendent unlocked a drawer in his desk and took out a small red manuscript book. Each page was ruled with double columns and filled with Mr. Campion's own elegant handwriting. Oates ran a forefinger down the left-hand column on the third page.

'Carrie ... Catherine ... Charles. ...'

His eye ran across the page.

'Someone you want,' he read and looked on down the list.

The legend against the word 'George' was brief. 'Two,' it said simply.

Oates turned to the back of the book. There were several messages under the useful word 'lunch.' 'Come to lunch' meant 'Send two men.' 'Lunch with me' was translated 'Send men armed,' and 'Cannot lunch' was 'Come yourself.'

'Tuesday' was on another page. The superintendent did not trouble to look it up. He knew its meaning. It was 'hurry.'

He wrote the whole message out on a pad.

'Unexpected developments. Come down immediately. Someone you want (two). Come yourself. Hurry. Campion.'

He sighed. 'Energetic chap,' he commented and pressed a bell for Sergeant Bloom.

As it happened, it was Mr Gervaise Papulous himself who caught the first glimpse of the police car which pulled up outside the lonely little hotel. He was standing by the window in an upper room whose floor was so flimsily constructed that he could listen with ease to the discussion taking place in the lounge below. There the unfortunate experts were still arguing. The only point on which they all agreed was the absolute necessity of avoiding a scandal.

As the car stopped and the superintendent sprang out and made for the door Papulous caught a glimpse of his official-looking figure. He swung round savagely to the forlorn little figure who sat hunched up on the bed.

'You peached, damn you!' he whispered.

'Me?' The man who had been calling himself 'Jessant' sat up in indignation. 'Me peach?' he repeated, his foreign accent fading into honest South London. 'Don't be silly. And you pay up, my lad. I'm fed up with this. First I do me stuff, then you chloroform me, then you bandage me, then you keep me shut up 'ere, and now you accuse me of splitting. What you playing at?'

'You're lying, you little rat.' Papulous's voice was dangerously soft and he strode swiftly across the room towards the man on the bed, who shrank back in sudden alarm.

'Here—that'll do, that'll do. What's going on here?'

It was Oates who spoke. Followed by Campion and the sergeant he strode across the room.

'Let the fellow go,' he commanded. 'Good heavens, man, you're choking him.'

Doubling his fist, he brought it up under the other man's wrists with a blow which not only loosed their hold but sent their owner staggering back across the room.

The man on the bed let out a howl and stumbled towards the door into the waiting arms of Sergeant Bloom, but Oates did not notice. His eyes were fixed upon the face of the tall man on the other side of the room.

'The Widow!' he ejaculated. 'Well I'll be damned!'

The other smiled.

'More than probably, my dear Inspector. Or have they promoted you?' he said. 'But at the moment I'm afraid you're trespassing.'

The superintendent glanced enquiringly at the mild and elegant figure at his side.

'False pretences is the charge,' murmured Mr Campion affably. 'There are certain rather unpleasant traces of blackmail in the matter, but false pretences will do. There are six witnesses and myself.'

The man whose alias was The Widow stared at his accuser.

'Who are you?' he demanded, and then, as the answer dawned upon him, he swore softly. 'Campion,' he said. 'Albert Campion . . . I ought to have recognised you from your description.'

Campion grinned. 'That's where I had the advantage of you,' he said.

Mr Campion and the superintendent drove back to London together, leaving a very relieved company of experts to travel home in their own ways. Oates was jubilant.

'Got him,' he said. 'Got him at last. And a clear case. A pretty little swindle, too. Just like him. If you hadn't been there all those poor devils would have paid up something. They're the kind of people he goes for, folk whose business depends on their absolute integrity. They all represent small firms, you see, with old, conservative clients. When did you realise that he wasn't the real Gervaise Papulous?'

'As soon as I saw him I thought it unlikely.' Campion grinned as he spoke. 'Before I left town I rang up the publishers of the Papulous monograph. They had lost sight of him, they said, but from their publicity department I learned that Papulous was born in '72. So as soon as I saw our friend The Widow I realised that he was a good deal younger than the real man. However, like a fool I didn't get on to the swindle until this morning. It was when he was putting on that brilliant final act of his. I suddenly recognised him and, of course, the whole thing came to me in a flash.'

'Recognised him?' Oates looked blank. 'I never described him to you.'

Mr Campion looked modest. 'Do you remember showing off to a very pretty girl I brought up to your office, and so far forgetting yourself as to produce an advertisement from an evening paper?' he enquired.

'I remember the ad,' Oates said doggedly. 'The fellow advertised for a kids' entertainer. But I don't remember him including a photograph of himself.'

'He printed his name,' Campion persisted. 'It's a funny nickname. The significance didn't occur to me until I looked at him this morning, knowing that he was a crook. I realised that he was tricking us, but couldn't see how. Then his face gave him away.'

'His face?'

'My dear fellow, you haven't spotted it yet. I'm glad of that. It didn't come to me for a bit. Consider that face. How do crooks get their names? How did Beaky Doyle get his name? Why was Cauliflower Edwards so called? Think of his forehead, man. Think of his hair.'

'Peak,' said the superintendent suddenly. 'Of course, a widow's peak! Funny I didn't think of that before. It's obvious when it comes to you. But even so,' he added more seriously, 'I wonder you cared to risk sending for me on that alone. Plenty of people have a widow's peak. You'd have looked silly if he'd been on the level.'

'Oh, but I had the advertisement as well,' Campion objected. 'Taken in conjunction, the two things are obvious. That demonstration last night was masterly. Young brandy went in at one end of the apparatus and old brandy came out at the other, and we saw, or thought we saw, the spirit the whole time. There was only one type of man who could have done it—a children's party entertainer.'

Oates shook his head.

'I'm only a poor demented policeman,' he said derisively. 'My mind doesn't work. I'll buy it.'

Campion turned to him. 'My good Oates, have you ever been to a children's party?'

'No.'

'Well, you've been a child, I suppose?'

'I seem to remember something like that.'

'Well, when you were a child what entertained you? Singing? Dancing? *The Wreck of the Hesperus*? No, my dear friend, there's only one kind of performer who goes down well with children and that is a member of the brotherhood of which Jessant is hardly an ornament. A magician, Oates. In other words, a conjurer. And a damned good trick he showed us all last night!'

He trod on the accelerator and the car rushed on again.

The superintendent sat silent for a long time. Then he glanced up.

'That *was* a pretty girl,' he said. 'Nice manners, too.'

'Leonie?' Campion nodded. 'That reminds me, I must phone her when we get back to town.'

'Oh?' The superintendent was interested. 'Nothing I can do for you, I suppose?' he enquired archly.

Campion smiled. 'Hardly,' he said. 'I want to tell her she owes me two pounds.'

TO THE WIDOW

Christianna Brand

Champagne, as the favourite drink of my publisher and myself, has been saved to the last in this section. The story's author, Christianna Brand (1907-), is also in the champagne league of crime writers, receiving this praise from Anthony Boucher a few years ago: 'You have to reach for the greatest of the Great Names, Agatha Christie, John Dickson Carr and Ellery Queen, to find Brand's rivals in the subtleties of the trade.' She has also won several awards from the Mystery Writers of America and in 1984 was hailed as 'the Grand Lady of British mystery, suspense and main-stream fiction'. In 'To the Widow' she presents a bubbling mix of champagne, unusual characters, witty dialogue and ingenious plot twists which keep the reader guessing until the last page.

It fell to Dr Leo Theobald—described by himself, though not by any honest member of the profession, as a psychiatrist—to save a young woman's neck by giving evidence in court that at the time she slew her husband she had been in the grip of a compulsive urge to do so. From then on, he found his consulting room besieged by females confiding a variety of similar obsessions. He took down all they said on two sets of tapes which he humorously described (to himself) as *His* and *Hers,* and from then on prospered exceedingly.

It was not entirely astonishing, then, that on a Monday morning he should receive the confessions of no less than two pretty ladies, each declaring a compelling desire to murder her husband.

The second of these he took very seriously indeed. He *was* her husband.

Many of his patients introduced themselves cautiously as Mrs Brown, Smith, or Jones. These two were no exception. 'Ten thirty— a Mrs Brown,' said his secretary with a glint of humour. His secretary's name really was Mrs Jones. 'Mrs Ponsardine, actually.

Penelope. A well-to-do widow about to marry a gent called Lord Biggs, with a lot of money.'

'Money!' said Dr Theobald, to whom this was, bar none, the most beautiful word in the language.

Mrs (Ponsardine) Brown—Penelope—proved to be a very kempt and well-preserved lady. He invited her tenderly to relax upon the consulting-room couch. 'Relax, relaaaaaax! Fade away dreamily into semi-consciousness. Your hands are like jelly,' said Dr Theobald encouragingly, 'melted into one another. You can't feel your body, your legs. You can't feel your feet. . . .'

Oh, good! thought Penelope, earnestly endeavouring to fade away into semi-consciousness. Her new shoes were *killing* her.

Dr Theobald switched on his tape recorders—from the unconcealed one he would later extract the cassette and give it to her to take home, thus proving that all was safe and aboveboard—and switched off the lights. 'I shall sit at the head of the couch with only this tiny lamp on, to make my notes by—quite out of your sight so that you may forget all about me and just speak your thoughts aloud.'

He seated himself as described, and by the light of the tiny lamp gave himself over to the Quick Crossword. The cassette lasted forty minutes, which often gave him time to finish it. The maunderings of the average patient were of a tedium inexpressible. Anything of interest the invaluable Mrs Jones, his secretary, could extract from his secret tape when the patient was gone. It did not matter to Dr Theobald how tedious Mrs Jones might find them.

'Just speak your thoughts aloud, dear lady. Dreamily, dreeeeeeeeamily. . . .'

Mrs (Ponsardine) Brown—Penelope—dreamily obliged. She had, she said, this irresistible urge to murder her husband.

Dr Theobald abandoned the crossword. He suggested after a moment's thought, 'But your husband is dead.'

'I know,' said Penelope. 'That's what makes it so awful.'

'But then—why should you wish to murder him?'

'Well, to be free to marry Lord Briggs,' said Mrs Ponsardine reasonably.

'But you're going to marry Lord Briggs anyway.' (Goodness, how promising!) 'You do seem to be in some confusion. Tell me all about it.'

Dreamily, dreamily, Penelope told him about it.

An hour later, the lady having come to with a good deal of gasping and demanding to know where she was, she departed, clutching her highly inflammable cassette. Dr Theobald locked away *His* in his safe and inserted new ones. Mrs Jones ushered in the next patient. 'Mrs Smith,' said Mrs Jones, deadpan. 'Renée.'

Dr Theobald received his lady wife without demonstration. Such syndromes were by no means unknown in the profession where, indeed, all things are possible if you only get the right psychiatrist. This time, however, he did not trouble himself with the crossword but, when her extremities were sufficiently congealed, exhorted her just to speak her thoughts aloud.

'Dreamily,' crooned Dr Theobald, all agog at the head of the couch. 'Dreeeeeeeeamily. . . .'

Mrs (Theobald) Smith—Renée—spoke her thoughts aloud. 'I seem to have this irresistible urge to murder my husband.'

'Oh,' said the doctor rather blankly. The feeling was creeping up on him that this was becoming an increasingly curious day. He said at last, 'But why?'

'He is such an odious little man,' said Renée, more dreamy by the minute. 'Rather paunchy, you know, as bald as a coot, and his nose is all peppered with tiny black dots, as though the little hairs had come to the surface and suddenly given up in despair.'

'Perhaps he shaves them,' said Dr Theobald, as this was what he did.

'No one but my husband would have to shave his nose,' said Renée. 'Besides, his eyes are like frog spawn.'

'He can hardly help his appearance,' said the doctor, nettled. Nor, he suggested, was it quite sufficient reason for murder.

'Oh, but it's worse than that,' said Renée. 'He's awful. So uncouth. He puts ice into everything—even into a liqueur brandy. And mean about money—which happens to be *my* money. And so cold and uncaring. . . .'

Dr Theobald brought the session to an early close and did not offer a cassette to be taken home with her. He thought it wise, however, to propose a further session as early as possible.

'Oh, yes,' said his patient blissfully. 'And then I can tell you all about my lovely new lover.'

The patient having departed to cook his lunch—his consulting rooms were part of his private house, though approached by a separate entrance—he summoned his secretary, for he felt badly shaken and in need of comfort. 'Get up on the couch,' said Dr Theobald and scrambled up after her. He was not so cold and uncaring as all *that*.

The couch was narrow and, for two, unaccommodating, but over several years he had found this problem not insurmountable. Nowadays, however, Mrs Jones was proving somewhat narrow and unaccommodating, too. 'Oh, Muriel, you never used to make this fuss!'

'But, Leo, I'm a married lady now. I simply can't go on with it.'

'That weed, all books and artiness! How could you have married him? A lot of affectations about smoked salmon and vintages. Sit him down to a good slab of Canadian tinned and a bottle of plonk and he'd never know the difference. *I* wouldn't.'

'I know,' said Muriel. 'That's why I married *him*.'

'I'd have married you in a minute, Mu, you know that, if it hadn't been for Renée. I mean, Renée's got the money, hasn't she? But you know I'm mad about you. Always have been.' As Mu showed signs of returning to her office desk, he implored, 'Tomorrow night, then?'

'No, Leo, I'm staying at home.'

'But on Tuesdays he goes off to this horticultural club of his.'

'Nothing horticultural about it,' said Muriel. 'I've told you. It's just a sort of literary joke. The Herbiferous Club. They meet to discuss the works of an author they're interested in called Herbert Ferris. Herb Ferris, you see. But you wouldn't understand.'

'What I would understand would be a night on the tiles with you. Tomorrow evening, Mu—please do!'

'Not tomorrow or ever again,' said Muriel. 'That's all done with. My husband wouldn't like it.'

Dr Theobald, left alone, lay back on the couch and gave himself over to an irresistible urge to murder Mu's husband.

Mrs Ponsardine's promising sessions went on apace. Mrs Ponsardine had dropped the 'Brown' now and become simply Penelope, who was going to marry rich Lord Briggs. At least she was if Dr Theobald kept very, very quiet about these consulting-room revelations. For, as he had explained to her, clearly a guilt complex had arisen in regard to some earlier misdemeanour, and nothing but a full confession could let her off this subterraneously irritant hook. Penelope, therefore, in an extremity of dreaminess, unburdened herself.

The late Ponsardine had been a research chemist who had—predictably late in life, for really was he not asking for trouble?—evolved a concoction which, taken with alcohol, would bring about a rapid though painless death. And she, driven to madness by her passion for Lord Briggs, had administered a sufficient dose to the unsuspecting apothecary in a plate of soup, closely followed by a postprandial brandy. Since none but he had known of his discovery, and the symptoms might be variously ascribed, no following suspicion had attached to her.

Dr Theobald's fees took a sudden upward thrust, and he

strongly advised her to hand over to him the remains of the
dangerous potion. And just in case, he said, her subconscious
should be playing tricks on her, he would test what she brought
on a suitable animal, and she should then wrap up the remains
securely herself, and herself stow it away in his safe.

A very small dose indeed—leaving lots over—put a happily
peaceful end to his neighbour's very old and, as it happened, very
disagreeable dog. It rebelled against a stiffish lacing of flavourless
vodka in its bowl of milk, but made no protest at all against
Brand-X, as the doctor had now christened it—more wittily than
he knew.

'And it seems to have no taste at all,' he said, sniffing at the
little bottle—holding it, however, wrapped carefully in a handkerchief. (To have the phial liberally covered with his own finger-
prints was no part of the doctor's vaguely forming plan.) 'And no
odour.'

'That's why my Everard thought it might be so dangerous. And
why, as he could see no purpose for it—but killing people,' said
his relict, faltering a little, 'he described that no one else should
ever know about it.'

'He was a public benefactor,' said Dr Theobald reverently—not
referring, however, to the late Everard's concern for posterity.

So Penelope sat down and, all too freely handling it, carefully
parcelled up the little phial and saw it bestowed in the doctor's
private safe. If it seemed a little odd that, having ascertained its
authenticity, he should not immediately destroy the stuff, she said
nothing. With the exalted marriage now imminent, her situation
was clearly dicey in the extreme, and she meekly paid up a further
astronomical fee and went through to the office. Mu reappeared,
now with Renée. 'Mrs Smith,' said Muriel, ushering her in.

Renée—notwithstanding that she had just arrived in fact from
the same house—wore a hat and coat and carried a handbag and
gloves, together with a book, which she placed with the gloves
on a corner of the desk before disposing herself upon the couch
and losing touch with her hands and feet and drooling off into
the darkness on the eternal subject of her unlovable husband
and the miraculously contrasting boyfriend. Dr Theobald deafened
himself to the former, but was becoming increasingly riveted by
the latter. They had a little love nest, it seemed, and once a week
would spend the evening there. More was impossible, for he was,
alas, a married man and she, in fact, a married woman. 'But my
husband. . . .'

'Never mind *him*,' said the doctor, who had no great wish for
further recorded revelations of his own shortcomings. 'You've
never told me this man's name.'

'I call him Tybalt—Romeo and Juliet, you know. . . .'

'Where do they come in?' said the doctor, who was not on the whole of a highly literary bent.

'Well, Mercutio's Tybalt, you know. "Good King of Cats." '

'Tibbles. That's what old women call their pussycats.'

'And he's *my* pussycat,' said Renée fondly. 'I shall call him Tibbles, too.'

'And what would be dear Tibbles' surname?'

'Well, Smith,' said Mrs Smith. She explained that Smith wasn't really her name. Nor his either, as a matter of fact. They'd just made it up between them. She'd have preferred Lyon, herself, or something noble and appropriate like that, but no, he had said that his real name was plain Jones and the next plainest thing was plain Smith. So there they were, plain Mr and Mrs Smith.

I only wish you were, thought Dr Theobald. But a glimmer of light which had recently begun to glow in his consciousness was growing steadily brighter. 'Well, so tell me about your Tibbles.'

Mrs Smith was only too happy to oblige. As feline as his name, it seemed—a very lion of svelteness and strength. (Mrs Smith here roused herself sufficiently from her semi-hypnotic condition to be able to open one eye and cast it rather anxiously towards Dr Theobald's half-hidden chair, as though to assure herself that this time she hadn't gone too far, then relaxed again.) And so tremendously handsome. The complexion very fair, yet manly. The splendid mane of hair, the Grecian nose. . . . And intellectual! 'He does the crossword every day—not that childish little quick thing some people do, but the *Times*!' And all the Arts. But most of all, Tibbles was devoted to literature—to literature and to painting. 'The Impressionists! His little Renoir, he calls me. Not just Renée, but Renoir, his precious Renoir. . . .'

'You call him Tibbles and he calls you Renwar?' said Dr Theobald. A right pair; he thought—Tibbles and Renwar.

'Well, the painter, you know. One of those young girls with their little half-open mouths, so deliciously smiling, half-innocent, half-naughty, so inscrutable. . . .'

Dr Theobald had indeed observed of late a tendency in his lady to go around with her mouth hanging slightly open, but simply registered that she looked, if anything, a little more gormless than ever. 'So once a week, you and Tibbles engage in these intellectual evenings?'

'Well, I know it's rather wicked but, you see, on Tuesday nights my husband is always out. . . .'

'On Tuesdays?' said Dr Theobald, and the sudden incandescence of the glimmer almost blinded him. Tuesdays had been the regular days of his evenings out with Mu—her husband being absent at this precious club of his, where they met and discussed the immortal works of this writer they were so keen on. The Herbiferous Club.

On an inspiration, he rose and passed silently by the corner of his desk where lay the book his wife had brought with her. Accustomed to the gloom, his eyes could just discern the title. BLEST PAIR OF LOVERS. Well, that seemed appropriate enough. By—sure enough—some fellow calling himself Herbert Ferris.

How many evenings, he asked himself with chill calculation, had Mu's husband—who called himself plain Smith when his name was plain Jones—found himself obliged to miss the meetings with his cronies of the Herbiferous Club?

He crept back to his place. No doubt wearing, in the encircling gloom, the little Renwar smile, his lady wife was blathering on. '. . . and such delicious little dinners. I do them myself, of course. Such a change to have someone who can appreciate anything above tinned soup and hashed mutton with lots of Dad's Relish. . . .'

'What's wrong with Dad's Relish?' said Dr Theobald, whose favourite sauce, by a strange coincidence, this was. But Renée was rattling on, regardless. '. . . and with the dinner, a perfect champagne. Just half a bottle because I don't drink, you know; though of course it's *not* quite the same as the full bottle. And then a glass of the very best brandy that money can buy. . . .'

'Whose money?' asked Dr Theobald, apprehensively.

'Well, it's mine, really,' said Renée, automatically on the defensive. 'Tybalt—Tibbles—rebels. He's such a *man* you know, the real gentleman, and wildly generous with money. But I insist on playing hostess, whatever it costs me.'

Dr Theobald perceived that Tibbles was going to have to quit the scene of these revels even sooner than one had hitherto vaguely anticipated, and for reasons other than those connected solely with Mu. He began to build upon what had come to seem very promising foundations. 'And after dinner? . . .'

'Well, we just say good-night and go home,' said Renwar, suddenly rather bleak.

'What, no love-play?' Dr Theobald plunged for five minutes into a fairly deep pond of weedy analysis. 'No sex-u-al activity?' The psychiatrist in him rose in revolt against so uncharacteristic a minnow fished up from the analytical pond.

'Well, but he *is* a married man. And I'm afraid the wife is rather—demanding. It's not very nice for *me*,' said Renée disconsolately. 'Is it?'

It was not very nice for Dr Theobald either. His Mu! But the thing was becoming more and more promising. 'You mean he is—

let us say overtired?' It sounded not at all that leonine and manly, but then such a vision reposed largely in the mind of the infatuate Renwar. Dr Theobald, briefly introduced to Mu's Mr Jones, had judged him to be a good deal more high-browed than high-powered. 'Or at any rate—*too* tired!' He lowered his voice conspiratorially. 'You'll never have heard, dear lady, of Brand-X?'

'Brand-X?'

'That's just my name for it. To save embarrassment. So many of my lady patients. . . . These little difficulties are not uncommon. I tell them, "What your gentleman needs, my dear, is a drop of jolly old Brand-X. Pop a dose into his glass tonight," I say, "and then a good snort of something after dinner—and away we go!" ' He kept a supply of the stuff by him. Nicer for the ladies than trotting off to the chemist's on so delicate an errand. 'And you shall have a little bottle of it right now and next Tuesday—why, that's tomorrow! Just empty the whole thing into Tibbles' champagne— it's quite tasteless. And then, afterwards, he'll be having his fine, expensive,' said Dr Theobald, grinding his teeth, 'liqueur brandy. . . . It won't work without quite a bit of alcohol.'

'You don't think he might feel a little humiliated?'

'But you wouldn't *tell* him!' cried her husband, almost fainting. 'A proud man like that! Such a lion! Of course don't tell him. Don't tell a soul!' He laboured the point for some minutes. 'Tip it into his glass, but secretly. The champagne and the glass of fine brandy, and you'll find that all of a sudden, my dear—whacko!' Quite whacko'd himself by the shock she had given him—*tell* the wretched fellow, indeed!—he almost yanked her off the couch, allowed her to help herself to the small package in the safe, and accepted her almost maudlin thanks. On feet perhaps not yet quite sufficiently thawed from their gelatinous condition, she tottered off through the door leading to the patients' entrance.

Dr Theobald tottered to the door leading to the private part of his house and so to the dining room. He felt he could do with a very stiff whiskey and soda.

The decanter was empty. Rooting round for replenishment, he found, tucked not too unobtrusively away, a half-bottle of champagne. Viewve Clikott it seemed to be called. A lot of French nonsense. He had a vague idea that Viewve meant a widow and the champagne was so familiarly called—by those who cared to show off about that kind of thing. Well, well—by day after tomorrow, that should apply very nicely to his Mu; and with Renée proved clearly to have administered the dose! . . . A little advance celebration would by no means come amiss. His favourite dinner was on tonight's menu—oxtail soup, mince and 'mushy peas,' and a couple of cartons of Chokletrife. The champers would go down a treat with that lot. He poured himself out a handsome tot of whiskey, meanwhile, and sat back to contemplate the joys of this evening's meal.

His secretary, having ushered Renwar into the consulting room, had returned to her desk where Penelope Ponsardine awaited her. 'Your next appointment?' As she scribbled it down she said, not looking up from the desk diary, 'You settle your fees personally with the doctor, Mrs Ponsardine? And in cash?'

'I prefer it that way,' said Mrs Ponsardine, cagily.

'So many patients seem to, I find,' said Mrs Jones. 'After the first few sessions with Dr Theobald. He prefers it, too—very much prefers it. I gather from the ladies,' she added casually, 'that the fees are rising.'

'You can say that again,' said Penelope. But giving her no time to do so, suggested as though on an impulse, 'You wouldn't be free for dinner tonight, Mrs Jones? And a little chat?'

'I might,' said Dr Theobald's secretary. 'In a very good cause.'

They met in a restaurant of Mrs Ponsardine's choice. 'You've saved me a nice private table, Henri? And a bottle of the One and Only?'

'Caviar on the table, Madame Ponsardin, and the champagne coming up. *Bien frais!*' said Henri, tossing a kiss into the air, in a gesture not perhaps owing a great deal to his native Blackpool. 'But first, with the caviar, the two tiny glasses of vodka. . . .'

Mrs Jones, settling herself into the nice private corner, watched fondly the approach of the ice bucket, the small head gold-wrapped on its long Modigliani neck and sloping green glass shoulders. 'You are a connoisseur?'

'The veuve Cliquot was a forebear of mine.' She raised her glass. 'To the Widow!'

Mrs Jones also raised her glass. 'As one imminently threatened with that condition, may I drink to your coming release from it, Mrs Ponsardine?'

'Whatever do you mean—threatened? But do please call me Penelope, Mrs Jones.'

'And do please call me Muriel, Penelope.'

'Not Mu?' said Penelope archly. She explained: 'He does sometimes slip up a bit and give things away.'

'Yes, well—I used to fancy him, you know. We were both a lot younger. But now I'm married and trying to put an end to it all. Not easy.'

'A touch of the backmails?'

'For years, now. And if my husband ever dreamed! . . . So Leo could make things very unpleasant. But *you* know that, Penelope. That's why we're here.'

'I was in a state. I blurted out past—misdoings. Like the confessional, I thought. And he does get one very dopey—or did while one was still secure and trustful. He recorded it all, but I didn't worry. He gave me the cassette to take away with me. I couldn't know, what I've since realised must be the case, that he was keeping a duplicate locked away in his safe.'

'*He* couldn't know that I also had a duplicate,' said his secretary. 'Of the key.'

Penelope went exceedingly pale. 'Oh, my God!—you've played back the tapes?'

'Every last one. He takes such nice long lunch hours, the greedy old pig! The dull ones he makes me read anyway, but I wasn't standing for that. . . .'

'If he should tell George—Lord Briggs! If he should go to the police! I mean—I know to you I may seem to have been very wicked, Muriel. . . .'

'That's between you and the late Ponsardine,' said Muriel. 'For the rest—it's very simple. Dr Theobald has discovered your deep, dark secret. You murdered your husband.'

'Oh, Muriel. . . .'

'Don't worry too much,' said Muriel. 'You see, I have discovered *his* deep, dark secret. He has made all arrangements to murder mine.'

So neat. So easy. So safe. 'He gets the little phial from you, Penelope—the widow's curse, we might aptly call it? Tries it out on the wretched dog—just what he would do, though certainly it was a horrid old thing and better off dead anyway—'

'A pretty fair description of my late husband, Muriel. Do believe me!'

'. . . making sure it can never be proved that he's handled the poison. If he ever gets to use it, *you* aren't going to tell anyone about it, are you?—complete with your prints and with all those dangerous cassettes locked away in his safe.' She recounted the contents of Renée's tape, made that afternoon. 'The plan being that poor Renée shall dump the stuff into my husband's drink at tomorrow's tryst, and later ply him with brandy. Then she gets a life sentence, probably in a criminal lunatic bin—and he gets me. Can you beat it?'

Penelope might be said in her time indeed to have beaten it. She was shocked and horrified nevertheless. 'But she would explain.'

'Who's going to believe her? All those lovely tapes about urges to murder her husband—confided *to* her husband under the delusion that he's never set eyes on her before. Batty as a crumpet. And then on and on about her so-called lover—i.e., my husband.'

'You don't believe that your husband was her lover?'

'Not for a moment. But the point is that Leo believes it.'

'I wonder he didn't advise Renée to take a dose of the stuff, too,' said Penelope, 'and get rid of them both, at one fell swoop.'

'You have to take alcohol with it, and Renée doesn't drink,' said Muriel, at the same time registering a conclusion that rich Lord Briggs had better behave himself if he wished to attain to a ripe old age.

Penelope herself may have felt her intervention to have smacked a trifle too much of the professional, for she rather hastily suggested that the Law would surely have doubted any impulsion on Renée's part to have murdered beloved Tibbles. The tapes would hardly have prepared them for that.

'Leo will suggest a shift in aggressions. He can wipe from the tape the part where she confesses that, after she's exhausted herself whipping up the little dinners and what not, Tibbles just slopes off home to the demanding wife. So now, only with a change of object, back she comes with the compulsive urge. With which, in the past, you yourself have been all too familiar.'

'As you are, my dear, in the present. To murder Dr Theobald.'

'Common to both of us,' agreed Muriel, unruffled. 'I'm only saying that that makes twice for you.' Fortunately, she added, they need do nothing positive about it. Just by sitting here, they were letting it happen. 'At this very moment, I wouldn't be surprised. . . .'

And indeed, at that very moment, Dr Theobald, having surveyed the steaming bowl of canned oxtail, was issuing orders. 'I just fancy a drop of champagne for my supper. And don't tell me there's none, because I've sussed out your fine, precious bottle. So fetch it from the icebox, and a couple of lumps of ice with it.'

'Oh, Leo, you found? . . . I just thought. . . .'

'Well, don't think. Fetch the bottle and some ice.'

'But, Leo—not ice! It's a vintage Veuve Cliquot. In the 'fridge! Oh, no! And then—you're not going to insist on putting ice in it?'

'Of course I damn well insist. And don't stand there with your mouth open,' said Leo, irritably, 'looking what I suppose you imagine is. . . .' What had been the word? The Renwar smile. Yes, that had been it—inscrutable. 'Don't stand there looking inscrutable. Go and get the bottle and some lumps of ice.'

'Yes, Leo,' said Renwar, looking not noticeably any more scrutable.

He took a bit longer than the poor old dog, to die. There was no pain but, equally, no point in resistance. Nothing was known of the poison nor, therefore, of any antidote—and anyway, how confess to knowledge of its existence? The bitch! he thought. She's done for me. His failing mind wandered, blundering, over recent recollections. The lover. Blond, handsome, svelte. . . . And an intellectual. All that guff about meetings at the Herbiferous Club. On the other hand—it had been Mu who had said he went out to the club. Renée had never mentioned it. 'Y'r boyfriend. . . . Thought you meant . . . Mu's husband. . . .'

'I can't hear you too well, Leo. But Mr Jones—good heavens, no!'

'Then how could you? . . . Highbrowshtuff. . . .'

He lay, an unlovely log, on the dining-room floor. She sat quietly, curled up beside him. 'Well, I'm not really such a dud, you know, as you've always suggested I was. I'm quite capable of understanding a bit about food and wine—and about music and painting and so on. Even of appreciating a book by Herbert Ferris.'

He mumbled out, 'But—s'lover. . . .'

'Oh, Leo! Well, you see. . . . I described him to the psychiatrist. Everything. Nothing to do with Muriel's Mr Jones—just everything my husband was not. Splendid physique—you should see his horrid little paunch! Fairskinned—my husband has little black dots. . . .'

'Ll'r't, ll'r't,' groaned Dr Theobald.

'And—leonine. Tibbles, I called him in my mind. I'm sort of vague about how that name arose. I seem to be very vague about a lot of things. But Tibbles is a cat, and a cat can be a lion, and a lion is a leo, Leo.' And she seemed all of a sudden to emerge from a sort of—dream. 'But how could you know about my lover? Only if you were—oh, my goodness, Leo! What a muddle I've been in. That psychiatrist—that was you all the time!'

If Leo could have spoken to be understood, he would have been understood to say, 'As you bloody well knew.'

'So you really should have caught on to it. All those clues. I mean, Tibbles—it was you who invented Tibbles. From Tybalt. Only you don't know your Shakespeare, Leo, do you? I think you thought Romeo and Juliet were some people I'd dragged into the conversation. Mercutio's Tybalt, I told you—"Good King of Cats." And the king of cats is a lion, and a lion is a leo—a Leo. So you see, it was all there, all laid out in front of you—my fantasy creation of a lover whom you could well have recognised as everything that I'd have liked you to be, and you were not. I mean—putting ice in a beautiful champagne! Insisting. Admit that I did beg you not to. I did give you a chance. The stuff was *in* the ice, you see.' She added, leaning over him a little puzzled, 'This seems a funny way for it to be beginning to work.'

'For *what* to be beginning to work?' screamed Dr Theobald without a single sound.

'Well, the aphrodisiac,' said Renwar. 'Jolly old Brand-X.'

The three ladies met at Penelope's wedding. She found the other two ensconced at a nice little table—well in the path of the waiters circulating freely with their cool green bottles—and sat down to spend a moment with them. 'Well, my dears!'

'Well, my dear!' Muriel waited until Henri had departed—after placing before them their own ice bucket and bottle. Handing over a small brown paper packet, she said, 'A wedding present for you, Penelope.'

'Oh, Muriel—my cassettes?'

'Their remains.' That mysterious little conflagration in the consulting-room safe, said Muriel. She couldn't imagine what had happened. And just before the police had got there. So embarrassing for her. But meanwhile, the confidences of all those other poor sinners, she said limpidly—burnt to ashes.

'Poor Leo,' said Renée. 'To think of so much potential blackmail money in ashes!'

'Where poor Leo almost certainly is now,' said his Mu, 'it will have been in ashes long ago, anyway.'

'Renée,' said Penelope. 'You give me a wedding present, too. Put an end to my suspense. All that time—you were leading him along by the nose?'

'Oh, Penelope, not by the nose. *His* nose! . . .'

'Yes, yes, we know all about his nose. By—a noose, then?'

'Oh, no,' said Renée, allowing her mouth to hang very slightly open. 'Only teasing him. To be able to tell him to his face exactly what I thought of him.'

'Yes, but later,' said Muriel. 'You, also, had access to the tapes.'

'Who, me? How could I have?'

'Oh, come off it, Renée! Living in the same house—keys nipped out of his trousers pocket while he snored away. . . . And you listened to Penelope's tapes, too. . . .'

Penelope experienced a moment of anxiety, but reflected that Dr Theobald's widow was hardly in less dangerous case than herself. 'So you knew what Brand-X really was.'

'Well, an aphrodisiac, wasn't it? That's what he'd told me—the police found it all on my tapes. Jolly old Brand-X. He *told* me,' insisted Renée.

'And persuaded you to give a dose to your fantasy lover.'

'Ah, my fantasy lover! Only somehow—I simply can't think

how—Leo had quite misinterpreted the fantasy, hadn't he? My husband—tricking me into giving a dose of Brand-X in a glass of champagne to my lover. And all the time, my husband *was* my lover.'

Brand-X. Penelope and Renwar and Mu—all safe and sound and happy now, thanks to jolly old Brand-X. The champagne seethed and shimmered in its golden haze. Almost in awe, two ladies lifted their glasses to the third. 'To the widow!' they said.

Half-innocent, half-naughty—inscrutable. With deliciously parted lips, the relict of the late Dr Theobald bestowed upon the ice bucket the little Renoir smile. 'To the Widow!' she said.

3

MAKE MINE MURDER

Cases of the Drinking Detectives

A MATTER OF TASTE

Dorothy L. Sayers

Lord Peter Wimsey, the witty and aristocratic amateur detective, is probably second only to Sherlock Holmes as London's (even England's) most famous detective. He may well be the most discerning connoisseur of wine among all the fictional crime fighters – indeed, it has been said of him, 'Is it not a matter of common notoriety that Lord Peter has a palate for wine almost unequalled in Europe?' Since his first appearance seventy years ago in the book Whose Body? *(1923), Lord Peter has become a legend, featuring in novels and short stories, films (played by Peter Haddon and Robert Montgomery), plays and on the radio, and most recently on television where he has been portrayed by Ian Carmichael and Edward Petherbridge. The case of 'A Matter of Taste' certainly puts the dashing and sophisticated detective on his mettle as a wine connoisseur when he is invited to dinner to sample and identify six outstanding vintages – and, in so doing, bring an imposter to justice . . .*

'Halte-là! . . . Attention! . . . F—e!'

The young man in the grey suit pushed his way through the protesting porters and leapt nimbly for the footboard of the guard's van as the Paris-Evreux express steamed out of the Invalides. The guard, with an eye to a tip, fielded him adroitly from among the detaining hands.

'It is happy for monsieur that he is so agile,' he remarked. 'Monsieur is in a hurry?'

'Somewhat. Thank you. I can get through by the corridor?'

'But certainly. The *premières* are two coaches away, beyond the luggage-van.'

The young man rewarded his rescuer, and made his way forward, mopping his face. As he passed the piled-up luggage something caught his eye, and he stopped to investigate. It was a suitcase, nearly new, of expensive-looking leather, labelled conspicuously:

LORD PETER WIMSEY
Hôtel Saumon d'Or,
Verneuil-sur-Eure.

and bore witness to its itinerary thus:

LONDON — PARIS
(Waterloo) (Gare St. Lazare)
via Southampton—Havre
PARIS — VERNEUIL
(Ch. De Fer de L'Ouest)

The young man whistled, and sat down on a trunk to think it out.

Somewhere there had been a leakage, and they were on his trail. Nor did they care who knew it. There were hundreds of people in London and Paris who would know the name of Wimsey, not counting the police of both countries. In addition to belonging to one of the oldest ducal families in England, Lord Peter had made himself conspicuous by his meddling with crime detection. A label like this was a gratuitous advertisement.

But the amazing thing was that the pursuers were not troubling to hide themselves from the pursued. That argued very great confidence. That he should have got into the guard's van was, of course, an accident, but, even so, he might have seen it on the platform, or anywhere.

An accident? It occurred to him—not for the first time, but definitely now, and without doubt—that it was indeed an accident for them that he was here. The series of maddening delays that had held him up between London and the Invalides presented itself to him with an air of prearrangement. The preposterous accusation, for instance, of the woman who had accosted him in Piccadilly, and the slow process of extricating himself at Marlborough Street. It was easy to hold a man up on some trumped-up charge till an important plan had matured. Then there was the lavatory door at Waterloo, which had so ludicrously locked itself upon him. Being athletic, he had climbed over the partition, to find the attendant mysteriously absent. And, in Paris, was it by chance that he had had a deaf taxi-driver, who mistook the direction 'Quai d'Orléans' for 'Gare de Lyon,' and drove a mile and a half in the wrong direction before the shouts of his fare attracted his attention? They were clever, the pursuers, and circumspect. They had accurate information; they would delay him, but without taking any overt step; they knew that, if only they could keep time on their side, they needed no other ally.

Did they know he was on the train? If not, he still kept the advantage, for they would travel in a false security, thinking him to be left, raging and helpless, in the Invalides. He decided to make a cautious reconnaissance.

The first step was to change his grey suit for another of inconspicuous navy-blue cloth, which he had in his small black bag. This he did in the privacy of the toilet, substituting for his grey soft hat a large travelling cap, which pulled well down over his eyes.

There was little difficulty in locating the man he was in search of. He found him seated in the inner corner of a first-class compartment, facing the engine, so that the watcher could approach unseen from behind. On the rack was a handsome dressing-case, with the initials P. D. B. W. The young man was familiar with Wimsey's narrow, beaky face, flat yellow hair, and insolent dropped eyelids. He smiled a little grimly.

'He is confident,' he thought, 'and has regrettably made the mistake of underrating the enemy. Good! This is where I retire into a *seconde* and keep my eyes open. The next act of this melodrama will take place, I fancy, at Dreux.'

It is a rule on the Chemin de Fer de l'Ouest that all Paris-Evreux trains, whether of the Grande Vitesse or what Lord Peter Wimsey preferred to call Grande Paresse, shall halt for an interminable period at Dreux. The young man (now in navy-blue) watched his quarry safely into the refreshment room, and slipped unobtrusively out of the station. In a quarter of an hour he was back—this time in a heavy motoring coat, helmet, and goggles, at the wheel of a powerful hired Peugeot. Coming quietly on to the platform, he took up his station behind the wall of the *lampisterie*, whence he could keep an eye on the train and the buffet door. After fifteen minutes his patience was rewarded by the sight of his man again boarding the express, dressing-case in hand. The porters slammed the doors, crying: 'Next stop Verneuil!' The engine panted and groaned; the long train of grey-green carriages clanked slowly away. The motorist drew a breath of satisfaction, and, hurrying past the barrier, started up the car. He knew that he had a good eighty miles an hour under his bonnet, and there is no speed limit in France.

Mon Souci, the seat of that eccentric and eremitical genius the Comte de Rueil, is situated three kilometres from Verneuil. It is a sorrowful and decayed château, desolate at the termination of its neglected avenue of pines. The mournful state of a nobility without an allegiance surrounds it. The stone nymphs droop greenly over their dry and mouldering fountains. An occasional peasant creaks with a single waggonload of wood along the ill-forested glades. It has the atmosphere of sunset at all hours of the day. The woodwork is dry and gaping for lack of paint. Through the *jalousies* one sees the prim *salon*, with its beautiful and faded furniture. Even the last of its ill-dressed, ill-favoured women has withered away from Mon Souci, with her inbred, exaggerated features and her long white gloves. But at the rear of the château a chimney smokes incessantly. It is the furnace of the laboratory, the only living and modern thing among the old and dying: the only place tended and loved, petted and spoiled, heir to the long solicitude which counts of a more light-hearted day had given to stable and kennel, portrait gallery and ballroom. And below, in the cool cellar, lie, row upon row, the dusty bottles, each an enchanted glass coffin in which the Sleeping Beauty of the vine grows ever more ravishing in sleep.

As the Peugeot came to a standstill in the courtyard, the driver observed with considerable surprise that he was not the count's only visitor. An immense super-Renault, like a *merveilleuse* of the Directoire, all bonnet and no body, had been drawn so ostentatiously across the entrance as to embarrass the approach of any newcomer. Its glittering panels were embellished with a coat of arms, and the count's elderly servant was at that moment staggering beneath the weight of two large and elaborate suitcases, bearing in silver letters that could be read a mile away the legend: 'LORD PETER WIMSEY.'

The Peugeot driver gazed with astonishment at this display, and grinned sardonically. 'Lord Peter seems rather ubiquitous in this country,' he observed to himself. Then, taking pen and paper from his bag, he busied himself with a little letter-writing. By the time that the suit-cases had been carried in, and the Renault had purred its smooth way to the outbuildings, the document was complete and enclosed in an envelope addressed to the Comte de Rueil. 'The hoist with his own petard touch,' said the young man, and, stepping up to the door, presented the envelope to the manservant.

'I am the bearer of a letter of introduction to monsieur le comte,' he said. 'Will you have the obligingness to present it to him? My name is Bredon—Death Bredon.'

The man bowed, and begged him to enter.

'If monsieur will have the goodness to seat himself in the hall for a few moments. Monsieur le comte is engaged with another gentleman, but I will lose no time in making monsieur's arrival known.'

The young man sat down and waited. The windows of the hall looked out upon the entrance, and it was not long before the château's sleep was disturbed by the hooting of yet another motor horn. A station taxi-cab came noisily up the avenue. The man from the first-class carriage and the luggage labelled P. D. B. W. were deposited upon the doorstep. Lord Peter Wimsey dismissed the driver and rang the bell.

'Now,' said Mr Bredon, 'the fun is going to begin.' He effaced himself as far as possible in the shadow of a tall *armoire normande*.

'Good evening,' said the newcomer to the manservant, in admirable French, 'I am Lord Peter Wimsey. I arrive upon the invitation of Monsieur le comte de Rueil. Monsieur le comte is at liberty?'

'Milord Peter Wimsey? Pardon, monsieur, but I do not understand. Milord de Wimsey is already arrived and is with monsieur le comte at this moment.'

'You surprise me,' said the other, with complete imperturbability 'for certainly no one but myself has any right to that name. It seems as though some person more ingenious than honest has had the bright idea of impersonating me.'

The servant was clearly at a loss.

'Perhaps,' he suggested, 'monsieur can show his *papiers d'identité*.'

'Although it is somewhat unusual to produce one's credentials on the doorstep when paying a private visit,' replied his lordship, with unaltered good humour, 'I have not the slightest objection. Here is my passport, here is a *permis de séjour* granted to me in Paris, here my visiting-card, and here a quantity of correspondence addressed to me at the Hôtel Meurice, Paris, at my flat in Piccadilly, London, at the Marlborough Club, London, and at my brother's house at King's Denver. Is that sufficiently in order?'

The servant perused the documents carefully, appearing particularly impressed by the *permis de séjour*.

'It appears there is some mistake,' he murmured dubiously; 'if monsieur will follow me, I will acquaint monsieur le comte.'

They disappeared through the folding doors at the back of the hall, and Bredon was left alone.

'Quite a little boom in Richmonds today,' he observed, 'each of us more unscrupulous than the last. The occasion obviously calls for a refined subtlety of method.'

After what he judged to be a hectic ten minutes in the count's library, the servant reappeared, searching for him.

'Monsieur le comte's compliments, and would monsieur step this way?'

Bredon entered the room with a jaunty step. He had created for himself the mastery of this situation. The count, a thin, elderly man, his fingers deeply stained with chemicals, sat, with a perturbed expression, at his desk. In two armchairs sat the two Wimseys. Bredon noted that, while the Wimsey he had seen in the train (whom he mentally named Peter I) retained his unruffled smile, Peter II (he of the Renault) had the flushed and indignant air of an Englishman affronted. The two men were superficially alike—both fair, lean, and long-nosed, with the nondescript, inelastic face which predominates in any assembly of well-bred Anglo-Saxons.

'Mr Bredon,' said the count, 'I am charmed to have the pleasure of making your acquaintance, and regret that I must at once call upon you for a service as singular as it is important. You have presented to me a letter of introduction from your cousin, Lord Peter Wimsey. Will you now be good enough to inform me which of these gentlemen he is?'

Bredon let his glance pass slowly from the one claimant to the other, meditating what answer would best serve his own ends. One, at any rate, of the men in this room was a formidable intellect, trained in the detection of imposture.

'Well?' said Peter II. 'Are you going to acknowledge me, Bredon?'

Peter I extracted a cigarette from a silver case. 'Your confederate does not seem very well up in his part,' he remarked, with a quiet smile at Peter II.

'Monsieur le comte,' said Bredon, 'I regret extremely that I cannot assist you in the matter. My acquaintance with my cousin, like your own, has been made and maintained entirely through correspondence on a subject of common interest. My profession,' he added, 'has made me unpopular with my family.'

There was a very slight sigh of relief somewhere. The false Wimsey—whichever he was—had gained a respite. Bredon smiled.

'An excellent move, Mr Bredon,' said Peter I, 'but it will hardly explain—Allow me.' He took the letter from the count's hesitating hand. 'It will hardly explain the fact that the ink of this letter of recommendation, dated three weeks ago, is even now scarcely dry—though I congratulate you on the very plausible imitation of my handwriting.'

'If *you* can forge my handwriting,' said Peter II, 'so can this Mr Bredon.' He read the letter aloud over his double's shoulder.

' "Monsieur le comte—I have the honour to present to you my friend and cousin, Mr Death Bredon, who, I understand, is to be travelling in your part of France next month. He is very anxious to view your interesting library. Although a journalist by profession, he really knows something about books." I am delighted to learn for the first time that I have such a cousin. An interviewer's trick, I fancy, monsieur le comte. Fleet Street appears well informed about our family names. Possibly it is equally well informed about the object of my visit to Mon Souci?'

'If,' said Bredon boldly, 'you refer to the acquisition of the de Rueil formula for poison gas for the British Government, I can answer for my own knowledge, though possibly the rest of Fleet Street is less completely enlightened.' He weighed his words carefully now, warned by his slip. The sharp eyes and detective ability of Peter I alarmed him far more than the caustic tongue of Peter II.

The count uttered an exclamation of dismay.

'Gentlemen,' he said, 'one thing is obvious—that there has been somewhere a disastrous leakage of information. Which of you is the Lord Peter Wimsey to whom I should entrust the formula I do not know. Both of you are supplied with papers of identity; both appear completely instructed in this matter; both of your handwritings correspond with the letters I have previously received from Lord Peter, and both of you have offered me the sum agreed upon in Bank of England notes. In addition, this third gentleman arrives endowed with an equal facility in handwritings, an introductory letter surrounded by most suspicious circumstances, and a degree of acquaintance with this whole matter which alarms me. I can see but one solution. All of you must remain here at the château while I send to England for some elucidation of this mystery. To the genuine Lord Peter I offer my apologies, and assure him that I will endeavour to make his stay as agreeable as possible. Will this satisfy you? It will? I am delighted to hear it. My servants will show you to your bedrooms, and dinner will be at half-past seven.'

'It is delightful to think,' said Mr Bredon, as he fingered his glass and passed it before his nostrils with the air of a connoisseur, 'that whichever of these gentlemen has the right to the name which he assumes is assured tonight of a truly Olympian satisfaction.' His impudence had returned to him, and he challenged the company with an air. 'Your cellars, monsieur le comte, are as well known among men endowed with a palate as your talents among men of science. No eloquence could say more.'

The two Lord Peters murmured assent.

'I am the more pleased by your commendation,' said the count, 'that is suggests to me a little test which, with your kind co-operation, will, I think, assist us very much in determining which of you gentlemen is Lord Peter Wimsey and which his talented impersonator. Is it not matter of common notoriety that Lord Peter has a palate for wine almost unequalled in Europe?'

'You flatter me, monsieur le comte,' said Peter II modestly.

'I wouldn't like to say unequalled,' said Peter I, chiming in like a well-trained duet; 'let's call it fair to middling. Less liable to misconstruction and all that.'

'Your lordship does yourself an injustice,' said Bredon, addressing both men with impartial deference. 'The bet which you won from Mr Frederick Arbuthnot at the Egotists' Club, when he challenged you to name the vintage years of seventeen wines blindfold, received its due prominence in the *Evening Wire*.'

'I was in extra form that night,' said Peter I.

'A fluke,' laughed Peter II.

'The test I propose, gentlemen, is on similar lines,' pursued the count, 'though somewhat less strenuous. There are six courses ordered for dinner tonight. With each we will drink a different wine, which my bulter shall bring in with the label concealed. You shall each in turn give me your opinion upon the vintage. By this means we shall perhaps arrive at something, since the most brilliant forger—of whom I gather I have at least two at my table tonight—can scarcely forge a palate for wine. If too hazardous a mixture of wines should produce a temporary incommodity in the morning, you will, I feel sure, suffer it gladly for this once in the cause of truth.'

The two Wimseys bowed.

'*In vino veritas*,' said Mr Bredon, with a laugh. He at least was well seasoned and foresaw opportunities for himself.

'Accident, and my butler, having placed you at my right hand, monsieur,' went on the count, addressing Peter I, 'I will ask you to begin by pronouncing as accurately as may be, upon the wine which you have just drunk.'

'That is scarcely a searching ordeal,' said the other with a smile. 'I can say definitely that it is a very pleasant and well-matured Chablis Moutonne; and, since ten years is an excellent age for a Chablis—a real Chablis—I should vote for 1916, which was perhaps the best of the war vintages in that district.'

'Have you anything to add to that opinion, monsieur?' inquired the count, deferentially, of Peter II.

'I wouldn't like to be dogmatic to a year or so,' said that gentleman critically, 'but if I must commit myself, don't you know, I should say 1915—decidedly 1915.'

The count bowed, and turned to Bredon.

'Perhaps you, too, monsieur, would be interested to give an opinion,' he suggested, with the exquisite courtesy always shown to the plain man in the society of experts.

'I'd rather not set a standard which I might not be able to live up to,' replied Bredon, a little maliciously. 'I know that it is 1915, for I happened to see the label.'

Peter II looked a little disconcerted.

'We will arrange matters better in the future,' said the count. 'Pardon me.' He stepped apart for a few moments' conference with the butler, who presently advanced to remove the oysters and bring in the soup.

The next candidate for attention arrived swathed to the lip in damask.

'It is your turn to speak first, monsieur,' said the count to Peter II. 'Permit me to offer you an olive to cleanse the palate. No haste, I beg. Even for the most excellent political ends, good wine must not be used with disrespect.'

The rebuke was not unnecessary, for, after a preliminary sip, Peter II had taken a deep draught of the heady white richness. Under Peter I's quizzical eye he wilted quite visibly.

'It is—it is Sauterne,' he began, and stopped. Then, gathering encouragement from Bredon's smile, he said, with more aplomb, 'Château Yquem, 1911—ah! the queen of white wines, sir, as what's-his-name says.' He drained his glass defiantly.

The count's face was a study as he slowly detached his fascinated gaze from Peter II to fix it on Peter I.

'If I had to be impersonated by somebody,' murmured the latter gently, 'it would have been more flattering to have had it undertaken by a person to whom all white wines were *not* alike. Well, now, sir, this admirable vintage is, of course, a Montrachet of—let me see'—he rolled the wine delicately upon his tongue—'of 1911. And a very attractive wine it is, though, with all due deference to yourself, monsieur le comte, I feel that it is perhaps slightly too sweet to occupy its present place in the menu. True, with this excellent *consommé marmite*, a sweetish wine is not altogether out of place, but, in my own humble opinion, it would have shown to better advantage with the *confitures*.'

'There, now,' said Bredon innocently, 'it just shows how one may be misled. Had not I had the advantage of Lord Peter's expert opinion—for certainly nobody who could mistake Montrachet for Sauterne has any claim to the name of Wimsey—I should have pronounced this to be, not the Montrahet-Aîné, but the Chevalier-Montrachet of the same year, which is a trifle sweeter. But no doubt, as your lordship says, drinking it with the soup has caused it to appear sweeter to me than it actually is.'

The count looked sharply at him, but made no comment.

'Have another olive,' said Peter I kindly. 'You can't judge wine if your mind is on other flavours.'

'Thanks frightfully,' said Bredon. 'And that reminds me—' He launched into a rather pointless story about olives, which lasted out the soup and bridged the interval to the entrance of an exquisitely cooked sole.

The count's eye followed the pale amber wine rather thought-fully as it trilled into the glasses. Bredon raised his in the approved manner to his nostrils, and his face flushed a little. With the first sip he turned excitedly to his host.

'Good God, sir—' he began.

The lifted hand cautioned him to silence.

Peter I sipped, inhalted, sipped again, and his brows clouded. Peter II had by this time apparently abandoned his pretensions. He drank thirstily, with a beaming smile and a lessening hold upon reality.

'*Eh bien*, monsieur?' inquired the count gently.

'This,' said Peter I, 'is certainly hock, and the noblest hock I have ever tasted, but I must admit that for the moment I cannot precisely place it.'

'No?' said Bredon. His voice was like bean honey now, sweet and harsh together. 'Nor the other gentleman? And yet I fancy I could place it within a couple of miles, though it is a wine I had hardly looked to find in a French cellar at this time. It is hock, as your lordship says, and at that it is Johannisberger. Not the plebian cousin, but the *echter* Schloss Johannisberger from the castle vine-yard itself. Your lordship must have missed it (to your great loss) during the war years. My father laid some down the year before he died, but it appears that the ducal cellars at Denver were less well furnished.'

'I must set about remedying the omission,' said the remaining Peter, with determination.

The *poulet* was served to the accompaniment of an argument over the Lafitte, his lordship placing it at 1878, Bredon maintaining it to be a relic of the glorious 'seventy-fives, slightly over-matured, but both agreeing as to its great age and noble pedigree.

As to the Clos-Vougeot, on the other hand, there was complete agreement; after a tentative suggestion of 1915, it was pronounced finally by Peter I to belong to the equally admirable though slightly lighter 1911 crop. The *pré-salé* was removed amid general applause, and the desert was brought in.

'Is it necessary,' asked Peter I, with a slight smile in the direction of Peter II—now happily murmuring, 'Damn good wine, damn good dinner, damn good show'—'is it necessary to prolong this farce any further?'

'Your lordship will not, surely, refuse to proceed with the dis-cussion?' cried the count.

'The point is sufficiently made, I fancy.'

'But no one will surely ever refuse to discuss wine,' said Bredon, 'least of all your lordship, who is so great an authority.'

'Not on this,' said the other. 'Frankly, it is a wine I do not care about. It is sweet and coarse, qualities that would damn any wine in the eyes—the mouth, rather—of a connoisseur. Did your excellent father have this laid down also, Mr Bredon?'

Bredon shook his head.

'No,' he said, 'no. Genuine Imperial Tokay is beyond the opportunities of Grub Street, I fear. Though I agree with you that it is horribly overrated—with all due deference to yourself, monsieur le comte.'

'In that case,' said the count, 'we will pass at once to the liqueur. I admit that I had thought of puzzling these gentlemen with the local product, but, since one competitor seems to have scratched, it shall be brandy—the only fitting close to a good wine-list.'

In a slightly embarrassing silence the huge, round-bellied balloon glasses were set upon the table, and the few precious drops poured gently into each and set lightly swinging to release the bouquet.

'This,' said Peter I, charmed again into amiability, 'is, indeed, a wonderful old French brandy. Half a century old, I suppose.'

'Your lordship's praise lacks warmth,' replied Bredon. 'This is *the* brandy—the brandy of brandies—the superb—the incomparable—the true Napoleon. It should be honoured like the emperor it is.'

He rose to his feet, his napkin in his hand.

'Sir,' said the count, turning to him, 'I have on my right a most admirable judge of wine, but you are unique.' He motioned to Pierre, who solemnly brought forward the empty bottles, unswathed now, from the humble Chablis to the stately Napoleon, with the imperial seal blown in the glass. 'Every time you have been correct as to growth and year. There cannot be six men in the world with such a palate as yours, and I thought that but one of them was an Englishman. Will you not favour us, this time, with your real name?'

'It doesn't matter what his name is,' said Peter I. He rose. 'Put up your hands, all of you. Count, the formula!'

Bredon's hands came up with a jerk, still clutching the napkin. The white folds spurted flame as his shot struck the other's revolver cleanly between trigger and barrel, exploding the charge, to the extreme detriment of the glass chandelier. Peter I stood shaking his paralysed hand and cursing.

Bredon kept him covered while he cocked a wary eye at Peter II, who, his rosy visions scattered by the report, seemed struggling back to aggressiveness.

'Since the entertainment appears to be taking a lively turn,' observed Bredon, 'perhaps you would be so good, Count, as to search these gentlemen for further firearms. Thank you. Now, why should we not all sit down again and pass the bottle round?'

'You—*you* are—' growled Peter I.

'Oh, my name is Bredon all right,' said the young man cheerfully. 'I loathe aliases. Like another fellow's clothes, you know—never seem quite to fit. Peter Death Bredon Wimsey—a bit lengthy and all that, but handy when taken in instalments. I've got a passport and all those things, too, but I didn't offer them, as their reputation here seems a little blown upon, so to speak. As regards the formula, I think I'd better give you my personal cheque for it—all sorts of people seem able to go about flourishing Bank of England notes. Personally, I think all this secret diplomacy work is a mistake, but that's the War Office's pigeon. I suppose we all brought similar credentials. Yes, I thought so. Some bright person seems to have sold himself very successfully in two place at once. But you two must have been having a lively time, each thinking the other was me.'

'My lord,' said the count heavily, 'these two men are, or were, Englishmen, I suppose. I do not care to know what Governments have purchased their treachery. But where they stand, I, alas! stand too. To our venal and corrupt Republic, I, as a Royalist, acknowledge no allegiance. But it is in my heart that I have agreed to sell my country to England because of my poverty. Go back to your War Office and say I will not give you the formula. If war should come between our countries—which may God avert!—I will be found on the side of France. That, my lord, is my last word.'

Wimsey bowed.

'Sir,' said he, 'it appears that my mission has, after all, failed. I am glad of it. This trafficking in destruction is a dirty kind of business after all. Let us shut the door upon these two, who are neither flesh nor fowl, and finish the brandy in the library.'

RAFFLES AND OPERATION CHAMPAGNE

Barry Perowne

It is perhaps no surprise that the favourite drink of Raffles, the man who has been described as 'the greatest cracksman in the history of roguery', should be champagne. Created just over one hundred years ago in The Amateur Cracksman *by Ernest William Hornung (1866–1921), Raffles was hugely popular not only in book form, but also on the screen where he has been portrayed by several famous film stars including John Barrymore, Ronald Colman and David Niven. In 1950 the crime writer, Barry Perowne (1908-) revived him in a series of cases which a number of critics believe are actually superior to the original Hornung stories. In one of the best of these, 'Raffles and Operation Champagne', written in 1981, the intrepid cracksman and his faithful assistant-chronicler Bunny Manders set out on what at first seems like a simple mission to deliver twelve cases of champagne—but instead turns into an adventure of mounting tension and danger.*

'Does the name Gouvion Frères mean anything to you?' demanded Colonel Godfrey Lees-Garland.

'Champagne,' said A. J. Raffles promptly.

Summoned to Paris by a coded telegram, Raffles and I, arriving at the Gare du Nord, had found a November mist dimming the streetlamps; but we had managed to get a taxi and had had ourselves driven to the Ritz, in the Place Vendôme.

Receiving us in his suite—for in his private capacity he was a member of the landed gentry and suites at the Ritz were his lifestyle—the Colonel immediately flung his question at us.

'Yes,' he said, confirming Raffles' reply, 'Gouvion Frères is one of the great champagne firms of the city of Rheims.'

Gaunt and bald, leathery and deeply furrowed of face, with shrewd eyes, the Colonel poured three whiskies from a decanter on the sideboard.

'I'll now tell you, Raffles and Manders,' he said, handing us our glasses, 'why I've called you chaps over from London. Very early this morning I was confidentially informed that within an hour or two of the signing of the Armistice at eleven a.m. yesterday, the eleventh of November, bringing an end at last to this damnable war, General Sir Douglas Haig, commanding the British sector in France, invited King George the Fifth to visit his troops in the line. The King's acceptance of the invitation was at once signalled to Sir Douglas.'

Glass in hand, the Colonel prowled the room.

'As a matter of protocol,' he went on, 'the King's visit to France had, of course, to be cleared with the French Premier, old "Tiger" Clemenceau—who, in approving the visit, added a suggestion of his own. Already in Paris, or on their way here, are certain eminent Allied statesmen—men of the calibre of President Wilson's adviser, the influential Colonel House. These eminent men are here for preliminary discussions on the terms of a definitive Treaty to be drawn up at a Peace Conference soon to convene formally at the Palace of Versailles. Premier Clemenceau suggested that King George, while in France, take the opportunity to meet some of these eminent statesmen. One hardly needs a prophetic eye to see that on the wisdom of these distinguished men depends the future, probably for generations to come.'

Raffles nodded, intent. My heart was beginning to thump.

'I'm informed,' Colonel Lees-Garland continued, 'that a meeting has been rather hastily arranged. A luncheon is to take place two days hence at a rendezvous mutually convenient to the King, who will be at Haig's headquarters at St. Omer, and to the statesmen who are now in Paris. Twelve cases of champagne, a gross of magnums, have been ordered from Gouvion Frères. I'm told that this champagne is of a quite exceptional *cuvée*. Trust the French to know where to look for it! At this time when half the world is celebrating the Armistice, this wine is virtually priceless—liquid gold.'

The Colonel gave us a searching look.

'The luncheon rendezvous, classified Most Secret,' he said, 'is the Château Rèmy-Latour, a secluded mansion in the forest just north of Versailles itself, between St. Omer and Paris. Because the rendezvous is secret, I've been instructed, as current head of Section O, the special-tasks unit of the Allies' clandestine intelligence organization, to arrange for the collection and delivery of the required champagne—which is why I've sent for you.'

I took a gulp of my whisky.

'As soon as I got my orders this morning,' Colonel Lees-Garland went on, 'I telephoned to Count Jules Gouvion, head of Gouvion Frères. He had news for me. Now, as you know, until Uncle Sam threw his stovepipe hat into the ring, things looked grim for the Allies. It seemed that we'd lose Rheims. Consequently, though Count Gouvion himself is at his Rheims establishment, the required wine is not. He told me that most of the great champagne firms shifted their wines to safer areas. Gouvions shifted theirs well away to Normandy, where they own a deconsecrated Priory, the Prieuré de St. Gabriel, in the historic old town of St. Lô. They're using the Priory as emergency cellars.

'Count Gouvion told me to get in touch with his Cellarer, a Monsieur Yvonnec, who's been with the firm for many years. He is at the Priory with his Wine Porter, and has full authority there. I've spoken with the Cellarer on the telephone and arranged everything with him.'

'And our orders, sir?' Raffles said.

'This persistent November mist,' said the Colonel, 'failed to damp the joy when the bells of half the world rang out in tumultuous thanksgiving at eleven a.m. yesterday. But the mist threatens fog to come, so your quickest way to Normandy will be by rail. You will spend the night here at the Ritz and leave for St. Lô, via Caen, by the first train in the morning. A compartment's been booked for you. On arrival at the Priory you'll find that the Cellarer has had the consignment loaded into Gouvion Frères transport, ready for instant collection.'

Colonel Lees-Garland unlocked a drawer of the sideboard, took out an envelope and a military mapcase.

'I've marked the forest luncheon rendezvous, the Château Rèmy-Latour, on this map,' he said. 'In this envelope is authority for the Cellarer at St. Lô to hand over the consignment to you. You will deliver the consignment as early as possible to the majordomo in charge of preparations at the Château. I've impressed upon the Cellarer at St. Lô that in no circumstances whatever is he to release the consignment to anybody except two of my officers, uniformed and armed. That's why I instructed you, in my telegram, to wear the uniform of your substantive military ranks. Apropos—the war's over now, thank God, but I take it those revolvers in your holsters are still loaded?'

Seldom as Raffles and I wore uniform for our Section O work, our khaki was immaculate, our Sam Browne belts and our revolver holsters highly polished—and our revolvers, Raffles assured the Colonel, were indeed loaded.

'Not that I anticipate,' said the Colonel, 'any trouble for you on this job—Operation Champagne. Compared with some of the missions you've done for me, this one should be a cakewalk. It'll be your last job before you're demobilised and return to your civilian way of life.'

Our civilian way of life as, ostensibly, gentlemen of independent means, had been financed by opportunistic larcenies, but Colonel Lees-Garland did not know this, or he might have had second thoughts before making us responsible for a consignment of liquid gold. I took a final gulp of my whisky.

'Just on the off-chance of your running into any difficulty, Raffles,' said the Colonel, 'I've obtained a formal Order of Mission for you from my superior, General De Sauvagnac, of Allied High Command. Before we go down to dine, you'd better take a look at this Order.'

The document which Colonel Lees-Garland handed to Raffles could hardly have been more comprehensive. In French and in English, it read:

> To: All Ranks, Allied Armies.
> On production of this Order of Mission, the bearer, *Major A. J. Raffles* (I.D. S/4/828), is to be provided, immediately and unquestioned, with assistance of whatsoever nature he may stand in need.
> (Sgd.): R. De Sauvagnac, GSO(I), for
>   *FERDINAND FOCH*, Marshal of France,
>   *GENERALISSIMO, ALLIED ARMIES.*

Over the wet green fields of northern France, on the day following our first postwar dinner at the Ritz, the mist steadily thickened. The train was crowded with Allied troops. Veterans of General Pershing's campaign in the Argonne sector, they were bound—an American officer who shared our first-class compartment told us— for early repatriation via Cherbourg.

'They've certainly earned it, Major,' Raffles said. 'Your dough-boys have put up a damned fine show.'

'I'm happy to say the same for your tommies, Major,' replied the American courteously.

We exchanged hip-flasks and cigarettes with him and discussed the probable shape of the world to come.

'I guess it all depends,' the American major said shrewdly, 'on this forthcoming Peace Conference at Versailles.'

Agreeing, Raffles and I exchanged significant glances.

As the day wore on, the train's speed was reduced. More and more frequently the locomotive sounded its warning howl, and the audible jubilation of the homeward-bound troops began to give way to impatience. At prolonged, unscheduled stops at blurred red signals, the troops put their heads out of the windows and expressed their opinion of the Chemin-de-Fer de L'Etat by vehement outbursts which the American major referred to as 'raspberries.'

At Caen, Raffles and I left the troop train to continue its slow journey to Cherbourg—and by the time we ourselves reached St. Lô at last, the murky daylight was gone. Unseen in the darkness and fog that blanketed the old Norman town, a church clock was sonorously striking the hour, 6:00 p.m. Here and there dim lights showed, each ringed with a nimbus. A caped gendarme, of whom we inquired the whereabouts of the Prieuré de St. Gabriel, shone the ray of his bull's-eye over our khaki.

'Come with me,' he said.

He guided us along a dark, meandering, cobblestoned street, where he soon halted, and with his bull's-eye, showed us a knocker on one of a pair of massive doors, rustily iron-studded, centuries old, set in an arch of lichened stone.

'Voilà, messieurs,' he said, touched two fingers to his kepi, and left us.

Using the heavy knocker, Raffles pounded on the door. The iron reverberations died away in the fog. We waited. All was still. Raffles was about to knock again, but suddenly a spyslot in the door snapped open and a bright light shone out, dazzling us.

'Bon soir,' said Raffles. 'We have business with Monsieur Yvonnec, the Cellarer.'

I sensed an eye looking over our khaki, then a voice said, in tolerable English, 'What is your business with me?'

'This,' said Raffles, and thrust into the slot our written authorisation to collect the champagne consignment.

The paper vanished, the slot snapped shut. In darkness we waited, then bolts and bars clattered. The ponderous doors creaked open just widely enough to permit our entry into the glare of a pressure-lamp. Two men, revolvers in hand, held us at gunpoint.

'I am the Cellarer,' said the taller man, slender of build, wearing a white coat of the laboratory-technician kind, and a belt of keys. His tone was peremptory. 'Your military identifications?'

We produced them. He snatched them from us. The other man, squat and muscular, a green baize apron over his sweater, was obviously the Wine Porter. His revolver in one fist, the pressure-lamp dangling from the other, he kept us covered as the Cellarer examined our credentials. The light shone on his smooth hair and thin, unlined, ascetic face, and his tension visibly relaxed as he returned our papers to us.

'Ça va, Jacques,' he said to the Wine Porter, and gave us a bleak smile. 'Strange days, gentlemen, these of the war's immediate aftermath. In the wake of victory come its camp followers—bacchanalia, rape, Army deserters steal out from their boltholes. In anticipation of high profits, black-marketeer gangs grow bold.

They raid supply dumps and loot liquor storerooms—especially such as I have here in this Priory's cellars. You will understand my caution.'

With his Wine Porter carrying the pressure-lamp, the tall Cellarer led us to a vehicle looming nearby in the fog of this cobble-toned courtyard.

'Transport is hard to come by these days,' he said. 'We use this sparingly, for local haulage, but it will serve your purpose.'

The transport, a coupé of a model long outmoded, had a two-wheeled trailer attached, and the Cellarer, unfastening the rope that secured the trailer-cover, showed us the twelve wooden cases, firmly packed in the trailer and prominently stencilled Gouvion Frères, Rheims.

'As a matter of course,' he said, refastening the trailer-cover, 'champagne, bottled and in bin, is turned once daily – if the Cellarer knows his business. Where are you travelling to with this consignment?'

Raffles had taken the driver's seat in the coupé and, with his flashlamp, was examining the controls.

'The Persian poet, Omar Khayyam,' said the Cellarer, 'remarked that he "often wondered what the vintner buys one half so precious as the goods he sells." I could have told him in one word—gasoline. I have managed to provide you with a full tank. It should suffice. I take it you are going to Paris?'

'Bunny,' Raffles said to me, 'give the starting handle a crank.'

He switched on the brassbound headlamps, which bloomed feebly, staining the fog a bilious yellow. I cranked again and again with the starting-handle. Finally, the motor came to life, and I ran around and joined Raffles in the throbbing coupé, which was as cramped as a London hansom. Adjusting a lever on the steering-wheel quadrant, reducing the din, Raffles thanked the Cellarer for his services.

He replied, with frigid hauteur, 'I expect this transport to be returned in due course—with a full tank.'

'It will be,' said Raffles.

Jacques, the musclebound Wine Porter, trundled open the archaic doors of the courtyard. The unseen church clock was striking again. Two resonant chimes, vibrating deeply in the fog, proclaimed the hour, 6:30 p.m., as we left the Prieuré de St. Gabriel and sought the road to Versailles.

Visibility, even when we had found our way on to the *route nationale*, was almost zero. I could not help remembering prewar times, when we had chosen just such nights as this for our ventures in crime.

'Raffles,' I said, 'our old London friend and "fence," Ivor Kern, would pay us a high price for this freight we're hauling.'

The thought amused me. But Raffles, his tone meditative, said, 'Bunny, the man I keep thinking of, in connection with this freight, would also pay us a high price for it, and he's not so far off as London. He's in Paris. What's more, he's a wine merchant, a prosperous one, and as you and I have reason to know, from one of our past ventures, he's a crook.'

I felt a twinge of uneasiness.

'Raffles,' I said, 'we've kept an unblemished record throughout our war service—'

'So we'd be fools, now that we're practically on the eve of demobilisation,' Raffles said, 'to risk blotting our character records? Sound thinking, Bunny! Any such risk, in the present circumstances, is out of the question. But the risk of a collision in this damned fog is well in the cards, so keep your eyes peeled.'

He was watching the grassy road-edge himself, steering by what little could be seen of it in the glimmer of our debilitated headlamps. Very infrequently, vehicles—mostly Army type—came looming out of the fog. They passed us as cautiously as we passed them. But there was little traffic on the road, and gradually, as we kept steadily on for mile after mile, the strain of peering ahead into the fog began to tell on my eyes.

Cramped in our rattletrap coupé, I now and then—to keep myself awake—used my pocket flashlight to consult the map in the mapcase on my knees. I was none the wiser for doing so. Nor, in spite of my best efforts to the contrary, did I succeed in keeping my glazed eyes open.

It was a sense of cessation of movement that brought my lolling head up with a jerk that almost dislocated my neck.

The coupé, its lamps wanly illuminating the fog, was at a standstill, with the motor running, and Raffles was saying, 'We're at a Y-fork in the road. There's a signpost there, but I can't read it. Get out with your flashlight, Bunny, and see what's on the post.'

The touch of the fog, chill on my face as I stumbled out of the coupé, somewhat revived me. Shining my ray of light up at the signpost, I called to Raffles, 'Left for Argentan. Straight on for Vernoeuil and Versailles.'

'Good,' said Raffles. 'We're well on our way.'

As I moved back to the coupé, my flashlight-ray swivelled over it. My heart lurched. I stopped dead. My legs almost gave way.

'What's the matter?' said Raffles.

I hardly knew how to tell him. I had to clear my throat.

'The trailer,' I said. 'It's come uncoupled.'

He got out of the coupé and added the ray of his flashlight to mine. He drew in his breath, deeply.

'We'll have to go back,' he said, 'and find the damned thing.'

His theory was that our separation from the trailer must have occurred at one of the bad patches of *pavé* on the road.

'My fault,' he said. 'I ought to have realised this damned noisy rattletrap was pulling a bit easier.'

Scanning the road-edges, Raffles the one on his side, me the one on mine, we made our slow way back for kilometer after kilometer over our route, and we found the trailer. It was standing, with a marked list, on the grassy road-marge. We got out of the coupé and with our flashlights examined the trailoer. Its canvas cover still was roped down intact over the freight.

'No great harm done, after all,' I said.

'Provided,' Raffles said drily, 'we can tow a two-wheeled trailer that has only one wheel.'

I saw then, my heart sinking, what must have happened. Uncoupled from the coupé, the trailer must have continued its journey independently, got onto a downslope, gathered speed, and struck an adjacent telegraph pole a glancing blow. This evidently had deprived one wheel of its hubcap, thus freeing the wheel to go rolling on, but abruptly halting the headlong progress of the trailer.

We spent a half-hour vainly searching the roadside ditches for the missing wheel, but it probably had rolled on for a long distance, leaving Operation Champagne stalled in the fog here—wherever here might be. Personally, I had no idea. But Raffles, standing by the coupé, was using his flashlight to consult the map in the map-case.

'While you were asleep,' he said to me, 'we passed through a small town that, as far as I can judge from this map, must have been Flers. I noticed a garage there. I'd better stay with the trailer and its freight, now that we've recovered it. You take the coupé, go to Flers, find that garage, and see if you can hire a van of some kind. Leave the coupé at the garage, for later collection, and get back here with alternative transport as quickly as—' He broke off. 'No! Wait! Listen!'

I heard the sound of a motor. The sound grew louder.

'This is probably another Army vehicle,' Raffles said.

Signalling with his flashlight, he stepped out into the middle of the road. Powerful headlamps penetrated the fog. A limousine, chauffeur-driven, pulled up sharply. A domelight came on in the tonneau, the window was lowered, and a hatless head appeared. Looking out, and seeing that we were in khaki, the passenger demanded, 'What's this—a road check?' He sounded American, and by the look of the fur coat he was wearing and the fragrance of the cigar he was smoking, he was a civilian of considerable importance. He added, 'Hurry it up. I've got to get on to Cherbourg.'

'In that case, sir,' said Raffles, moving round to look in at the window, 'you'll shortly be passing through Flers. I don't think it's far on. I'd be grateful if you'd drop off my lieutenant there.'

'Surely,' said the American. He opened the tonneau door. 'Get in, Lieutenant.'

'You'll get to Flers quicker this way, Bunny,' Raffles said. 'In you get!'

As I went off in the American's limousine, I thought that probably he was a member of the Diplomatic Corps, and involved with the Versailles Treaty preliminaries, he was on his way to embark at Cherbourg for consultations at the White House in Washington, D.C. But no. Cordially enough, he introduced himself as Alexander Woollcott, a correspondent on the staff of the American Expeditionary Force journal, *Stars and Stripes*.

'Published in Paris,' he said. 'I'm on my way to Cherbourg to report on the embarkation of the first A.E.F. contingent to be going home. What with this fog, I've got a nasty hunch I'll find that the troopship's weighed anchor and gone.'

I was glad to be able to set his mind at rest.

'As it happens,' I told him, 'I saw your A.E.F. chaps on the train from Paris to-day. They're probably still quite a way from Cherbourg. They're on a very slow train.'

Reassured, the correspondent told me that he had started late from Paris, owing to the difficulty in getting a car.

'With all these parties going on, celebrating the Armistice,' he said, 'transport's at a premium. I had to bribe the U.S. Motor Pool sergeant in Paris to let *Stars and Stripes* have this limousine for just this one journey to Cherbourg and back. The car had been requisitioned, along with its French civilian chauffeur, for use by Colonel House, a brass hat very big politically. He's on his way from Washington, but he's not expected in Paris till late to-morrow.'

I could have told the correspondent that Colonel House would need his limousine the day after to-morrow to take him to an important luncheon engagement in the forest near Versailles. But I said nothing. Security was involved here.

'I've got to get the car back to the Pool not later than four p.m. to-morrow,' said the correspondent, 'or that crook of a Transport Sergeant is liable to find himself in the brig.'

'This is a very fine car, Mr Woollcott,' I said.

'It was probably requisitioned from some war profiteer,' said the correspondent. 'He'd left his fur coat in the car, and it's just the coat for a night like this.'

A well-informed man, the correspondent was rich in A.E.F. anecdotes and remarkably up-to-date on the subject of the New York theatre. He predicted that Broadway was on the eve of being revitalised by the dazzling talent of new dramatists returning from the war.

'Some of them probably embarking right now,' he said, 'at Cherbourg.'

Fascinating as I found the correspondent, I was anxious to return to Raffles with alternative transport for Operation Champagne, and Flers was further on than we had thought. I was relieved when at last the limousine reached Flers and I saw, in the glow of the limousine's headlamps, a solitary pump. It marked a garage of sorts, and I asked the correspondent to drop me off here.

The garage doors were shut, but a window above them showed a dim light in the fog. I shouted up at the window. There was no response.

'Lieutenant,' said the correspondent, putting on his hat and getting out of the limousine, 'there's a bell hanging there by the pump.'

Agitating the bell-clapper by its dangling cord, he produced a clangour that must have been heard all over this fogbound little French town. He did it again. The din seemed to inspire him.

'Hey,' he said, 'this gives me a title—The Town Crier. How about that for a gossip column—or maybe for radio, the coming thing now the war's over.'

'Great title, Mr Woollcott,' I said.

'A natural,' he said, and clanged again with evident enthusiasm.

Suddenly the lighted window over the garage doors was flung up and a man leaned out, yelling, *'Fermé! Fermé! Pas de l'essence!'*

'Do you happen to have a van for hire?' I called up to him.

'Van?' he shouted. 'Every motor van in Flers has been jacked up for years. No tyres. *Allez vous en!'*

The window banged shut.

Reluctant as any old-time Town Crier to leave off ringing, the correspondent gave the bell one more resounding clang.

'Well, Lieutenant,' he said to me regretfully, 'I'd have liked to see you squared away, but meantime the A.E.F.'s embarking at Cherbourg, so I can't help you any longer.' About to get back into the limousine he paused abruptly, a foot on the running-board. 'I think I hear a truck coming!'

The approaching vehicle certainly sounded like a big one, but what came rattling to a standstill, with a rasp of the hand-brake, was the diminutive coupé belonging to Gouvion Frères. Raffles stepped out. He looked at me inquiringly. I shook my head.

'No luck,' I told him, 'and not much prospect of any.'

'This gentleman?' said Raffles.

'Mr Alexander Woollcott,' I said. 'He's on the way to report on the A.E.F. contingent's embarkation. He's on the staff of *Stars and Stripes*.'

'An Army journal,' said Raffles.

'Excuse me, gentlemen,' said the correspondent, 'I must be getting along.'

'Just a moment, Mr Woollcott,' Raffles said. 'Almost as soon as you'd driven off in your limousine, kindly taking my lieutenant along, an impression came to me—an impression that, when I spoke to you through your car window, there'd been a hat on the seat. Your much more conspicuous fur coat made my belated impression that the hat I'd unconsciously seen was a U.S. Army hat, with chin-strap, seem rather improbable. Still, I thought it as well, just in case my lieutenant should have had no luck on his errand, to see if I could overtake you. You're now wearing your hat, and my original impression of it is confirmed, I see now, by your regulation U.S. Army boots and leggings. That fur coat conceals both your uniform and your rank.'

'I'm a private,' said the correspondent, bewildered, 'but—'

'It's nothing to do with me what you wear,' Raffles said, with a smile. 'The point is this—I'm going to have to do a swap with you.'

'This coat for yours?' said the mystified correspondent.

'No,' Raffles said. 'Your car for ours.'

'With respect, Major,' exclaimed the correspondent, aghast, 'you can't *do* that!'

'With no less respect,' Raffles said, 'I must tell you that I can. Let me explain. I'm under orders to deliver an important freight to a specified map reference at a stated hour. The trailer containing the freight has been crippled by a mishap. The coupé we've been using to tow the trailer hasn't enough space in it to carry the freight, but your limousine has, so I'm obliged to requisition it.'

'It's already been requisitioned,' protested the correspondent. 'It ranks, temporarily, as a U.S. Army vehicle on charge to our Motor Pool in Paris. If you seize this—'

'Seize?' Raffles said. 'Exchange is no seizure, soldier. I'm leaving you this coupé. Here, you'd better take a look at this Order of Mission. It's issued by Allied Supreme Headquarters on the authority of Marshal Foch, Generalissimo, Allied Armies.'

Raffles handed the Order to the correspondent who, his

expresson bemused, read the document in the light of the limousine's headlamps.

'Now that you understand the position,' Raffles said, taking back the Order and pocketing it, 'let's waste no more time. The coupé will get you to Cherbourg, given reasonable luck, and you're probably as anxious to be on your way as we are to be on ours.'

Turning to the civilian chauffeur, who had been listening while rolling a cigarette, Raffles told him in French to get out of the limousine and into the coupé. He obeyed, with a shrug, and Raffles and I got into the limousine. Raffles took the wheel, pressed the self-starter.

Above the rich purring of the motor Raffles said to the fur-coated correspondent, who was standing nonplussed, 'I'm sincerely sorry about this, but we're all three of us similarly placed. We're the pawns of High Command.'

As we drove off in the fog a sudden clamour broke out behind us. It was the furious clanging, urgent as a fire alarm, of the garage bell.

'What good does Woollcott think he's doing,' Raffles said, 'by kicking up that row?'

'He's probably doing it in a tantrum of frustration, rage, and panic,' I said, 'and I fully sympathise with him. I happen to know that if this limousine isn't back in the U.S. Motor Pool in Paris by four p.m. to-morrow, Woollcott could be in trouble.'

'We don't want that,' said Raffles. 'What we'll do, Bunny, when we've delivered the freight to the Château Rémy-Latour, is drive on into Paris and turn in this car to the Motor Pool.'

'Good idea,' I said, relieved. 'That'll keep Woollcott in the clear. He's an interesting chap—an able journalist, very quick in the uptake. The first time he rang that bell, it gave him a notion for a witty sort of news-and-comment project. He plans to call it The Town Crier.'

'Then it's lucky I spotted that A.E.F. hat of his,' Raffles said, 'before he'd thought of changing it for a tricorne of Rip Van Winkle's time.'

The clanging of the bell in the fog died away behind us.

The limousine originally requisitioned for the use of Colonel House, the enigmatic politico on his way from Washington, purred along at a better speed than had been possible in the rattletrap coupé. The limousine's headlamps were superior to those of the coupé and, as we went on and on in the fog without seeing the trailer, I began to be puzzled. So did Raffles.

'Where we left the trailer,' he said, 'there was a dip in the road. I could have sworn we just passed that dip. I remember there was a heap of gravel there at the roadside. I think we'll take another look.'

Steering with the road-edge for guide, he backed the limousine for fifty yards or so down to the dip in the road—and abruptly applied the brakes.

'There it is,' he said. 'No wonder we didn't see it!'

The trailer's position had changed. It no longer was standing lopsidedly on the grassy road-marge. With its one remaining wheel barely visible in the glow of the limousine's headlamps, the trailer lay on its side in the deep ditch beyond the marge.

We got quickly out of the limousine, and our flashlights showed us at once what had happened.

The trailer had been looted. Its canvas cover had been ripped off. The twelve cases of champagne were gone.

My heart thumped like a drum. I stood rooted, incredulous, shining my flashlight down onto the trailer, capsized and empty, its cover lying in the ditchwater.

'The damned thieves,' I heard Raffles say. 'There was more than one of them. Look at this!'

I shone my flashlight down on to the muddy grass he was examining.

'Tracks!' I exclaimed.

'As plain as a pikestaff,' said Raffles. 'Bootmarks, cartwheel tracks, a horse's hoofprints. The thieves spotted the tralier, emptied it, and shoved it into the ditch for concealment. Come on, we've only to follow the tracks!'

We got back into the limousine. Raffles turned it. The headlamps clearly showed the cartwheel tracks in the muddy *pavé* of the road. Driving slowly, we followed the tracks for almost two kilometres, then they turned to the right, through a decrepit gateway standing open. The tracks led us on up a rutted and puddled drive, and Raffles halted the limousine as its headlamps, diluting the fog, revealed the cart that had made the tracks. It was a farm tumbril, tilted down on its shafts, the horse gone from it. Dimly visible beyond was a long low farmhouse with a roof of sodden thatch.

'Have your gun handy,' Raffles whispered, as we got out of the limousine.

Squelching through farmyard slush, we approached the house cautiously. To the left of its door was a pungent midden, to the right a dimlit window. From within sounded a rumble of voices. Stealthily Raffles lifted the crude door-latch, pressed slightly on the door. It was unlocked. He flung it open. Revolvers in hand, we charged in—upon a scene of rustic debauchery.

We were in a kitchen. Three hulking peasants, sprawled on

chairs around a table littered with the remains of some insanitary
repast, were in the act of guzzling champagne from magnums.

'*A votre santé, messieurs,*' said Raffles.

They stared at us with jaws agape. A poker dropped with a
clatter from the hand of a brawny woman surprised in the act of
tending a turf fire smouldering sullenly in the chimney place. On
the uneven flagstones of the kitchen floor the stolen champagne
cases were stacked. One of them had been broken into. Straw
sleeves from pilfered magnums were scattered around on the
flagstones, where one magnum lay smashed and a pointer dog
speckled with fleas was lapping up a puddle of the spilled
champagne.

The brawny woman, wringing her hands in her sleazy pinafore,
her feet in wooden *sabots* and her scanty hair done up in twists of
newspaper, wailed at us that her sons had found the wine when
returning late from the village.

'We are honest people, messieurs,' she assured us. 'The Inspector
will vouch for us. I was just about to call the police on the Inspector's telephone and inform him of the find.'

'Were you indeed?' Raffles said.

He was watching the dog with a curious intensity.

'I swear it, m'sieu,' insisted the woman, as the dog slunk off,
an occasional lurch in its gait, to some sacking in a corner. 'Admit-
tedly, my sons should not have opened one of the cases, but—*que
voulez vous?*' Her shrug proclaimed a mother's helplessness. 'They
had been at the *estaminet*, celebrating the Armistice, and their
minds were befuddled as to right and wrong.'

With a sign of alcoholic repletion the dog sank down voluptu-
ously on the sacking in the corner. Raffles looked from the dog to
the three thieves around the table. They simpered at him ingratiat-
ingly, conscious of their guilt. They did not look too intelligent.

'Pardon,' Raffles said, politely relieving one of the guzzlers of
his magnum and turning it upside down. It was empty. '*C'est bon,
le vin?*' Raffles asked, with a smile.

The uncouth clowns smirked and nodded, their heads seeming
loose on their necks. They were obviously feeling the effects of
their potations.

'Bunny,' Raffles said, looking thoughtfully at the three sots,
'keep an eye on these gentry. Madame, where's the telephone you
were about to call the police on?'

'In my parlour, m'sieu. The provincial Inspector for the Agricul-
tre Ministry had the telephone put in for use on his rounds.
Inspectors must communicate, is it not so?'

'Lead me to it, madame,' said Raffles.

Left alone with the three inebriates, I kept a wary eye on them.

They sat gazing at me stupidly, but they ventured no comment except for occasional belchings, which seemed to make the champagne fumes more potent in their addled heads. Their condition visibly deteriorated. They swayed in their chairs. One of them fell off, overturning his chair, and lay with his legs outstretched. His brothers peered down at him, then blinked accusingly at my revolver, as though I had shot the miserable clod with it.

Their mother returned, her *sabots* clonking on the flagstones.

'Tiens,' she exclaimed, disgusted, 'what a drunken spectacle!! M'sieu, I am saddened that my sons should make such an exhibition of themselves. They are not used to champagne. *C'est l'Armistice que fait mal!'*

She went on gabbling excuses for her sons' lapse from virtue, and I was relieved when Raffles came back. He stooped over the fallen yokel, twitched his eyelid back, felt his pulse, then looked at the chap's hapless brothers.

'Spiflicated,' Raffles said, 'to put it mildly.' He shrugged. 'Come on, Bunny, we shall have to load the freight into the limousine ourselves.'

The brawny mother of sons insisted on helping us, and we carried the eleven intact champagne-cases out to the limousine and stacked them in the tonneau. We took our seats in front, and driving off down the farm track, got once more onto the *route nationale*, bound for Versailles.

There was no diminution of the fog, and I was beginning to wonder about the champagne. It had had a good deal more movement than we had bargained for, and I wondered if, by the time we delivered it to the major-domo anxiously awaiting it at the Château Rèmy-Latour, the wine would have recovered sufficiently from its journey to be at its best for drinking at the luncheon the day after. I asked Raffles what he thought.

'I'm wondering myself, Bunny,' he said. 'That's what I telephoned about.' Concentrated on his driving, he added, 'Keep your eyes open ahead.'

A thought occurred to me. I used my flashlight for a brief glance at my wrist watch. It was long past midnight, so the date was not now the 13th. I did not mention this to Raffles, who had no superstitions that I ever noticed, but personally I felt that we were now out of the woods and our luck would change for the better. I was therefore dismayed when, the limousine having purred along smoothly for heaven knew how many kilometres, I saw in the fog ahead three stationary red lights spaced across the road, barring our way.

'Oh, dear God,' I said, 'what now?'

Raffles brought the limousine purring to a halt. Near the middle one of the three red lanterns that obstructed the road stood a caped gendarme. On the grassy road-marge three bicycles stood propped against each other, and two more gendarmes approached the limousine, one of them on Raffles' side, one on mine. They shone their flashlights in at us, then onto the wooden cases stacked in the tonneau, then onto us again—and my heart skipped a beat at the menace of the gendarmes' revolvers.

'We've had a long cold wait for you,' said the gendarme on Raffles' side sardonically. 'Switch off your motor and get out of that car with your hands up.'

'Now, just a moment, officer,' Raffles said. 'As you see, we're in uniform. We're on an official journey—as you will further see from this Order of Mission issued on the authority of—'

'Of Marshal Foch, no less,' said the gendarme. 'That accords with the warning telephoned to our station. You are in possession of an automobile stolen from a member of the American Expeditionary Force!'

'The Town Crier,' Raffles murmured. 'Your friend's been ringing bells again, Bunny—telephone type—to broadcast his news.'

'You are wearing stolen uniforms, carrying a forged Order of Mission,' rasped the gendarme, 'and are heading for Paris with freight of some kind for the black market!'

'Well, well,' said Raffles. 'So he's broadcast not only his news but his comments on it.'

'Get out of that car instantly,' ordered the gendarme, 'or you'll be shot for resisting arrest!'

'Force majeure, Bunny,' Raffles said, with a sigh.

He made as though to switch off the purring motor. Instead, he let in the clutch, and with the limousine roaring in low gear, swerved it, bouncing, onto the road-marge. The three bicycles were knocked flying and the limousine crunched over them with a jolt that flung me forward in my seat. My head met the windshield with a mighty impact. I saw a brief brilliant galaxy of stars, then nothing more.

A certain famous statue of the Emperor Napoleon, regal in robes of bronze, a chaplet of bronze laurel leaves crowning his brow, stands on top of a tall pillar. Recognising the statue, at which I found myself looking up through a shattered windshield, in wintry daylight, I realised gradually where I was.

'Paris,' I heard myself say, my tongue feeling swollen, as though inadvertently I had bitten it. 'Place Vendôme—'

'We've just this minute arrived at the Ritz,' said Raffles' voice. 'It's about nine a.m.'

I became aware that I was semi-recumbent in the front seat

of what, I recalled, was the limousine we had requisitioned for Operation Champagne.

Raffles, at the wheel of the stationary limousine, was looking at me anxiously.

'You need a shave,' I said.

'You should see yourself,' he said, relief in his smile.'You have three stitches in your scalp and you've a beautiful black eye. Otherwise, you seem all right. But you'd better stay where you are. Don't worry about a thing. I've delivered the champagne, and I'm just going to pop into the Ritz and report to Colonel Lees-Garland. Just stay where you are and take it easy.'

'No,' I said. 'I want to hear if I've missed much. I'm coming in with you. I feel fine.'

I did not, actually. My head ached, and when I sat up to put my cap on, I found that it was too small, my head having been bandaged. All the same, I got out of the limousine, straightened my tunic and Sam Browne belt, to make myself as presentable as possible, and my legs feeling a trifle shaky, accompanied Raffles into the Ritz. The reception-desk attendants eyed me rather oddly, but a pageboy was summoned to conduct us up to the Colonel's suite, where we found him at breakfast.

'Good God, Manders,' he said, rising at the sight of me, 'I thought the bloody war was over!'

He poured coffee for us, putting a particularly good dollop of brandy into mine, and he said, 'Well now, Raffles, I got your telephone call from that farmhouse place. It was then about one fifteen a.m. You explained to me about your exchange of cars with the *Stars and Stripes* correspondent, but I'd like to know exactly what prompted the request you made to me when you telephoned me from the farmhouse.'

'It was the orgy we found in progress there, Colonel,' Raffles said. 'Those simpletons at the farm were guzzling that champagne, found by chance at the roadside, with no more knowledge of it than a kid why accepts goodies from a stranger, or a dog that picks up stray bones. They could have been poisoned. It was a fleeting thought, Colonel, but it brought me a sudden memory of something you'd told us. You said that the Cellarer at St. Lô. had been *many years* with Gouvion Frères. But, Colonel, that was impossible! The man we talked to at the Priory hadn't a grey hair on his head or a line in his face. He was a *young* man—under thirty, I'd say. So I telephoned to you and asked you to get through on the phone to the Police Chief at St. Lô and request him to confirm that the man we'd talked to at the Priory was, in fact, Monsieur Yvonnec, the Cellarer.'

'I got through to the Police Chief,' said Colonel Lees-Garland.

'He called me back at four a.m. He'd been to the Priory with two of his men. They got no reply to their knocking. They forced an entrance and searched the place. They found Monsieur Yvonnec and his Wine Porter. They'd been shot and thrown into the deepest of cellars. Monsieur Yvonnec's still alive, is in hospital, and will recover. He says that the seizure of the Priory by the two men you saw occurred on the eleventh, the very day the Armistice was signed. Undoubtedly those two men were enemy agents.'

'Diehards,' said Raffles, 'refusing to accept the stark face of defeat—'

'And determined to strike a final blow—a low blow *after* the bell had rung!' The furrows were deep in the Colonel's face. 'God help me,' he said bitterly, 'it was *I* who gave that bogus Cellarer exactly the chance he was waiting for. He's in the wine trade. Monsieur Yvonnec recognised him as a young salesman of Rhenish wines and French champagnes who came into Gouvion Frères' place at Rheims, just before the war, and offered to represent them in England. He didn't get the job. But of course, being in the trade, he knew just where the great champagne firms had emergency cellars. He knew he had only to wait and that special *cuvée* wine would be required—for some quite exceptional Armistice occasion. And it was *I* who gave him the order, and told him it would be collected by two of my men of *officer* rank, thus emphasising the importance *and* the secrecy of the occasion.'

'He was certainly curious to know exactly where his wine was going,' Raffles said. 'Eh, Bunny?'

'Absolutely, Raffles,' I said, my bandaged head throbbing.

'But what I don't understand,' the Colonel said to Raffles, 'are your actions subsequent to your telephone call to me at one fifteen a.m. from the farmhouse.'

'We continued our journey, sir,' Raffles said. 'I was worried. Those chaps at the farmhouse hadn't been poisoned. Neither had their dog. They were merely drunk. But another possibility gnawed at me. What if one or more of those eleven remaining champagne cases had been booby-trapped—Russian-roulette style—to explode on opening?'

I almost dropped my cup. I stared at Raffles.

He said, 'We had a little trouble, evading a road check by gendarmes, but that was incidental, Colonel. The important thing was that I thought it inadvisable to deliver the suspect champagne consignment to the major-domo at the Château Rèmy-Latour. I brought the consignment straight on, through Versailles, into Paris, and delivered the eleven cases to the Duty Officer at Allied Supreme Headquarters.'

'I know you did,' Colonel Lees-Garland said grimly. 'I had a call, an hour or so ago, from General De Sauvagnac. He told me that you explained the position to the Night Duty Officer and instructed him—on the authority of your high-level Order of Mission—to have the eleven cases taken immediately to the nearest ballistics testing-range, have the cases set out in a row, and have them machine-gunned.'

I listened, open-mouthed, my heart hammering.

'I hope I did right, Colonel?' Raffles said.

'Absolutely right,' said the Colonel, 'and General De Sauvagnac agrees. In your place, we'd have done the same thing. The fact remains—there was *no* explosion when the champagne cases were machine-gunned.'

'No explosion, sir?' Raffles' keen face was a study in consternation. Never had I seen him so taken aback.

'I don't know what to make of it,' said the Colonel. 'But there it is—what's done is done. The magnums have been riddled with machine-gun bullets, shot to smithereens, and the wine's sunk into the ground. I shall have a big squawk from Section O's Paymaster when I show him Gouvion Frères' bill for a gross of magnums of their finest *cuvée* champagne. He'll yell murder—especially when he hears that the luncheon's been cancelled.'

'Cancelled, sir?' Raffles said.

'So General De Sauvagnac told me on the phone this morning. The luncheon was arranged in haste. King George is in France, all right—he's at Sir Douglas Haig's headquarters at St. Omer. But some Allied statesmen might not arrive in time for the luncheon—Colonel House, for instance, who's believed to be bringing from Washington, for discussion, a draft of Fourteen Points that President Wilson feels could provide a sound basis for the forthcoming Versailles Peace Treaty. Apparently, on second thoughts, it was decided that if late-arriving statesmen heard that some of their Allied opposite numbers had already conferred privately together, it could give rise to inter-Allied jealousies. Quite enough of those will probably emerge at the formal Peace Conference. Anyway, the luncheon's been cancelled—wisely, in my opinion,' the Colonel said.

A knock sounded on the door, and he called, 'Come in!'

The newcomer was the pageboy who had brought Raffles and me up to the suite.

'Please, Colonel, sir,' the boy said, 'there are two Military Policemen down in the foyer. They belong to the U.S. Army Provost Corps. They're inquiring about a limousine that's standing outside. They say its licence-plate number was reported to their headquarters and they were ordered to watch out for it. They have been told at the reception-desk that the limousine was brought here by two officers.' The boy studiously avoided looking at Raffles and me. 'The M.P.s want to speak to the two officers, Colonel, sir.'

'Tell the M.P.s to wait just a minute, Jean-Claude,' said the Colonel, frowning at us as the boy went out. 'What's this, then?'

Raffles smiled ruefully. 'The *Stars and Stripes* correspondent, Colonel—our friend The Town Crier. He's still ringing bells, telephone bells, possibly from as far away as Cherbourg. Either because he genuinely believes Manders and I are crooks, or because he's trying to alibi himself and the Motor Pool sergeant if the limousine's not back in the Pool by four p.m. today, he's broadcasting the news far and wide that the car was stolen from him.'

'Exchange is no robbery,' said the Colonel.

'I explained that to him, sir,' Raffles said, 'but he doesn't seem to have been convinced. This is just one of those inter-Allied misunderstandings. Don't you think, Colonel, that you'd better have a word with these M.P.s yourself? You know just how much or how little they should be told about Operation Champagne. You could ask them to return the limousine to the Motor Pool, and you could show them this Order of Mission—which should put everything right.'

'Except that the bogus Cellarer hasn't been caught,' the Colonel said grimly, 'and with all this war aftermath movement of displaced persons and prisoners of war, across international frontiers, he's very unlikely to be caught. I'm still wondering just what the devil he had up his sleeve.'

The Colonel stood up.

'I suppose I'd better have a word with these M.P.s,' he said. 'You fellows will lunch with me here at the Ritz, then catch the night train back to London and report to your Army depot, in Buckingham Palace Road, for early demobilisation.'

Colonel Godfrey Lees-Garland left us, and Raffles looked at me with concern.

'That shiner of yours is swelling a bit, Bunny,' he said. 'We'll see if the Ritz kitchen has a raw beefsteak handy. I had the medical orderly at Supreme Headquarters stitch and bandage your scalp wound while I was arranging with the Night Duty Officer to have the champagne machine-gunned. How're you feeling now?'

'Mystified,' I said, 'and it's making my headache worse. Raffles, if the champagne consignment was neither poisoned nor booby-trapped with explosives, what was the bogus Cellarer's object?'

'That's a good question, Bunny,' Raffles said. 'The fact is that when we reached Paris, with you unconscious in the seat beside me, I made a call before going to Supreme Headquarters. I visited that crooked wine merchant we've had dealings with before, remember? He was in bed, but I got him up. I asked him if he had any Gouvion Frères champagne in stock. He told me he had sixteen cases of one of their less expensive champagnes. I offered to take eleven cases of it off his hands, in exchange for eleven cases of Gouvion's finest *cuvée* wine—provided he paid me the difference in the value of the two wines.'

Raffles took a thick sheaf of Banque de France thousand-franc notes from his tunic pocket.

'These should help cure your headache, Bunny,' he said. 'It's all very simple. There's a saying that "circumstances alter cases"—so I altered the cases to suit the circumstances, then went directly to Supreme Headquarters and delivered the consignment.'

I was so shocked that, for a moment, I forgot my black eye and my headache.

'But that wine merchant,' I faltered, 'if those cases we hauled from St. Lô *are* booby-trapped—'

'I've no doubt some of them are,' said Raffles. 'But he's been warned. He received an anonymous telephone call shortly after he'd done his deal. Some excited-sounding person seemed to know of it, and warned him, if he valued his life, not to play Russian roulette by opening those cases, but to cart them out of Paris and drop them, intact, into a deep place in the Seine. He's a crook, not a hero. We know very well what choice he'll make—and he knows we know too much about him for him to try any crafty reprisal.'

Raffles divided the sheaf of banknotes into two equal shares.

'So you see, Bunny, now that the war's over, we can return with clear consciences to our civilian way of life—as gentlemen,' said A. J. Raffles pleasantly, 'of independent means.'

AUTHOR'S NOTE

In connection with the Manders narrative, found recently among his long-hidden records of criminal adventure in peace and war, it may possibly be of interest to remark that the physical appearance of the bogus Cellarer at St. Lô, as described by Manders, bears some resemblance to that of an individual who later achieved world-wide notoriety.

Should the resemblance be more than merely coincidental, which unfortunately cannot at this late date be proven one way or the other, it is a very great pity that the individual in question was not apprehended while clandestinely active in France during World War One.

For this arrogant, ambitious man subsequently became a prominent Nazi, was appointed Foreign Minister by Adolf Hitler, significantly assisted in destroying the well-meaning efforts of the eminent treaty makers of Versailles, and with consummate skill manipulated a foreign policy that inevitably resulted in World War Two.

Born in the Rhineland in 1893, the individual in question was hanged at Nuremburg in 1946.

So ended the ex-champagne salesman, Joachim Von Ribbentrop.

THE UNBLEMISHED BOOTLEGGER

Leslie Charteris

In one of his early adventures, the Saint—otherwise known as Simon Templar—described the raison d'être *of his life in these words: 'I want something elementary and honest—battle, murder, sudden death and plenty of good beer and damsels in distress.' As his fame grew, the palate of this 'modern day Robin Hood' became somewhat more sophisticated and he was more likely to be seen with a glass of wine, scotch or champagne in his hand than a pint of bitter. This was especially true when his adventures were adapted for television with the urbane Roger Moore. Alcohol features in several of the Saint's adventures written by Leslie Charteris (1907–1993), himself a devotee of the best wines and spirits. They include 'The Unlicensed Victuallers', 'The Intemperate Reformer' and 'The Unblemished Bootlegger', of which the third has been selected for this book. It is set in the Twenties and deals with the Prohibition Era in the United States presenting a case that requires all Simon Templar's legendary powers at deception to solve.*

Mr Melford Croon considered himself a very prosperous man. The brass plate outside his unassuming suite of offices in Gray's Inn Road described him somewhat vaguely as a 'Financial Consultant'; and while it is true that the gilt-edged moguls of the City had never been known to seek his advice, there is no doubt that he flourished exceedingly.

Out of Mr Croon's fertile financial genius emerged, for example, the great Tin Salvage Trust. In circulars, advertisements, and statements to the Press, Mr Croon raised his literary hands in horror at the appalling waste of tin that was going on day by day throughout the country. 'Tins', of course, as understood in the ordinary domestic vocabulary to mean the sepulchres of Heinz's 57 Varieties, the Crosse & Blackwell vegetable garden, or the Chef soup kitchen, are made of thin sheet iron with the most economical possible plating of genuine tin; but nevertheless (Mr Croon pointed out) *tin was used*. And what happened to it? *It was thrown away*. The dustman removed it along with the other contents of the dustbin, and the municipal incinerators burnt it. And tin was a precious metal—not quite so valuable as gold and platinum, but not very far behind silver. Mr Croon invited his readers to think of it. Hundreds of thousands of pounds being poured into dustbins and incinerators every day of the week from every kitchen in the land. Individually worthless 'tins' which in the accumulation represented an enormous potential wealth.

The great Tin Salvage Trust was formed with a capital of nearly a quarter of a million to deal with the problem. Barrows would collect 'tins' from door to door. Rag-and-bone men would lend their services. A vast refining and smelting plant would be built to recover the pure tin. Enormous dividends would be paid. The subscribers would grow rich overnight.

The subscribers did not grow rich overnight; but that was not Mr Croon's fault. The Official Receiver reluctantly had to admit it, when the Trust went into liquidation eighteen months after it was formed. The regrettable capriciousness of fortune discovered and enlarged a fatal leak in the scheme; without quite knowing how it all happened, a couple of dazed promoters found themselves listening to sentences of penal servitude; and the creditors were glad to accept one shilling in the pound. Mr Croon was overcome with grief—he said so in public—but he could not possibly be blamed for the failure. He had no connection whatever with the Trust, except as Financial Consultant—a post for which he received a merely nominal salary. It was all very sad.

In similar circumstances, Mr Croon was overcome with grief at the failures of the great Rubber Waste Products Corporation, the Iron Workers' Benevolent Guild, the Small Investors' Cooperative Bank, and the Universal Albion Film Company. He had a hard and unprofitable life; and if his mansion flat in Hampstead, his Rolls Royce, his shoot in Scotland, his racing stud, and his house in Marlow helped to console him, it is quite certain that he needed them.

'A very suitable specimen for us to study,' said Simon Templar.

The latest product of Mr Croon's indomitable inventiveness was spread out on his knee. It took the form of a very artistically typewritten letter, which had been passed on to the Saint by a chance acquaintance.

Dear Sir,

As you cannot fail to be aware, a state of Prohibition exists at present in the United States of America. This has led to a highly profitable trade in the forbidden alcoholic drinks between countries not so affected and the United States.

A considerable difference of opinion exists as to whether this traffic is morally justified. There can be no question, however, that from the standpoint of this country it cannot be legally attacked; nor that the profits, in proportion to the risk, are exceptionally attractive.

If you should desire further information on the subject, I shall be pleased to supply it at the above address.

Yours faithfully,

MELFORD CROON

Simon Templar called on Mr Croon one morning by appointment; and the name he gave was not his own. He found Mr Croon to be a portly and rather pale-faced man, with the flowing iron-grey mane of an impresario; and the information he gave—after a few particularly shrewd inquiries about his visitor's status and occupation—was very much what the Saint had expected.

'A friend of mine,' said Mr Croon—he never claimed personally to be the author of the schemes on which he gave Financial Consultations—'a friend of mine is interested in sending a cargo of wines and spirits to America. Naturally, the expenses are somewhat heavy. He has to charter a ship, engage a crew, purchase the cargo, and arrange to dispose of it on the other side. While he would prefer to find the whole of the money—and, of course, reap all the reward—he is unfortunately left short of about two thousand pounds.'

'I see,' said the Saint.

He saw much more than Mr Croon told him, but he did not say so.

'This two thousand pounds,' said Mr Croon, 'represents about one-fifth of the cost of the trip, and in order to complete his arrangements my friend is prepared to offer a quarter of his profits to anyone who will go into partnership with him. As he expects to make at least ten thousand pounds, you will see that there are not many speculations which offer such a liberal return.'

If there was one rôle which Simon Templar could play better than any other, it was that of the kind of man whom financial consultants of every size and species dream that they may meet one day before they die. Mr Croon's heart warmed towards him as Simon laid on the touches of his self-created character with a master's brush.

'A very charming man,' thought the Saint, as he paused on the pavement outside the building which housed Mr Croon's offices.

Since at various stages of the interview Mr Croon's effusive bonhomie had fairly bubbled with invitations to lunch with Mr Croon, dine with Mr Croon, shoot with Mr Croon, watch Mr

Croon's horses win at Goodwood with Mr Croon and spend week-ends with Mr Croon at Mr Croon's house on the river, the character which Simon Templar had been playing might have thought that the line of the Saint's lips was unduly cynical; but Simon was only thinking of his own mission in life.

He stood there with his walking-stick swinging gently in his fingers, gazing at the very commonplace street scene with thoughtful blue eyes, and became aware that a young man with the physique of a pugilist was standing at his shoulder. Simon waited.

'Have you been to see Croon?' demanded the young man suddenly.

Simon looked round with a slight smile.

'Why ask?' he murmured. 'You were outside Croon's room when I came out, and you followed me down the stairs.'

'I just wondered.'

The young man had a pleasantly ugly face with crinkly grey eyes that would have liked to be friendly; but he was very plainly nervous.

'Are you interested in bootlegging?' asked the Saint; and the young man stared at him grimly.

'Listen. I don't know if you're trying to be funny, but I'm not. I'm probably going to be arrested this afternoon. In the last month I've lost about five thousand pounds in Croon's schemes—and the money wasn't mine to lose. You can think what you like. I went up there to bash his face in before they get me, and I'm going back now for that same reason. But I saw you come out, and you didn't look like a crook. I thought I'd give you a word of warning. You can take it or leave it. Goodbye.'

He turned off abruptly into the building, but Simon reached out and caught him by the elbow.

'Why not come and have some lunch first?' he suggested. 'And let Croon have his. It'll be so much more fun punching him in the stomach when it's full of food.'

He waved away the young man's objections and excuses without listening to them, hailed a taxi, and bundled him in. It was the kind of opportunity that the Saint lived for, and he would have had his way if he was compelled to kidnap his guest for the occasion. They lunched at a quiet restaurant in Soho; and in the persuasive warmth of half a litre of Chianti and the Saint's irresistible personality the young man told him what he knew of Mr Melford Croon.

'I suppose I was a complete idiot—that's all. I met Croon through a man I used to see in the place where I always had lunch. It didn't occur to me that it was all a put-up job, and I thought Croon was all right. I was fed to the teeth with sitting about in an office copying figures from one book to another, and Croon's stunts looked like a way out. I put three thousand quid into his Universal Albion Film Company: it was only on paper, and the way Croon talked about it made me think I'd never really be called on for the money. They were going to rent the World Features studio at Teddington—the place is still on the market. When the Universal Albion went smash I had to find the money, and the only way I could get it was to borrow it out of the firm. Croon put the idea into my head, but—Oh, hell! It's easy enough to see how things have happened after the damage is done.'

He had borrowed another two thousand pounds—without the cashier's knowledge—in the hope of retrieving the first loss. It had gone into a cargo of liquor destined for the thirsty States. Six weeks later Mr Croon broke the news to him that the coastal patrols had captured the ship.

'And that's what'll happen to any other fool who puts money into Croon's bootlegging,' said the young man bitterly. 'He'll be told that the ship's sunk, or captured, or caught fire, or grown wings and flown away. He'll never see his money back. My God— to think of *that* slimy swab trying to be a bootlegger! Why, he told me once that the very sight of a ship made him feel sick, and he couldn't cross the Channel for a thousand pounds.'

'What are you going to do about it?' asked the Saint, and the young man shrugged.

'Go back and try to make him wish he'd never been born—as I told you. They're having an audit today at the office, and they can't help finding out what I've done. I stayed away—said I was ill. That's all there is to do.'

Simon took out his cheque-book and wrote a cheque for five thousand pounds.

'Whom shall I make it payable to?' he inquired, and his guest's eyes widened.

'My name's Peter Quentin. But I don't want any of your damned—'

'My dear chap, I shouldn't dream of offering you charity.' Simon blotted the pink slip and scaled it across the table. 'This little chat has been worth every penny of it. Besides, you don't want to go to penal servitude at your age. It isn't healthy. Now be a good fellow and dash back to your office—square things up as well as you can—'

The young man was staring at the name which was scribbled in the bottom right-hand corner of the paper.

'Is that name Simon Templar?'

The Saint nodded.

'You see, I shall get it all back,' he said.

He went home with two definite conclusions as the result of his day's work and expenses: first, that Mr Melford Croon was in every way as undesirable a citizen as he had thought, and second, that Mr Melford Croon's contribution to the funds of righteousness was long overdue. Mr Croon's account was, in fact, exactly five thousand pounds overdrawn; and that state of affairs could not be allowed to continue.

Nevertheless, it took the Saint twenty-four hours of intensive thought to devise a poetic retribution; and when the solution came to him it was so simple that he had to laugh.

Mr Croon went down to his house on the river for the week-end. He invariably spent his week-ends there in the summer, driving out of London on the Friday evening and refreshing himself from his labours with three happy days of rural peace. Mr Croon had an unexpected appetite for simple beauty and the works of nature: he was rarely so contented as when he was lying out in a deck chair and spotless white flannels, directing his gardener's efforts at the flower-beds, or sipping an iced whisky and soda on his balcony while he watched supple young athletes propelling punts up and down the stream.

This week-end was intended to be no exception to his usual custom. He arrived at Marlow in time for dinner, and prepared for an early night in anticipation of the tireless revels of a mixed company of his friends who were due to join him the next day. It was scarcely eleven o'clock when he dismissed his servant and mixed himself a final drink before going to bed.

He heard the front door bell ring, and rose from his armchair grudgingly. He had no idea who could be calling on him at that hour; and when he had opened the door and found that there was no one visible outside he was even more annoyed.

He returned to the sitting-room, and gulped down the remainder of his nightcap without noticing the bitter tang that had not been there when he poured it out. The taste came into his mouth after the liquid had been swallowed, and he grimaced. He started to walk towards the door, and the room spun round. He felt himself falling helplessly before he could cry out.

When he woke up, his first impression was that he had been buried alive. He was lying on a hard narrow surface, with one shoulder squeezed up against a wall on his left, and the ceiling seemed to be only a few inches above his head. Then his sight cleared a little, and he made out that he was in a bunk in a tiny unventilated compartment lighted by a single circular window. He struggled up on one elbow, and groaned. His head was one reeling whirligig of aches, and he felt horribly sick.

Painfully he forced his mind back to his last period of consciousness. He remembered pouring out that last whisky and soda—the ring at the front door—the bitter taste in the glass ... Then nothing but an infinity of empty blackness ... How long had he been unconscious? A day? Two days? A week? He had no means of telling.

With an agonising effort he dragged himself off the bunk and staggered across the floor. It reared and swayed sickeningly under him, so that he could hardly keep his balance. His stomach was somersaulting nauseatingly inside him. Somehow he got over to the one round window: the pane was frosted over, but outside he could hear the splash of water and the shriek of wind. The explanation dawned on him dully—he was in a ship!

Mr Croon's knees gave way under him, and he sank moaning to the floor. A spasm of sickness left him gasping in a clammy sweat. The air was stiflingly close, and there was a smell of oil in it which made it almost unbreathable. Stupidly, unbelievingly, he felt the floor vibrating to the distant rhythm of the engines. A ship! He'd been drugged—kidnapped—shanghaied! Even while he tried to convince himself that it could not be true, the floor heaved up again with the awful deliberateness of a seventh wave; and Mr Croon heaved up with it ...

He never knew how he managed to crawl to the door between the paroxysms of torment that racked him with every movement of the vessel. After what seemed like hours he reached it, and found strength to try the handle. The door failed to budge. It was locked. He was a prisoner—and he was going to die. If he could have opened the door he would have crawled up to the deck and thrown himself into the sea. It would have been better than dying of that dreadful nausea that racked his whole body and made his head swim as if it were being spun round on the axle of a dynamo.

He rolled on the floor and sobbed with helpless misery. In another hour of that weather he'd be dead. If he could have found a weapon he would have killed himself. He had never been able to stand the slightest movement of the water—and now he was a prisoner in a ship that must have been riding one of the worst storms in the history of navigation. The hopelessness of his position made him scream suddenly—scream like a trapped hare— before the ship slumped suckingly down into the trough of another seventh wave and left his stomach on the crest of it.

Minutes later—it seemed like centuries—a key turned in the locked door, and a man came in. Through the bilious yellow mists that swirled over his eyes, Mr Croon saw that he was tall and wiry, with a salt-tanned face and far-sighted twinkling blue eyes. His double-breasted jacket carried lines of dingy gold braid, and he balanced himself easily against the rolling of the vessel.

'Why, Mr Croon—what's the matter?'

'I'm sick,' sobbed Croon, and proceeded to prove it.

The officer picked him up and laid him on the bunk.

'Bless you, sir, this isn't anything to speak of. Just a bit of a blow—and quite a gentle one for the Atlantic.'

Croon gasped feebly.

'Did you say the Atlantic?'

'Yes, sir. The Atlantic is the ocean we are on now, sir, and it'll be the same ocean all the way to Boston.'

'I can't go to Boston,' said Croon pathetically. 'I'm going to die.'

The officer pulled out a pipe and stuffed it with black tobacco. A cloud of rank smoke added itself to the smell of oil that was contributing to Croon's wretchedness.

'Lord, sir, you're not going to die!' said the officer cheerfully. 'People who aren't used to it often get like this for the first two or three days. Though I must say, sir, you've taken a long time to wake up. I've never known a man be so long sleeping it off. That must have been a very good farewell party you had, sir.'

'Damn you!' groaned the sick man weakly. 'I wasn't drunk—I was drugged!'

The officer's mouth fell open.

'Drugged, Mr Croon?'

'Yes, drugged!' The ship rolled on its beam ends, and Croon gave himself up for a full minute to his anguish. 'Oh, don't argue about it! Take me home!'

'Well, sir, I'm afraid that's—'

'Fetch me the captain!'

'I am the captain, sir. Captain Bourne. You seem to have forgotten, sir. This is the *Christabel Jane*, eighteen hours out of Liverpool with a cargo of spirits for the United States. We don't usually take passengers, sir, but seeing that you were a friend of the owner, and you wanted to make the trip, why, of course we found you a berth.'

Croon buried his face in his hands.

He had no more questions to ask. The main details of the conspiracy were plain enough. One of his victims had turned on him for revenge—or perhaps several of them had banded together for the purpose. He had been threatened often before. And somehow his terror of the sea had become known. It was poetic justice— to shanghai him on board a bootlegging ship and force him to take the journey of which he had cheated their investments.

'How much will you take to turn back?' he asked; and Captain Bourne shook his head.

'You still don't seem to understand, sir. There's ten thousand pounds' worth of spirits on board—at least, they'll be worth ten thousand pounds if we get them across safely—and I'd lose my job if I—'

'Damn your job!' said Melford Croon.

With trembling fingers he pulled out a cheque-book and fountain pen. He scrawled a cheque for fifteen thousand pounds and held it out.

'Here you are, I'll buy your cargo. Give the owner his money and keep the change. Keep the cargo. I'll buy your whole damned ship. But take me back. D'you understand? *Take me back*—'

The ship lurched under him again, and he choked. When the convulsion was over the captain had gone.

Presently a white-coated steward entered with a cup of steaming beef tea. Croon looked at it and shuddered.

'Take it away,' he wailed.

'The Captain sent me with it, sir,' explained the steward. 'You must try to drink it, sir. It's the best thing in the world for the way you're feeling. Really, sir, you'll feel quite different after you've had it.'

Croon put out a white flabby hand. He managed to take a gulp of the hot soup; then another. It had a slightly bitter taste which seemed familiar. The cabin swam round him again, more dizzily than before, and his eyes closed in merciful drowsiness.

He opened them in his own bedroom. His servant was drawing back the curtains, and the sun was streaming in at the windows.

The memory of his nightmare made him feel sick again, and he clenched his teeth and swallowed desperately. But the floor underneath was quite steady. And then he remembered something else, and struggled up in the bed with an effort which threatened to overpower him with renewed nausea.

'Give me my cheque-book,' he rasped. 'Quick—out of my coat pocket—'

He opened it frantically, and stared at a blank counterfoil with his face growing haggard.

'What's today?' he asked.

'This is Saturday, sir,' answered the surprised valet.

'What time?'

'Eleven o'clock, sir. You said I wasn't to call you—'

But Mr Melford Croon was clawing for the telephone at his bedside. In a few seconds he was through to his bank in London. They told him that his cheque had been cashed at ten.

Mr Croon lay back on the pillows and tried to think out how it could have been done.

He even went so far as to tell his incredible story to Scotland Yard, though he was not by nature inclined to attract the attention of the police. A methodical search was made in Lloyd's Register, but no mention of a ship called the *Christabel Jane* could be found.

Which was not surprising; for the *Christabel Jane* was the name temporarily bestowed by Simon Templar on a dilapidated Thames tug which had wallowed very convincingly for a few hours in the gigantic tank at the World Features studio at Teddington for the filming of storm scenes at sea, which would undoubtedly have been a great asset to Mr Croon's Universal Albion Film Company if the negotiations for the lease had been successful.

THE UNKNOWN PEER

E. C. Bentley

Philip Trent is a youthful artist-cum-detective who is fond of good living and far from infallible in his deductions—facts which caused the first novel about his exploits, published in 1913 with the perverse title Trent's Last Case, *to be hailed as a landmark in crime fiction. Indeed, the author, Edmund Clerihew Bentley (1875–1956) was thereafter described as 'the father of the contemporary detective story'. Bentley, who is also famous for his invention of four-line nonsense verses known as 'clerihews' (after his middle name), was a close friend of G. K. Chesterton and Hilaire Belloc and, like them, an enthusiastic* bon vivant. *He is said to have had a better understanding of wine than many men of his time—a talent which he also bestowed on Philip Trent, as is revealed in this tale about the mysterious disappearance of a wine-loving nobleman.*

When Philip Trent went down to Lackington, with the mission of throwing some light upon the affair of Lord Southrop's disappearance, it was without much hope of adding anything to the simple facts already known to the police and made public in the newspapers. Those facts were plain enough, pointing to but one sad conclusion.

In the early morning of Friday, the 23rd of September, a small touring car was found abandoned by the shore at Merwin Cove, some three miles along the coast from the flourishing Devonian resort of Brademouth. It had been driven off the road over turf to the edge of the pebble beach.

Examined by the police, it was found to contain a heavy overcoat, a folding stool, and a case of sketching materials with a sketching-block on the back seat; a copy of Anatole France's *Mannequin d'Osier*, two pipes, some chocolate, a flask of brandy, and a pair of binoculars in the shelves before the driving-seat; and in the pockets a number of maps and the motoring papers of Lord Southrop, of Hingham Blewitt, near Wymondham, in Norfolk.

Inquiries in the neighbourhood led to the discovery that a similar car and its driver were missing from the Crown Inn at Lackington, a small place a few miles inland; and later the car was definitely recognised.

In the hotel register, however, the owner had signed his name as L. G. Coxe; and it was in that name that a room had been booked by telephone early in the day. A letter too, addressed to Coxe, had been delivered at the Crown, and had been opened by him on his arrival about 6.30. A large suitcase had been taken up to his room, where it still lay, and the mysterious Coxe had deposited an envelope containing £35 in banknotes in the hotel safe. He had dined in the coffee-room, smoked in the lounge for a time, then gone out again in his car, saying nothing of his destination. No more had been seen or heard of him.

Some needed light had been cast on the affair when Lord Southrop was looked up in *Who's Who*—for no one in the local force had ever heard of such a peer. It appeared that his family name was Coxe, and that he had been christened Lancelot Graham; that he was the ninth baron, was thirty-three years old, and had succeeded to the title at the age of twenty-six; that he had been educated at Harrow and Trinity, Cambridge; that he was unmarried, and that his heir was a first cousin, Lambert Reeves Coxe. No public record of any kind, nor even any 'recreation', was noted in this unusually brief biography, which, indeed, bore the marks of having been compiled in the office, without any assistance from its subject.

Trent, however, had heard something more than this about Lord Southrop. Sir James Molloy, the owner of the *Record*, who had sent Trent to Lackington, had met everybody, including even the missing peer, who was quite unknown in society. Society, according to Molloy, was heartily detested and despised by Lord Southrop. His interests were exclusively literary and artistic, apart from his taste in the matter of wine, which he understood better than most men. He greatly preferred Continental to English ways of life, and spent much of his time abroad. He had a very large income, for most of which he seemed to have no use. He had good health and a kindly disposition; but he had a passion for keeping himself to himself, and had indulged it with remarkable success. One of his favourite amusements was wandering about the country alone in his car, halting here and there to make a sketch, and staying always at out-of-the-way inns under the name he had used at Lackington.

Lord Southrop had been, however, sufficiently like other men to fall in love, and Molloy had heard that his engagement to Adela Tindal was on the point of being announced at the time of his disappearance. His choice had come as a surprise to his friends; for though Miss Tindal took art and letters as seriously as himself, she was, as an authoress, not at all averse to publicity. She enjoyed being talked about, Molloy declared; and talked about she had certainly been—especially in connection with Lucius Kelly, the playwright. Their relationship had not been disguised; but a time came when Kelly's quarrelsome temper was no longer to be endured, and she refused to see any more of him.

All this was quite well known to Lord Southrop, for he and Kelly had been friends from boyhood; and the knowledge was a signal proof of the force of his infatuation. On all accounts, in Molloy's judgment, the match would have been a complete disaster; and Trent, as he thought the matter over in the coffee-room of the Crown, was disposed to agree with him.

Shortly before his arrival that day, a new fact for his first dispatch to the Record had turned up. A tweed cap had been found washed up by the waves on the beach between Brademouth and Merwin Cove, and the people at the Crown were sure that it was Lord Southrop's. He had worn a suit of unusually rough, very light-grey homespun tweed, the sort of tweed that, as the head waiter at the Crown vividly put it, you could smell half a mile away; and his cap had been noted because it was made of the same stuff as the suit. After a day and a half in salt water it still had an aroma of Highland sheep. Apart from this and its colour, or absence of colour, there was nothing by which it could be identified; not even a maker's name; but there was no reasonable doubt about its being Lord Southrop's, and it seemed to settle the question, if question there were, of what had happened to him. It was, Trent reflected, just like an eccentric intellectual—with money—to have his caps made for him, and from the same material as his clothes.

It was these garments, together with the very large horn-rimmed spectacles which Lord Southrop affected, which had made the most impression on the head waiter. Otherwise, he told Trent, there was nothing unusual about the poor gentleman, except that he seemed a bit absent-minded like. He had brought a letter to the table with him—the waiter supposed it would be the one that came to the hotel for him—and it had seemed to worry him. He had read and re-read it all through his dinner, what there was of it; he didn't have only some soup and a bit of fish. Yes, sir: consommé and a nice fillet of sole, like there is this evening. There was roast fowl, but he wouldn't have that, nor nothing else. Would Trent be ordering his own dinner now?

'Yes, I want to—but the fish is just what I won't have,' Trent decided, looking at the menu. 'I will take the rest of the hotel dinner.' An idea occurred to him. 'Do you remember what Lord Southrop had to drink? I might profit by his example.'

The waiter produced a fly-blown wine list. 'I can tell you that, sir. He had a bottle of this claret here, Château Margaux 1922.'

'You're quite sure? And did he like it?'

'Well, he didn't leave much,' the waiter answered. Possibly, Trent thought, he took a personal interest in unfinished wine. 'Were you thinking of trying some of it yourself, sir? It's our best claret.'

'I don't think I will have your best claret,' Trent said, thoughtfully scanning the list. 'There's a Beychevelle 1924 here, costing eighteen-pence less, which is good enough for me. I'll have that.' The waiter hurried away, leaving Trent to his reflections in the deserted coffee-room.

Trent had learned from the police that the numbers of the notes left in the charge of the hotel had been communicated by telephone to Lord Southrop's bank in Norwich, the reply being that these notes had been issued to him in person ten days before. Trent had also been allowed to inspect the objects, including the maps, found in the abandoned car. Lackington he found marked in pencil with a cross; and working backwards across the country he found similar crosses at the small towns of Hawbridge, Wringham, and Candley. The police, acting on these indications, had already established that 'L. G. Coxe' had passed the Thursday, Wednesday, and Tuesday nights respectively at inns in these places; and they had learned already of his having started from Hingham Blewitt on the Monday.

Trent, finding no more to be done at Lackington, decided to follow this designated trail in his own car. On the morning after his talk with the waiter at the Crown he set out for Hawbridge. The distances in Lord Southrop's progress, as marked, were not great by the most direct roads; but it could be guessed that he had been straying about to this and that point of interest—not, Trent imagined, to sketch, for there had been no sketches found among his belongings. Hawbridge was reached in time for lunch; and at the Three Bells Inn Trent again found matter for thought in a conversation—much like that which he had already enjoyed at the Crown Inn—with the head waiter. So it was again at the Green Man in Wringham that evening. The next day, however, when Trent dined at the Running Stag in Candley, the remembered record of Lord Southrop's potations took a different turn. What Trent was told convinced him that he was on the right track.

The butler and housekeeper at Hingham Blewitt, when Trent spoke with them the following day, were dismally confident that

Lord Southrop would never be seen again. The butler had already given to the police investigator from Devon what little information he could. He admitted that none of it lent the smallest support to the idea that Lord Southrop had been contemplating suicide; that he had, in fact, been unusually cheerful, if anything, on the day of his departure. But what, the butler asked, could a person think? Especially, the housekeeper observed, after the cap was found. Lord Southrop was, of course, eccentric in his views; and you never knew—here the housekeeper, with a despondent head-shake, paused, leaving unspoken the suggestion that a man who did not think or behave like other people might go mad at any moment.

Lord Southrop, they told Trent, never left any address when he went on one of these motoring tours. What he used to say was, he never knew where he was going till he got there. But this time he did have one object in mind, though what it was or where it was the butler did not know; and the police officer, when he was informed, did not seem to make any more of it. What had happened was that, a few days before Lord Southrop started out, he had been rung up by someone on the phone in his study; and as the door of the room was open, the butler, in passing through the hall, had happened to catch a few words of what he said.

He had told this person he was going next Tuesday to visit the old moor; and that if the weather was right he was going to make a sketch. He had said, 'You remember the church and chapel'— the butler heard that distinctly; and he had said that it must be over twenty years. 'What must be over twenty years?' Trent wanted to know. Impossible to tell: Lord Southrop had said just that.

The butler had heard nothing further. He thought the old moor might perhaps be Dartmoor or Exmoor, seeing where it was that Lord Southrop had disappeared. Trent thought otherwise, but he did not discuss the point. 'There's one thing you can perhaps tell me,' he said. 'Lord Southrop was at Harrow and Cambridge, I believe. Do you know if he went to a preparatory school before Harrow?'

'I can tell you that, sir,' the housekeeper said. 'I have been with the family since I was a girl. It was Marsham House he went to, near Sharnsley in Derbyshire. The school was founded by his lordship's grand-father's tutor, and all the Coxe boys have gone there for two generations. It stands very high as a school, sir; the best families send their sons there.'

'Yes, I've heard of it,' Trent said. 'Should you say, Mrs Pillow, that Lord Southrop was happy as a schoolboy—popular, I mean, and fond of games, and so forth?'

Mrs Pillow shook her head decisively. 'He always hated school, sir; and as for games, he had to play them, of course, but he couldn't abide them. And he didn't get on with the other boys— he used to say he wouldn't be a sheep, just like all the other something sheep—he learned bad language at school if he didn't learn anything else. But at Cambridge—that was very different. He came alive there for the first time—so he used to say.'

In Norwich, that same afternoon, Trent furnished himself with a one-inch Ordnance Survey map of a certain section of Derbyshire. He spent the evening at his hotel with this and a small-scale map of England, on which he marked the line of small towns which he had already visited; and he drew up, not for publication, a brief and clear report of his investigation so far.

The next morning's run was long. He had lunch at Sharnsley, where he made a last and very gratifying addition to his string of coffee-room interviews. Marsham House, he learned, stood well outside Sharnsley on the verge of the Town Moor; which, as the map had already told him, stretched its many miles away to the south and west. He learned, too, what and where were 'the Church and Chapel', and was thankful that his inquiring mind had not taken those simple terms at their face value.

An hour later he halted his car at a spot on the deserted road that crossed the moor; a spot whence, looking up the purple slope, he could see its bareness broken by a huge rock, and another less huge, whose summits pierced the skyline. They looked, Trent told himself, not more unlike what they were called than rocks with names usually do. Away to the right of them was a small clump of trees, the only ones in sight, to which a rough cart-track led from the road; and from that point, he thought an artist might well consider the Church and Chapel and their background made the best effect. He left his car and took the path through the heather.

Arrived at the clump, which stood well above the road, he looked over a desolate scene. If any one had met Lord Southrop there, they would have had the world to themselves. Not a house or hut was in sight, and no live thing but the birds. He looked about for traces of any human visitor; and he had just decided that nothing of the sort could reasonably be expected, after the lapse of a week, when something white, lodged in the root of a fir tree, caught his eye.

It was a small piece of torn paper, pencilled on one side with lines and shading, the look of which he knew well. A rapid search discovered another piece nearby among the heather. It was all that the wind had left undispersed of an artist's work, but for Trent, as he scanned the remnants closely, it was enough.

His eyes turned now over a wider range; for this, though to him it spelt certainty, was not what he had been looking for. Slowly following the track over the moor, he came at length to the reason for its existence—a small quarry, to all appearance long abandoned. A roughly circular pond of muddy water, some fifty yards across, filled the lower part of it; and about the margin was a confusion of stony fragments, broken and rusted implements, bits of rotting wood and smashed earthenware—a typical scene of industrial litter. With his arm bare to the shoulder Trent could feel no bottom to the pond. If it held any secret, that opaque yellow water kept it well.

There was no soil to take a footprint near the pond. For some time he raked among the débris in which the track ended, finding nothing. Then, as he turned over a broken fire-bucket, something flashed in the sunlight. It was a small, flat fragment of glass, about as large as a farthing, with one smooth and two fractured edges. Trent examined it thoughtfully. It had no place in his theory; it might mean nothing. On the other hand . . . he stowed it carefully in his note-case along with the remnants of paper.

Two hours later, at the police headquarters in Derby, he was laying his report and maps, with the objects found on the moor, before Superintendent Allison, a sharp-faced, energetic officer to whom Trent's name was well known.

It was well known also to Mr Gurney Bradshaw, head of the firm of Bradshaw & Co., legal advisers to Lord Southrop and to his father before him. He had at Trent's telephoned request, given him an appointment at three o'clock; and he appeared at that hour on the day after his researches in Derbyshire. Mr Bradshaw, a courteous but authoritative old gentleman, wore a dubious expression as they shook hands.

'I cannot guess,' he said, 'what it is that you wish to put before me. It seems to me a case in which we should get the Court to presume death with the minimum of difficulty; and I wish I thought otherwise, for I had known Lord Southrop all his life, and I was much attached to him. Now I must tell you that I have asked a third party to join us here—Mr Lambert Coxe, who perhaps you know is the heir to the title and to a very large estate. He wrote me yesterday that he had just returned from France, and wanted to know what the position was; and I thought he had better hear what you have to say, so I asked him for the same time as yourself.'

'I know of him as a racing man,' Trent said, 'I had no idea he was what you say until I saw it in the papers.'

The buzzer on the desk-telephone sounded, and Bradshaw put it to his ear. 'Show him in,' he said.

Lambert Coxe was a tall, spare, hard-looking man with a tanned, clean-shaven face and a cordless monocle screwed into his left eye. As they were introduced he looked at the other with a keen and curious scrutiny.

'And now,' Bradshaw said, 'let us hear your statement, Mr Trent.'

Trent put his folded hands on the table. 'I will begin by making a suggestion which may strike you gentlemen as an absurd one. It's this. The man who drove that car to Lackington, and afterwards down to the seashore, was not Lord Southrop.'

Both men stared at him blankly; then Bradshaw, composing his features, said impassively, 'I shall be interested to hear your reasons for thinking so. You have not a name for making absurd suggestions, Mr Trent, but I may call this an astonishing one.'

'I should damned well think so,' observed Coxe.

'I got the idea originally,' Trent said, 'from the wine which this man chose to drink with his dinner at the Crown Inn before the disappearance. Do you think that absurd?'

'There is nothing absurd about wine,' Mr Bradshaw replied with gravity. 'I take it very seriously myself. Twice a day, as a rule,' he added.

'Lord Southrop, I am told, also took it seriously. He had the reputation of a first-rate connoisseur. Now this man I'm speaking of had little appetite that evening, it seems. The dinner they offered him consisted mainly of soup, fillet of sole, and roast fowl.'

'I am sure it did,' Bradshaw said grimly. 'It's what you get nine times out of ten in English hotels. Well?'

'This man took only the soup and the fish. And with it he had a bottle of claret.'

The solicitor's composure deserted him abruptly.

'Claret!' he exclaimed.

'Yes, claret, and a curious claret, too. You see, mine host of the Crown kept a perfectly good Beychevelle 1924—I had some myself. But he had also a Château Margaux 1922; and I suppose because it was an older wine he thought it ought to be dearer, so he marked it in his list eighteen-pence more than the other. That was the wine which was chosen by our traveller that evening. What do you think of it? With a fish dinner he had claret, and he chose a wine of a notoriously bad year when he could have had a wine of 1924 for less money.'

While Coxe looked his bewilderment, Mr Bradshaw got up and began to pace the room slowly. 'I will admit so much,' he said. 'I cannot conceive of Lord Southrop doing such a thing if he was in his right mind.'

'If you still think it was he, and that he was out of his senses,'

Trent rejoined, 'there was a method in his madness. Because the night before, at Hawbridge, he chose one of those wines bearing the name of a château which doesn't exist, and is merely a label that sounds well; and the night before that, at Wringham, he had two whiskies and soda just before dinner, and another inferior claret at an excessive price on top of them. I have been to both the inns and got these facts. But when I worked back to Candley, the first place where Lord Southrop stayed after leaving home, it was another story. I found he had picked out about the best thing on the list, a Rhine wine, which hardly anybody ever asked for. The man who ordered that, I think, was really Lord Southrop.'

Bradshaw pursed up his mouth. 'You are suggesting that someone in Lord Southrop's car was impersonating him at the other three places, and that, knowing his standing as a connoisseur, this man did his ignorant best to act up to it. Very well; but Lord Southrop signed the register in his usual way at those places. He received and read a letter addressed to him at Lackington. The motor tour as a whole was just such a haphazard tour as he had often made before. The description given of him at Lackington was exact—the clothes, the glasses, the abstracted manner. The cap that was washed up was certainly his. No, no, Mr Trent. We are bound to assume that it was Lord Southrop; and the presumption is that he drove down to the sea and drowned himself. The alternative is that he was staging a sham suicide, so as to be able to disappear, and there is no sense in that.'

'Just so,' observed Lambert Coxe. 'What you say about the wine may be all right as far as it goes, Mr Trent, but I agree with Mr Bradshaw. Southrop committed suicide; and if he was insane enough to do that, he was insane enough to go wrong about his drinks.'

Trent shook his head. 'There are other things to be accounted for. I'm coming to them. And the clothes and the cap and the rest are all part of my argument. This man was wearing Lord Southrop's tweed suit just because it was so easily identifiable. He knew all about Lord Southrop and his ways. He had letters from Lord Southrop in his possession, and had learned to imitate his writing. It was he who wrote and posted that letter addressed to L. G. Coxe; and he made a pretence of being worried by it. He knew that Lord Southrop's notes could be traced; so he left them at the bureau to clinch the thing. And, of course, he did not drown himself. He only threw the cap into the sea. What he may have done is to change out of those conspicuous clothes, put them in a bag which he had in the car, and which contained another suit in which he proceeded to dress himself. He may then have walked, with his bag, the few miles into Brademouth, and travelled to

London by the 12.15—quite a popular train, in which you can get a comfortable sleeping-berth.'

'So he may,' Bradshaw agreed with some acidity, while Lambert Coxe laughed shortly. 'But what I am interested in is facts, Mr Trent.'

'Well, here are some. A few days before Lord Southrop set out from his place in Norfolk, someone rang him up in his library. The door was ajar, and the butler heard a little of what he said to the caller. He said he was going on the following Tuesday to a visit a place he called the old moor, as if it was a place as well known to the other as to himself. He said "You remember the church and the chapel," and that it must be over twenty years; and that he was going to make a sketch.'

Coxe's face darkened. 'If Southrop was alive,' he sneered, 'I am sure he would appreciate your attention to his private affairs. What are we supposed to gather from all this keyhole business?'

'I think we can gather,' Trent said gently. 'that some person, ringing Lord Southrop up about another matter, was told incidentally where Lord Southrop expected to be on that Tuesday—the day, you remember, when he suddenly developed a taste for bad wine in the evening. Possibly the information gave this person an idea, and he had a few days to think it over. Also we can gather that Lord Southrop was talking to someone who shared his recollection of a moor which they had known over twenty years ago—that's to say, when he was at prep. school age, as he was thirty-three this year. And then I found out that he had been at a school called Marsham House, on the edge of Sharnsley Town Moor in Derbyshire. So I went off there to explore, and I discovered that the Church and Chapel were a couple of great rocks on the top of the moor, about two miles from the school. If you were there with your cousin, Mr Coxe, you may remember them.'

Coxe was drumming on the table with his fingers. 'Of course I do,' he said aggressively. 'So do hundreds of others who were at Marsham House. What about it?'

Bradshaw, who was now fixing him with an attentive eye, held up a hand. 'Come, come, Mr Coxe,' he said; 'don't let us lose our tempers. Mr Trent is helping to clear up what begins to look like an even worse business than I thought. Let us hear him out peaceably, if you please.'

'I am in the sketching business myself,' Trent continued, 'so I looked about for what might seem the best view-point for Lord Southrop's purpose. When I went to the spot, I found two pieces of torn-up paper, the remains of a pencil sketch; and that paper is of precisely the same quality as the paper Lord Southrop's sketching-block, which I was able to examine at Lackington. The sketch was torn from the block and destroyed, I think, because it was evidence of his having been to Sharnsley. That part of the moor is a wild, desolate place. If someone went to meet Lord Southrop there, as I believe, he could hardly have had more favourable circumstances for what he meant to do. I think it was he who appeared in the car at Wringham that evening; and I think it was on Sharnsley Moor, not at Lackington, that Lord Southrop—disappeared.'

Bradshaw half-rose from his chair. 'Are you not well, Mr Coxe?' he asked.

'Perfectly well, thanks,' Coxe answered. He drew a deep breath, then turned to Trent. 'And so that's all you have to tell us. I can't say that—'

'Oh no, not nearly all,' Trent interrupted him. 'But let me tell you now what I believe it was that really happened. If the man who left the moor in Lord Southrop's car was not Lord Southrop, I wanted an explanation of the masquerade that ended at Lackington. What would explain it was the idea that the man who drove the car down to Devonshire had murdered him, and then staged a sham suicide for him three hundred miles away. That would have been an ingenious plan. It would have depended on everyone making the natural assumption that the man in the car was Lord Southrop. And how was any one to imagine that he wasn't?

'Lord Southrop was the very reverse of a public character. He lived quite out of the world; he had never been in the news; very few people knew what he looked like. He depended on all this for maintaining his privacy in the way he did when touring in his car—staying always at small places where there was no chance of his being recognised, and pretending not to be a peer. The murderer knew all about that, and it was the essence of his plan. The people at the inns would note what was conspicuous about the traveller; all that they could say about his face would be more vague, and would fit Lord Southrop well enough, so long as there was no striking difference in looks between the two men. Those big horn-rims are a disguise in themselves.'

Bradshaw rubbed his hands slowly together. 'I suppose it could happen so,' he said. 'What do you think, Mr Coxe?'

'It's just a lot of ridiculous guesswork,' Coxe said impatiently. 'I've heard enough of it, for one.' He rose from his chair.

'No, no, don't go, Mr Coxe,' Trent advised him. 'I have some more of what you prefer—facts, you know. They are important, and you ought to hear them. Thinking as I did, I looked about for any places where a body could be concealed. In that bare and featureless expanse I could find only one: an old abandoned quarry in the hillside, with a great pond of muddy water at the bottom of it. And by the edge of it I picked up a small piece of broken glass.

'Yesterday evening this piece of glass was shown by a police officer and myself to an optician in Derby. He stated that it was a fragment of a monocle—what they call a spherical lens—so that he could tell us all about it from one small bit. Its formula was not a common one—minus 5; so that it had been worn by a man very short-sighted in one eye. The police think that as very few people wear monocles, and hardly any of them would wear one of that power, an official inquiry should establish the names of those who had been supplied with such a glass in recent years. You see,' Trent went on, 'this man had dropped and broken his glass on the stones while busy about something at the edge of the pond. Being a tidy man, he picked up all the pieces that he could see; but he missed this one.'

Lambert Coxe put a hand to his throat. 'It's infernally stuffy in here,' he muttered. 'I'll open a window, if you don't mind.' Again he got to his feet, but the lawyer's movement was quicker. 'I'll see to that,' he said, and stayed by the window when he had opened it.

Trent drew a folded paper from his pocket. 'This is a telegram I received just before lunch from Superintendent Allison of the Derbyshire police. I have told him all I am telling you.' He unfolded the paper with deliberation. 'He says that the pond was dragged this morning, and they recovered the body of a man who had been shot in the head from behind. It was stripped to the underclothing and secured by a chain to a pedal bicycle.

'That, you see, clears up the question how the murderer got to the remote spot where Lord Southrop was. He couldn't go there in a car, because he would have had to leave it there. He used a cycle, because there was to be a very practical use for the machine afterwards. The police believe they can trace the seller of the cycle, because it is in perfectly new condition, and he may give them a line on the buyer.'

Bradshaw, his hands thrust into his pockets, stared at Coxe's ghastly face as he inquired, 'Has the body been identified?'

'The superintendent says the inquest will be the day after tomorrow. He knows whose body I believe it is, so he will already be sending down to Hingham Blewitt about evidence of identity. He says my own evidence will probably not be required until a later stage of the inquest, after a charge has been—'

A sobbing sound came from Lambert Coxe. He sprang to his feet, pressing his hands to his temples, then crashed unconscious to the floor.

While Trent loosened his collar, the lawyer splashed water from the bottle on his table upon the upturned face. The eyelids began to flicker. 'He'll do,' Bradshaw said coolly. 'My congratulations, Mr Trent. This man is not a client of mine, so I may say that I don't think he will enjoy the title for long—or the money, which was what really mattered, I have reason to believe. He's dropped his monocle again, you see. I happen to know, by the way, that he has been half-blind of that eye since it was injured by a cricket ball at Marsham.'

THE ADVENTURE OF THE TELL-TALE BOTTLE

Ellery Queen

American amateur detective Ellery Queen, who shares the same name as the pseudonym of his creators, has been described as an extremely erudite, knowledgeable but rather arrogant young man and 'the logical successor to Sherlock Holmes' by virtue of these qualities. The two writers behind the pen-name, Frederic Dannay (1905-) and Manfred Lee (1905–1971), made Ellery Queen famous as both a character and as the figurehead of a New York-based magazine which has been publishing the best in crime and mystery fiction ever since 1941. Both men liked to celebrate any special achievement in their distinguished career by sharing a bottle of Chateau d'Yquem—and small wonder that this very special vintage should be the focus of the following story of a crime committed on that most famous of American holidays, Thanksgiving, when fine meals are eaten and superb wines drunk . . .

'Now regarding this folksy fable, this almost-myth, this canard upon history,' continued Ellery, 'what are the facts? The facts, my dear Nikki, are these:

'It was *not* a good harvest. Oh, they had twenty acres planted to seed corn, but may I remind you that the corn had been pilfered from the Cape Indians? And had it not been for Tisquantum—'

'Tis-who?' asked Inspector Queen feebly.

'—corruptly known as Squanto—there would have been no harvest that year at all. For it took the last of the more-or-less noble Patuxet to teach our bewildered forefathers how to plant it properly.'

'Well, you can't deny they decreed *some* sort of holiday,' flashed Nikki, 'so that they might "rejoyce" together!'

'I have no desire to distort the facts,' replied Ellery with dignity. 'To the contrary. They had excellent reason to "rejoyce"—some of them were still alive. And tell me: Who actually participated in that first American festival?'

'Why, the Pilgrims,' said Inspector Queen uneasily.

'And I suppose you'll tell me that as they stuffed themselves with all the traditional goodies other revered forefathers came running out of the woods with arrows through their hats?'

'I remember a picture like that in my grade-school history book—yes,' said Nikki defiantly.

'The *fact* is,' grinned Ellery, 'they were on such good terms with the Indians during that fall of 1621 that the most enthusiastic celebrants at the feast were Massasoit of the Wampanoag and ninety of his braves!—all very hungry, too. And tell me this: What was the menu on that historic occasion?'

'Turkey!'

'Cranberry sauce!'

'Pumpkin pie!'

'And—so forth,' concluded the Inspector. He was at home that day receiving Madame La Grippe and he had been—until Ellery unleashed his eloquence—the most ungracious host in New York. But now he was neglecting Madame beautifully.

'I accept merely the and-so-forths,' said Ellery indulgently. 'If they had "Turkies" at that feast, there is no mention of them in the record. Yes, there were plenty of cranberries in the bogs—but it is more than doubtful that the Pilgrim ladies knew what to do with them. And we can definitely assert that the pastry possibilities of the Narraganset *askútasquash* were not yet dreamed of by the pale green females who had crept off the *Mayflower*.'

'Listen to him,' said the Inspector comfortably.

'I suppose,' said Nikki, grinding her teeth, 'I suppose they just sat there and munched on that old corn.'

'By no means. The menu was regal, considering their customary diet of wormy meal. They gorged themselves on eels—'

'*Eels!*'

'And clams, venison, water-fowl, and so on. For dessert—wild plums and dried berries; and—let's face it—wild grape wine throughout,' said Ellery, looking sad. 'And—oh, yes. How long did this first thanksgiving celebration last?'

'Thanksgiving day? How long would a day *be*? A day!'

'Three days. And why do we celebrate Thanksgiving in the month of November?'

'Because—because—'

'Because the Pilgrims celebrated it in the month of October,' concluded Ellery. 'And there you have it, Nikki—the whole sordid record of historical misrepresentation, simply another example of our national vainglory. I say, if we must celebrate Thanksgiving, let us give thanks to the red man, whose land we took away. I say—let us have facts!'

'And *I* say,' cried Nikki, 'that you're a factual show-off, a—a darned old talking encyclopedia, Ellery Queen, and I don't care what your precious "facts" are because all I wanted to do was take Thanksgiving baskets of turkeys and cranberries and stuff to those people down on the East side that I take baskets to every year because they're too poor to have decent Thanksgiving dinners tomorrow, and especially this year with prices sky-high and so many refugee children here who ought to learn the American traditions and who's to teach them if . . . And, anyway, one of them *is* an Indian—way back—so there!'

'Why, Nikki,' mourned Ellery, joining Nikki on the floor, where she was now hugging the carpet, in tears, 'why didn't you tell me one of them is an Indian? That makes all the difference—don't you see?' He sprang erect, glowing fiercely with the spirit of Thanksgiving. 'Turkeys! Cranberries! Pumpkin pies! To Mr Sisquencchi's!'

The affair of the Telltale Bottle was a very special sort of nastiness culminating in that nastiest of nastiness, murder; but it is doubtful if, even had Ellery been a lineal descendant of Mother Shipton, he would have called the bountiful excursion off or in any other wise tarnished that silvery day.

For Mr Sisquencchi of the market around the corner made several glittering suggestions regarding the baskets; there was a lambency about Miss Porter which brightened with the afternoon; and even Manhattan shone, getting into a snowy party dress as Ellery's ancient Duesenberg padded patiently about the East side.

Ellery lugged baskets and assorted packages through medieval hallways and up donjon staircases until his arms protested; but this was a revolt of the flesh only—the spirit grew fresher as they knocked on the doors of O'Keefes, Del Florios, Cohens, Wilsons, Olsens, Williamses, Pomerantzes, and Johnsons and heard the cries of various Pats, Sammies, Antonios, Olgas, Clarences, and Petunias.

'But where's the Indian?' he demanded, as they sat in the car while Nikki checked over her list. The sun was setting, and several thousand ragamuffins were crawling over the Duesenberg, but it was still a remarkable day.

'Check,' said Nikki. 'Orchard Street. That's the Indian, Ellery. I mean—oh, she's not an *Indian*, just has some Indian blood way back, Iroquois, I think. She's the last.'

'Well, I won't quibble,' frowned Ellery, easing old Duesey through the youth of America. 'Although I *do* wish—'

'Oh, shut up. Mother Carey's the darlingest old lady—scrubs floors for a living.'

'Mother Carey's!'

But at the Orchard Street tenement, under a canopy of ermine-trimmed fire escapes, a janitor was all they found of Ellery's Indian.

'The old hag don't live here no more.'

'Oh, dear,' said Nikki. 'Where's she moved to?'

'She lammed outa here with all her junk in a rush the other day—search me.' The janitor spat, just missing Nikki's shoe.

'Any idea where the old lady works?' asked Ellery, just missing the janitor's shoe.

The janitor hastily withdrew his foot. 'I think she cleans up some Frog chow joint near Canal Street regular.'

'I remember!' cried Nikki. 'Fouchet's, Ellery. She's worked there for years. Let's go right over there—maybe they know her new address.'

'Fouchet's!' said Ellery gaily; and so infected was he by the enchantment of the fairy-tale afternoon that for once his inner voice failed him.

Fouchet's Restaurant was just of Canal Street, a few blocks from Police Headquarters—squeezed between a button factory and a ship chandler's. Cars with Brooklyn accents whished by its plate glass front, and it looked rather frightened by it all. Inside they found round tables covered with chequered oilcloths, a wine bar, walls decorated with prewar French travel posters, a sharp and saucy odour, and a cashier named Clothilde.

Clothilde had a large bosom, a large cameo on it, a large black-velvet ribbon in her hair, and when she opened her mouth to say: 'The old woman who clean up?' Nikki saw that she also had a large gold tooth. 'Ask Monsieur Fouchet. 'E will be right back.' She examined Nikki with very sharp black eyes.

'If the Pilgrims could eat eels,' Ellery was mumbling, over a menu, 'Why not? *Escargots!* Nikki, let's have dinner here!'

'Well,' said Nikki doubtfully. 'I suppose ... as long as we have to wait for Mr Fouchet, anyway. . . .' A waiter with a long dreary face led them to a table, and Ellery and the waiter conferred warmly over the menu, but Nikki was not paying attention—she was too busy exchanging brief feminine glances with Clothilde. It was agreed: the ladies did not care for each other. Thereafter, Clothilde wore an oddly watchful expression, and Nikki looked uneasy.

'Ellery . . .' said Nikki.

'—only the very best,' Ellery was saying baronially. 'Now where the devil did that waiter go? I hadn't got to the wine. Pierre!'

'*Un moment, Monsieur,*' came the voice of the waiter with the long, dreary face.

'You know, Nikki, less than five per cent of all the wine produced in the world can be called really fine wine—'

'Ellery, I don't like this place,' said Nikki.

'The rest is *pour la soif*—'

'Let's . . . not eat here after all, Ellery. Let's just find out about Mother Carey and—'

Ellery looked astonished. 'Why, Nikki, I thought you loved French food. Consequently, we'll order the rarest, most exquisitely balanced, most perfectly fermented wine. Pierre! Where the deuce has he gone? A Sauterne with body, bouquet, breeding . . .'

'Oh!' squeaked Nikki, then she looked guilty. It was only Pierre breathing down her neck.

'After all, it's a special occasion. Ah, there you are. *La carte des vins!* No, never mind. I know what I want. Pierre,' said Ellery magnificently, 'a bottle of . . . *Château d'Yquem!*'

The dreary look on the waiter's face rather remarkably vanished.

'But, monsieur,' he murmured, '*Château d'Yquem* . . .? That is an expensive wine. We do not carry so fine a wine in our cellar.'

And still, as Pierre said this, he contrived to give the impression that something of extraordinary importance had just occurred. Nikki glanced anxiously at Ellery to see if he had caught that strange overtone; Ellery was merely looking crushed.

'Carried away by the spirit of Thanksgiving Eve. Very stupid of me, Pierre. Of course. Give us the best you have—which,' Ellery added as Pierre walked rapidly away, 'will probably turn out to be *vin ordinaire.*' And Ellery laughed.

Something is horribly wrong, thought Nikki, and she wondered how long it would take Ellery to become himself again.

It happened immediately after the *pêches flambeaux* and the *demitasse*. Or, rather, two things happened. One involved the waiter. The other involved Clothilde.

The waiter seemed confused: Upon handing Ellery *l'addition*, he simultaneously whisked a fresh napkin into Ellery's lap! This astounding *non sequitor* brought Mr Queen to his slumbering senses. But he made no remark, merely felt the napkin and, finding something hard and flat concealed in its folds, he extracted it without looking at it and slipped it into his pocket.

As for the cashier, she too seemed confused. In payment of *l'addition*, Ellery tossed a twenty-dollar bill on the desk. Clothilde made change, chattering pleasantly all the while about *Monsieur* and *Mad'moiselle* and 'ow did they like the dinner?—and she made change very badly. She was ten dollars short.

Ellery had just pointed out this deplorable unfamiliarity with the

American coinage system when a stout little whirlwind arrived, scattering French before him like leaves.

'*Mais Monsieur Fouchet, je fais une méprise . . .* '

'*Bête à manger du foin—silence!*' And M. Fouchet fell upon Ellery, almost weeping. '*Monsieur*, this 'as never 'appen before. I give you my assurance—'

For a chilled moment Nikki thought Ellery was going to produce what lay in his pocket for M. Fouchet's inspection. But Ellery merely smiled and accepted the missing ten-dollar bill graciously and asked for Mother Carey's address. M. Fouchet threw up his hands and ran to the rear of the restaurant and ran back to press an oil-stained scrawl upon them, chattering in French at Ellery, at Nikki, at his cashier; and then they were on the street and making for the Duesenberg in a great show of postprandial content . . . for through the plate glass M. Fouchet, and Clothilde, and—yes— Pierre of the long face were watching them closely.

'Ellery, what . . .?'

'Not now, Nikki. Get into the car.'

Nikki kept glancing nervously at the three Gallic faces as Ellery tried to start the Duesenberg. 'Huh?'

'I said it won't start, blast it. Battery.' Ellery jumped out into the snow and began tugging at the basket. 'Grab those other things and get out, Nikki.'

'But—'

'Cab!' A taxicab parked a few yards beyond Fouchet's shot forward. 'Driver, get this basket and stuff in there beside you, will you? Nikki, hop to it. Get into the cab!'

'You're leaving the *car*?'

'We can pick it up later. What are you waiting for, driver?'

The driver looked weary. 'Ain't you startin' your Thanksgivin' celebratin' a little premature?' he asked. 'I ain't no fortune-teller. Where do I go?'

'Oh. That slip Fouchet gave me. Nikki, where . . .? Here! 214-B Henry Street, cab. The East Side.'

The cab slid away. 'Wanna draw me diagrams?' muttered the driver.

'Now, Nikki. Let's have a look at Pierre's little gift.'

It was a stiff white-paper packet. Ellery unfolded it.

It contained a large quantity of a powdery substance—a white crystalline powder.

'Looks like snow,' giggled Nikki. 'What is it?'

'That's what it is.'

'*Snow?*'

'Cocaine.'

'That's the hell of this town,' the cab-driver was remarking. 'Anything can happen. I remember once—'

'Apparently, Nikki,' said Ellery with a frown, 'I gave Pierre some password or other. By accident.'

'He thought you're an addict! That means Fouchet is—'

'A depot for the distribution of narcotics. I wonder what I said that made Pierre . . . *The wine!*'

'I don't follow you,' complained the driver.

Ellery glared. The driver looked hurt and honked at an elderly Chinese in a black straw hat.

'*Château d'Yquem*, Nikki. That was the password! Pearls in a swinery . . . of course, of course.'

'I *knew* something was wrong the minute we walked in there, Ellery.'

'Mmm. We'll drop this truck at Mrs Carey's, then we'll shoot back uptown and get Dad working on this Fouchet nastiness.'

'Watch the Inspector snap out of that cold,' laughed Nikki; then she stopped laughing. 'Ellery . . . do you suppose all this has anything to do with Mother Carey?'

'Oh, nonsense, Nikki.'

It was a bad day for the master.

For when they got to 214-B Henry Street and knocked on the door of Apartment 3-A and a voice as shaky as the stairs called out, 'who's there?' and Nikki identified herself . . . something happened. There were certain sounds. Strange rumbly, sliding sounds. The door was not opened at once.

Nikki bit her lip, glancing timidly at Ellery. Ellery was frowning.

'She don't act any too anxious to snag this turk-bird,' said the cab-driver, who had carried up the pumpkin pie and the bottle of California wine which had been one of Mr Sisquencchis' inspirations, while Nikki took odds and ends and Ellery the noble basket. 'My old lady'd be tickled to death—'

'I'd rather it were you,' said Ellery violently. 'When she opens the door, dump the pie and wine inside, then wait for us in the cab—'

But at that instant the door opened, and a chubby little old woman with knobby forearms and flushed cheeks stood there, looking not even remotely like an Indian.

'Miss Porter!'

'Mother Carey.'

It was a poor little room with an odour. Not the odour of poverty; the room was savagely clean. Ellery barely listened to the chirrupings of the two women; he was too busy using his eyes and his nose. He seemed to have forgotten Massasoit and the Wampanoag.

When they were back in the cab, he said abruptly: 'Nikki, do you happen to recall Mother Carey's old apartment?'

'The one on Orchard Street? Yes—why?'

'How many rooms did she have there?'

'Two. A bedroom and a kitchen. Why?'

Ellery asked casually: 'Did she always live alone?'

'I think so.'

'Then why has she suddenly—so very suddenly, according to that Orchard Street janitor—moved to a *three*-room flat?'

'You mean the Henry Street place has—?'

'Three rooms—from the doors. Now why should a poor old scrubwoman living alone suddenly need an *extra* room?'

'Cinch,' said the cab-driver. 'She's takin' in boarders.'

'Yes,' murmured Ellery, without umbrage. 'Yes, I suppose that might account for the odour of cheap cigar smoke.'

'Cigar smoke!'

'Maybe she's runnin' a horse parlour,' suggested the driver.

'Look, friend,' said Nikki angrily, 'how about letting us take the wheel and you coming back here?'

'Keep your bra on, lady.'

'The fact is,' mused Ellery, 'before she opened the door she moved furniture away from it. Those sounds? She'd barricaded that door, Nikki.'

'Yes,' said Nikki in a small voice. 'And that doesn't sound like a boarder, does it?'

'It sounds,' said Ellery, 'like a hideout.' He leaned forward just as the driver opened his mouth. 'And don't bother,' he said. 'Nikki, it's somebody who can't go out—or doesn't dare to. . . . I'm beginning to think there's a connection between the cigar-smoker your Mrs Carey's hiding, and the packet of drugs Pierre slipped me at Fouchet's by mistake.'

'Oh, no, Ellery,' moaned Nikki.

Ellery took her hand. 'It's a rotten way to wind up a heavenly day, honey, but we have no choice. I'll have Dad give orders to arrest Pierre tonight the minute we get home, and let's hope . . . Hang the Pilgrims!'

'That's subversive propaganda, brother,' said the driver.

Ellery shut the communicating window, violently.

Inspector Queen sniffled: 'She's in it, all right.'

'Mother Carey?' wailed Nikki.

'Three years ago,' nodded the Inspector, drawing his bathrobe closer about him, 'Fouchet's was mixed up in a drug-peddling case. And a Mrs Carey was connected with it.'

Nikki began to cry.

'Connected how, Dad?'

'One of Fouchet's waiters was the passer—'

'Pierre?'

'No. Pierre was working there at that time—or at least a waiter of that name was—but the guilty waiter was an old man named Carey . . . whose wife was a scrubwoman.'

'Lo the poor Indian,' said Ellery, and he sat down with his pipe. After a moment, he said: 'Where's Carey now, Dad?'

'In the clink doing a tenner. We found a couple of hundred dollars' worth of snow in the old geezer's bedroom—they lived on Mulberry then. Carey claimed he was framed—but they all do.'

'And Fouchet?' murmured Ellery, puffing.

'Came out okay. Apparently he hadn't known. It was Carey all by himself.'

'Strange. It's still going on.'

The Inspector looked startled, and Ellery shrugged.

Nikki cried: 'Mr Carey was *framed*!'

'Could be,' muttered the old gentleman. 'Might have been this Pierre all the time—felt the heat on and gave us a quick decoy. Nikki, hand me the phone.'

'I knew it, I knew it!'

'And while you're on the phone, Dad,' said Ellery mildly, 'you might ask why Headquarters hasn't picked up Carey.'

'Picked him up? I told you, Ellery, he's in stir. Hello?'

'Oh, no, he's not,' said Ellery. 'He's hiding out in Apartment 3-A at 214-B Henry Street.'

'The cigar smoke,' breathed Nikki. 'The barricade. The extra room!'

'Velie!' snarled the Inspector. 'Has a con named Frank Carey broken out of stir?'

Sergeant Velie, bewildered by this clairvoyance stammered: 'Yeah, Inspector, a few days ago, ain't been picked up yet, we're tryin' to locate his wife but she's moved and—But you been home sick!'

'She's moved,' sighed the Inspector. 'Well, well, she's probably moved to China.' Then he roared: 'She's hiding him out! But never mind—you take those Number Fourteens of yours right down to Fouchet's Restaurant just off Canal and arrest a waiter named Pierre! And if he isn't there, don't take two weeks finding out where he lives. I want that man tonight!'

'But Carey—'

'I'll take care of Carey myself. Go on—don't waste a second!' The old man hung up, fuming. 'Where's my pants, dad blast the—'

'Dad!' Ellery grabbed him. 'You're not going out *now*. You're still sick.'

'I'm picking up Carey personally,' said his father gently. 'Do you think you're man enough to stop me?'

The old scrubwoman sat at her kitchen table stolidly, and this time the Iroquois showed.

There was no one else in the Henry Street flat.

'We know your husband was here, Mrs Carey,' said Inspector Queen. 'He got word to you when he broke out of jail, you moved, and you've been hiding him here. Where's he gone to now?'

The old lady said nothing.

'Mother Carey, please,' said Nikki. 'We want to help you.'

'We believe your husband was innocent of that drug-passing charge, Mrs Carey,' said Ellery quietly.

The bluish lips tightened. The basket, the turkey, the pumpkin pie, the bottle of wine, the packages were still on the table.

'I think, Dad,' said Ellery, 'Mrs Carey wants a bit more evidence of official good faith. Mother, suppose I tell you I not only believe your husband was framed three years ago, but that the one who framed him was—'

'That Pierre,' said Mother Carey in a hard voice. 'He was the one. He was the brains. He used to be "friendly" with Frank.'

'The one—but not the brains.'

'What d'ye mean, Ellery?' demanded Inspector Queen.

'Isn't Pierre working alone?' asked Nikki.

'If he is, would he have handed me—a total stranger—a packet of dope worth several hundred dollars ... without a single word about payment?' asked Ellery dryly.

Mother Carey was staring up at him.

'*Those were Pierre's instructions*,' said the Inspector slowly.

'Exactly. So there's someone behind Pierre who's using him as the passer, payment being arranged for by some other means—'

'Probably in advance!' The Inspector leaned forward. 'Well, Mrs Carey, won't you talk now? Where is Frank?'

'Tell the Inspector, Mother,' begged Nikki. 'The truth!'

Mother Carey looked uncertain. But then she said, 'We told the truth three years ago,' and folded her lacerated hands.

There is a strength in the oppressed which yields to nothing.

'Let it go,' sighed the Inspector. 'Come on, son—we'll go over to Fouchet's and have a little chin with Mr Pierre, find out who his bossman is—'

And it was then that Mother Carey said, in a frightened quick voice: 'No!' and put her hand to her mouth, appalled.

'Carey's gone to Fouchet's,' said Ellery slowly. 'Of course, Mrs Carey would have a key—she probably opens the restaurant. Carey's gone over with some desperate idea that he can dig up some evidence that will clear him. That's it, Mother, isn't it?'

But Inspector Queen was already out in the unsavoury hall.

Sergeant Velie was standing miserably in the entrance to Fouchet's when the squad car raced up.

'Now Inspector, don't get mad—'

The Inspector said benignly: 'You let Pierre get away.'

'Oh, no!' said Sergeant Velie. 'Pierre's in there, Inspector. Only he's dead.'

'*Dead!*'

'Dead of what, Sergeant?' asked Ellery swiftly.

'Of a carvin' knife in the chest, that's of what, Maestro. We came right over here like you said, Inspector, only some knife artist beat us to it.' The Sergeant relaxed. It was all right. The Old Man was smiling.

'Frank Carey did it, of course?'

The Sergeant stopped relaxing. 'Heck, no, Inspector. Carey didn't do it.'

'Velie—!'

'Well, he didn't! When we rolled up we spot Carey right here at the front door. Place is closed for the night—just a night-light. He's got a key. We watch him unlock the door, go in, and wham! he damn' near falls over this Pierre. So the feeble-minded old cluck bends down and takes the knife out of Pierre's chest and stands there in a trance lookin' at it. He's been standin' like that ever since.'

'Without the knife, I hope,' said the Inspector nastily; and they went in.

And found an old man among the detectives in the posture of a question-mark leaning against an oilcloth-covered table under a poster advertising Provençal, with his toothless mouth ajar and his watery old eyes fixed on the extinct *garçon*. The extinct *garçon* was still in his monkey-suit; his right palm was upturned, as if appealing for mercy, or the usual *pourboire*.

'Carey,' said Inspector Queen.

Old man Carey did not seem to hear. He was fascinated by Ellery; Ellery was on one knee, peering at Pierre's eyes.

'Carey, who killed the Frenchman?'

Carey did not reply.

'Plain case of busted gut,' remarked Sergeant Velie.

'You can hardly blame him!' cried Nikki. 'Framed for dope-peddling three years ago, convicted, jailed for it—and now he thinks he's being framed for murder!'

'I wish we could get something out of him,' said the Inspector thoughtfully. 'It's a cinch Pierre stayed after closing time because he had a date with somebody.'

'His boss!' said Nikki.

'Whoever he's been passing the snow for, Nikki.'

'Dad.' Ellery was on his feet looking down at the long dreary face that now seemed longer and drearier. 'Do you recall if Pierre was ticketed as a drug addict three years ago?'

'I don't think he was.' The Inspector looked surprised.

'Look at his eyes.'

'Say!'

'Far gone, too. If Pierre wasn't an addict at the time of Carey's arrest, he'd taken to the habit in the past three years. And that explains why he was murdered tonight.'

'He got dangerous,' said the Inspector grimly. 'With Carey loose and Pierre pulling that boner with you tonight, the boss knew the whole Fouchet investigation would be reopened.'

Ellery nodded. 'Felt he couldn't trust Pierre any longer. Weakened by drugs, the fellow would talk as soon as the police pulled him in, and this mysterious character knew it.'

'Yeah,' said the Sergeant sagely. 'Put the heat on a smecker and he squirts like whipped cream.'

But Ellery wasn't listening. He had sat down at one of the silent tables and was staring over at the wine-bar.

M. Fouchet flew in in a strong tweed overcoat, showing a dent in his Homburg where it should not have been.

'Selling of the dope—again! This *Pierre* . . .!' hissed M. Fouchet, and he glared down at his late waiter with quite remarkable venom.

'Know anything about this job, Fouchet?' asked the Inspector courteously.

'Nothing, *Monsieur l'inspecteur*. I give you my word, nothing. Pierre stay late tonight. He says to me he will fix up the tables for tomorrow. He stays and—pfft! *il se fait tuer!*' M. Fouchet's fat lips began to dance. 'Now the bank will give me no more credit.' He sank into a chair.

'Oh? You're not in good shape financially, Fouchet?'

'I serve *escargots* near Canal Street. It should be pretzels! The bank, I owe 'im five thousand dollar.'

'And that's the way it goes,' said the Inspector sympathetically. 'All right, Mr Fouchet, go home. Where's that cashier?'

A detective pushed Clothilde forward. Clothilde had been

weeping into her make-up. But not now. Now she glared down at Pierre quite as M. Fouchet had glared. Pierre glared back.

'Clothilde?' muttered Ellery, suddenly coming out of deep reverie.

'Velie turned up something,' whispered the Inspector.

'She's in it. She's got something to do with it,' Nikki said excitedly to Ellery. 'I knew it!'

'Clothilde,' said the Inspector, 'how much do you make in this restaurant?'

'Forty-five dollar a week.'

Sergeant Velie drawled. 'How much dough you got in the bank, mademazelle?'

Clothilde glanced at the behemoth very quickly indeed. Then she began to sniffle, shaking in several places. 'I 'ave no money in the bank. Oh, maybe a few dollars—'

'This is your bank book, isn't it, Clothilde?' asked the Inspector.

Clothilde stopped sniffling just as quickly as she had begun. 'Where do you get that? Give it to me!'

'Uh-uh-uh,' said the Sergeant, embracing her. 'Say . . .!'

She flung his arm off. 'That is my bank book!'

'And it shows,' murmured the Inspector, 'deposits totalling more than seventeen thousand dollars, Clothilde. Rich Uncle?'

'*Voleurs!* That is my money! I save!'

'She's got a new savings system, Inspector,' explained the Sergeant. 'Out of forty-five bucks per week, she manages to sock away, some weeks, sixty, some weeks eighty-five. . . . It's wonderful. How do you do it, Cloey?'

Nikki glanced at Ellery, startled. He nodded gloomily.

'*Fils de lapin! Jongleur! Chienloup!*' Clothilde was screaming. 'All right! Some time I short-change the customer. I am cashier, *non?* But—nothing else!' She jabbed her elbow into Sergeant Velie's stomach. 'And take your 'and off me!'

'I got my duty, mademazelle,' said the Sergeant, but he looked a little guilty. Inspector Queen said something to him in an undertone, and the Sergeant reddened, and Clothilde came at him claws first, and detectives jumped in, and in the midst of it Ellery got up from the table and drew his father aside and said: 'Come on back to Mother Carey's.'

'What for, Ellery? I'm not through here—'

'I want to wash this thing up. Tomorrow's Thanksgiving, poor Nikki is out on her feet—'

'*Ellery,*' said Nikki.

He nodded, still gloomily.

The sight of his wife turned old man Carey into a human being again, and he clung to her and blubbered that he had done nothing and they were trying to frame him for the second time, only this time it was the hot seat they were steering him into. And Mrs Carey kept nodding and picking lint off his jacket collar. And Nikki tried to look invisible.

'Where's Velie?' grumbled the Inspector. He seemed irritated by Carey's blubbering and the fact that Ellery had insisted on sending all the detectives home, as if this were a piece of business too delicate for the boys' sensibilities.

'I've sent Velie on an errand,' Ellery replied, and then he said: 'Mr and Mrs Carey, would you go into that room there and shut the door?' Mother Carey took her husband by the hand without a word. And when the door had closed behind them, Ellery said abruptly: 'Dad, I asked you to arrest Pierre tonight. You phoned Velie to hurry right over to Fouchet's. Velie obeyed—and found the waiter stabbed to death.'

'So?'

'Police Headquarters is on Centre Street. Fouchet's is just off Canal. A few blocks apart.'

'Hey?'

'Didn't it strike you as extraordinary,' murmured Ellery, 'that Pierre should have been murdered so quickly? Before Velie could negotiate those few blocks?'

'You mean the boss dope-peddler struck so fast to keep his man from being arrested? We went through all that before, son.'

'Hm,' said Ellery. 'But what did Pierre's killer have to know in order to strike so quickly tonight? Two things: That Pierre had slipped me a packet of dope by mistake this evening; and that I was intending to have Pierre pulled in tonight.'

'But Ellery,' said Nikki with a frown, 'nobody knew about either of those things except you, me, and the Inspector . . .'

'Interesting?'

'I don't get it,' growled his father. 'The killer knew Pierre was going to be picked up even before Velie reached Fouchet's. He must have because he beat Velie to it. But if only the three of us knew—'

'Exactly—then how did the killer find out?'

'I give up,' said the Inspector promptly. He had discovered many years before that this was, after all, the best way.

But Nikki was young. 'Someone overheard you talking it over with me and the Inspector?'

'Well, let's see, Nikki. We discussed it with Dad in our apartment when we got back from Mrs Carey's . . .'

'But nobody could have overheard there,' said the Inspector.

'Then Ellery, you and I must have been overheard before we got to the apartment.'

'Good enough, Nikki. And the only place you and I discussed the case—the only place we *could* have discussed it . . .'

'Ellery!'

'We opened the packet in the cab on our way over to Henry Street here,' nodded Ellery, 'and we discussed its contents quite openly—in the cab. In fact,' he added dryly, 'if you'll recall, Nikki, our conversational cab-driver joined our discussion with enthusiasm.'

'*The cab-driver, by Joe,*' said Inspector Queen softly.

'Whom we had picked up just outside Fouchet's, Dad, where he was parked. It fits.'

'The same cab-driver,' Ellery went on glumly,' who took us back uptown from here, Nikki—remember? And it was on that uptown trip that I told you I was going to have Dad arrest Pierre tonight. . . . Yes, the cab-driver, and only the cab-driver—the only outsider who could have overheard the two statements which would make the boss dope-peddler kill his pusher quickly to prevent an arrest, a police grilling, and an almost certain revelation of the boss's identity.'

'Works a cab,' muttered the Inspector. 'Cute dodge. Parks outside his headquarters. Probably hacks his customers to Fouchet's and collects beforehand. Let Pierre pass the white stuff afterwards. Probably carted them away.' He looked up, beaming. 'Great work, son! I'll nail that hack so blasted fast—'

'You'll nail whom, Dad?' asked Ellery, still glum.

'The cab-driver!'

'*But who is the cab-driver?*'

Ellery is not proud of this incident.

'You're asking *me*?' howled his father.

Nikki was biting her lovely nails. 'Ellery, I didn't even *notice*—'

'Ha, ha,' said Ellery. 'That's what I was afraid of.'

'Do you mean to say,' said Inspector Queen in a terrible voice, 'that *my son* didn't read a hack police-identity card?'

'Er . . .'

'It's the LAW!'

'It's Thanksgiving Eve, Dad,' muttered Ellery. 'Squanto—the Pilgrims—the Iroquois heritage of Mother Carey—'

'Stop drivelling! Can't you give me a description?'

'Er . . .'

'No description,' whispered his father. It was really the end of all things.

'Inspector, *nobody* looks at a cab-driver,' said Nikki brightly. 'You know. A cab-driver? He—he's just *there*.'

'The invisible man,' said Ellery hopefully. 'Chesterton?'

'Oh, so you do remember his name!'

'No, no, Dad—'

'I'd know his voice,' said Nikki. 'If I ever heard it again.'

'We'd have to catch him first, and if we caught him we'd hardly need his voice!'

'Maybe he'll come cruising back around Fouchet's.'

The Inspector ejaculated one laughing bark.

'Fine thing. Know who did it—and might's well not know. Listen to me, you detective. You're going over to the Hack Licence Bureau with me, and you're going to look over the photo of every last cab jockey in—'

'Wait. Wait!'

Ellery flung himself at Mother Carey's vacated chair. He sat on the bias, chin propped on the heel of his hand, knitting his brows, unknitting them, knitting them again until Nikki thought there was something wrong with his eyes. Then he shifted and repeated the process in the opposite direction. His father watched him with great suspicion. This was not Ellery tonight; it was someone else. All these gyrations . . .

Ellery leaped to his feet, kicking the chair over. 'I've got it! We've got him!'

'How? What?'

'Nikki.' Ellery's tone was mysterious, dramatic—let's face it, thought the old gentleman: corny. 'Remember when we lugged the stuff from the cab up to Mother Carey's kitchen here? The cab-driver helped us up—*carried this bottle of wine*.'

'Huh?' gaped the Inspector. Then he cried: 'No, no, Nikki, don't touch it!' And he chortled over the bottle of California wine. '*Prints*. That's it, son—that's my boy! We'll just take this little old bottle of grape back to Headquarters, bring out the fingerprints, compare the prints on it with the file sets at the Hack Bureau—'

'Oh, yeah?' said the cab-driver.

He was standing in the open doorway, there was a dirty handkerchief tied around his face below the eyes and his cap was pulled low, and he was pointing a Police Positive midway between father and son.

'I thought you were up to somethin' when you all came back here from Fouchet's,' he sneered. 'And then leavin' this door open so I could hear the whole thing. You—the old guy. Hand me that bottle of wine.'

'You're not very bright,' said Ellery wearily. 'All right, Sergeant, shoot it out of his hand.'

And Ellery embraced his father and his secretary and fell to Mother Carey's spotless floor with them as Sergeant Velie stepped into the doorway behind the cab-driver and very carefully shot the gun out of the invisible man's hand.

'Happy Thanksgivin', sucker,' said the Sergeant.

WRY HIGHBALL

Craig Rice

*John J. Malone is a Chicago lawyer who has a greater passion for whisky
than the law. The file in his office marked 'Personal' invariably contains
a bottle of rye, and one of his favourite spots for wrestling with the clues
to a crime—over more than a highball or two—is Joe Angel's City Hall
Bar. Despite this apparent lack of interest in his profession, Malone is
an incisive and clever investigator as his various cases in novel and
short story form demonstrate. The lawyer-detective was created during
the years of the Second World War by Craig Rice (the pseudonym of
Georgiana Ann Randolph, 1908–1957), a former public relations consultant and radio broadcaster who lived for most of her life in Chicago,
although she did spend some time in Hollywood writing film scripts.
The stories of Malone were undoubtedly the most successful of all her
crime novels, although she is also remembered for having ghosted two
popular murder mysteries by the film star Gypsy Rose Lee,* The G-
String Murders *(1941) and* Mother Finds A Body *(1942). Two mysteries about Craig Rice have persisted since her death: the origin of her
pen name, and the precise number of times she was married—varying
accounts give her between four and seven husbands! Such a puzzle
would certainly have delighted John J. Malone who sets out in 'Wry
Highball' to investigate a murder involving two beautiful girls, both
very much to his taste . . .*

'You've got to believe me,' the beautiful girl said. 'I had nothing
to do with it. I was just as surprised as Arthur—'

She produced a handkerchief from her purse and cried into it,
softly. John J. Malone sat behind his desk feeling uncomfortable.
'Now, now,' he said. The girl went on sobbing. Malone said, 'There,
there.'

'But it's terrible,' the girl said at last. 'Arthur is dead, and—'
She went back to the handkerchief.

Malone sighed. 'I'd like to help you,' he said untruthfully, 'but you'll have to tell me all about it. Now, let's start from the beginning. Your name is Sheila Manson.'

The girl stopped sobbing as if someone had thrown a switch. She brushed hair the colour of cornsilk away from her tear-stained face, looked up at Malone, and said, 'But how did you know?'

Malone didn't think it was worthwhile telling Sheila Manson that a good description of her had been in every Chicago newspaper for the past forty-eight hours. 'I have my methods,' he said airily, trying to look mysterious.

'Then you must know about Arthur, too,' Shelia Manson said.

'Suppose you tell me,' Malone suggested diplomatically.

Sheila nodded. She put the handkerchief away in her purse and said, 'He was my fiancé. Arthur Bent. We were going to be married next week.'

'And now he's dead,' Malone encouraged her sympathetically.

She nodded again. 'And the police think I did it, but I didn't. You believe me, don't you, Mr Malone?'

'Why do the police think you killed your fiancé?' Malone said, side-stepping neatly.

Sheila Manson shook her head. 'I don't know why,' she said. 'But I can tell you who really did kill him.'

There was a little silence. At last Malone prodded, 'Who?'

'Mae Ammon,' Sheila said. 'After all, she was right there, too. And if I didn't do it, she must have.'

'Mae Ammon?'

'She's just no good,' Sheila said. 'She would murder anybody if she thought she could get something out of it.'

'And what could she get out of murdering Arthur Bent?' Malone asked.

Sheila shrugged. She was beautiful even when she shrugged, Malone thought.

He decided he had to take the case—even if there wasn't any money in it. Even if he owed the telephone company, his landlord, the electric company, and three restaurants. They could wait, but Sheila Manson was the kind of vision that dropped into a man's office once in a lifetime.

'She was just jealous,' Sheila said. 'I was Arthur's fiancé, and she was jealous.'

To Malone it sounded as if Mae Ammon had a better motive for murdering Sheila than for doing away with Arthur. However, this was no time for fine distinctions. 'I'll do what I can for you,' he said decisively.

'I can't pay you very much—'

'Don't you worry your pretty head about that,' Malone said.

'Just give me your address, so that I can get in touch with you—
and then go home and try to relax.'

'Mr Malone.' Sheila stood up. Her figure was slim and breath-
taking. The last shreds of monetary regret disappeared from the
little lawyer's thoughts. 'If the police come—what shall I do?'

'Shoot it out,' Malone said. Then he caught himself. 'Sorry—I
must have been thinking of something else. If they come, just call
me. I'll be right here, or else my secretary will find me. Now, you
just relax and stop worrying.'

'All right, Mr Malone.' She started for the door, under the
lawyer's breathless scrutiny. At the door she turned. 'Malone,' she
said, and her voice dropped an octave, 'I'm—very grateful to you.'

The door banged and she was gone.

After a minute Malone wiped the smile guiltily off his face, put
on a businesslike frown, and told himself that precious time was
passing.

He leaned back in his chair, closed his eyes, and tried hard to
think about Arthur Bent.

Of course, he had read about it in the newspapers. Bent had been
a rich man—and just recently rich, Malone reminded himself. On
his twenty-fifth birthday he had become heir to the Bent fortune,
as provided in his father's will. Two weeks later Arthur Bent was
dead. He'd been poisoned with arsenic, placed in a rye-and-
ginger-ale highball. He had taken this fatal drink in his own home,
and no one else had been present except Sheila Manson and Mae
Ammon.

But neither the bottle of ginger ale nor the bottle of expensive
rye had been tampered with. The poison had been only in Bent's
highball.

It certainly looked as if there were only two possible suspects:
Sheila Manson and Mae Ammon. Well, he was working for Sheila
Manson, Malone told himself; that meant he had to see Mae
Ammon at once.

It was perfectly obvious, when you thought about it, that Mae
Ammon had committed the murder. After all, Sheila was a beautiful young girl, and beautiful young girls just didn't do things like
that. Or, at any rate, Malone was convinced this one hadn't done it.

Unfortunately for Malone's first theory, Mae Ammon was
beautiful too.

Her address was, conveniently, in the Chicago telephone direc-
tory. Malone took a cab to the quiet brownstone, walked up the
steps, and rang the bell.

The girl who answered the door had short black hair and a
figure that made Malone almost stop breathing. She was not slim,

like Sheila Manson, but Malone decided that he preferred cur-
vaceous and cuddly brunettes. She wore a dark-green dress that
clung to her figure like adhesive tape.

'I'm looking for Mae Ammon,' Malone said. 'But I'd rather be
looking for you.'

The girl smiled. 'In that case,' she said, 'you're lucky. I'm Mae
Ammon. Come in.'

Malone followed her, in a daze, through a hallway and up one
flight of dim stairs. 'Most of the people who live here work during
the day,' she said as she pushed open the door of a large bright
room. 'I'm the only one here, so I answer the bell.'

Malone said, 'Ah,' in an intelligent fashion, and followed her
inside. The room was high-ceilinged and sunny. Magazines were
scattered everywhere—on the blonde-wood coffee table, over the
light-green couch and chairs, piled on the hi-fi and the television
set. There was even a large bundle of them stacked on the yellow
spread of the single daybed.

'So you're Mae Ammon,' Malone said, for lack of anything else
to say.

'That's right.' She smiled again. 'Just put some of the magazines
on the floor and sit down. Who are you, by the way?'

Malone took a stack of Lifes and Looks from the couch and sat
down. 'I'm John J. Malone,' he said.

'The John J. Malone?' Mae Ammon's face showed surprise.

Malone nodded. 'The lawyer, anyway,' he said with what he
hoped was modesty.

'And you're here about poor Arthur,' Mae said. Her smile disappeared. 'I hope that woman gets the chair,' she burst out. 'Killing
Arthur—and out of sheer jealousy, that's all it was—just because
he was my fiancé—'

Malone said, 'Stop.'

Mae looked down at him. 'Stop?'

'Did you say Arthur Bent was your fiancé?'

'That's right,' the girl said.

Malone sighed. Things were getting a little complicated, he
realised. 'I'd heard that he was Sheila Manson's fiancé,' he said
cautiously.

'Sheila Manson!' Mae looked around the room suddenly, and
saw a china dog lying on the floor. She picked it up and threw it
against the wall. Malone ducked. The dog landed over his head
with a sharp crash, and little pieces of china drifted down the
back of his collar.

'That's what I think of Sheila Manson!' Mae said. 'I hope she
gets the chair! Arthur Bent was my fiancé, and I don't intend to
forget it!'

Malone rose slowly. 'I was only asking,' he said mildly.

Mae came over to him and put a hand on his shoulder. 'Oh, I wouldn't hurt you,' she said. 'I don't have anything against you. After all, you know I didn't kill Arthur. Why should I—we were going to be married week after next.'

'Sure,' Malone said. This didn't seem like the proper time to tell Mae Ammon that he was working for Sheila Manson. But Sheila had said she was going to marry Arthur Bent next week. That gave her a week's priority on Mae Ammon. Malone decided, in a hurry, that he'd better not mention that either.

'I just want to find out the truth,' he said.

'Well, you know the truth,' Mae said. 'It was that hussy Sheila Manson, that's who it was. She slipped poison into his drink and he died. And now she's going to be caught and tried and convicted, and I hope she gets the chair—' She bent down and Malone ducked again. But she was only picking up a magazine. 'They sometimes give women the chair,' Mae said. 'This magazine has some stories—but that's not important. I *want* Shelia Manson to get the chair.'

Malone took a deep breath. 'Suppose,' he said gently, 'that she didn't do it.'

'But she did,' Mae said. 'I was there. I know.'

'Did you see her actually put poison into his drink?'

'Well,' Mae said, 'not exactly. But I saw him mix the drink—take out the bottles and everything—take his own little stirrer out of the glass, and then drink it. And if *I* didn't kill him, then *she* must have! We were the only ones there.'

Malone nodded. There was, he felt sure, another question he should ask, but he didn't come up with it. 'Was there ice in the drink?' he said at random.

'Of course there was,' Mae said. 'But the police checked the ice tray. There was no poison in it.'

That, Malone thought, eliminated another possibility. But it had been a good idea. 'Suppose Sheila Manson didn't murder your— suppose she didn't murder Arthur Bent,' he said. 'Who else might have had a motive?'

'Everybody loved Arthur,' Mae said. 'He was a wonderful man.'

'Sure,' Malone said. 'But he was rich. Who's going to inherit his money?'

'I was his fiancé,' Mae said. 'I'm going to inherit.'

'Did he make a will?'

Mae shrugged. She too was beautiful when she shrugged. 'I don't know,' she said with insouciance.

'How about any close relatives?' Malone said.

'He only had two cousins,' Mae said. 'Charlie Bent and J. O.

Hanlon. They both live in Chicago. But they weren't even at
Arthur's place. I tell you, I saw everything. He put in the ice, then
the rye, then the ginger ale, then he stirred it all up and drank
it—'

'I'll do what I can,' Malone said diplomatically.

'I'm sure you will,' Mae said. 'By the way, why are you asking
questions? Are you working with the police? Because I told them
all of this—'

'I'm just a friend,' Malone lied smoothly. 'I'm interested in
justice.'

'So am I,' Mae said. 'And justice means giving that hussy the
chair.'

Well, Malone thought when he arrived at his own office again,
there's still J. O. Hanlon and Charlie Bent.

He didn't feel much like seeing them, but somebody had to be
the murderer. As things stood, the only suspects were a beautiful
blonde and a beautiful brunette. Both, it seemed, had been fiancées
of the dead man. And each was convinced the other had committed the murder—unless, Malone thought, they were both awfully
good actresses.

But if neither girl had murdered Arthur Bent, Malone thought
slowly, then how did he die? The arsenic was in his drink. It
wasn't in the bottle of rye or in the bottle of ginger ale. It wasn't,
according to Mae Ammon, in the ice cubes. So somebody had put
it in the particular glass Arthur had used.

Unless he only used one particular glass—and somebody had
painted the inside with arsenic beforehand. You could do that,
Malone knew, if you used an arsenic-in-water solution. The poison
would dry as a thin film, and dissolve again in any liquid.

Of course, it would make the glass look a little filmy . . .

Malone sighed and reached for the telephone.

Five minutes later he put it down. Von Flanagan had been exceptionally polite and courteous—for von Flanagan, that is. He'd
actually told Malone what he wanted to know, and hadn't
threatened even once to arrest the little criminal lawyer.

There was no arsenic residue in the glass above the level of the
drink.

So the glass hadn't been painted with arsenic.

And that meant that either Mae or Sheila had murdered Arthur
Bent.

The only trouble was that Malone was sure neither had.

Of course, the glass might have been painted only at the bottom.
Malone wondered if von Flanagan had thought of that, and started

to call him back before he realised it wouldn't have made any
difference.

'It's a funny thing,' von Flanagan had said. 'Here's a guy who
monograms everything he owns—got his own special monogrammed coasters, for instance. Nobody else uses his coaster. But
he didn't monogram the glasses. So there'd be no way for anyone
to tell in advance which glass he'd use.'

And that, Malone thought, made the cheese even more binding.

He reached for the telephone again.

J. O. Hanlon, it developed, would be right over. He sounded on
the telephone like the gruff and overbearing type, and Malone
wondered if he were in for more trouble. Charlie Bent, unfortunately, couldn't be reached. His housekeeper said he'd been in
Central Africa for the last six months on a safari.

And that's where I should be, Malone told himself sadly.

J. O. Hanlon charged into the office like a bull. Behind him the
door slammed shut and rattled. 'You wanted to see me?' he asked
Malone in a voice that sounded as if it had come from the quarter-
deck of the *Bounty*.

'Sit down,' Malone said nervously. 'And relax.'

Hanlon dropped into a chair and stared belligerently across the
desk. 'What can I do for you?' he roared.

Malone winced. 'I'm investigating the death of Arthur Bent—'

'I spoke to the police,' Hanlon said. 'Told 'em everything. You
ask the police about it.' He started to rise.

'I'd like to ask just a few questions,' Malone said. 'This won't
take much of your time.'

'All right,' Hanlon said, and dropped back into the chair with
a thud. 'Ask away. I'm a fair and reasonable man. Willing to help
if I can.'

Malone cleared his throat, then said, 'I understand you were
Arthur's cousin.'

'That's correct—mother's side of the family. My mother was
Arthur's mother's sister.'

Malone tried to work it out in his head and gave up. 'Cousin'
would have to do. 'Do you know if Arthur Bent made a will?'
Malone said.

'Told that to the police, too,' Hanlon bellowed. 'Charlie gets it
all—good old Charlie.'

'Charlie Bent?'

'Right,' Hanlon shouted. 'Charlie's in Africa now—hunting or
some such foolishness. He'll find out when he gets back.'

'Ah,' Malone said. Hanlon, then, was motiveless. And that still
left only two suspects—neither of whom, Malone assured himself

dismally, was guilty. But maybe he could clear up a few of the cloudy points.

'I understand your cousin was engaged,' he probed cautiously.

'Engaged?' Hanlon broke into gusts of laughter. Malone sat patiently, waiting for the outbursts to stop. At last Hanlon said, 'Those two girls, right? Good game of Arthur's, poor man. Engaged to nobody—but he let the girls *think* he was engaged to them. That's why the three of them met up at his apartment that night—to compare notes.'

'They had found out about each other?' Malone said.

'Oversight of Arthur's,' Hanlon explained. 'They both went to his apartment that night to talk things out with him.'

Malone suddenly thought of another question. 'How do you know about all this?'

'Me?' Hanlon said. 'Been going with one of 'em myself—Arthur took her away. She told me all about it before she went to his apartment.' 'Which one?' Malone leaned forward.

'Sheila,' Hanlon said. 'Good old Sheila. I'm sure she didn't do it. Must have been the other one—what's her name—Mae. Sheila wouldn't do a thing like that.'

Malone closed his eyes for a long time. At last they opened. 'My advice to you,' he said, 'is to hire a good lawyer. Me.'

'Lawyer?'

'To defend you on a charge of murder,' Malone said. 'You see, I knew there was something—I knew I'd heard *something* that explained the whole killing. But I had to wait until now, when I saw a motive, to remember it and put all the pieces together.'

'You're not making any sense,' Hanlon said.

'Wait,' Malone promised, 'and I will. Hanlon, you murdered your cousin—so you could get your girl back.'

'What?' Hanlon bounced up.

Malone said, 'Relax. I'm going to defend you. Never lost a client yet.'

'But I wasn't even there!' Hanlon exclaimed.

'You didn't have to be. Arthur Bent made the perfect victim— for a clever killer. Each of you had some kind of a motive—both girls, and you, and Charlie. But the girls didn't do it—they'd have killed each other first. And Charlie's in Africa. Arthur Bent monogrammed everything except—for some reason—his drinking glasses.'

'They were new—he hadn't got around to having his special monogram put on them,' Hanlon said.

'And Mae kept talking about Arthur's own individual little stirrer.'

Hanlon began to wilt.

'All right,' he said, at last, like a balloon gasping out its final breath. 'I painted the arsenic on his stirrer . . . I had to get rid of him—so Sheila would come back to me.'

'Don't worry about a thing,' Malone said. 'And admit nothing to the police. You were overwrought. You didn't know what you were doing.'

'What?'

'Of course, my services come high,' Malone went on persuasively.

'I'll take care of you, Malone,' Hanlon said. 'I've got some money of my own . . .'

Malone leaned back with satisfaction. Maybe, he thought, he'd get paid by everybody—each in his, or her, own fashion . . .

THE MAN WHO STIRRED CHAMPAGNE

Hugh Pentecost

John Jericho is a tall, 17-stone hard man whose bright red Viking beard and moustache seem to attract violence wherever he goes. He doubles as an artist and detective, and has a ready thirst for bourbon whiskey which he refers to as 'anti-freeze'. His creator, Hugh Pentecost (real name, Judson Pentecost Philips, 1903-), is also something of a larger-than-life character whose prolific writing career spans the era of the pulp magazines to the present day. He was a founding member of the Mystery Writers of America and was made a 'Grand Master' in 1973 in recognition of his achievements as a crime novelist and short story writer. Jericho, the crusader against crime, made his debut in the novel Dead Woman of the Year *(1967), but of late has appeared more frequently in short stories like 'The Man Who Stirred Champagne' (1979), in which his finer sensibilities towards drinking enable him to solve a vicious racecourse crime.*

It has been said that the reason there are so many stray dogs in the town of Saratoga Springs, New York, during the month of August, is that they have rented their dog-houses to visiting canines. It is the custom of the human residents of the town to rent their gracious homes, surrounded by lush green lawns and shaded by ancient elms, to people who come there in August for the month of racing. It has been said that the rents for the month could amount to half of the purchase price of the property. But the racing buffs ignore the costs. There is only one Saratoga, only one place on earth for the genuine horse player to be in the month of August. From these undeniable facts comes the probable apocrypha about stray dogs.

'Like the horses,' Jericho would say when he was asked, 'I come to Saratoga in August to eat the grass.'

Since Jericho was considered to be an eccentric, some people thought he might actually be telling the truth. He was a giant of a man, well over six feet tall with 240 pounds of well muscled body. His red hair, red beard, and moustache gave him the look of an old-time Viking warrior. Perhaps, some people thought, a diet of sweet clover and grass might account for his aura of incredible good health. Anything could be true in Saratoga if you said it with authority—for instance, who will win the fifth race? There will always be someone to tell you, and it will be true until a different horse makes it a lie.

Going to Saratoga in August, wrote the late Joe Palmer, incomparable chronicler of the world of horses, 'is a successful turning back of the pages, a stroll through the mirror, the slow drop of Alice down the rabbit hole. It is a month of living in about 1910.'

Jericho, sitting in the grass, his back propped against a giant elm, making casual charcoal sketches of grooms cooling thoroughbreds who had just been working out on the track, of horses looking at him curiously over the tops of box-stall doors, felt that he was living comfortably in another age. He knew that the famous Mrs Langtry, the Jersey Lily, and the probably infamous Diamond Jim Brady had walked in the grass right where he sat more than three quarters of a century ago.

In a world of turmoil and violence, of crime and man's inhumanity to man, there was an old-world grace, a strange peaceful tradition, a kind of forgotten style here at Saratoga that let you relax and forget—for the month of August. Horse people will tell you that after eleven months of racing in the big cities, at tracks like Aqueduct and Belmont, surrounded by cement and macadam and carbon monoxide fumes, Saratoga was good for man and beast. For the horses there was grass to eat; for the people the grandstand wasn't as crowded as those at the city tracks; for the State the share of the betting money was smaller, but surely there should be one time in the racing year when the prime concern was not the cash register. As Joe Palmer also wrote, 'Any man who would change that would stir champagne.'

On that morning when Jericho sat propped against a tree, sketching, there was, not far away, a man preparing to stir champagne.

Saratoga is not guarded by armed troops, like the city tracks. You don't need a pass to walk into Shed Row, where the horses are kept, fed, groomed, pampered, and even worshipped. You don't need an introduction to the person standing next to you. You presumably both belong to the same club, have a mutual interest in horses and the life that goes with them. You could have no other reason to be there and, therefore, you are friends with everyone. Saratoga in August.

The truth is that John Jericho is not a passionate devotee of the horse, but of the way of life that surrounds them, particularly at Saratoga in August. He is a man who has travelled the world,

painting in brilliant colours and with a kind of fierce outrage the
daily history of violence. The result is that he is not only a painter
but a persistent and deadly fighter against men who destroy their
brothers for the sake of profit and power. Thieves, murderers, and
war-makers of all races and creeds are his enemies, and a great
many of them have learned, too late, that they would be well
advised to stay out of his way. Saratoga in August is the place
where, once a year, he takes time to regroup his energies, refresh
his enormous vitality; where he sits in the shade, totally relaxed,
idly sketching the horses and the people who surround them. It
is his way of preparing for the next turn of the wheel. Violence is
inconceivable in this old-world setting.

And yet, there was a man preparing to stir champagne.

Willie Jacobs, known as Slick to his friends, was one of the delights
Jericho looked forward to each August at Saratoga. Jericho was a
man who detested phonies and Willie Slick Jacobs was a total
fraud. But a harmless one, an engaging one, Jericho noted. Slick
was a character straight out of a Damon Runyan story. His language was a combination of Runyanese and the eloquent prose of
the aforementioned Joe Palmer. Jericho, taken in from time to time,
discovered after a little research that Slick was loaded with direct
quotes from those two great men, quotes he appropriated as his
own colourful inventions, and that he acted a role invented by
those great men from the past.

There was nothing sinister about Willie the Slick. He knew
horses. He worked at the business of being a character for the
simple reason that it gave him entree to the world of people who
live with and by horses. Willie the Slick didn't want to steal from
them, or defraud them. He just wanted to be one of them.

Jericho had met Willie one day, half a dozen years ago. Jericho
had been propped against his favourite elm tree, sketching. He
found himself attracted to a little man with a sharp ferret's face
wearing a chequered cap and a rather gaudy, vested summer suit.
A tout, Jericho thought, and drew a wicked caricature of the little
man.

Slick Jacobs approached him. 'You drawin' a picture of me?' he
asked.

Jericho handed him his sketch pad.

Slick looked stunned. 'Gawd a'mighty, do I look like that?' he
asked.

Jericho grinned at him. 'To me,' he said.

Slick shook his head. 'Maybe I oughta steer clear of you,' he
said. But he was fascinated by the other sketches of horses and

people on the pages of the sketch pad. He sat down in the grass beside Jericho.

'They really pamper the horses,' Slick said. 'A hundred and fifty years ago they'd rub 'em down with whiskey and let 'em drink it, too. Twenty eggs the day they exercised. Some people believed in a pound of butter each day, washed down with a quart of English claret.' Slick gave Jericho a sly look. 'In those days when they said a horse was stiff, he was stiff!'

Jericho smiled back. 'As Joe Palmer wrote in one of his inimitable columns.'

'Jeese, I better steer clear of you,' Slick said.

'Expert plagiarism is a gift,' Jericho said.

It was the beginning of a beautiful friendship.

On that day, six years later, when trouble was brewing, Slick sought out Jericho under his favourite tree.

'Time to head for the grandstand, Dad,' he said. He called Jericho 'Dad' for no particular reason. They had a date to watch Foreclosure, considered the greatest horse of the day, run the seventh race.

Jericho rarely watched the races. His concern was with the backstage of the world of horses, but Slick had insisted that he simply couldn't bypass the chance to see the great Foreclosure do his stuff.

Slick and Jericho made their way around the far end of the track to the grandstand. The parade to the post for the seventh race had already begun.

'Look at him!' Slick said. 'Ever see anything like it? He looks like a plow horse.'

Different horses had a different approach to the moment of truth. Some of them, tense, prancing, are led to the starting gate by an outrider on a stable pony. Some of them, with only the jockey in control, seem prepared to take off for the moon at any moment. Then there is the rare one, like Foreclosure, who just ambles down the track, relaxed, unexcited by the noise of the crowd or the nearness of the contest for which he is prepared, coddled, trained.

Foreclosure, a big bay stallion, unbeaten in three years of racing, was the picture of relaxation. Jimmy Coombs, the jockey who had ridden him in all his big races, exerted no pressure on the reins. Foreclosure just ambled along, fourth in the parade.

'He don't waste anythin' on the way to work,' Slick said. He obviously loved the big horse, as did the applauding spectators in the grandstand and along the rail. Foreclosure turned his head, ears pricked, as if to acknowledge the cheers that he evidently knew were meant for him.

The horses turned at the far end of the track and approached the starting gate, where handlers on foot waited to lead them into their appointed starting stalls.

'In like a lamb and out like a lion,' Slick said.

Foreclosure walked into the Number 4 slot and stood quietly while the other horses, exhibiting varying degrees of tension and excitement, were led into place, the gates closed behind them.

'The horses are in place,' the track loudspeaker told the crowd. 'Hammerlock in the Number 6 spot is giving the handlers a little trouble and—*they're off!*'

The horses broke from the gate, and at the same moment the crowd was on its feet, screaming. The great Foreclosure, normally a fast starter from the gate, had gone completely haywire. He came out bucking and kicking. He barged into the Number 5 horse on his right, knocking that one off stride. He swerved in and smashed into the Number 3 horse, unseating the jockey. He headed outside again and charged into the rail, throwing Jimmy Coombs over his head and into the crowd.

Then Foreclosure raced down the track, nostrils flaring, dark with sweat, still bucking like a rodeo horse broken loose from a cattle pen. Riderless, he pounded his way through the horses that were ahead of him and then, at the first turn, he kept right on to the fence and sailed over it and into the screaming crowd.

Slick, jumping up and down in an effort to see over the heads of the people in front of him, was swearing, tears streaming down his cheeks. The crazed Foreclosure was a symbol of everything he cared for on this earth.

Very few people, except perhaps those who had bet on him, noticed that Slim Jim, a 40–1 outsider, won the seventh race at Saratoga that afternoon by six lengths.

Rumours spread like a forest fire around the track. An ambulance had taken Jimmy Coombs to the hospital. Some said he was dead. Some said he had broken limbs or a concussion. What about the jockey who had been knocked off the Number 3 horse? He'd walked away from the spill, miraculously unhurt.

But the big question was Foreclosure. Had he been caught without serious injury? What could have driven him into such a frenzy?

'Only pain—pain he couldn't stand,' Slick said, as he and Jericho wedged their way through the crowd toward Shed Row where there would be answers.

Foreclosure had finally been brought down by cowboy skills as he reared and kicked his way through the crowd at the far end of the track. A couple of dozen people had been injured—how seriously there were no reports as yet—before some stablehands managed to lassoo the berserk horse and bring him down, sweat-smeared, bleeding from the mouth and from wounds in his fore-legs where he had hit the fence breaking out of the track. A track veterinarian had managed to sedate the struggling Foreclosure and he had been carried back to his stable on Shed Row in a horse ambulance.

A huge crowd had gathered around the stable, waiting for some news about the horse's condition. Slick Jacobs knew everyone backstage, including the security men who had roped off the area to keep the curious from barging right into the animal's stall.

Eventually an old man, his face tear-stained, came out of the stall. He was Mike Greenleaf, the groom whose job it was to care for the champion thoroughbred. He seemed to grab onto Slick, someone he knew and trusted.

'You wouldn't believe,' he said, nodding to Jericho when Slick introduced them. 'His mouth. Of course Jimmy Coombs tried to stop him when he bolted, yanked him around pretty bad. But that isn't what did it. It's like his mouth was burned out with acid.'

'Acid!'

'That's what the vet thinks. Burned the poor baby's mouth raw as hamburger.'

'How?' Slick asked, not believing. 'He walked into the starting gate quiet enough, Mike.'

Mike Greenleaf nodded. 'Either it was squirted into his mouth at the last minute, or it was contained in a capsule, maybe fastened to his bit, that he bit into, or that dissolved just as the starting gate opened.'

'You saddled him for the race, didn't you, Mike?' Slick asked. 'Wouldn't you have noticed if anything was fastened to his bit?'

'You'd think I would, wouldn't you? Well, I didn't. I got to go, Slick. The track stewards are holding an inquiry.'

'The only person who could have squirted anything into his mouth is the handler who led him into the starting gate,' Slick said.

Greenleaf nodded. 'Eddie Stevens. They're trying to locate him.'

'What about Foreclosure? Is he going to make it all right?'

'Who knows?' Greenleaf said bitterly. 'He may never let anyone put a bit in his mouth again—we may never be able to handle him in another race.'

'The horse's owner?' Jericho asked, speaking for the first time.

'Jeb Faulkner,' Greenleaf said. 'He's out on the West Coast. He has a couple of horses running out there. They're trying to get him on the phone now.'

Slick and Jericho watched the old groom walk off.

'Acid!' Slick said. 'Some bum really did stir the champagne.'

Jericho had made friends over the years of his visits to Saratoga. Finding a place to stay for a month wasn't easy. Among the people who rented estates there for August was Ruth Prentiss, one of the great ladies in the world of racing. Mrs Prentiss was also a patron of the arts and the owner of several of Jericho's paintings. There was a small apartment over the garage of the estate she rented and it was Jericho's for the asking. Slick and Jericho went there.

'I've got some forty-year-old bonded anti-freeze there that I think I could use,' Jericho told Slick. 'Anti-freeze' was a synonym for bourbon whiskey. Jericho didn't want to drink in a bar surrounded by mobs of people all talking about the disaster to Foreclosure. A deep anger was burning in his gut. The senseless cruelty to the great horse, who could be worth more than a million dollars to his owner when he was syndicated and put out to stud, was as evil a crime as anything Jericho had seen man do to man.

'Someone probably made a killing on that race,' he said to Slick as he poured the bourbon over ice in two old-fashioned glasses. Neither man wanted his liquor diluted. 'That Slim Jim paid forty-to-one.'

'The totalisator will show that up if there was any heavy betting on him at the track,' Slick said.

'Offtrack betting parlours all over the country,' Jericho said. 'Hundreds of hundred-dollar bets scattered around the country. Would they show up?'

'In time,' Slick said. 'But let me tell you about Slim Jim. He's a sprinter, not a distance horse. That race was a mile and a quarter. Slim Jim can't run that far. He was in there to set a fast pace for the first few furlongs. Foreclosure would have run him into the ground over the distance. He'd have been at the end of the parade when the race ended if it hadn't been that all hell broke loose.'

'But if someone knew it was going to happen?'

'Slim Jim is owned by a guy named Rod Cross. Decent guy, good young owner. His father was Martin Cross who raced good horses ever since I was a kid. No shenanigans from him. What happened? Slim Jim broke fast from the gate, like he was supposed to. He was ahead of the field when Foreclosure stampeded. Everyone behind him was pulling up, trying to get out of Foreclosure's way. Slim Jim just kept running with nobody able to take out after him until it was too late. I'll bet if you look at a film of the race you'll see that Slim Jim was staggering the last quarter mile, but he was ten lengths ahead by then in the confusion. I'll bet you Rod Cross didn't have two bucks on him. Slim Jim wasn't supposed to win, just set the early pace.'

'It wouldn't have to be anyone who owned or trained Slim Jim, would it?' Jericho asked. 'Anyone who knows racing, like you, would know that Slim Jim would be in the lead at the start. If the race could be disrupted behind him—?'

Slick Jacobs didn't seem to hear. He'd picked up Jericho's sketch pad which the big man had tossed down on a table when he set about making drinks.

'When did you do this?' he asked. He'd been flipping the pages, casually interested. Now he was riveted on a sketch of two men, leaning against a fence rail somewhere, watching a horse who was being walked cool in the background.

'Why?' Jericho asked. 'What about it? Sometime just after breakfast this morning. Friends of yours?'

Slick's finger wasn't quite steady as he pointed at one figure dressed in blue jeans, a plaid sports shirt, and Western boots.

'That one is Eddie Stevens,' Slick said. 'He's the guy they're looking for. He handled Foreclosure in the starting gate.'

'You know the other one?'

'Sure I know him,' Slick said. 'He's Joe Salmin, gangster type who isn't very popular around race tracks anywhere. Strong-arm wheeler-dealer. You suppose—?'

'That horse in the background,' Jericho said. 'That's Foreclosure. Just finished an easy canter on the track, preparing for this afternoon's race.'

'And two and two makes four,' Slick said.

'If you can prove it,' Jericho said.

'The track stewards would like to see that sketch, I'll bet,' Slick said. 'And the State Police, too.'

Over the years John Jericho had developed a healthy respect for the professional skills of the police, but the legal restrictions under which they operated were another matter. You had to read a criminal his rights. You couldn't third-degree a confession out of a man, no matter how monstrous his crime. *'Poor baby's mouth raw as hamburger,'* old Greenleaf had said. An innocent animal ruthlessly tortured—for profit!' *'Read the prisoner his rights.'* Damn his rights, Jericho thought.

'Where can we find Eddie Stevens?' he asked.

'Somewhere between here and Mexico,' Slick said. 'Paid off and took off.'

'And this Joe Salmin? He wouldn't take a powder, would he? It might draw attention to him.'

'He rents a cottage down at the south end of town for the month of August,' Slick said. 'Some local yokel lets him have it each summer. Probably knows he'll get his arm broke if he doesn't.'

'Let's see if Mr Salmin will be interested in my sketch,' Jericho said.

'That's not a safe idea, Dad,' Slick said. 'Joe Salmin's apt to blow your head off when he sees it.'

A muscle along Jericho's jaw rippled under his red beard. 'That could be dangerous if I wasn't ready for it,' he said.

The Lyman cottage at the south end of Saratoga was a pleasant little place, surrounded by a white picket fence. At the rear of it was a small garden, bright with summer flowers. Joe Salmin, overlord of crime, sat there in a wicker armchair, drinking what looked like a pleasantly cool gin and tonic. Counting his money, Jericho thought. He was a big man, dark-haired, wearing a gaudy sports shirt and light beige slacks. His size pleased Jericho, who never liked to fight a smaller man.

Salmin turned his head as he heard the garden gate open. 'What the hell are you doing here, Slick?' he asked.

'Friend of mine wanted to meet you, Mr Salmin,' Slick said. 'He has something I thought you'd like to see.' He held out Jericho's sketchbook, opened at the right drawing.

Salmin took the drawing and looked at it, a nerve twitching at the corner of his mouth.

'I remember seeing you out at the track this morning,' he said to Jericho. 'You do this for fun, or you make your living at it?'

'You might say both,' Jericho said. He moved casually, so that he was standing behind the gangster, looking over his shoulder.

'It's good,' Salmin said. 'How much you want for it?'

'Oh, the price isn't prohibitive, Mr Salmin,' Jericho said. 'Just some information—like, where is Eddie Stevens? And what are the names of the people who placed bets on Slim Jim for you all around the country?'

Salmin started to heave up out of his chair. Jericho's left arm went around his neck, jerking him back. His right hand closed on Salmin's right wrist and twisted the arm behind the man's back. In spite of himself the gangster cried out in pain.

'Be good enough to pull Mr Salmin's tooth, will you, Slick?' Jericho said softly. 'He's carrying a gun in a holster under his left arm.'

Slick, as if he were walking on eggs, came slowly forward. Salmin lashed out at him with a booted foot.

'Now, now, Mr Salmin, none of that,' Jericho said. 'I can start out by breaking your arm. And if you insist, I can break your neck. If you please, Slick.'

Slick came forward and snatched the gun out of Salmin's holster. He backed away, holding the gun in a shaking hand.

'Be good enough to point that somewhere else, Slick,' Jericho said. 'And now, Mr Salmin, where is Eddie Stevens?'

'I don't know any Eddie Stevens,' Salmin said, half strangling for breath.

'The other man in my sketch,' Jericho said. 'The man you were talking to about acid.'

The gangster started to struggle, but Jericho pulled up painfully on his arm.

'I guess you can stand pain, Mr Salmin,' Jericho said. 'But I think I have something that you can't stand.' He looked steadily at Slick. 'Be good enough, Slick, to hand me that little bottle of acid we found in Eddie Stevens' room.'

Slick stared at his friend like a man in a trance, his eyes wide with disbelief.

'Come on, Slick, we haven't got all day,' Jericho said.

Slick put a hand in his pocket and brought it out, his fist closed around something. He came forward, stiff-legged, and held out that fist to Jericho. Jericho put his knee into the middle of Salmin's back and jerked his head back. He released the gangster's right arm and reached out for what Slick apparently was holding in his closed fist. Salmin, his head bent back so that he looked up into the sky, struggled weakly.

'What I've got here, Mr Salmin, is the acid you prescribed for Foreclosure. When I start to pour it into your eyes you will never see another summer sunset, or the flowers in this garden, or another horserace, or the profit figures at the bottom of the accounting sheet your men send you.'

'All right! All right!' Salmin cried out, a pent-up scream. 'Eddie's on his way to the Albany airport where a chartered plane is waiting to fly him out of the country.'

'Go into the cottage, Slick, and call the police,' Jericho said. 'Tell them to stop any chartered plane preparing to leave the Albany airport. Meanwhile, Mr Salmin, the names of the people who placed bets for you, please.' He held his closed fist over the gangster's terrified eyes.

'I thought you must have gone out of your mind!' Slick said. 'Asking me for acid we found in Eddie's room. What room? What acid? I almost blew it.'

The two men were back in Jericho's room, sipping the bonded anti-freeze again. The Saratoga cops had carted off Joe Salmin. Airport security people had snatched Eddie Stevens when he arrived there.

'It turned out to be a great tongue loosener,' Jericho said. 'I knew I could count on you, Slick. You spend your life acting a role, and I knew you'd improvise well when it was required of you.'

'Brother! I almost asked you what the hell you were talking about!' Slick shook his head. 'How could he believe that you'd really pour acid in his eyes?'

'I suspect Mr Salmin has done just as terrible things as that to other men,' Jericho said. 'A man who is capable of brutal torture has to believe that other men are capable of the same monstrous actions.' He raised his glass. 'It seems our Mr Salmin stirred the champagne once too often.'

UNDER THE HAMMER

Georges Simenon

Inspector Jules Maigret is arguably the detective most associated with drinking because of his wide appreciation of wine and spirits. Indeed, he often pursues his inquiries into crime in bars and cafés and usually drinks draught beer or calvados although if he is eating lunch or dinner, he is likely to have wine, pernod or an aperitif. Maigret is, in fact, at his most effective, and disarming, when gently questioning suspects over a drink or two. His life of wine is particularly evident in Maigret and the Wine Merchant *(1970) which also reveals the keen interest in fine vintages of his creator, Georges Simenon (1903–1989). Alcohol likewise features in the Maigret short stories such as 'The Inn of the Drowned', 'Missing Miniatures' and 'Under the Hammer', in which the Inspector pits his wits against an inn-keeper who is not all that he seems . . .*

Maigret pushed away his plate, got up from the table, grunted, shook himself, went over to the stove, and raised the lid mechanically.

'Well, now, let's get to work. We're going to be in bed early.'

And the others, sitting around the big table in the inn, looked at him with resignation. Frédéric Michaux, the proprietor, three days' stubble on his chin, was the first to get up and move to the bar. 'What'll you—?'

'No,' cried Maigret. 'No more. We've had enough. White wine, calvados, more wine and—'

They had all reached that stage of weariness where one's eyes smart and one's whole body aches. Julia, who passed for Frédéric's wife, went into the kitchen with a platter that bore the congealed remains of a dish of baked beans. Thérèse, the servant girl, wiped her eyes, but not because she was crying: she had a cold in the head.

'Where do we go back to?' she asked. 'Where I've cleared away?'

'It's eight o'clock now, so we pick it up from eight o'clock in the evening.'

'Then I'll bring the tablecloth and the cards.'

It was hot in the inn, too hot in fact, but outside the wind was driving gusts of icy rain through the darkness.

'Nicholas, you sit where you were last night. Monsieur Groux, you hadn't yet arrived.'

'It was when I heard Groux's footsteps outside, the innkeeper interrupted, 'that I said to Thérèse, "Put the cards out."'

'Have I got to pretend to come in all over again?' groaned Groux, a six-foot farmer, solid as a kitchen dresser.

You would have thought they were actors rehearsing a play for the twentieth time—their minds blank, their gestures limp, their eyes vacant. Maigret himself, in his role of stage manager, had some difficulty in believing it was all real. Even the place itself—imagine spending three days in an inn miles from the nearest village, in the middle of the fens of the Vendée!

The place was called Pont-du-Grau, and there was in fact a bridge, a long wooden bridge over a sort of muddy canal, filled twice a day by the tide. But the sea could not be seen: all there was to see was fenland, crisscrossed by ditches, and far away on the horizon flat roofs, farms—called 'cabins' in these parts.

Why this inn here by the roadside? For sportsmen after duck and plover? There was a red-painted petrol pump in the yard, and on the gable end there was a big blue advertisement for a brand of chocolate.

On the other side of the bridge, a hovel—nothing more than a rabbit hutch—the home of old Nicholas, who was an eel-fisher. Three hundred yards away, quite a big farm, with long single-storey buildings: Groux's place.

January 15th . . . 1 p.m. sharp at the place known as La Mulatière, sale by auction . . . farm, 30 hectares, equipment and stock . . . farm machinery, furniture, china . . . The transaction will be by cash.

That is how it had all started. For years life at the inn had been the same every evening. Old Nicholas would arrive, always half drunk, and before he settled down with his pint, he would go over for a drink at the bar. Then Groux would arrive from his farm. Thérèse would spread a red cloth on the table, and bring the cards and the counters. They still had to wait for the excise man to make the fourth: if he didn't turn up, Julia took his place.

Now, on the 14th, the eve of the sale, there were two other customers, farmers who had come from farther away—one of them a man called Borchain, from near Angoulême, the other a certain Canut, from Saint Jean-d'Angély.

'Just a minute,' said Maigret, as the innkeeper was about to shuffle the cards. 'Borchain went to bed before eight o'clock— that's to say, straight after his supper. Who was it who took him to his room?'

'I did,' Frédéric answered.

'He'd been drinking?'

'Not too much. A little, of course. He asked me who the chap was who looked so glum, and I told him it was Groux, the man whose property was going to be sold ... Then he asked me how Groux had come to fail with such good land, and I—'

'That's enough of that,' Groux groaned. The big fellow was in a gloomy mood. He refused to admit that he had never looked after his land and his beasts, and he blamed fate for his failure.

'All right! By that time who had seen his wallet?'

'All of us. He had taken it out of his pocket during the meal to show us a photograph of his wife ... so we saw it was full of notes. Even if we hadn't seen them we would have known, as he had come with the intention of buying, and the sale had been advertised as a cash one.'

'Same thing for you, Canut? You, too had over a hundred thousand francs on you?'

'A hundred and fifty. I did not mean to go any higher ...'

Ever since his arrival there Maigret, who was at that time in charge of the flying squad at Nantes, had been studying Frédéric Michaux thoughtfully. Michaux, who was about forty-five, hardly looked like a country innkeeper, with his boxer's jersey and his broken nose.

'Tell me, don't you have the feeling we've seen one another before somewhere?'

'It's not worth beating about the bush—you're quite right, Inspector. But I'm going straight now.'

Loitering with intent in the Ternes district of Paris, assault and battery, illegal bets, slot machines ... In short, Frédéric Michaux, innkeeper at Pont-du-Grau in the depths of the Vendée, was better known to the police under the name of Fred the Boxer.

'You'll recognise Julia, too, no doubt ... You put the two of us away ten years ago. But you can see she's a respectable woman now ...'

It was true. Bloated and flabby, blowsy, her hair greasy, shuffling back and forth between kitchen and dining-room, Julia in no way resembled the girl of the Place des Ternes, and, what was more unexpected, she was a first-class cook.

'We brought Thérèse with us. She's an orphanage kid.'

Eighteen years old, slim and tall, with a sharp nose and a funny little mouth, and a bold stare.

'Have we got to play in earnest?' asked the excise man, whose names was Gentil.

'Play as you did then. You, Canut, why haven't you gone to bed?'

'I was watching the game,' the farmer muttered.

'Or, rather, he kept running after me,' snapped Thérèse, 'making me promise to go to his room afterwards.'

Maigret noted that Fred threw a black look at the man, and that Julia was watching Fred.

Good, they were all in their places. And the other night it had been raining, too. Borchain's room was on the ground floor, at the far end of the passage. In that corridor there were three doors: one that led into the kitchen, another that opened on to the cellar stairs, and a third numbered 100.

Maigret sighed and ran his hand wearily over his brow. In the three days he had been there, the smell of the place had been soaking into him, the atmosphere clung to his skin until it sickened him. And yet what else could he do?

A little before midnight on the 14th, while the card game was going on quietly, Fred had sniffed once or twice, and shouted to Julia in the kitchen, 'Is there something burning on the stove?'

He had got up and opened the door into the passage.

'Heavens, it reeks of burning out here!'

Groux had followed him, and Thérèse, too. It was coming from Borchain's room. He had banged on the door, then he had opened it, for it had no lock.

It was the mattress that was smouldering, a wool mattress, which gave off an acrid fatty smell. On the bed, in shirt and drawers, Borchain lay stretched out, his skull smashed in.

Then the telephone. At one in the morning Maigret had been roused. By four he was arriving, in the middle of a downpour, his nose red with cold, his hands frozen.

Borchain's wallet had disappeared. The window of the room was closed. No one could have come in from outside, for Michaux had a disagreeable Alsatian dog.

Impossible to arrest them all. They were all under suspicion, except Canut, the only one who had not left the inn parlour the whole evening.

'Come, now, my friends! I'm listening to you, and I'm watching . . . Do exactly what you did at this time on the 14th.'

The sale had been postponed to a later date. All day on the 15th people had been passing up and down in front of the house, whose doors the inspector had had closed.

Now it was the 16th. Maigret had hardly left the room, except to get a few hours' sleep. The same for the rest of them. They were sick to death of seeing each other from morning to night, of hearing the same question over and over again, of going through the same actions time after time.

Julia was cooking. The rest of the world was forgotten. It was hard to realise that that were people in other places, in the towns, who were not saying the same things over and over, endlessly. 'Let's see . . . I had just cut hearts . . . Groux threw down his hand, saying: 'It's not worth playing . . . I haven't a single card . . . Just my luck! He got up—'

'Get up, Groux,' ordered Maigret, 'just as you did that night.'

The big man shrugged. 'How many more times are you going to send me along that corridor?' he grumbled. 'Ask Frédéric—ask Nicholas—don't I go along there at least twice most evenings? Eh? What do you think I do with the four or five bottles of white wine I drink during the day?'

He spat, and went towards the door, slouched along the passage, and banged open the door marked 100 with his fist. 'There! Have I got to stay here, at this time of night?'

'As long as necessary, yes . . . Now, what did the rest of you do while he was out?'

The excise man laughed nervously at Groux's show of temper, and his laughter sounded forced. He was the least tough of them all. It was as if his nerves were too near the surface.

'I said to Gentil and Nicholas that no good would come of it,' said Fred.

'No good would come of what?'

'Groux and his farm . . . He never really believed the sale would take place. He was sure he would find some way to borrow the money . . . When they came to put up the notice he threatened the bailiff with his gun. At his age, when you've always been your own master, it's not easy to go back to being somebody else's farmhand . . .'

Groux had come back without a word and was looking at them balefully.

'Now what?' he shouted. 'Have you got it all fixed? Was it me who killed him and set fire to the mattress? Say so now, and chuck me into prison! Having got this far . . .'

'Where were you, Julia?' Maigret asked. 'It seems to me you're not where you should be . . .'

'I was cleaning the vegetables in the kitchen. We were expecting a lot of people to lunch because of the sale. I had ordered two gigots, and we've only just finished one of them now . . .'

'And you, Thérèse?'

'I went up to my room . . .'

'When, exactly?'

'A little after Monsieur Groux came back ...'

'All right, we'll go up together. The rest of you carry on—you started playing again?'

'Not right away: Groux didn't want to. We talked ... I went to get a packet of cigarettes from the bar.'

'Come along, Thérèse ...'

The room where Borchain had died was certainly strategically placed. The staircase was barely six feet away, so Thérèse could have ...

A narrow room, an iron bed, clothes and underwear on a chair.

'What did you come up for?'

'To write.'

'To write what?'

'That we certainly wouldn't have a moment alone together the next day ...' She was looking him straight in the eye, defiantly. 'You know very well what I'm talking about—I could tell from the looks you gave me and from your questions ... The old woman suspects something. She's always on top of us. I begged Fred to take me away, and we had made up our minds to clear off in the spring ...'

'Why the spring?'

'I don't know—Fred fixed the date. We were to go to Panama, where he once lived, and open a bistro ...'

'How long did you stay in your room?'

'Not long. I heard the old woman coming upstairs. She asked me what I was doing. I answered, 'Nothing.' She hates me and I hate her—I'd swear she suspected what we were planning ...'

And Thérèse returned Maigret's gaze. She was a girl who knew what she wanted, and she wanted it badly.

'You don't think Julia would rather see Fred in prison than have him go off with you?'

'She's capable of it!'

'What was she going to her room for?'

'To take off her corset. She has to wear a rubber one to keep what's left of her figure ...'

Thérèse's pointed teeth reminded him of some small animal; she had the same unfeeling cruelty. Her lips curled as she spoke of the woman who had preceded her in Fred's affections.

'In the evenings, especially when she has eaten too much—it's revolting how she stuffs herself!—her corset kills her, and she goes upstairs to take it off ...'

'How long did she stay?'

'Maybe ten minutes. When she came down again I helped her with the vegetables. The others were still playing cards ...'

'The door was open between the kitchen and the parlour?'

'It's always open.'

Maigret gave her a last look, then tramped heavily down the creaking stairs. From the courtyard came the sound of the dog pulling at its chain.

Just behind the cellar door was a heap of coal, and it was there that the murder weapon had been found—a heavy coal hammer.

No fingerprints. The killer must have picked up the tool with a cloth. Through the rest of the house, including the doorknob of Borchain's room, innumerable blurred prints belonging to all those who were there on the night of the 17th.

As for the wallet, ten of them had looked for it, even in the unlikeliest places—all men accustomed to searches of this kind—and the day before the sanitary department had been called in to drain the cesspool.

The unfortunate Borchain had come from his place to buy Groux's farm. Until then he had been only a farmer; he wanted to become a landowner. He was married and had three daughters. He had had dinner at one of the tables. He had chatted with Canut, who was another prospective buyer. He had shown around his wife's photograph.

Weighed down with too heavy a meal and liberal helpings of drink, he had made for bed, the way country people do when they feel sleep coming on. No doubt he had slipped the wallet under his pillow.

In the inn parlour, four men playing *belote*, as on any other evening, and drinking white wine: Fred, Groux, old Nicholas, whose face turned purplish when he had drunk his fill, and the excise man Gentil, who would have been better off doing his rounds.

Behind them, straddling a chair, Canut, dividing his attention between the cards and Thérèse, in the hope that this night of his away from home would be marked by some adventure.

In the kitchen, two women: Julia and the young girl from the orphanage, at work on a pail of vegetables.

One of these people, at a given moment, went into the passage, on some pretext or other, opened first the cellar door, to take out the coal hammer, and then Borchain's door.

No one had heard anything. It could not have taken long as nobody had noticed any lengthy absence—even though the murderer had also to put the wallet in a safe place, for, as the mattress was set on fire, it would not be long before the alarm was given. They would telephone the police and each of them would be searched.

'When I think,' Maigret said plaintively on returning to the parlour, 'that you haven't even any decent beer . . .' A glass of cool, frothy beer straight from the barrel . . . instead of these contemptible bottles of so-called family brew.

'How about the game?'

Fred looked at the time on the clock with its sky-blue pottery frame and its advertising slogan. He was used to the police: he was tired, like the others, but rather less strung up.

'Twenty to ten . . . Not started yet. We were still talking. It was you, Nicholas, who wanted more wine?'

'That's possible.'

'I called through to Thérèse, "Go and draw some wine." Then I got up and went down to the cellar myself.'

'Why?'

He paused, then shrugged his shoulders. 'Oh well, can't be helped. What does it matter if she does hear it, after all? When all this is over, life won't carry on as it was before, anyway . . . I had heard Thérèse go up to her room. I thought she had probably left me a note. It would be put in the keyhole of the cellar door. Do you hear, Julia? I can't help it, old girl. The few happy moments we've spent together have been more than paid for by your endless scenes.'

Canut reddened. Only Nicholas sniggered into his ginger whiskers. Monsieur Gentil averted his eyes, for he, too, had often made a pass at Thérèse.

'Was there a note?' Maigret said.

'Yes. I read it down there while the bottle was filling. All Thérèse said was we probably wouldn't have a moment by ourselves the next day.'

Strange, but one sensed real feeling in Fred, and even a totally unexpected depth of emotion . . . In the kitchen Thérèse got up suddenly and came towards the card table.

'Haven't you had enough?' she said, with trembling lips. 'I'd rather they arrested us all and put us in prison. It would soon . . . But to go round and round like this, as if—as if . . .' She burst out sobbing, and ran over to bury her head in her arms against the wall.

'So you stayed in the cellar for several minutes?' Maigret went on imperturbably.

'Three or four minutes, yes,' Fred replied.

'What did you do with the note?'

'I burnt it in the candle.'

'Are you afraid of Julia?'

Fred strongly resented Maigret's questions. 'Surely you understand? You who arrested us ten years ago—don't *you* understand that when one's been through a lot together . . . Anyway, have it your own way. Don't you upset yourself, Julia dear.'

And a calm voice came from the kitchen: 'I'm not upset.'

As for motive—the classic motive that all the lectures on criminology stress—each one of these people had a motive. Groux even more than the others, as he was at the end of his tether, about to be sold up the day after, thrown out of house and home without even furniture or belongings, and with no alternative but to hire himself out as a labourer. He knew the house well—the way to the cellar, the coal, the hammer . . .

And Nicholas—an old drunk, certainly, but he was penniless. Although he had a daughter in service at Niort, all her earnings went to the upkeep of her child. So couldn't he have . . .? Besides, as Fred had just said, it was Nicholas who came in each week to chop the wood and break the coal.

Now, at about ten, Nicholas had gone along the passage, zigzagging drunkenly. Gentil had said, 'Hope he doesn't mistake the door.' It was an extraordinary coincidence: why had Gentil, sitting there, shuffling the cards mechanically, suddenly said that?

And why shouldn't Gentil have had the idea of committing the crime himself when a few moments later he followed in Nicholas' footsteps? Granted he was an excise officer, but everyone knew he didn't take that very seriously: he did his rounds at the café table, and was always ready to come to an arrangement . . .

'Listen, Inspector—' Fred started.

'One moment. It's five past ten. Where had we reached the other night?'

At that Thérèse, who was still sniffling, came and sat down behind Fred, her shoulder touching his back.

'You were sitting there?' Maigret asked.

'Yes. I had finished the vegetables. I took up the sweater I was knitting, but I didn't do any of it . . .'

Julia was still in the kitchen, but she couldn't be seen.

'What was it you wanted to say, Fred?' Maigret asked.

'Just an idea—it seems to me there's one point that proves it wasn't one of us who killed him, because—suppose—No, that's not what I mean . . . If I killed someone in my house, do you think I'd start a fire? What for? To draw attention . . .?'

Maigret had just filled his pipe, and was taking his time over lighting it. 'I think I'll have a calvados, after all, Thérèse,' he said. 'Now, Fred, why wouldn't you start a fire?'

'Well, because . . .' Fred was struck dumb.'If that fire hadn't started, we wouldn't have worried about the fellow. The others would have gone home . . . and . . .'

Maigret smiled; the stem of his pipe stretched his mouth into an odd grin. 'A pity you're proving exactly the opposite of what you wanted to prove, Fred. The start of that fire was the only real clue—it struck me immediately. Suppose you do kill the old man, as you say. Everyone knows he's at your place, so you wouldn't dream of disposing of the body ... The next morning you will just be compelled to open the door of his room and raise the alarm. When did he in fact ask to be called?'

'Six o'clock. He wanted to go over the farm and the fields before the sale.'

'So if the body had been found at six o'clock, there would be no one in the house but you, Julia, and Thérèse—I don't include Monsieur Canut, whom no one would have suspected. Nor would anyone have thought the crime could have been committed during the card game.'

Fred was following the Inspector's reasoning carefully, and it seemed to Maigret that he had grown paler. He even tore a playing-card absently into bits and dropped the pieces on the floor.

'Look what you're doing! Next time you try to play, you'll have a hard time finding the ace of spades. What was I saying? Ah, yes. How could one make sure the crime was discovered before the departure of Groux, Nicholas, and Monsieur Gentil, so that suspicion might fall on them? No reason for going into Borchain's room ... Except one—the fire ...'

This time Fred shot to his feet, fists clenched, grimfaced. 'In heaven's name!' he shouted.

There was dead silence: they were shocked to the core. They had become so exhausted that they had gradually ceased to believe in the murderer. They no longer grasped that he was there, in the house, talking to them, eating at the same table with them, perhaps playing cards with them, and raising his glass to them.

Fred strode up and down the inn parlour. Maigret seemed to have sunk into himself, his eyes almost closed; he wondered if he was going to succeed at last. For three days he had kept them on the go, hour after hour, making them repeat ten times over the same actions, the same words, partly in the hope that a forgotten detail would suddenly emerge, but above all to wear them down, to push the murderer to breaking-point.

'The whole thing—' His voice was quiet, the words punctuated by little puffs on his pipe—'hangs on knowing who had a safe enough hiding-place for the wallet never to be found ...'

Everyone had been searched. One after the other, that first night, they had been stripped stark naked. The coal behind the cellar door had been searched through. The walls had been tapped, and the casks sounded. In spite of that, a fat wallet holding more than a hundred thousand-franc notes ...

'You're making me dizzy, Fred, going round and round like that . . .'

'But, for heaven's sake, don't you understand—'

'Understand what?'

'That I didn't kill him! I'm not fool enough for that—me with a police record long enough to—'

'It was in the spring, then, you meant to take Thérèse to South America and buy a bistro?'

Fred glanced towards the kitchen door. 'So what?' he asked through clenched teeth.

'Where was the money coming from?'

Fred's eyes bored into Maigret's. 'So that's what you're getting at! You're on the wrong tack, Inspector. I'll have money on the 15th of May. It was a comfortable little idea that came to me when I was doing nicely as a boxing promoter. I took out an insurance policy for a hundred thousand francs to come at the age of fifty. I shall be fifty on the 15th of May—ah, yes, Thérèse, I'm a bit longer in the tooth than I usually let on.'

'Julia knew about this insurance?'

'That's nothing to do with a woman.'

'So, Julia, you didn't know Fred was coming into a hundred thousand francs?'

'I knew.'

'What?' Fred started.

'I also knew he wanted to go off with that trashy little—'

'And you would have let them go?'

Julia stayed quite still, her gaze fixed on Fred; there was a strange calm about her.

'You haven't answered me,' Maigret persisted.

She turned her gaze on him. Her lips moved, perhaps she was going to say something important—but instead she shrugged her shoulders. 'Can you ever tell what a man will do?'

Fred was not listening. He looked as if he was suddenly preoccupied with something else. Brows furrowed, he was deep in thought, and Maigret had the impression that they were thinking along the same lines.

'Well, now, Fred?'

'What?' It was as if he had been jolted out of a dream.

'About this insurance policy—this policy that Julia saw without your knowing—I'd also like to take a look at it.'

How oddly the truth can come to light! Maigret was sure he had thought of everything. Thérèse told him in her room about the departure, therefore there had to be money . . . Fred confessed to the existence of an insurance policy. And now—it was so simple, so obvious, that he almost burst out laughing—the house had been combed ten times over but no insurance policy had been found, no identity papers, no military service record.

'As you like, Inspector,' Fred answered calmly with a sigh. 'At least you'll be able to see how much I've saved up . . .' He went towards the kitchen.

'You can come in. When one lives at the back of beyond like this . . . Not to mention some papers I have that my pals from the old days wouldn't mind pinching . . .'

Thérèse followed them, astonished. Groux's heavy footsteps could be heard, and Canut getting up in turn.

'Don't think this is anything special,' Fred went on. 'I just happen to have been a coppersmith in my young days . . .'

To the right of the kitchen range there was an enormous dustbin of galvanised iron. Fred emptied the contents out right in the middle of the floor, and released the concealed double bottom in its base. He was the first to look inside. Slowly a frown spread over his face. Slowly he raised his head; his mouth hung open . . .

Lying there, among other papers, was a bulging wallet, grubby with use and held together with a band of red rubber out from an innertube.

'Well, Julia?' Maigret asked softly.

Then, it seemed to him, through the woman's flabby features he saw a flash of the old Julia. She looked round at them all, and her upper lip curled disdainfully. She looked as if the tears were not far away, but they did not come. Her voice was flat when she spoke. 'Well, that's that. I'm done for . . .'

The extraordinary thing was that it was Thérèse who suddenly burst into tears, like a dog howling in the presence of death. Meanwhile the woman who had done the killing asked, 'I suppose you're taking me off straight away? As you have the car? Can I bring my things?'

Maigret let her pack her bits and pieces. He felt sad: reaction, after prolonged nervous tension.

How long, he wondered, had Julia known about Fred's hiding-place? On seeing the insurance policy, which he had never told her about, she must have realised that the day that money came he would be off with Thérèse.

Then came her chance: more money even than Fred would be getting. And she would be the one who would bring it to him, a few days or a few weeks after the affair was all over—*Look, Fred, I know everything . . . You wanted to go away with her, didn't you? You thought I was no good any more . . . Take a look in your hiding place— It's your 'old girl' who . . .*

Maigret kept close watch over her as she moved about the bedroom where there was only a big mahogany bed and, above it, a photograph of Fred in boxing rigout. 'Have to put my corset on,' she said. 'You won't look, will you? It's not very pretty . . .'

It was not until she was in the car that she broke down. Maigret kept his eyes fixed on the raindrops sliding down the windows. He wondered what the others were doing now, back at the inn. And who would get Groux's farm when the auctioneer's voice rang out—going, going, gone!—and the hammer fell.

MEANS OF EVIL

Ruth Rendell

Scenes of Detective Chief Inspector Wexford appreciatively sipping a pint of beer in his local pub, the Olive and Dove in Kingsmarkham, are now familiar not only to countless readers of the novels and short stories in which he has featured, but also to the millions of viewers who have enjoyed the television series starring George Baker, which has been running since 1990. Wexford is rarely happier than when he is in the pub mulling over the clues of his latest crime investigation, in company with his astute assistant, Detective Inspector Mike Burden (played by Christopher Ravenscroft). The policemen were created by Ruth Rendell (1930-), one of the top selling crime writers, who lives in East Anglia, the home of some of the best beers and most inviting pubs in the country. She has admitted that her inspiration was the books of Georges Simenon, and so it is not surprising that Wexford, like Maigret, is aware how helpful a knowledge of drink can be in the solving of crimes, or that both men try to build up a psychological portrait of the criminal they are pursuing by observing their little foibles. 'Means of Evil' demonstrates both these elements at work in a story of a most ingenious case of poisoning which tests Wexford's powers of deduction to the limit. It also provides an outstanding last taste of murder by the glass . . .

'Blewits,' said Inspector Burden, 'parasols, horns of plenty, morels and boletus. Mean anything to you?'

Chief Inspector Wexford shrugged. 'Sounds like one of those magazine quizzes. What have these in common? I'll make a guess and say they're crustacea. Or sea anemones. How about that?'

'They are edible fungi,' said Burden.

'Are they now? And what have edible fungi to do with Mrs Hannah Kingman throwing herself off, or being pushed off, a balcony?'

The two men were sitting in Wexford's office at the police station, Kingsmarkham, in the County of Sussex. The month was

November, but Wexford had only just returned from his holiday. And while he had been away, enjoying in Cornwall an end of October that had been more summery than the summer, Hannah Kingman had committed suicide. Or so Burden had thought at first. Now he was in a dilemma, and as soon as Wexford had walked in that Monday morning, Burden had begun to tell the whole story to his chief.

Wexford, getting on for sixty, was a tall, ungainly, rather ugly man who had once been fat to the point of obesity but had slimmed to gauntness for reasons of health. Nearly twenty years his junior, Burden had the slenderness of a man who has always been thin. His face was ascetic, handsome in a frosty way. The older man, who had a good wife who looked after him devotedly, nevertheless always looked as if his clothes came off the peg from the War on Want Shop, while the younger, a widower, was sartorially immaculate. A tramp and a Beau Brummell, they seemed to be, but the dandy relied on the tramp, trusted him, understood his powers and his perception. In secret he almost worshipped him.

Without his chief he had felt a little at sea in this case. Everything had pointed at first to Hannah Kingman's having killed herself. She had been a manic-depressive, with a strong sense of her own inadequacy; apparently her marriage, though not of long duration, had been unhappy, and her previous marriage had failed. Even in the absence of a suicide note or suicide threats, Burden would have taken her death for self-destruction—if her brother hadn't come along and told him about the edible fungi. And Wexford hadn't been there to do what he always could do, sort out sheep from goats and wheat from chaff.

'The thing is,' Burden said across the desk, 'we're not looking for proof of murder so much as proof of *attempted* murder. Axel Kingman could have pushed his wife off that balcony—he has no alibi for the time in question—but I had no reason to think he had done so until I was told of an attempt to murder her some two weeks before.'

'Which attempt has something to do with edible fungi?'

Burden nodded. 'Say with administering to her some noxious substance in a stew made from edible fungi. Though if he did it, God knows how he did it, because three other people, including himself, ate the stew without ill effects. I think I'd better tell you about it from the beginning.'

'I think you had,' said Wexford.

'The facts,' Burden began, very like a Prosecuting Counsel, 'are as follows. Axel Kingman is thirty-five years old and he keeps a health-food shop here in the High Street called Harvest Home.

Know it?' When Wexford signified by a nod that he did, Burden went on, 'He used to be a teacher in Myringham, and for about seven years before he came here he'd been living with a woman named Corinne Last. He left her, gave up his job, put all the capital he had into this shop, and married a Mrs Hannah Nicholson.'

'He's some sort of food freak, I take it,' said Wexford.

Burden wrinkled his nose. 'Lot of affected nonsense,' he said. 'Have you never noticed what thin pale weeds these health-food people are? While the folks who live on roast beef and suet and whisky and plum cake are full of beans and rarin' to go.'

'Is Kingman a thin pale weed?'

'A feeble—what's the word?—aesthete, if you ask me. Anyway, he and Hannah opened this shop and took a flat in the high-rise tower our planning geniuses have been pleased to raise over the top of it. The fifth floor. Corinne Last, according to her and according to Kingman, accepted the situation after a while and they all remained friends.'

'Tell me about them,' Wexford said. 'Leave the facts for a bit and tell me about them.'

Burden never found this easy. He was inclined to describe people as 'just ordinary' or 'just like anyone else', a negative attitude which exasperated Wexford. So he made an effort. 'Kingman looks the sort who wouldn't hurt a fly. The fact is, I'd apply the word gentle to him if I wasn't coming round to thinking he's a cold-blooded wife-killer. He's a total abstainer with a bee in his bonnet about drink. His father went bankrupt and finally died of alcoholism, and our Kingman is an anti-booze fanatic.

'The dead woman was twenty-nine. Her first husband left her after six months of marriage and went off with some girl friend of hers. Hannah went back to live with her parents and had a part-time job helping with the meals at the school where Kingman was a teacher. That was where they met.'

'And the other woman?' said Wexford.

Burden's face took on a repressive expression. Sex outside marriage, however sanctioned by custom and general approval, was always distasteful to him. That, in the course of his work, he almost daily came across illicit sex had done nothing to mitigate his disapproval. As Wexford sometimes derisively put it, you would think that in Burden's eyes all the suffering in the world, and certainly all the crime, somehow derived from men and women going to bed together outside the bonds of wedlock. 'God knows why he didn't marry her,' Burden now said. 'Personally I think things were a lot better in the days when education authorities put their foot down about immorality among teachers.'

'Let's not have your views on that now, Mike,' said Wexford.

'Presumably Hannah Kingman didn't die because her husband didn't come to her a pure virgin.'

Burden flushed slightly. 'I'll tell you about this Corinne Last. She's very good-looking, if you like the dark sort of intense type. Her father left her some money and the house where she and Kingman lived, and she still lives in it. She's one of those women who seem to be good at everything they put their hands to. She paints and sells her paintings. She makes her own clothes, she's more or less the star in the local dramatic society, she's a violinist and plays in some string trio. Also she writes for health magazines and she's the author of a cookery book.'

'It would look then,' Wexford put in, 'as if Kingman split up with her because all this was more than he could take. And hence he took up with the dull little school-meals lady. No competition from her, I fancy.'

'I daresay you're right. As a matter of fact, that theory has already been put to me.'

'By whom?' said Wexford. 'Just where did you get all this information, Mike?'

'From an angry young man, the fourth member of the quartet, who happens to be Hannah's brother. His name is John Hood and I think he's got a lot more to tell. But it's time I left off describing the people and got on with the story.

'No one saw Hannah fall from the balcony. It happened last Thursday afternoon at about four. According to her husband, he was in a sort of office behind the shop doing what he always did on early-closing day—stock-taking and sticking labels on various bottles and packets.

'She fell on to a hard-top parking area at the back of the flats, and her body was found by a neighbour a couple of hours later between two parked cars. We were sent for, and Kingman seemed to be distraught. I asked him if he had had any idea that his wife might have wished to take her own life and he said she had never threatened to do so but had lately been very depressed and there had been quarrels, principally about money. Her doctor had put her on tranquillizers—of which, by the way, Kingman disapproved—and the doctor himself, old Dr Castle, told me Mrs Kingman had been to him for depression and because she felt her life wasn't worth living and she was a drag on her husband. He wasn't surprised that she had killed herself and neither, by that time, was I. We were all set for an inquest verdict of suicide while the balance of the mind was disturbed when John Hood walked in here and told me Kingman had attempted to murder his wife on a previous occasion.'

'He told you just like that?'

'Pretty well. It's plain he doesn't like Kingman, and no doubt he was fond of his sister. He also seems to like and admire Corinne Last. He told me that on a Saturday night at the end of October the four of them had a meal together in the Kingmans' flat. It was a lot of vegetarian stuff cooked by Kingman—he always did the cooking—and one of the dishes was made out of what I'm old-fashioned enough, or narrow-minded enough, to call toadstools. They all ate it and they were all OK but for Hannah who got up from the table, vomited for hours, and apparently was quite seriously ill.'

Wexford's eyebrows went up. 'Elucidate, please,' he said.

Burden sat back, put his elbows on the arms of the chair, and pressed the tips of his fingers together. 'A few days before this meal was eaten, Kingman and Hood met at the squash club of which they are both members. Kingman told Hood that Corinne Last had promised to get him some edible fungi called shaggy caps from her own garden, the garden of the house which they had at one time shared. A crop of these things show themselves every autumn under a tree in this garden. I've seen them myself, but we'll come to that in a minute.

'Kingman's got a thing about using weeds and whatnot for cooking, makes salads out of dandelion and sorrel, and he swears by this fungi rubbish, says they've got far more flavour than mushrooms. Give me something that comes in a plastic bag from the supermarket every time, but no doubt it takes all sorts to make a world. By the way, this cookbook of Corinne Last's is called *Cooking for Nothing*, and all the recipes are for making dishes out of stuff you pull up by the wayside or pluck from the hedgerow.'

These warty blobs or spotted puffets or whatever, had he cooked them before?'

'Shaggy caps,' said Burden, grinning, 'or *coprinus comatus*. Oh, yes, every year, and every year he and Corinne had eaten the resulting stew. He told Hood he was going to cook them again this time, and Hood says he seemed very grateful to Corinne for being so—well, magnanimous.'

'Yes, I can see it would have been a wrench for her. Like hearing "our tune" in the company of your ex-lover and your supplanter.' Wexford put on a vibrant growl. ' "Can you bear the sight of me eating our toadstools with another?" '

'As a matter of fact,' said Burden seriously, 'it could have been just like that. Anyway, the upshot of it was that Hood was invited round for the following Saturday to taste these delicacies and was told that Corinne would be there. Perhaps it was that fact which made him accept. Well, the day came. Hood looked in on his sister at lunchtime. She showed him the pot containing the stew which

Kingman had already made and she said *she had tasted it* and it was delicious. She also showed Hood half a dozen specimens of shaggy caps which she said Kingman hadn't needed and which they would fry for their breakfast. This is what she showed him.'

Burden opened a drawer in the desk and produced one of those plastic bags which he had said so inspired him with confidence. But the contents of this one hadn't come from a supermarket. He removed the wire fastener and tipped out four whitish scaly objects. They were egg-shaped, or rather elongated ovals, each with a short fleshy stalk.

'I picked them myself this morning,' he said, 'from Corinne Last's garden. When they get bigger, the egg-shaped bit opens like an umbrella, or a pagoda really, and there are sort of black gills underneath. You're supposed to eat them when they're in the stage these are.'

'I suppose you've got a book on fungi?' said Wexford.

'Here.' This also was produced from the drawer. *British Fungi, Edible and Poisonous.* 'And here we are—shaggy caps.'

Burden had opened it at the *Edible* section and at a line and wash drawing of the species he held it in his hand. He passed it to the chief inspector.

'Corprinus comatus,' Wexford read aloud, '*a common species, attaining when full-grown a height of nine inches. The fungus is frequently to be found, during late summer and autumn, growing in fields, hedgerows and often in gardens. It should be eaten before the cap opens and disgorges its inky fluid, but is at all times quite harmless.*' He put the book down but didn't close it. 'Go on, please, Mike,' he said.

'Hood called for Corinne and they arrived together. They got there just after eight. At about eight-fifteen they all sat down to table and began the meal with avocado *vinaigrette*. The next course was to be the stew, followed by nut cutlets with a salad and then an apple-cake. Very obviously, there was no wine or liquor of any sort on account of Kingman's prejudice. They drank grape juice from the shop.

'The kitchen opens directly out of the living-dining room. Kingman brought in the stew in a large tureen and served it himself at the table, beginning, of course, with Corinne. Each one of those shaggy caps had been sliced in half lengthwise and the pieces were floating in a thickish gravy to which carrots, onions and other vegetables had been added. Now, ever since he had been invited to this meal, Hood had been feeling uneasy about eating fungi, but Corinne had reassured him, and once he began to eat it and saw the others were eating it quite happily, he stopped worrying for the time being. In fact, he had a second helping.

'Kingman took the plates out and the tureen and immediately

rinsed them under the tap. Both Hood and Corinne Last have told me this, though Kingman says it was something he always did, being fastidious about things of that sort.'

'Surely his ex-girl friend could confirm or deny that,' Wexford put in, 'since they lived together for so long.'

'We must ask her. All traces of the stew were rinsed away. Kingman then brought in the nut concoction and the salad, but before he could begin to serve them Hannah jumped up, covered her mouth with her napkin, and rushed to the bathroom.

'After a while Corinne went to her. Hood could hear a violent vomiting from the bathroom. He remained in the living room while Kingman and Corinne were both in the bathroom with Hannah. No one ate any more. Kingman eventually came back, said that Hannah must have picked up some 'bug' and that he had put her to bed. Hood went into the bedroom where Hannah was lying on the bed with Corinne beside her. Hannah's face was greenish and covered with sweat and she was evidently in great pain because while he was there she doubled up and groaned. She had to go to the bathroom again and that time Kingman had to carry her back.

'Hood suggested Dr Castle should be sent for, but this was strenuously opposed by Kingman who dislikes doctors and is one of those people who go in for herbal remedies—raspbery leaf tablets and camomile tea and that sort of thing. Also he told Hood rather absurdly that Hannah had had quite enough to do with doctors and that if this wasn't some gastric germ it was the result of her taking 'dangerous' tranquillizers.

'Hood thought Hannah was seriously ill and the argument got heated, with Hood trying to make Kingman either call a doctor or take her to hospital. Kingman wouldn't and Corinne took his part. Hood is one of those angry but weak people who are all bluster, and although he might have called a doctor himself, he didn't. The effect on him of Corinne again, I suppose. What he did do was tell Kingman he was a fool to mess about cooking things everyone knew weren't safe, to which Kingman replied that if the shaggy caps were dangerous, how was it they weren't all ill? Eventually, at about midnight, Hannah stopped retching, seemed to have no more pain, and fell asleep. Hood drove Corinne home, returned to the Kingmans' and remained there for the rest of the night, sleeping on their sofa.

'In the morning Hannah seemed perfectly well, though weak, which rather upset Kingman's theory about the gastric bug. Relations between the brothers-in-law were strained. Kingman said he hadn't liked Hood's suggestions and that when he wanted to see his sister he, Kingman, would rather he came there when he was out or in the shop. Hood went off home, and since that day he hasn't seen Kingman.

'The day after his sister's death he stormed in here, told me what I've told you, and accused Kingman of trying to poison Hannah. He was wild and nearly hysterical, but I felt I couldn't dismiss this allegation as—well, the ravings of a bereaved person. There were too many peculiar circumstances, the unhappiness of the marriage, the fact of Kingman rinsing those plates, his refusal to call a doctor. Was I right?'

Burden stopped and sat waiting for approval. It came in the form of a not very enthusiastic nod.

After a moment Wexford spoke. 'Could Kingman have pushed her off that balcony, Mike?'

'She was a small fragile woman. It was physically possible. The back of the flats isn't overlooked. There's nothing behind but the parking area and then open fields. Kingman could have gone up by the stairs instead of using the lift and come down by the stairs. Two of the flats on the lower floors are empty. Below the Kingmans lives a bedridden woman whose husband was at work. Below that the tenant, a young married woman, was in but she saw and heard nothing. The invalid says she thinks she heard a scream during the afternoon but she did nothing about it, and if she did hear it, so what? It seems to me that a suicide, in those circumstances, is as likely to cry out as a murder victim.'

'OK,' said Wexford. 'Now to return to the curious business of this meal. The idea would presumably be that Kingman intended to kill her that night but that his plan misfired because whatever he gave her wasn't toxic enough. She was very ill but she didn't die. He chose those means and that company so that he would have witnesses to his innocence. They all ate the stew out of the same tureen, but only Hannah was affected by it. How then are you suggesting he gave her whatever poison he did give her?'

'I'm not,' said Burden frankly, 'but others are making suggestions. Hood's a bit of a fool, and first of all he would only keep on about all fungi being dangerous and the whole dish being poisonous. When I pointed out that this was obviously not so, he said Kingman must have slipped something into Hannah's plate, or else it was the salt.'

'What salt?'

'He remembered that no one but Hannah took salt with the stew. But that's absurd because Kingman couldn't have known that would happen. And, incidentally, to another point we may as well clear up now—the avocados were quite innocuous. Kingman halved them *at the table* and the *vinaigrette* sauce was served in a jug. The bread was not in the form of rolls but a home-made wholemeal loaf. If there was anything there which shouldn't have been it was in the stew all right.

'Corinne Last refuses to consider the possibility that Kingman might be guilty. But when I pressed her she said she was not actually sitting at the table while the stew was served. She had got up and gone into the hall to fetch her handbag. So she didn't see Kingman serve Hannah.' Burden reached across and picked up the book Wexford had left open at the description and drawing of the shaggy caps. He flicked over to the *Poisonous* section and pushed the book back to Wexford. 'Have a look at some of these.'

'Ah, yes,' said Wexford. 'Our old friend, the fly agaric. A nice-looking little red job with white spots, much favoured by illustrators of children's books. They usually stick a frog on top of it and a gnome underneath. I see that when ingested it causes nausea, vomiting, tetanic convulsions, coma and death. Lots of these agarics, aren't there? Purple, crested, warty, verdigris—all more or less lethal. Aha! The death cap, *amanita phalloides*. How very unpleasant. The most dangerous fungus known, it says here. Very small quantities will cause intense suffering and often death. So where does all that get us?'

'The death cap, according to Corinne Last, is quite common round here. What she doesn't say, but what I infer, is that Kingman could have got hold of it easily. Now suppose he cooked just one specimen separately and dropped it into the stew just before he brought it in from the kitchen? When he comes to serve Hannah he spoons up for her this specimen, or the pieces of it, in the same way as someone might select a special piece of chicken for someone out of a casserole. The gravy was thick, it wasn't like thin soup.'

Wexford looked dubious. 'Well, we won't dismiss it as a theory. If he had contaminated the rest of the stew and others had been ill, that would have made it look even more like an accident, which was presumably what he wanted. But there's one drawback to that, Mike. If he meant Hannah to die, and was unscrupulous enough not to mind about Corinne and Hood being made ill, why did he rinse the plates. To *prove* that it was an accident, he would have wanted above all to keep some of that stew for analysis when the time came, for analysis would have shown the presence of poisonous as well as non-poisonous fungi, and it would have seemed that he had merely been careless.

'But let's go and talk to these people, shall we?'

The shop called Harvest Home was closed. Wexford and Burden went down an alley at the side of the block, passed the glass-doored main entrance, and went to the back to a door that was labelled *Stairs and Emergency Exit*. They entered a small tiled vestibule and began to mount a steepish flight of stairs.

On each floor was a front door and a door to the lift. There was no one about. If there had been and they had had no wish to be seen, it would only have been necessary to wait behind the bend in the stairs until whoever it was had got into the lift. The bell by the front door on the fifth floor was marked *A. and H. Kingman*. Wexford rang it.

The man who admitted them was smallish and mild-looking and he looked sad. He showed Wexford the balcony from which his wife had fallen. It was one of two in the flat, the other being larger and extending outside the living-room windows. This one was outside a glazed kitchen door, a place for hanging washing or for gardening of the window-box variety. Herbs grew in pots, and in a long trough there still remained frost-bitten tomato vines. The wall surrounding the balcony was about three feet high, the drop sheer to the hard-top below.

'Were you surprised that your wife committed suicide, Mr Kingman?' said Wexford.

Kingman didn't answer directly. 'My wife set a very low valuation on herself. When we got married I thought she was like me, a simple sort of person who doesn't ask much from life but has quite a capacity for contentment. It wasn't like that. She expected more support and more comfort and encouragement than I could give. That was especially so for the first three months of our marriage. Then she seemed to turn against me. She was very moody, always up and down. My business isn't doing very well and she was spending more money than we could afford. I don't know where all the money was going and we quarrelled about it. Then she'd become depressed and say she was no use to me, she'd be better dead.'

He had given, Wexford thought, rather a long explanation for which he hadn't been asked. But it could be that these thoughts, defensive yet self-reproachful, were at the moment uppermost in his mind. 'Mr Kingman,' he said, 'we have reason to believe, as you know, that foul play may have been involved here. I should like to ask you a few questions about a meal you cooked on October 29th, after which your wife was ill.'

'I can guess who's been telling you about that.'

Wexford took no notice. 'When did Miss Last bring your these— er, shaggy caps?'

'On the evening of the 28th. I made the stew from them in the morning, according to Miss Last's own recipe.'

'Was there any other type of fungus in the flat at the time?'

'Mushrooms, probably.'

'Did you at any time add any noxious object or substance to that stew, Mr Kingman?'

Kingman said quietly, wearily. 'Of course not. My brother-in-law has a lot of ignorant prejudices. He refuses to understand that that stew, which I have made dozens of times before in exactly the same way, was as wholesome as, say, a chicken casserole. More wholesome, in my view.'

'Very well. Nevertheless, your wife was very ill. Why didn't you call a doctor?'

'Because my wife was not "very" ill. She had pains and diarrhoea, that's all. Perhaps you aren't aware of what the symptoms of fungus poisoning are. The victim doesn't just have pain and sickness. His vision is impaired, he very likely blacks out or has convulsions of the kind associated with tetanus. There was nothing like that with Hannah.'

'It was unfortunate that you rinsed those plates. Had you not done so and called a doctor, the remains of that stew would almost certainly have been sent for analysis, and if it was harmless as you say, all this investigation could have been avoided.'

'It was harmless,' Kingman said stonily.

Out in the car Wexford said, 'I'm inclined to believe him, Mike. And unless Hood or Corinne Last has something really positive to tell us, I'd let it rest. Shall we go and see her next?'

The cottage Corinne had shared with Axel Kingman was on a lonely stretch of road outside the village of Myfleet. It was a stone cottage with a slate roof, surrounded by a well-tended pretty garden. A green Ford Escort stood on the drive in front of a weatherboard garage. Under a big old apple tree, from which the yellow leaves were falling, the shaggy caps, immediately recognisable, grew in three thick clumps.

She was a tall woman, the owner of this house, with a beautiful square-jawed, high-cheekboned face and a mass of dark hair. Wexford was at once reminded of the Klimt painting of a languorous red-lipped woman, gold-neckleted, half covered in gold draperies, though Corinne Last wore a sweater and a denim smock. Her voice was low and measured. He had the impression she could never be flustered or caught off her guard.

'You're the author of a cookery book, I believe?' he said.

She made no answer but handed him a paperback which she took down from a bookshelf. *Cooking for Nothing, Dishes from Hedgerow and Pasture* by Corinne Last. He looked through the index and found the recipe he wanted. Opposite it was a coloured photograph of six people eating what looked like brown soup. The recipe included carrots, onions, herbs, cream, and a number of other harmless ingredients. The last lines read: *Stewed shaggy caps are best served piping hot with wholewheat bread. For drinkables, see page 171.* He glanced at page 171, then handed the book to Burden.

'This was the dish Mr Kingman made that night?'

'Yes.' She had a way of leaning back when she spoke and of half lowering her heavy glossy eyelids. It was serpentine and a little repellent. 'I picked the shaggy caps myself out of this garden. I don't understand how they could have made Hannah ill, but they must have done because she was fine when we first arrived. She hadn't got any sort of gastric infection, that's nonsense.'

Burden put the book aside. 'But you were all served stew out of the same tureen.'

'I didn't see Axel actually serve Hannah. I was out of the room.' The eyelids flickered and almost closed.

'Was it usual for Mr Kingman to rinse plates as soon as they were removed?'

'Don't ask me.' She moved her shoulders. 'I don't know. I do know that Hannah was very ill just after eating that stew. Axel doesn't like doctors, of course, and perhaps it would have—well, embarrassed him to call Dr Castle in the circumstances. Hannah had black spots in front of her eyes, she was getting double vision. I was extremely concerned for her.'

'But you didn't take it on yourself to get a doctor, Miss Last? Or even support Mr Hood in his allegations?'

'Whatever John Hood said, I knew it couldn't be the shaggy caps.' There was a note of scorn when she spoke Hood's name. 'And I was rather frightened. I couldn't help thinking it would be terrible if Axel got into some sort of trouble, if there was an inquiry or something.'

'There's an inquiry now, Miss Last.'

'Well, it's different now, isn't it? Hannah's dead. I mean, it's not just suspicion or conjecture any more.'

She saw them out and closed the front door before they had reached the garden gate. Farther along the roadside and under the hedges more shaggy caps could be seen as well as other kinds of fungi Wexford couldn't identify—little mushroom-like things with pinkish gills, a cluster of small yellow umbrellas, and on the trunk of an oak tree, bulbous smoke-coloured swellings that Burden said were oyster mushrooms.

'That woman,' said Wexford, 'is a mistress of the artless insinuation. She damned Kingman with almost every word, but she never came out with anything like an accusation.' He shook his head. 'I suppose Kingman's brother-in-law will be at work?'

'Presumably,' said Burden, but John Hood was not at work. He was waiting for them at the police station, fuming at the delay, and threatening 'if something wasn't done at once' to take his grievances to the Chief Constable, even to the Home Office.

'Something is being done,' said Wexford quietly. 'I'm glad you've come here, Mr Hood. But try to keep calm, will you, please?'

It was apparent to Wexford from the first that John Hood was in a different category of intelligence from that of Kingman and Corinne Last. He was a thick-set man of perhaps no more than twenty-seven or twenty-eight, with bewildered, resentful blue eyes in a puffy flushed face. A man, Wexford thought, who would fling out rash accusations he couldn't substantiate, who would be driven to bombast and bluster in the company of the ex-teacher and that clever subtle woman.

He began to talk now, not wildly, but still without restraint, repeating what he had said to Burden, reiterating, without putting forward any real evidence, that his brother-in-law had meant to kill his sister that night. It was only by luck that she had survived. Kingman was a ruthless man who would have stopped at nothing to be rid of her. He, Hood, would never forgive himself that he hadn't made a stand and called the doctor.

'Yes, yes, Mr Hood, but what exactly were your sister's symptoms?'

'Vomiting and stomach pains, violent pains,' said Hood.

'She complained of nothing else?'

'Wasn't that enough? That's what you get when someone feeds you poisonous rubbish.'

Wexford merely raised his eyebrows. Abruptly, he left the events of that evening and said, 'What had gone wrong with your sister's marriage?'

Before Hood replied, Wexford could sense he was keeping something back. A wariness came into his eyes and then was gone. 'Axel wasn't the right person for her,' he began. 'She had problems, she needed understanding, she wasn't . . .' His voice trailed away.

'Wasn't what, Mr Hood? What problems?'

'It's got nothing to do with all this,' Hood muttered.

'I'll be the judge of that. You made this accusation, you started this business off. It's not for you now to keep anything back.' On a sudden inspiration, Wexford said, 'Had these problems anything to do with the money she was spending?'

Hood was silent and sullen. Wexford thought rapidly over the things he had been told—Axel Kingman's fanaticism on one particular subject, Hannah's desperate need of an unspecified kind of support during the early days of her marriage. Later on, her alternating moods, and then the money, the weekly sums of money spent and unaccounted for.

He looked up and said baldly, 'Was your sister an alcoholic, Mr Hood?'

Hood hadn't liked this directness. He flushed and looked affronted. He skirted round a frank answer. Well, yes, she drank. She was at pains to conceal her drinking. It had been going on more or less consistently since her first marriage broke up.

'In fact, she was an alcoholic,' said Wexford.

'I suppose so.'

'Your brother-in-law didn't know?'

'Good God, no. Axel would have killed her!' He realised what he had said. 'Maybe that's why. Maybe he found out.'

'I don't think so, Mr Hood. Now I imagine that in the first few months of her marriage she made an effort to give up drinking. She needed a good deal of support during this time but she couldn't, or wouldn't, tell Mr Kingman why she needed it. Her efforts failed, and slowly, because she couldn't manage without it, she began drinking again.'

'She wasn't as bad as she used to be,' Hood said with pathetic eagerness. 'And only in the evenings. She told me she never had a drink before six, and after that she'd have a few more, gulping them down on the quiet so Axel wouldn't know.'

Burden said suddenly, 'Had your sister been drinking that evening?'

'I expect so. She wouldn't have been able to face company, not even just Corinne and me, without a drink.'

'Did anyone besides yourself know that your sister drank?'

'My mother did. My mother and I had a sort of pact to keep it dark from everyone so that Axel wouldn't find out.' He hesitated and then said rather defiantly, 'I did tell Corinne. She's a wonderful person, she's very clever. I was worried about it and I didn't know what to do. She promised she wouldn't tell Axel.'

'I see.' Wexford had his own reasons for thinking she hadn't done so. Deep in thought, he got up and walked to the other end of the room where he stood gazing out of the window. Burden's continuing questions, Hood's answers, reached him only as a confused murmur of voices. Then he heard Burden say more loudly, 'That's all for now, Mr Hood, unless the chief inspector has anything more to ask you.'

'No, no,' said Wexford abstractedly, and when Hood had somewhat truculently departed, 'Time for lunch. It's past two. Personally, I shall avoid any dish containing fungi, even *psalliota campestris*.'

After Burden had looked that one up and identified it as the common mushroom, they lunched and then made a round of such wineshops in Kingsmarkham as were open at that hour. At the Wine Basket they drew a blank, but the assistant in the Vineyard told them that a woman answering Hannah Kingman's description had been a regular customer, and that on the previous Wednesday, the day before her death, she had called in and bought a bottle of Courvoisier Cognac.

'There was no liquor of any kind in Kingman's flat,' said Burden. 'Might have been an empty bottle in the rubbish, I suppose.' He made a rueful face. 'We didn't look, didn't think we had any reason to. But she couldn't have drunk a whole bottleful on the Wednesday, could she?'

'Why are you so interested in this drinking business, Mike? You don't seriously see it as a motive for murder, do you? That Kingman killed her because he'd found out, or been told, that she was a secret drinker?'

'It was a means, not a motive,' said Burden. 'I know how it was done. I know how Kingman tried to kill her that first time.' He grinned. 'Makes a change for me to find the answer before you, doesn't it? I'm going to follow in your footsteps and make a mystery of it for the time being, if you don't mind. With your permission we'll go back to the station, pick up those shaggy caps and conduct a little experiment.'

Michael Burden lived in a neat bungalow in Tabard Road. He had lived there with his wife until her untimely death and continued to live there with his sixteen-year-old daughter, his son being away at university. But that evening Pat Burden was out with her boy friend, and there was a note left for her father on the refrigerator. *Dad, I ate the cold beef from yesterday. Can you open a tin for yourself? Back by 10.30. Love, P.*

Burden read this note several times, his expression of consternation deepening with each perusal. And Wexford could precisely have defined the separate causes which brought that look of weariness into Burden's eyes, that frown, that drooping of the mouth. Because she was motherless his daughter had to eat not only cold but leftover food, she who should be carefree was obliged to worry about her father, loneliness drove her out of her home until the appallingly late hour of half-past ten. It was all nonsense, of course, the Burden children were happy and recovered from their loss, but how to make Burden see it that way? Widowhood was something he dragged about with him like a physical infirmity. He looked up from the note, screwed it up and eyed his surroundings vaguely and with a kind of despair. Wexford knew that look of desolation. He saw it on Burden's face each time he accompanied him home.

It evoked exasperation as well as pity. He wanted to tell Burden—once or twice he had done so—to stop treating John and Pat like retarded paranoiacs, but instead he said lightly, 'I read somewhere the other day that it wouldn't do us a scrap of harm if we never ate another hot meal as long as we lived. In fact, the colder and rawer the better.'

'You sound like the Axel Kingman brigade,' said Burden, rallying and laughing which was what Wexford had meant him to do. 'Anyway, I'm glad she didn't cook anything. I shouldn't have been able to eat it and I'd hate her to take it as criticism.'

Wexford decided to ignore that one. 'While you're deciding just how much I'm to be told about this experiment of yours, d'you mind if I phone my wife?'

'Be my guest.'

It was nearly six. Wexford came back to find Burden peeling carrots and onions. The four specimens of *coprinus comatus*, beginning to look a little wizened, lay on a chopping board. On the stove a saucepanful of bone stock was heating up.

'What the hell are you doing?'

'Making shaggy cap stew. My theory is that the stew is harmless when eaten by non-drinkers, and toxic, or toxic to some extent, when taken by those with alcohol in the stomach. How about that? In a minute, when this lot's cooking, I'm going to take a moderate quantity of alcohol, then I'm going to eat the stew. Now say I'm a damned fool if you like.'

Wexford shrugged. He grinned. 'I'm overcome by so much courage and selfless devotion to the duty you owe the taxpayers. But wait a minute. Are you sure only Hannah had been drinking that night? We know Kingman hadn't. What about the other two?'

'I asked Hood that when you were off in your daydream. He called for Corinne Last at six, at her request. They picked some apples for his mother, then she made him coffee. He did suggest they call in at a pub for a drink on their way to the Kingmans', but apparently she took so long getting ready that they didn't have time.'

'OK. Go ahead then. But wouldn't it be easier to call in an expert? There must be such people. Very likely someone holds a chair of fungology or whatever it's called at the University of the South.'

'Very likely. We can do that after I've tried it. I want to know for sure *now*. Are you willing too?'

'Certainly not. I'm not your guest to that extent. Since I've told my wife I won't be home for dinner, I'll take it as a kindness if you'll make me some innocent scrambled eggs.'

He followed Burden into the living room where the inspector opened a door in the sideboard. 'What'll you drink?'

'White wine, if you've got any, or vermouth if you haven't. You know how abstemious I have to be.'

Burden poured vermouth and soda. 'Ice?'

'No, thanks. What are you going to have? Brandy? That was Hannah Kingman's favourite tipple apparently.'

'Haven't got any,' said Burden. 'It'll have to be whisky. I think we can reckon she had two double brandies before that meal, don't you? I'm not so brave I want to be as ill as she was.' He caught Wexford's eye. 'You don't think some people could be more sensitive to it than others, do you?'

'Bound to be,' said Wexford breezily. 'Cheers!'

Burden sipped his heavily watered whisky, then tossed it down. 'I'll just have a look at my stew. You sit down. Put the television on.'

Wexford obeyed him. The big coloured picture was of a wood in autumn, pale blue sky, golden beech leaves. Then the camera closed in on a cluster of red-and-white-spotted fly agaric. Chuckling, Wexford turned it off as Burden put his head round the door.

'I think it's more or less ready.'

'Better have another whisky.'

'I suppose I had.' Burden came in and re-filled his glass. 'That ought to do it.'

'What about my eggs?'

'Oh, God, I forgot. I'm not much of a cook, you know. Don't know how women manage to get a whole lot of different things brewing and make them synchronise.'

'It is a mystery, isn't it? I'll get myself some bread and cheese, if I may.'

The brownish mixture was in a soup bowl. In the gravy floated four shaggy caps, cut lengthwise. Burden finished his whisky at a gulp.

'What was it the Christians in the arena used to say to the Roman Emperor before they went to the lions?'

'*Morituri, te salutamus*,' said Wexford. ' "We who are about to die salute thee." '

'Well . . .' Burden made an effort with the Latin he had culled from his son's homework. '*Moriturus, te saluto*. Would that be right?'

'I daresay. You won't die, though.'

Burden made no answer. He picked up his spoon and began to eat.

'Can I have some more soda?' said Wexford.

There are perhaps few stabs harder to bear than derision directed at one's heroism. Burden gave him a sour look. 'Help yourself. I'm busy.'

Wexford did so. 'What's it like?' he said.

'All right. It's quite nice, like mushrooms.'

Doggedly he ate. He didn't once gag on it. He finished the lot and wiped the bowl round with a piece of bread. Then he sat up, holding himself rather tensely.

'May as well have your telly on now,' said Wexford. 'Pass the time.' He switched it on again. No fly agaric this time, but a dog fox moving across a meadow with Vivaldi playing. 'How d'you feel?'

'Fine,' said Burden gloomily.

'Cheer up. It may not last.'

But it did. After fifteen minutes had passed, Burden still felt perfectly well. He looked bewildered. 'I was so damned positive. I *knew* I was going to be retching and vomiting by now. I didn't put the car away because I was certain you'd have to run me down to the hospital.'

Wexford only raised his eyebrows.

'You were pretty casual about it, I must say. Didn't say a word to stop me, did you? Didn't it occur to you it might have been a bit awkward for you if anything had happened to me?'

'I knew it wouldn't. I said to get a fungologist.' And then Wexford, faced by Burden's aggrieved stare, burst out laughing. 'Dear old Mike, you'll have to forgive me. But you know, d'you honestly think I'd have let you risk your life eating that stuff? I knew you were safe.'

'May one ask how?'

'One may. And you'd have known too if you'd bothered to take a proper look at that book of Corinne Last's. Under the recipe for shaggy cap stew it said, *"For drinkables, see page 171."* Well, I looked at page 171, and there Miss Last gave a recipe for cowslip wine and another for sloe gin, both highly intoxicating drinks. Would she have recommended a wine and a spirit to drink with those fungi if there'd been the slightest risk? Not if she wanted to sell her book she wouldn't. Not unless she was risking hundreds of furious letters and expensive lawsuits.'

Burden had flushed a little. Then he too began to laugh.

After a little while they had coffee.

'A little logical thinking would be in order, I fancy,' said Wexford. 'You said this morning that we were not so much seeking to prove murder as attempted murder. Axel Kingman could have pushed her off that balcony, but no one saw her fall and no one heard him or anybody else go up to that flat during the afternoon. If, however, an attempt to murder her was made two weeks before, the presumption that she was eventually murdered is enormously strengthened.'

Burden said impatiently, 'We've been through all that. We know that.'

'Wait a minute. The attempt failed. Now just how seriously ill was she? According to Kingman and Hood, she had severe stomach pains and she vomited. By midnight she was peacefully sleeping and by the following day she was all right.'

'I don't see where all this is getting us.'

'To a point which is very important and which may be the crux of the whole case. You say that Axel Kingman attempted to murder her. In order to do so he must have made very elaborate plans— the arranging of the meal, the inviting of the two witnesses, the ensuring that his wife tasted the stew earlier in the same day, and the preparation for some very nifty sleight of hand at the time the meal was served. Isn't it odd that the actual method used should so signally have failed? That Hannah's *life* never seems to have been in danger? And what if the method had succeeded? At post-mortem some noxious agent would have been found in her body or the effects of such. How could he have hoped to get away with that since, as we know, neither of his witnesses actually watched him serve Hannah and one of them was even out of the room?

'So what I am postulating is that no one attempted to murder her, but someone *attempted* to make her ill so that, taken in conjunction with the sinister reputation of non-mushroom fungi and Hood's admitted suspicion of them, taken in conjunction with the known unhappiness of the marriage, *it would look as if there had been a murder attempt.*'

Burden stared at him. 'Kingman would never have done that. He would either have wanted his attempt to succeed or not to have looked like an attempt at all.'

'Exactly. And where does that get us?'

Instead of answering him, Burden said on a note of triumph, his humiliation still rankling, 'You're wrong about one thing. She *was* seriously ill, she didn't just have nausea and vomiting. King-man and Hood may not have mentioned it, but Corinne Last said she had double vision and black spots before her eyes and . . .' His voice faltered. 'My God, you mean . . .?'

Wexford nodded. 'Corinne Last only of the three says she had those symptoms. Only Corinne Last is in a position to say, because she lived with him, if Kingman was in the habit of rinsing plates as soon as he removed them from the table. What does she say?

That she doesn't know. Isn't that rather odd? Isn't it rather odd too that she chose that precise moment to leave the table and go out into the hall for her handbag?

'She knew that Hannah drank because Hood had told her so. On the evening that meal was eaten you say Hood called for her at her own request. Why? She has her own car, and I don't for a moment believe that a woman like her would feel anything much but contempt for Hood.'

'She told him there was something wrong with the car.'

'She asked him to come at six, although they were not due at the Kingmans' till eight. She gave him *coffee*. A funny thing to drink at that hour, wasn't it, and before a meal? So what happens when he suggests calling in at a pub on the way? She doesn't say no or say it isn't a good idea to drink and drive. She takes so long getting ready that they don't have time.

'She didn't want Hood to drink any alcohol, Mike, and she was determined to prevent it. She, of course, would take no alcohol and she knew Kingman never drank. But she also knew Hannah's habit of having her first drink of the day at about six.

'Now look at her motive, far stronger than Kingman's. She strikes me as a violent, passionate and determined woman. Hannah had taken Kingman away from her. Kingman had rejected her. Why not revenge herself on both of them by killing Hannah and seeing to it that Kingman was convicted of the crime? If she simply killed Hannah, she had no way of ensuring that Kingman would come under suspicion. But if she made it look as if he had previously attempted her life, the case against him would become very strong indeed.

'Where was she last Thursday afternoon? She could just as easily have gone up those stairs as Kingman could. Hannah would have admitted her to the flat. If she, known to be interested in gardening, had suggested that Hannah take her on to that balcony and show her the pot herbs, Hannah would willingly have done so. And then we have the mystery of the missing brandy bottle with some of its contents surely remaining. If Kingman had killed her, he would have left that there as it would greatly have strengthened the case for her suicide. Imagine how he might have used it. 'Heavy drinking made my wife ill that night. She knew I had lost respect for her because of her drinking. She killed herself because her mind was unbalanced by drink.'

'Corinne Last took that bottle away because she didn't want it known that Hannah drank, and she was banking on Hood's keeping it dark from us just as he had kept it from so many people in the past. And she didn't want it known because the fake murder attempt that *she* staged depended on her victim having alcohol present in her body.'

Burden sighed, poured the last dregs of coffee into Wexford's cup. 'But we tried that out,' he said. 'Or I tried it out, and it doesn't work. You knew it wouldn't work from her book. True, she brought the shaggy caps from her own garden, but she couldn't have mixed up poisonous fungi with them because Axel Kingman would have realized at once. Or if he hadn't, they'd all have been ill, alcohol or no alcohol. She was never alone with Hannah before the meal, and while the stew was served she was out of the room.'

'I know. But we'll see her in the morning and ask her a few more questions.' Wexford hesitated, then quoted softly, ' "Out of good still to find means of evil." '

'What?'

'That's what she did, isn't it? It was good for everyone but Hannah, you look as if it's done you a power of good, but it was evil for Hannah. I'm off now, Mike, it's been a long day. Don't forget to put your car away. You won't be making any emergency trips to hospital tonight.'

They were unable to puncture her self-possession. The languorous Klimt face was carefully painted this morning, and she was dressed as befitted the violinist or the actress or the author. She had been forewarned of their coming and the gardener image had been laid aside. Her long smooth hands looked as if they had never touched the earth or pulled up a weed.

Where had she been on the afternoon of Hannah Kingman's death? Her thick shapely eyebrows went up. At home, indoors, painting. Alone?

'Painters don't work with an audience,' she said rather insolently, and she leaned back, dropping her eyelids in that way of hers. She lit a cigarette and flicked her fingers at Burden for an ashtray as if he were a waiter.

Wexford said, 'On Saturday, October 29th, Miss Last, I believe you had something wrong with your car?'

She nodded lazily.

In asking what was wrong with it, he thought he might catch her. He didn't.

'The glass in the offside front headlight was broken while the car was parked,' she said, and although he thought how easily she could have broken that glass herself, he could hardly say so. In the same smooth voice she added, 'Would you like to see the bill I had from the garage for repairing it?'

'That won't be necessary.' She wouldn't have offered to show it to him if she hadn't possessed it. 'You asked Mr Hood to call for you here at six, I understand.'

'Yes. He's not my idea of the best company in the world, but I'd promised him some apples for his mother and we had to pick them before it got dark.'

'You gave him coffee but no alcohol. You had no drinks on the way to Mr and Mrs Kingman's flat. Weren't you a little disconcerted at the idea of going out to dinner at a place where there wouldn't even be a glass of wine?'

'I was used to Mr Kingman's ways.' But not so used, thought Wexford, that you can tell me whether it was normal or abnormal for him to have rinsed those plates. Her mouth curled, betraying her a little. 'It didn't bother me, I'm not a slave to liquor.'

'I should like to return to these shaggy caps. You picked them from here on October 28th and took them to Mr Kingman that evening. I think you said that?'

'I did. I picked them from this garden.'

She enunciated the words precisely, her eyes wide open and gazing sincerely at him. The words, or perhaps her unusual straightforwardness, stirred in him the glimmer of an idea. But if she had said nothing more, that idea might have died as quickly as it had been born.

'If you want to have them analysed or examined or whatever, you're getting a bit late. Their season's practically over.' She looked at Burden and gave him a gracious smile. 'But you took the last of them yesterday, didn't you? So that's all right.'

Wexford, of course, said nothing about Burden's experiment. 'We'll have a look in your garden, if you don't mind.'

She didn't seem to mind, but she had been wrong. Most of the fungi had grown into black-gilled pagodas in the twenty-four hours that had elapsed. Two new ones, however, had thrust their white oval caps up through the wet grass. Wexford picked them, and still she didn't seem to mind. Why, then, had she appeared to want their season to be over? He thanked her and she went back into the cottage. The door closed. Wexford and Burden walked out into the road.

The fungus season was far from over. From the abundant array by the roadside it looked as if the season would last weeks longer. Shaggy caps were everywhere, some of them smaller and greyer than the clump that grew out of Corinne Last's well-fed lawn. There were green and purple agarics, horn-shaped toadstools, and tiny mushrooms growing in fairy rings.

'She doesn't exactly mind our having them analysed,' Wexford said thoughtfully, 'but it seems she'd prefer the analysis to be done on the ones you picked yesterday than on those I picked today. Can that be so or am I just imagining it?'

'If you're imagining it, I'm imagining it too. But it's no good, that line of reasoning. We know they're not potentiated—or whatever the word is—by alcohol.'

'I shall pick some more all the same,' said Wexford. 'Haven't got a paper bag, have you?'

'I've got a clean handkerchief. Will that do?'

'Have to,' said Wexford who never had a clean one. He picked a dozen more young shaggy caps, big and small, white and grey, immature and fully grown. They got back into the car and Wexford told the driver to stop at the public library. He went in and emerged a few minutes later with three books under his arm.

'When we get back,' he said to Burden, 'I want you to get on to the university and see what they can offer us in the way of an expert in fungilogy.'

He closeted himself in his office with the three books and a pot of coffee. When it was nearly lunchtime, Burden knocked on the door.

'Come in,' said Wexford. 'How did you get on?'

'It's not fungologist or fungilogist,' said Burden with triumphant severity. 'It's *mycologist* and they don't have one. But there's a man on the faculty who's a toxicologist and who's just published one of those popular science books. This one's about poisoning by wild plants and fungi.'

Wexford grinned. 'What's it called? *Killing for Nothing*? He sounds as if he'd do fine.'

'I said we'd see him at six. Let's hope something will come of it.'

'No doubt it will.' Wexford slammed shut the thickest of his books. 'We need confirmation,' he said, 'but I've found the answer.'

'For God's sake! Why didn't you say?'

'You didn't ask. Sit down.' Wexford motioned him to the chair on the other side of the desk. 'I said you'd done your homework, Mike, and so you had, only your textbook wasn't quite comprehensive enough. It's got a section on edible fungi and a section on poisonous fungi—*but nothing in between*. What I mean by that is, there's nothing in your book about fungi which aren't wholesome yet don't cause death or intense suffering. There's nothing about the kind that can make people ill in certain circumstances.'

'But we know they ate shaggy caps,' Burden protested. 'And if by "circumstances" you mean the intake of alcohol, we know shaggy caps aren't affected by alcohol.'

'Mike,' said Wexford quietly, '*do* we know they ate shaggy caps?'

He spread out on the desk the haul he had made from the roadside and from Corinne Last's garden. 'Look closely at these, will you?'

Quite bewildered now, Burden looked at and fingered the dozen or so specimens of fungi. 'What am I to look *for*?'

'Differences,' said Wexford laconically.

'Some of them are smaller than the others, and the smaller ones are greyish. Is that what you mean? But, look here, think of the differences between mushrooms. You get big flat ones and small button ones and . . .'

'Nevertheless, in this case it is that small difference that makes all the difference.' Wexford sorted the fungi into two groups. 'All the small greyer ones,' he said, 'came from the roadside. Some of the larger whiter ones came from Corinne Last's garden and some from the roadside.'

He picked up between forefinger and thumb a specimen of the former. 'This isn't a shaggy cap, it's an ink cap. Now listen.' The thick book fell open where he had placed a marker. Slowly and clearly he read: *'The ink cap*, coprinus atramentarius, *is not to be confused with the shaggy cap*, coprinus comatus. *It is smaller and greyer in colour, but otherwise the resemblance between them is strong. While* coprinus atramentarius *is usually harmless when cooked, it contains however, a chemical similar to the active principle in* Antabuse, *a drug used in the treatment of alcoholics, and if eaten in conjunction with alcohol will cause nausea and vomiting.'*

'We'll never prove it.'

'I don't know about that,' said Wexford. 'We can begin by concentrating on the one lie we know Corinne Last told when she said she picked the fungi she gave Axel Kingman *from her own garden.'*

ACKNOWLEDGEMENTS

The editor and publishers are grateful to the following authors, publishers and agents for permission to use copyright material in this collection: Michael Joseph Ltd for 'A Connoisseur's Revenge' by Roald Dahl; the Estate of A. E. Coppard for 'Ale Celestial?'; Victor Gollancz Ltd for 'Bitter Almonds' and 'A Matter of Taste' by Dorothy L. Sayers, 'Marmalade Wine' by Joan Aiken and 'The Adventure of the Tell-tale Bottle' by Ellery Queen; Mercury Publications Ltd for 'The Income Tax Mystery' by Michael Gilbert and 'The Opener of the Crypt' by John Jakes; Ellery Queen's Mystery Magazine for 'In Vino Veritas' by Lawrence G. Blochman, 'The Last Bottle in the World' by Stanley Ellin and 'Wry Highball' by Craig Rice; Fleetway Publications for 'Cellar Cool' by Geoffrey Household and 'Under the Hammer' by Georges Simenon; Random Publishing Group for 'The Friends of Plonk' by Kingsley Amis and 'The Widow' by Margery Allingham; A. P. Watt Literary Agency for 'Before the Party' by Somerset Maugham; The author for 'A Bottle of Gin' by Robert Bloch; Methuen for 'The Wine Glass' by A. A. Milne; David Higham Associates for 'The Liqueur Glass' by Phyllis Bottome; Christianna Brand for her story 'To The Widow'; Davis Publications Inc for 'Raffles and Operation Champagne' by Berry Perowne and 'The Man Who Stirred Champagne' by Hugh Pentecost; Leslie Charteris for 'The Unblemished Bootlegger'; the Executors of the Estate of E. C. Bentley for 'The Unknown Peer'; Peters, Fraser & Dunlop for 'Means of Evil' by Ruth Rendell. While every care has been taken to clear permission for the use of the stories in this book, in the case of any accidental infringement, copyright holders are asked to write to the editor care of the publishers.